Pokémon™
Adventures
FireRed & LeafGreen

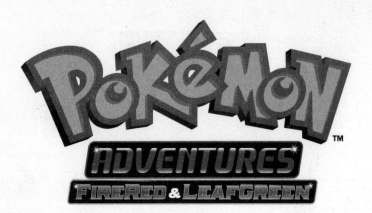

Pokémon ADVENTURES
FireRed & LeafGreen
Volume 24
Perfect Square Edition

Story by **HIDENORI KUSAKA**
Art by **SATOSHI YAMAMOTO**

© 2014 Pokémon.
© 1995–2014 Nintendo/Creatures Inc./GAME FREAK inc.
TM, ®, and character names are trademarks of Nintendo.
POCKET MONSTERS SPECIAL Vol. 24
by Hidenori KUSAKA, Satoshi YAMAMOTO
© 1997 Hidenori KUSAKA, Satoshi YAMAMOTO
All rights reserved.
Original Japanese edition published by SHOGAKUKAN.
English translation rights in the United States of America,
Canada, the United Kingdom, Ireland, Australia and
New Zealand arranged with SHOGAKUKAN.

English Adaptation/Bryant Turnage
Translation/Tetsuichiro Miyaki
Touch-up & Lettering/Annaliese Christman
Design/Shawn Carrico
Editor/Annette Roman

Printed in the U.S.A.

Published by VIZ Media, LLC
P.O. Box 77010
San Francisco, CA 94107

10 9 8 7 6 5 4 3 2 1
First printing, September 2014

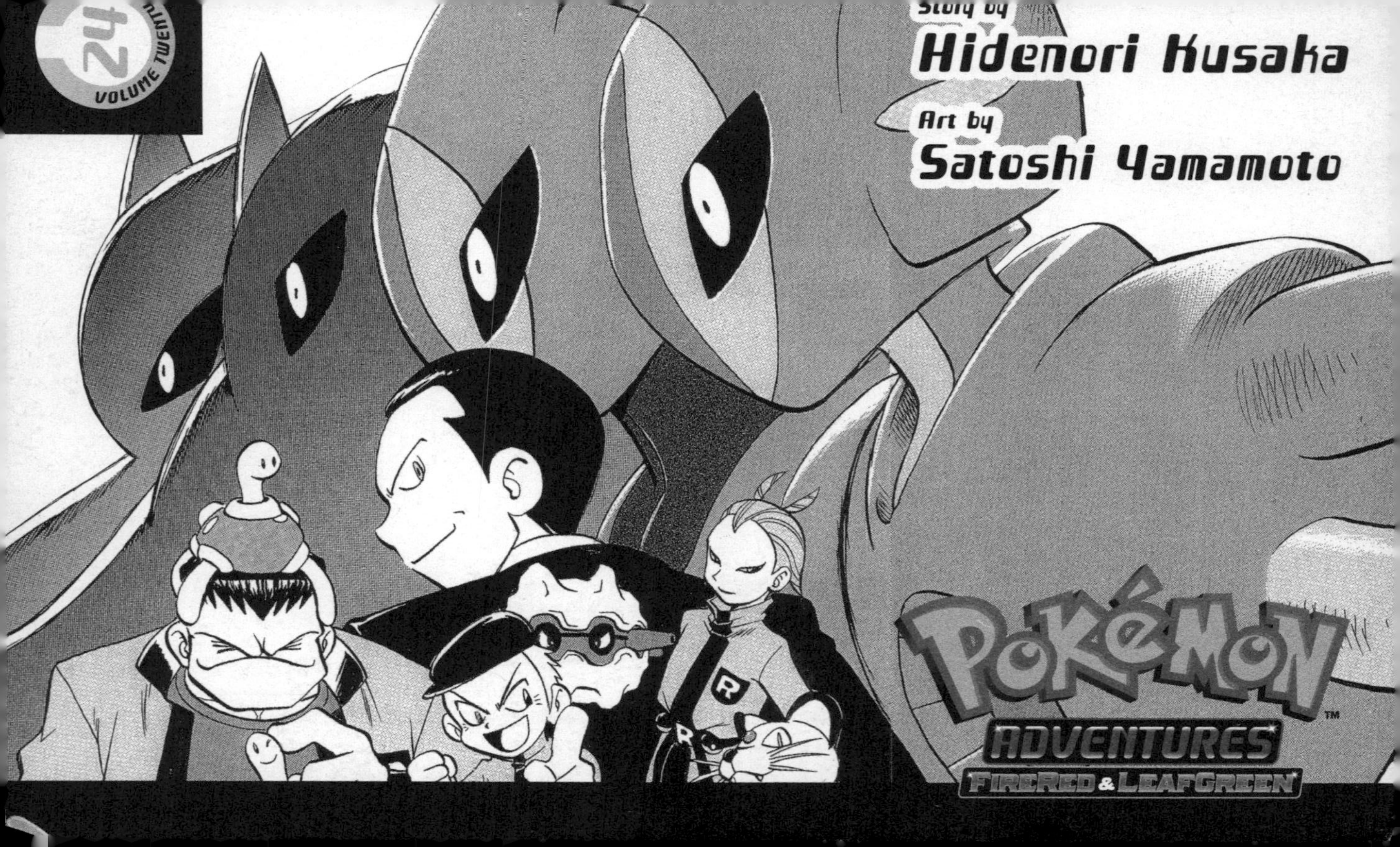
24
VOLUME TWENTY
Story by
Hidenori Kusaka
Art by
Satoshi Yamamoto
Pokémon™
ADVENTURES
FIRERED & LEAFGREEN

SPECIAL OBJECT

The Pokédex holders and their stories

Kanto region

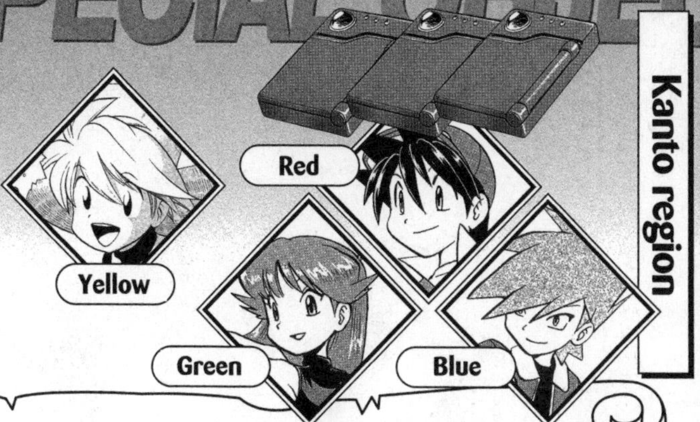
Red
Yellow
Green
Blue

1st Chapter

Red, a young boy from Pallet Town, receives a Pokédex from Professor Oak and heads out on a Pokémon training journey. Along the way, he meets two other Trainers, Blue, who becomes his rival, and Green. Red fights evil Team Rocket with his new friends and then becomes Champion of the Pokémon League.

2nd Chapter

Two years later, Red suddenly disappears and Yellow, a mysterious new Trainer, appears at Professor Oak's laboratory in search of him.

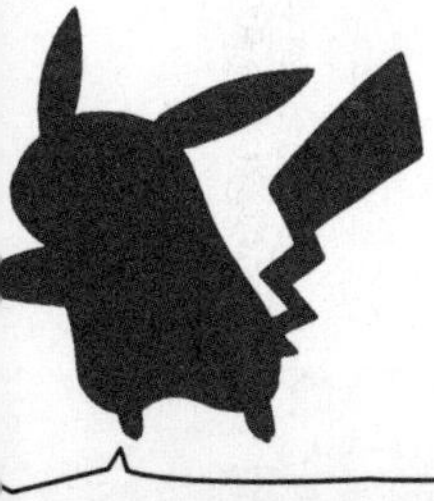

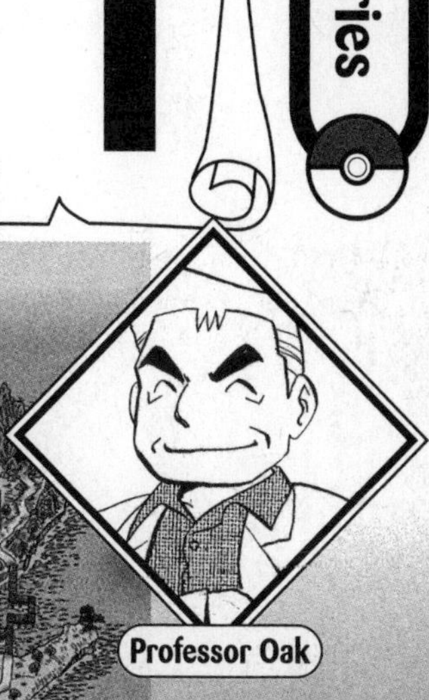
Professor Oak

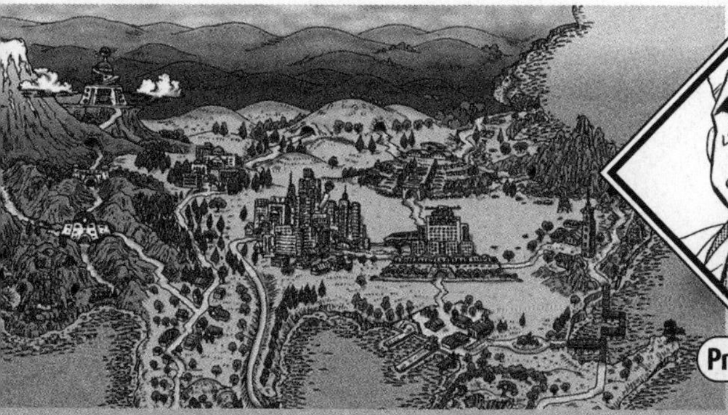

POKEMO

Johto region

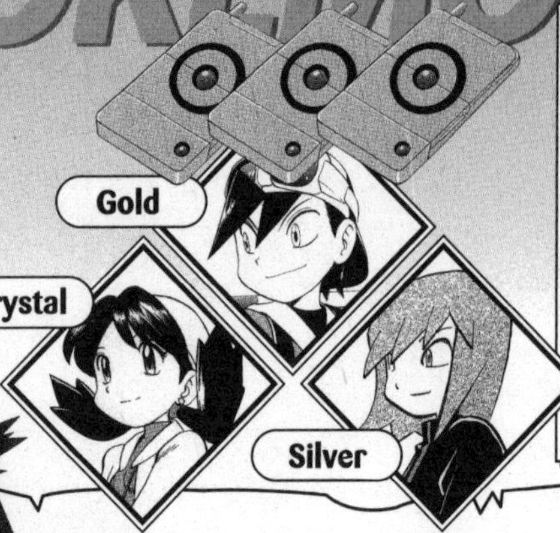
Gold
Crystal
Silver

Standing in
Yellow's way
is the Kanto
Elite Four,
led by Lance
In a major b
at Cerise Isla
Yellow mana
to stymie th
group's evil
ambitions.

3rd Chapter

A year later, Gold, a boy living in New Bark Town in a house full of Pokémon, sets out on a journey in pursuit of Silver, a Trainer who stole a Totodile from Professor Elm's laboratory. The two don't get along at first, but eventually they become partners fighting side by side. During their journey, they meet Crystal, the trainer who Professor Elm entrusts with the completion of his Pokédex. Together, the trio succeed to shatter the evil scheme of the Mask of Ice, a villain who leads what remains of Team Rocket.

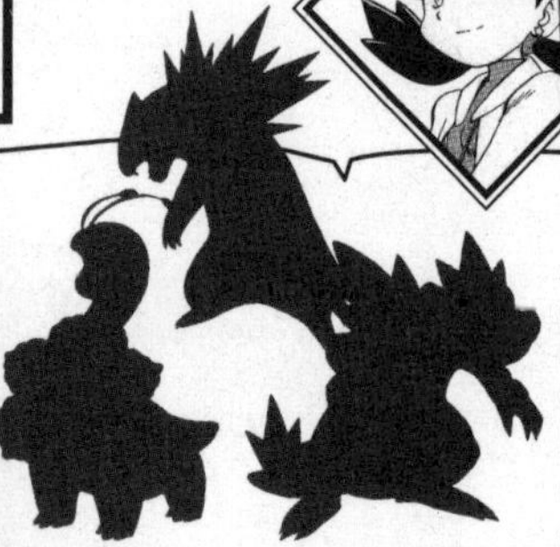

Hoenn region

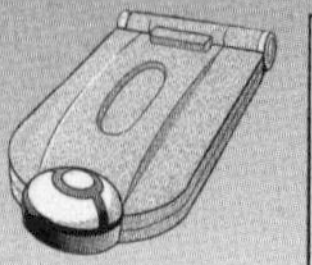

4th Chapter

Pokémon Trainer Ruby has a passion for Pokémon Contests. He runs away from home right after his family moves to Littleroot Town. He meets a wild girl named Sapphire and they pledge to compete with each other in an 80-day challenge to...

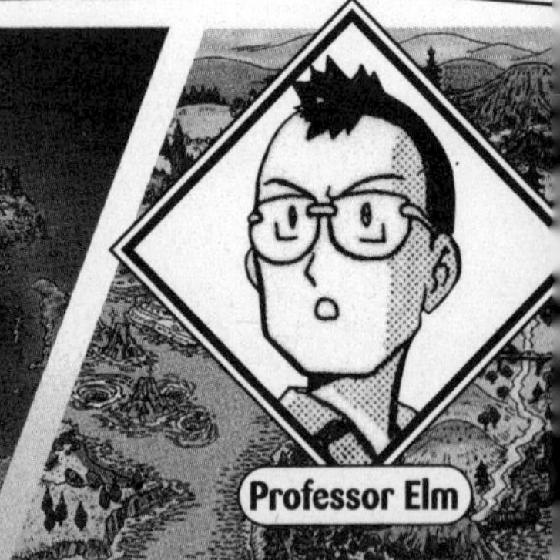
Professor Elm

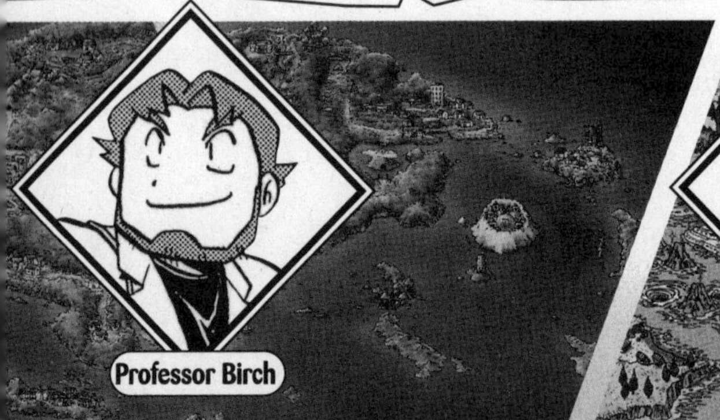
Professor Birch

SPECIAL OBJECT

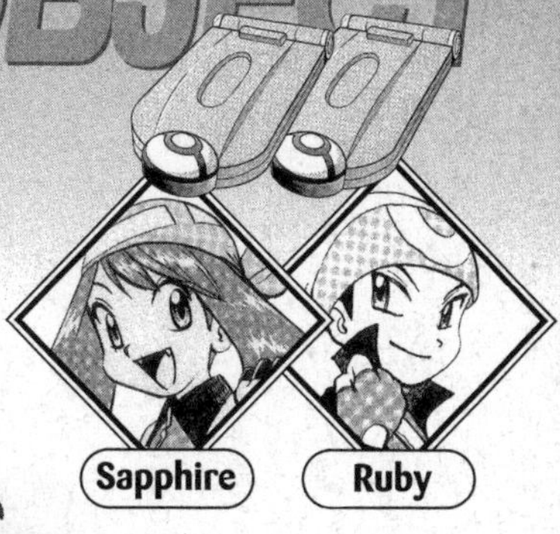
Sapphire
Ruby

...win every Pokémon Contest and every Pokémon Gym Battle, respectively. Meanwhile, in the Hoenn region, Team Aqua and Team Magma set their evil plot in motion. As a result, Legendary Pokémon Groudon and Kyogre are awakened and inflict catastrophic climate changes on Hoenn. In the end, thanks to Ruby and Sapphire's heroic efforts, the two legendary Pokémon go back into hibernation.

Kanto region

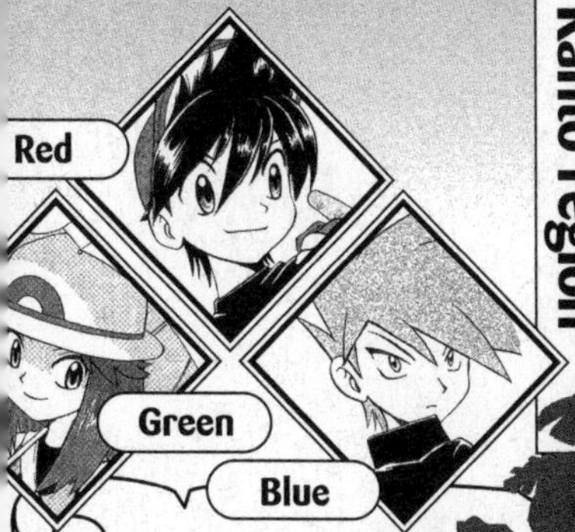
Red
Green
Blue

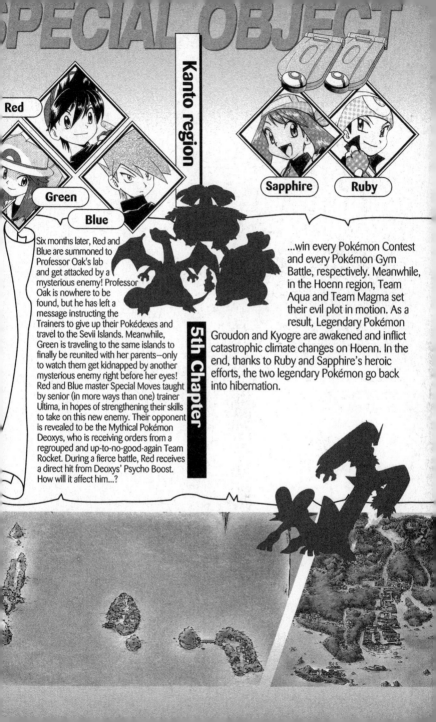

5th Chapter

Six months later, Red and Blue are summoned to Professor Oak's lab and get attacked by a mysterious enemy! Professor Oak is nowhere to be found, but he has left a message instructing the Trainers to give up their Pokédexes and travel to the Sevii Islands. Meanwhile, Green is traveling to the same islands to finally be reunited with her parents—only to watch them get kidnapped by another mysterious enemy right before her eyes! Red and Blue master Special Moves taught by senior (in more ways than one) trainer Ultima, in hopes of strengthening their skills to take on this new enemy. Their opponent is revealed to be the Mythical Pokémon Deoxys, who is receiving orders from a regrouped and up-to-no-good-again Team Rocket. During a fierce battle, Red receives a direct hit from Deoxys' Psycho Boost. How will it affect him...?

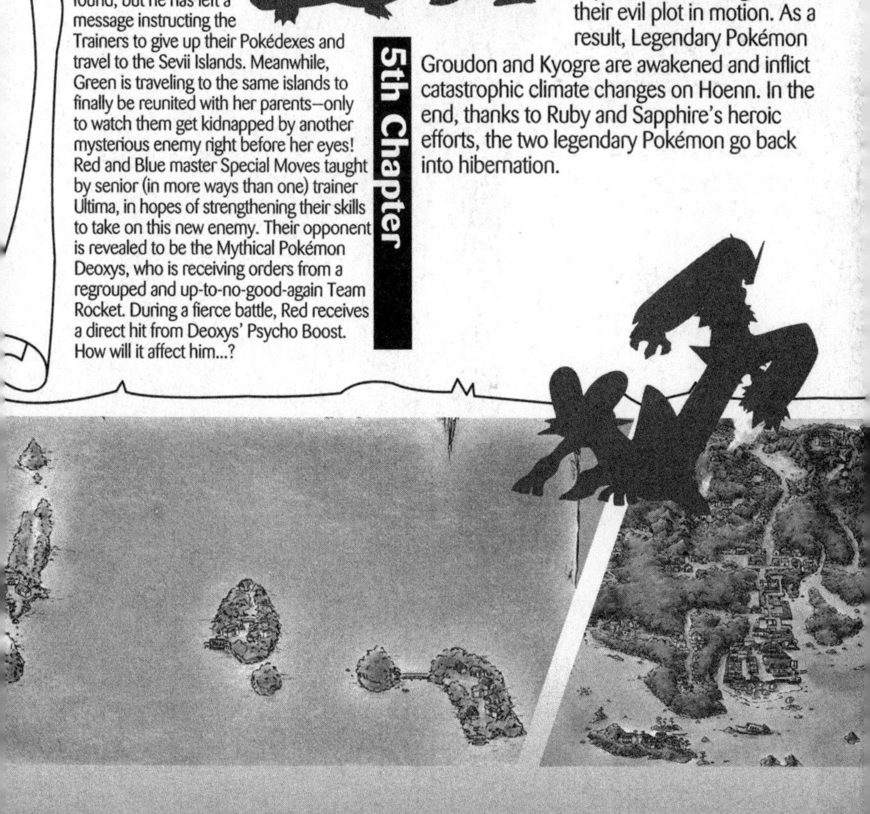

POKÉMON

ADVENTURES
FIRERED & LEAFGREEN

VOLUME TWENTY-FOUR

CONTENTS

• Adventure 280 •
Some Things Are Better Left Unown

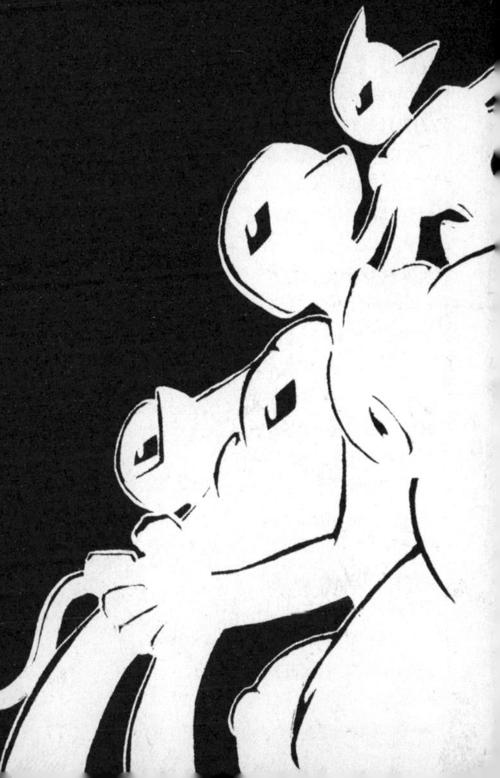

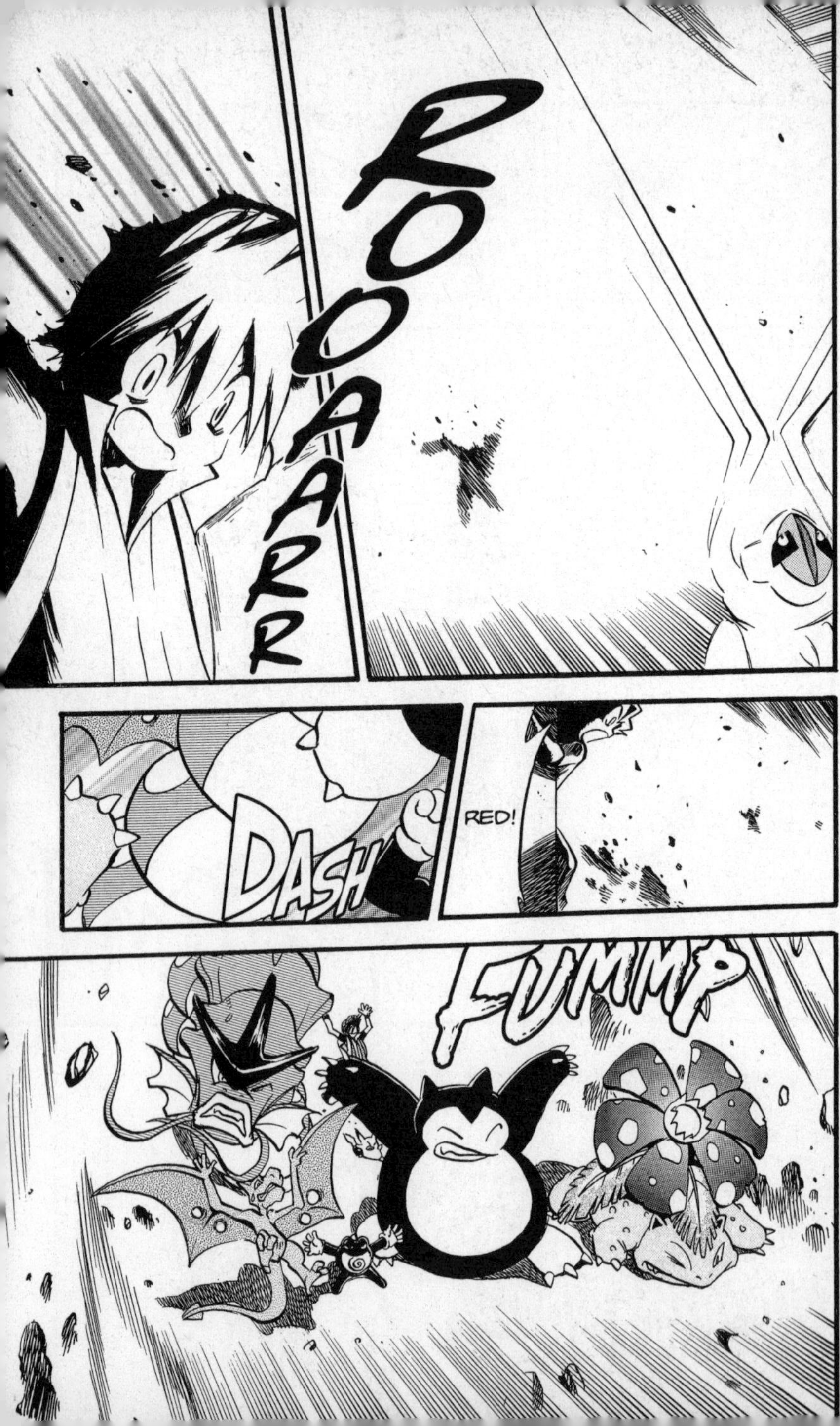
ROOOAARRR
RED!
DASH
FUMMP

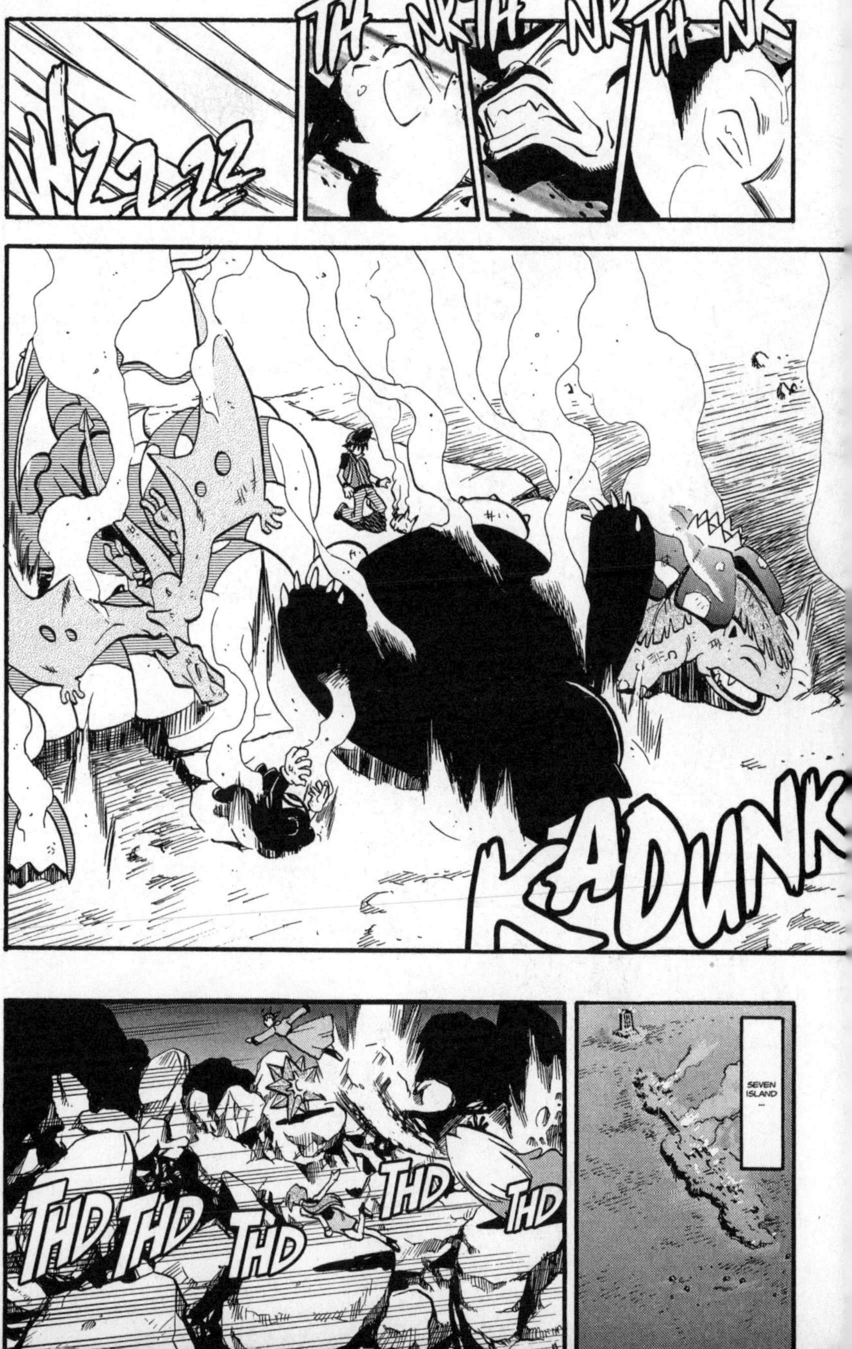

TH NK TH NK TH NK
WZZZZ
KADUNK
SEVEN ISLAND ...
THD THD THD THD THD

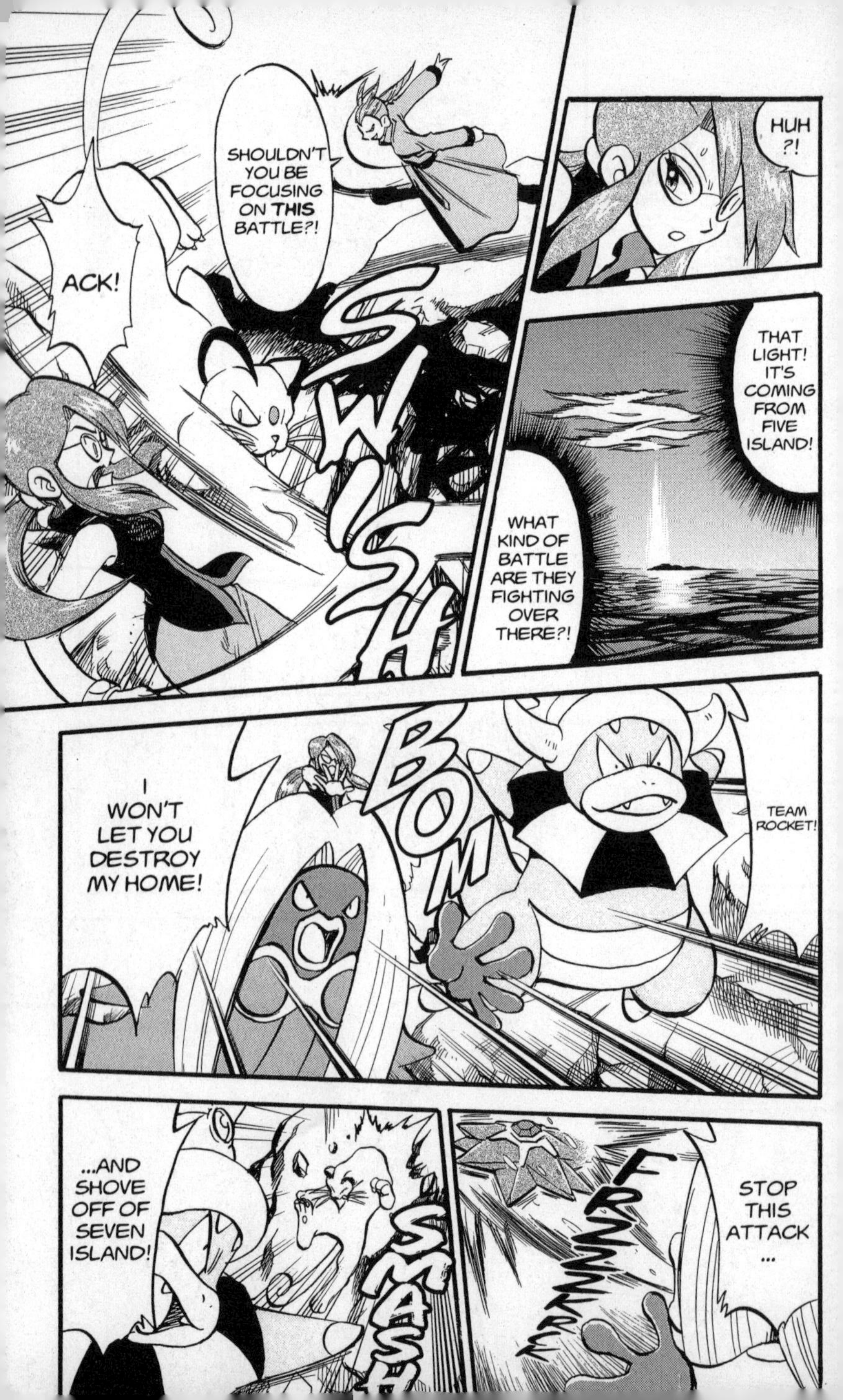
HUH ?!
THAT LIGHT! IT'S COMING FROM FIVE ISLAND!
WHAT KIND OF BATTLE ARE THEY FIGHTING OVER THERE?!
SHOULDN'T YOU BE FOCUSING ON **THIS** BATTLE?!
ACK!
SWISH
TEAM ROCKET!
I WON'T LET YOU DESTROY MY HOME!
STOP THIS ATTACK ...
...AND SHOVE OFF OF SEVEN ISLAND!
SMASH

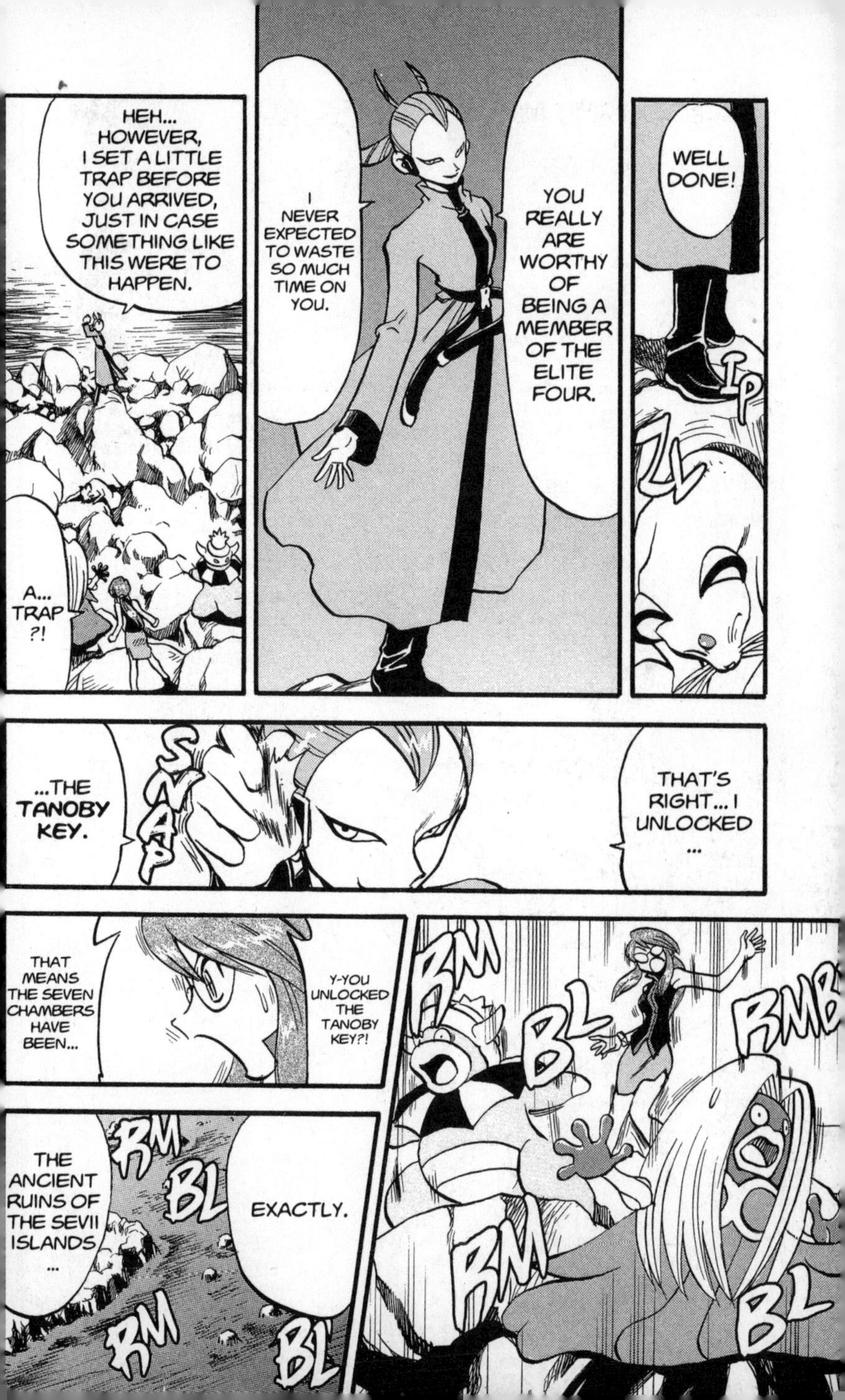
WELL DONE!
YOU REALLY ARE WORTHY OF BEING A MEMBER OF THE ELITE FOUR.
I NEVER EXPECTED TO WASTE SO MUCH TIME ON YOU.
HEH... HOWEVER, I SET A LITTLE TRAP BEFORE YOU ARRIVED, JUST IN CASE SOMETHING LIKE THIS WERE TO HAPPEN.
A... TRAP?!
THAT'S RIGHT... I UNLOCKED...
SNAP
...THE TANOBY KEY.
RMB
BM
BL
BM
BL
Y-YOU UNLOCKED THE TANOBY KEY?!
THAT MEANS THE SEVEN CHAMBERS HAVE BEEN...
EXACTLY.
RM
BL
THE ANCIENT RUINS OF THE SEVII ISLANDS...
BL
RM

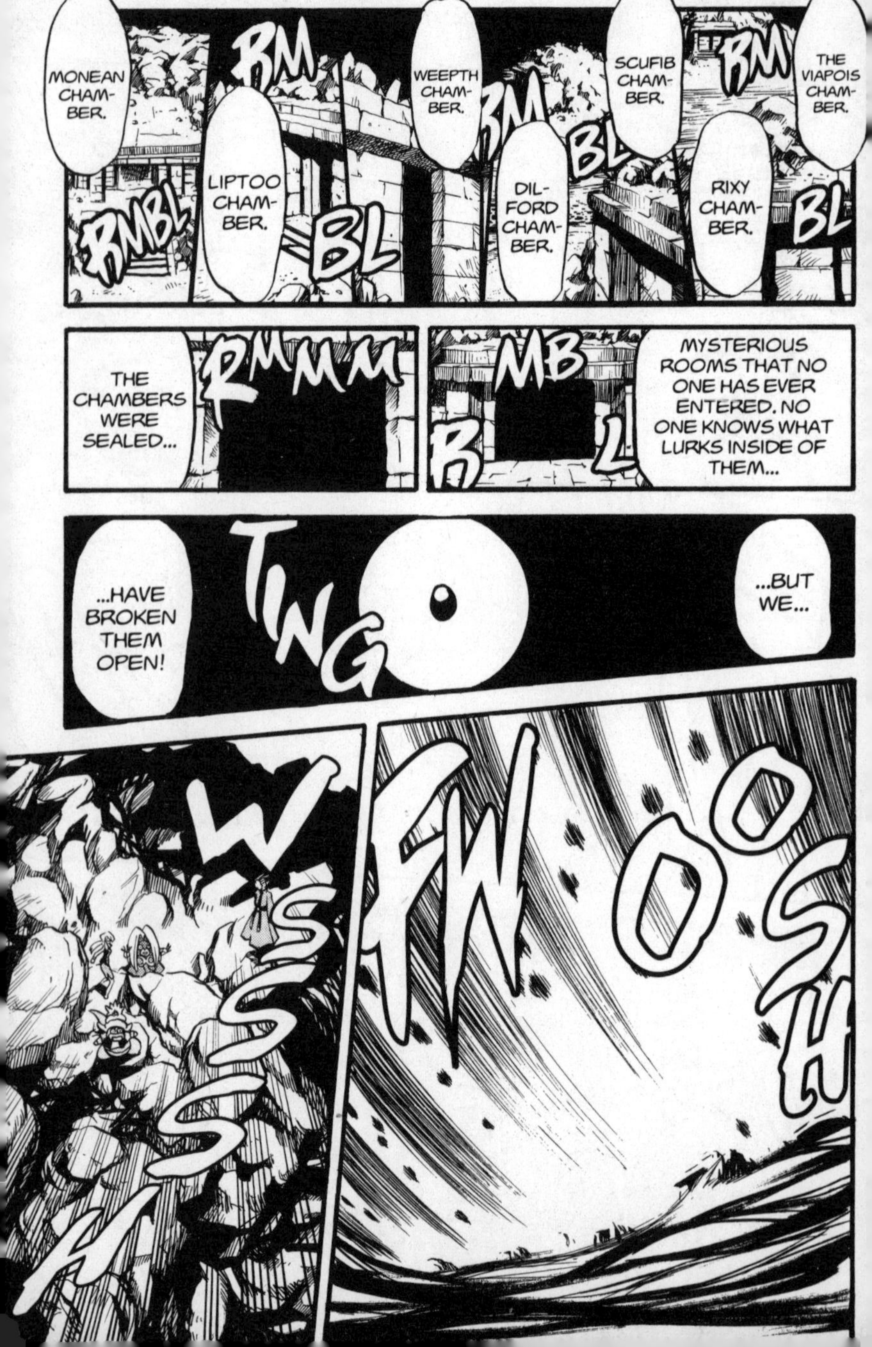

THE VIAPOIS CHAMBER.
BM
BL
RIXY CHAMBER.
SCUFIB CHAMBER.
BL
DILFORD CHAMBER.
BM
WEEPTH CHAMBER.
BL
LIPTOO CHAMBER.
BM
MONEAN CHAMBER.
RMBL
MYSTERIOUS ROOMS THAT NO ONE HAS EVER ENTERED. NO ONE KNOWS WHAT LURKS INSIDE OF THEM...
MB
BL
RMMMM
THE CHAMBERS WERE SEALED...
...BUT WE...
TING
...HAVE BROKEN THEM OPEN!
FWOOSH
WSSH

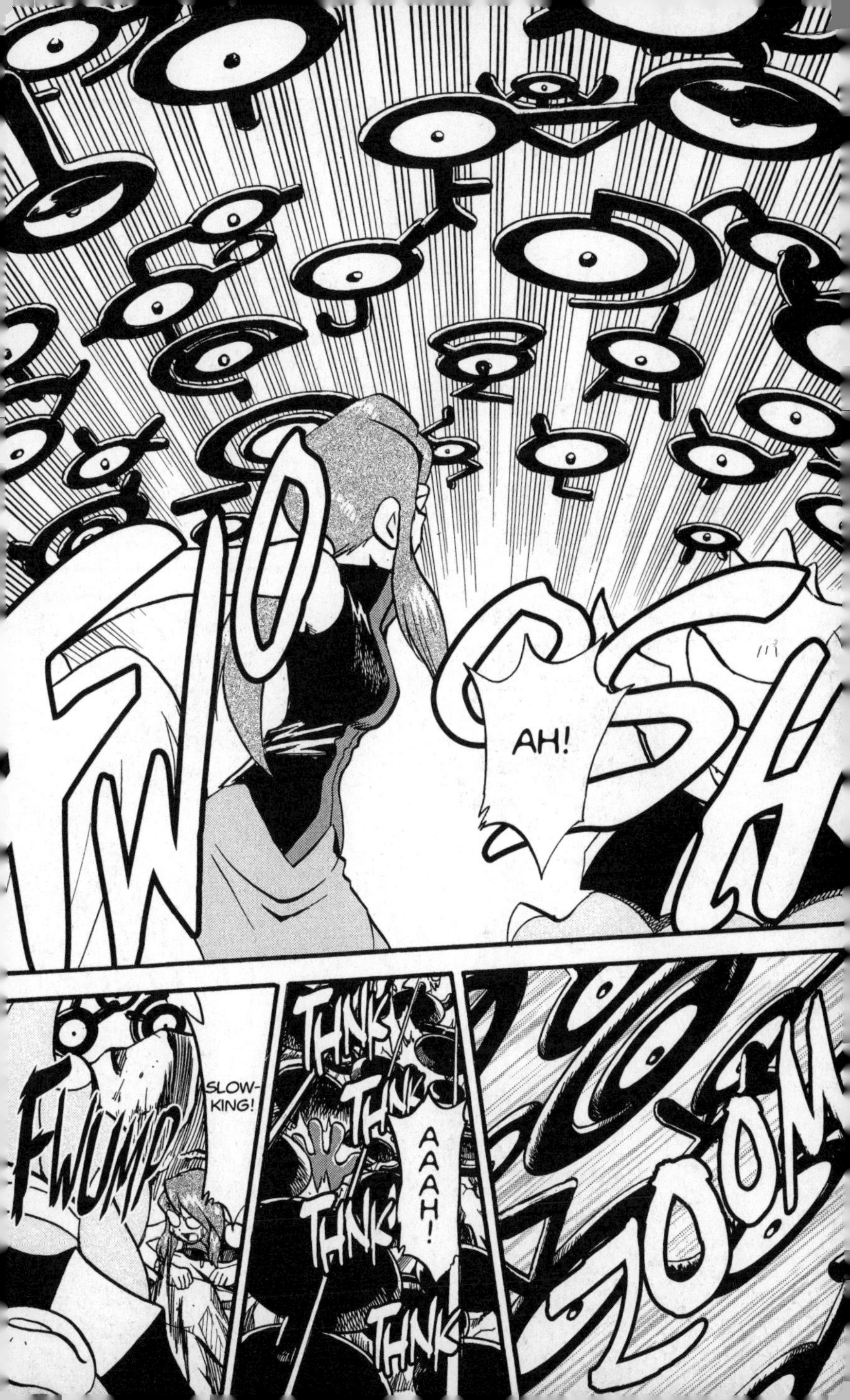
AH!
ZOOM
THNK
THNK
AAAH!
THNK
THNK
SLOW-KING!
FWUMP

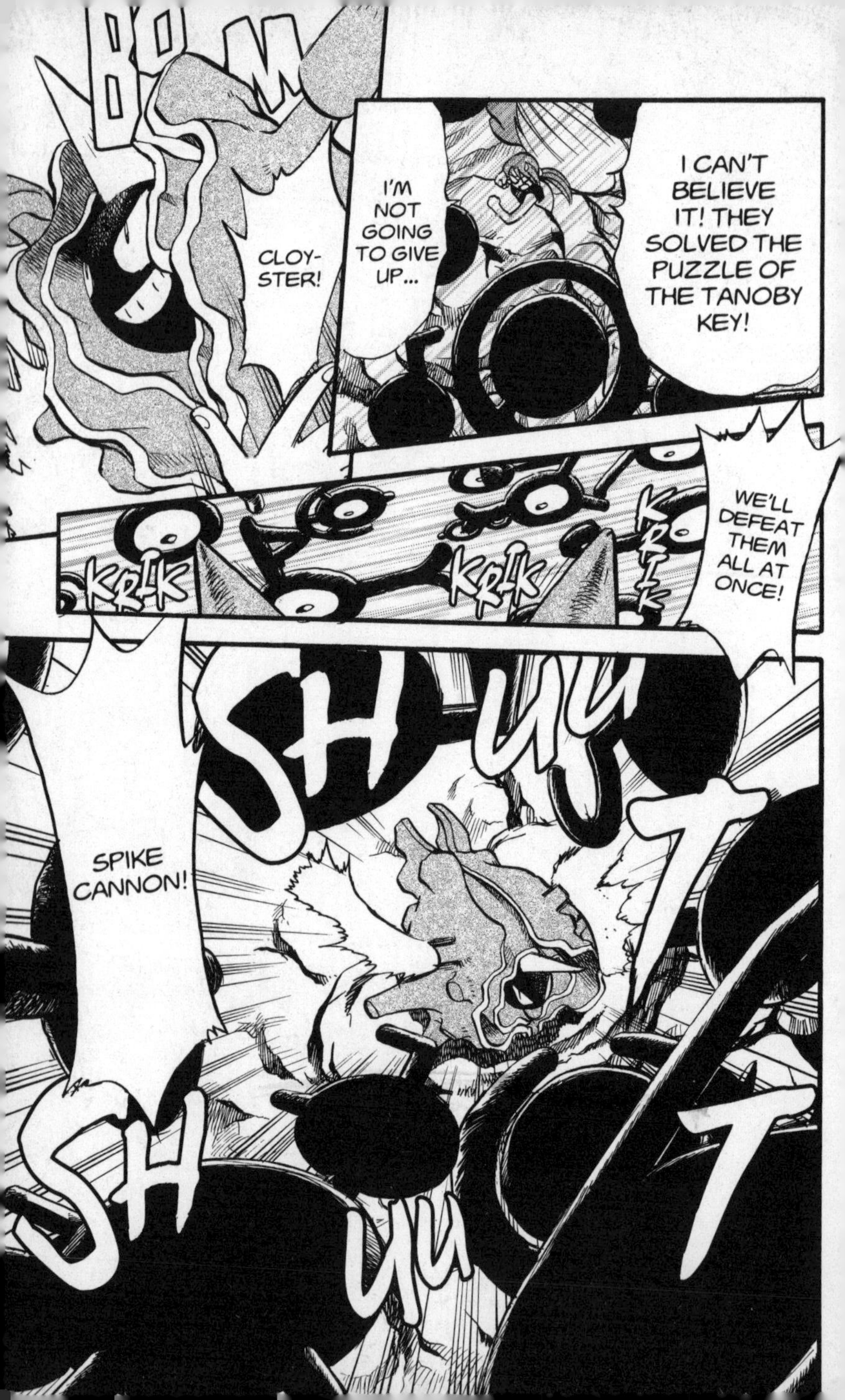
I CAN'T BELIEVE IT! THEY SOLVED THE PUZZLE OF THE TANOBY KEY!
I'M NOT GOING TO GIVE UP...
BOOM
CLOY-STER!
KRIK
KRIK
KRIK
WE'LL DEFEAT THEM ALL AT ONCE!
SHUUT
SPIKE CANNON!
SHUUT

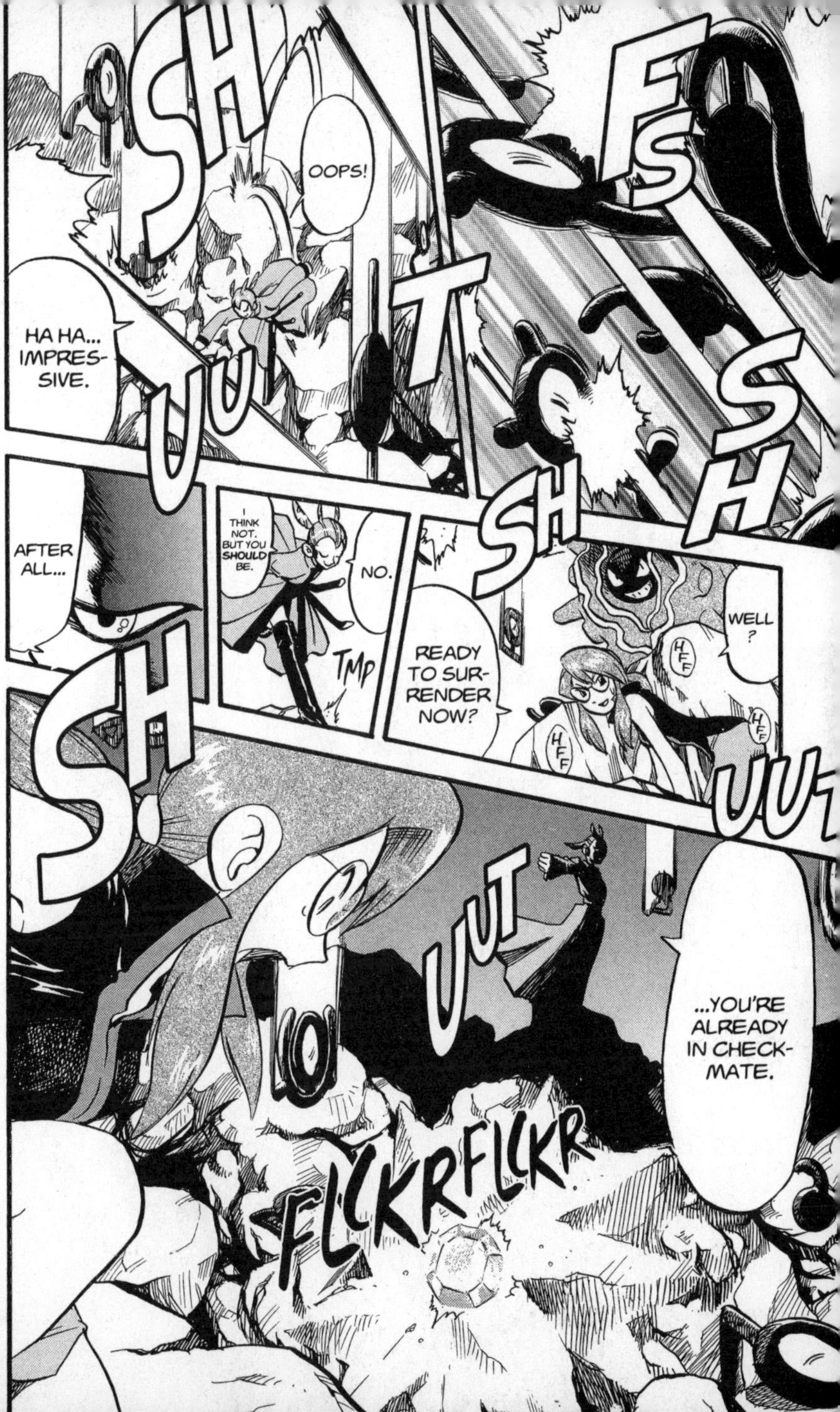
OOPS!
SHUUT
HA HA... IMPRESSIVE.
WELL?
HFF HFF HFF
READY TO SURRENDER NOW?
NO.
I THINK NOT. BUT YOU SHOULD BE.
TMP
AFTER ALL...
...YOU'RE ALREADY IN CHECKMATE.
FLCKRFLCKR

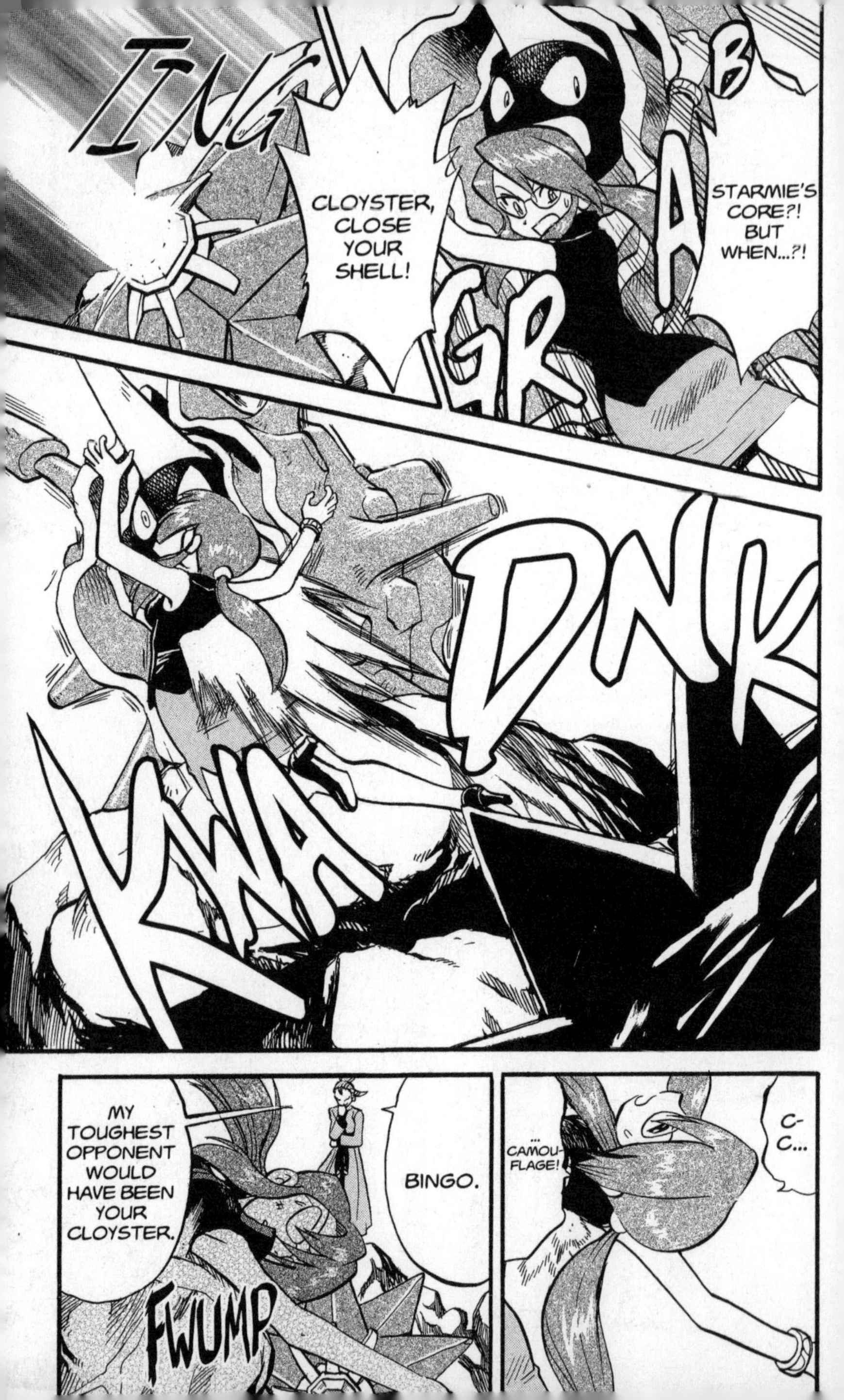
STARMIE'S CORE?! BUT WHEN...?!
CLOYSTER, CLOSE YOUR SHELL!
DNK
KWA
C- C...
... CAMOU-FLAGE!
BINGO.
MY TOUGHEST OPPONENT WOULD HAVE BEEN YOUR CLOYSTER.
FWUMP

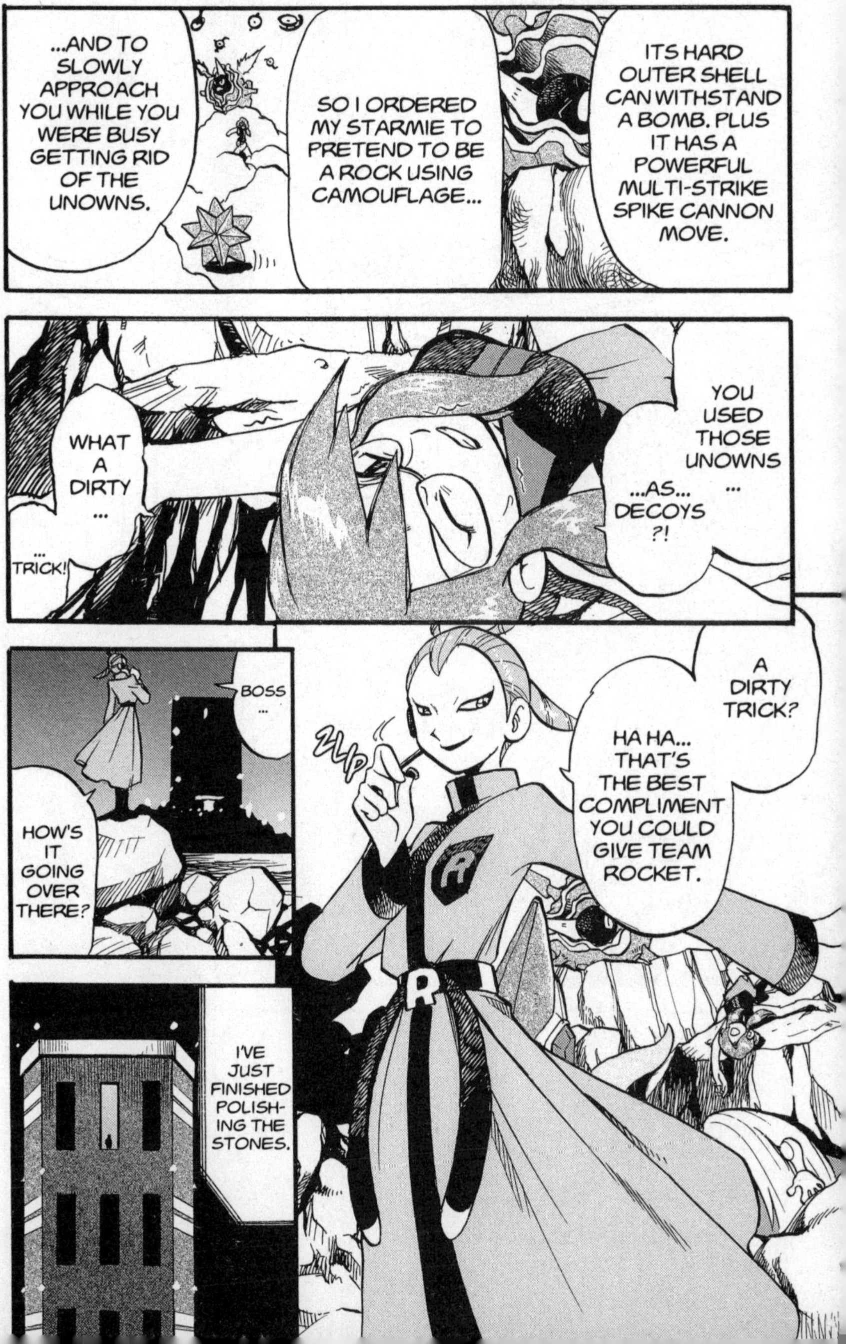
ITS HARD OUTER SHELL CAN WITHSTAND A BOMB. PLUS IT HAS A POWERFUL MULTI-STRIKE SPIKE CANNON MOVE.
SO I ORDERED MY STARMIE TO PRETEND TO BE A ROCK USING CAMOUFLAGE...
...AND TO SLOWLY APPROACH YOU WHILE YOU WERE BUSY GETTING RID OF THE UNOWNS.
YOU USED THOSE UNOWNS ...
...AS... DECOYS ?!
WHAT A DIRTY ...
... TRICK!
A DIRTY TRICK?
HA HA... THAT'S THE BEST COMPLIMENT YOU COULD GIVE TEAM ROCKET.
BOSS ...
HOW'S IT GOING OVER THERE?
I'VE JUST FINISHED POLISH-ING THE STONES.

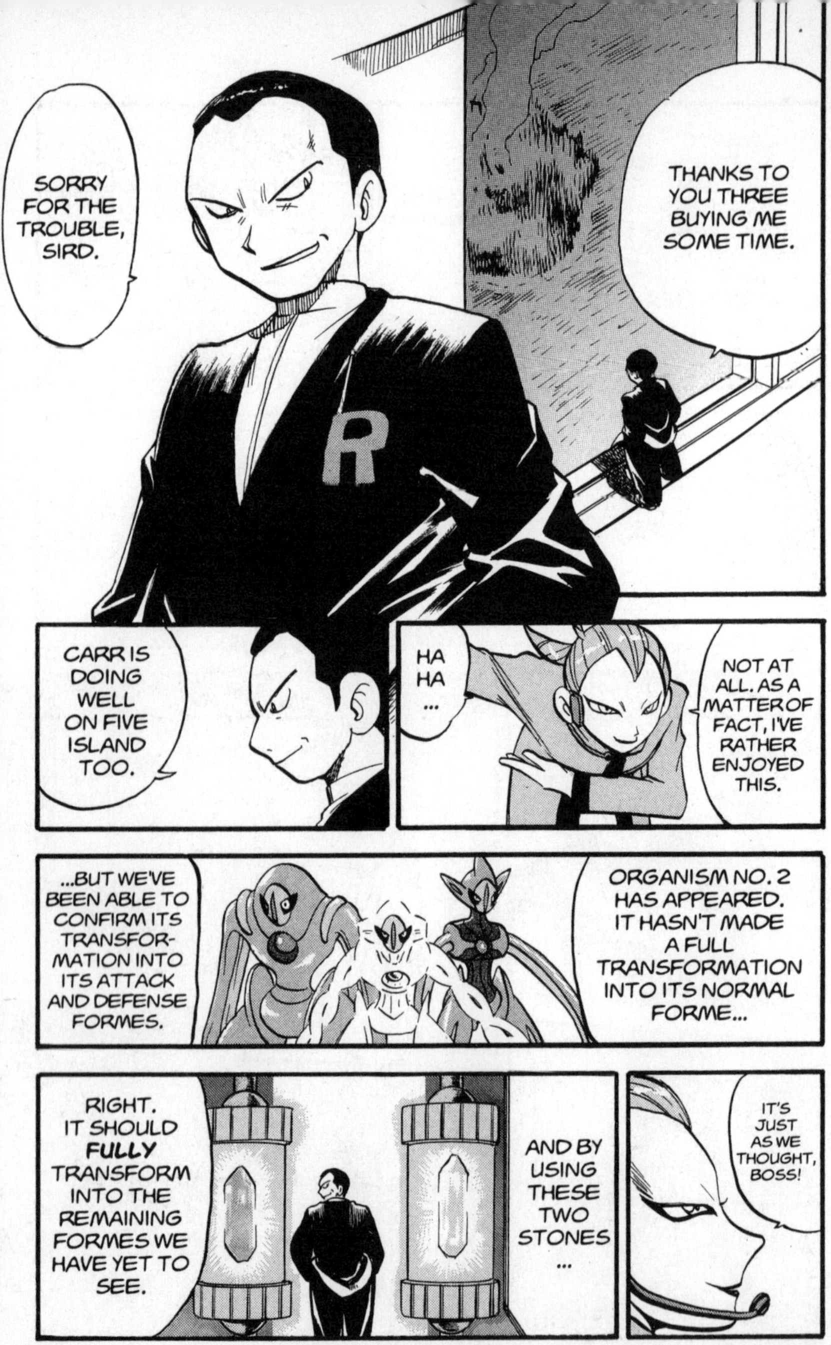
THANKS TO YOU THREE BUYING ME SOME TIME.
SORRY FOR THE TROUBLE, SIRD.
NOT AT ALL. AS A MATTER OF FACT, I'VE RATHER ENJOYED THIS.
HA HA ...
CARR IS DOING WELL ON FIVE ISLAND TOO.
ORGANISM NO. 2 HAS APPEARED. IT HASN'T MADE A FULL TRANSFORMATION INTO ITS NORMAL FORME...
...BUT WE'VE BEEN ABLE TO CONFIRM ITS TRANSFORMATION INTO ITS ATTACK AND DEFENSE FORMES.
IT'S JUST AS WE THOUGHT, BOSS!
AND BY USING THESE TWO STONES ...
RIGHT. IT SHOULD **FULLY** TRANSFORM INTO THE REMAINING FORMES WE HAVE YET TO SEE.

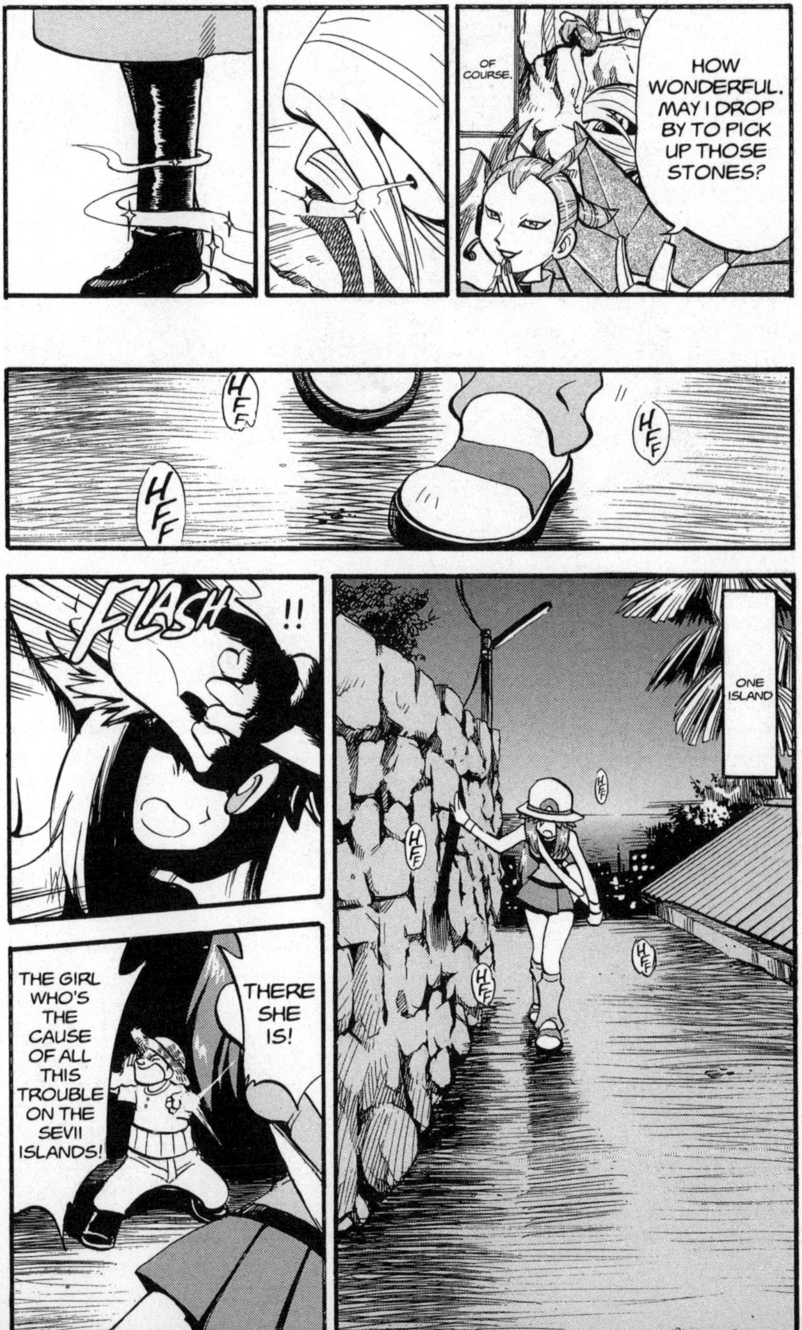
HOW WONDERFUL. MAY I DROP BY TO PICK UP THOSE STONES?
OF COURSE.
HFF
HFF
HFF
ONE ISLAND
HFF
HFF
HFF
HFF
FLASH
!!
THERE SHE IS!
THE GIRL WHO'S THE CAUSE OF ALL THIS TROUBLE ON THE SEVII ISLANDS!

AFTER HER!
GET HER!
HFF
HFF
HFF
HFF
HFF
HFF
HFF
HFF
HFF HFF... YOU CAN'T ESCAPE ANYMORE!
HFF
HFF
SPLASH
AAAAH!
OOOOOOH!
SPLASH

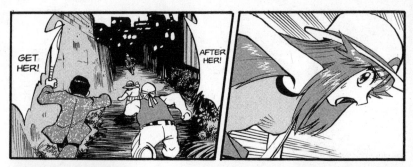

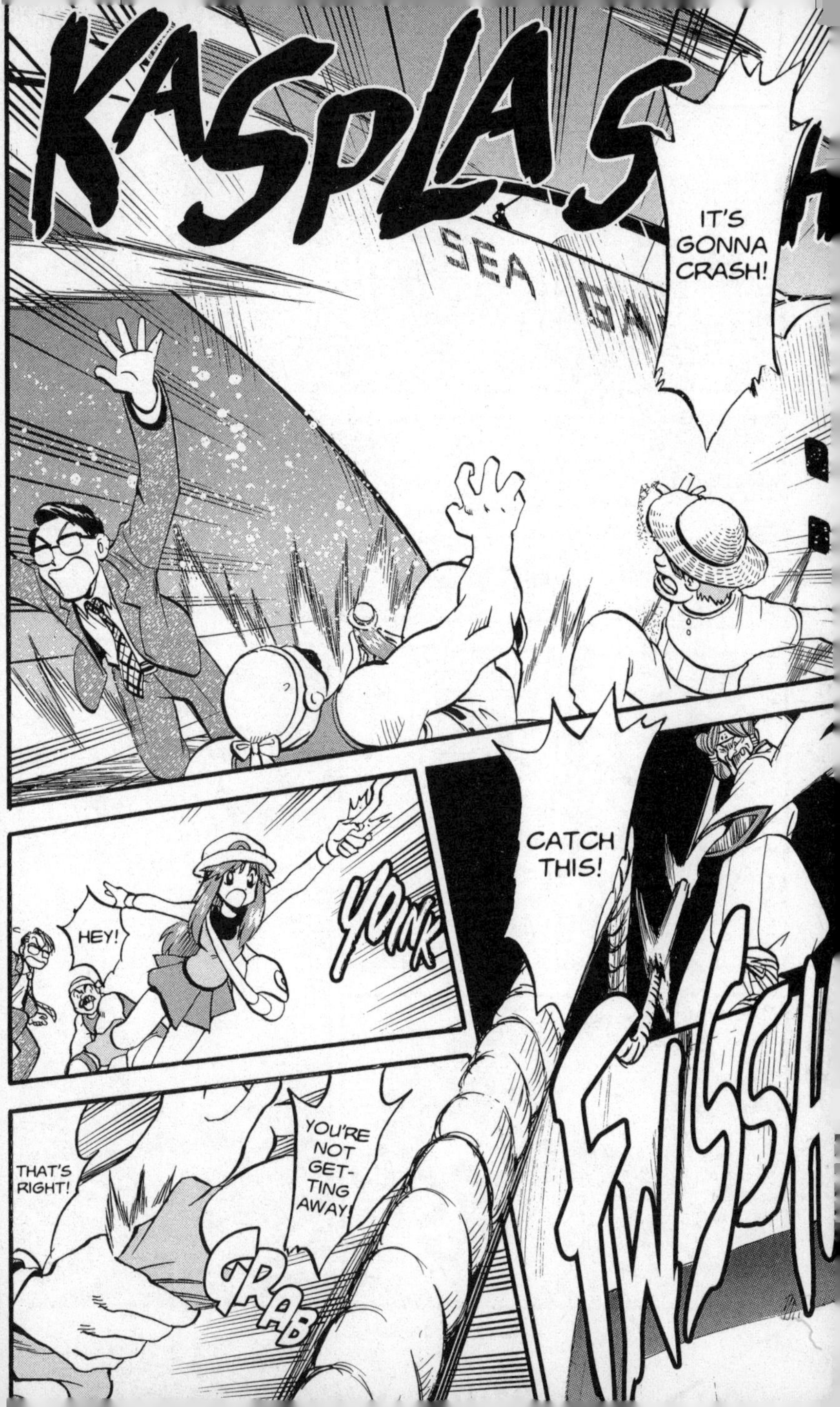
KASPLASH
IT'S GONNA CRASH!
CATCH THIS!
FWISSH
YOINK
HEY!
YOU'RE NOT GET-TING AWAY!
THAT'S RIGHT!
GRAB

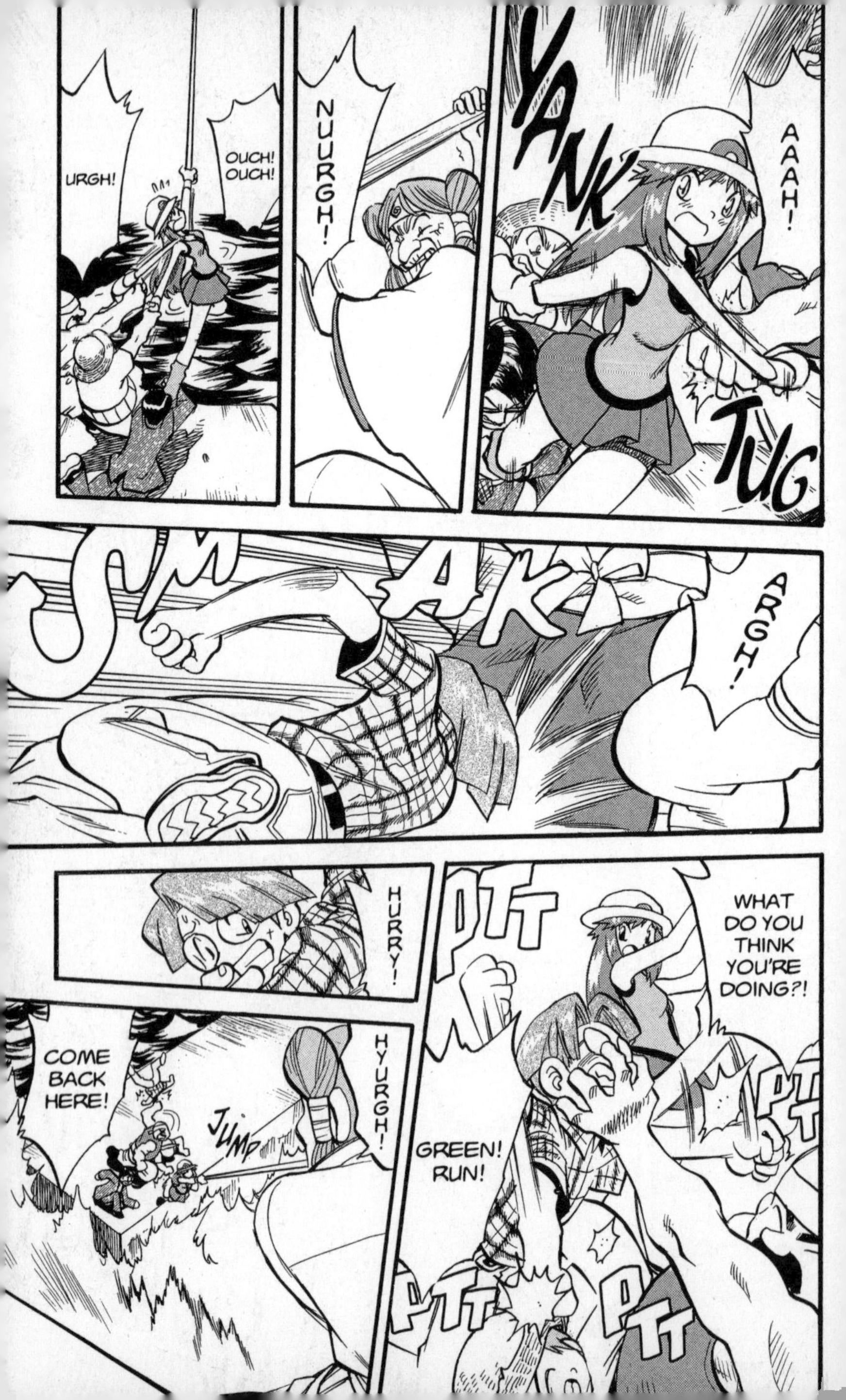

YANK
AAAAH!
TUG
NUURGH!
OUCH! OUCH!
URGH!
ARGH!
SMAK
PTT
WHAT DO YOU THINK YOU'RE DOING?!
PTT
GREEN! RUN!
PTT
PTT
HURRY!
HYURGH!
JUMP
COME BACK HERE!

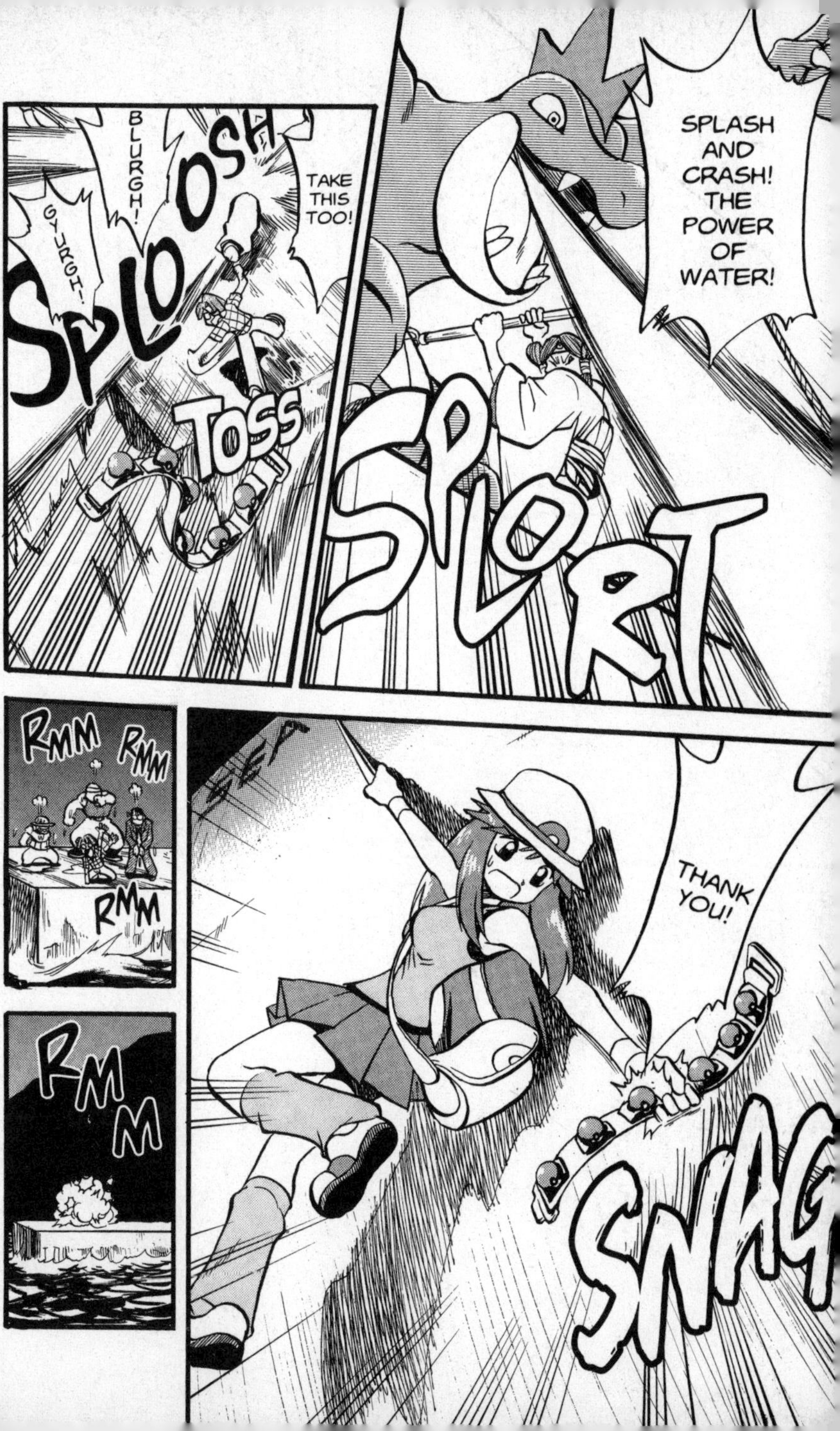
SPLASH AND CRASH! THE POWER OF WATER!
SPLORT
TAKE THIS TOO!
SPLOOSH
BLURGH!
GYURGH!
TOSS
THANK YOU!
SNAG
RMM RMM
RMM
RMM

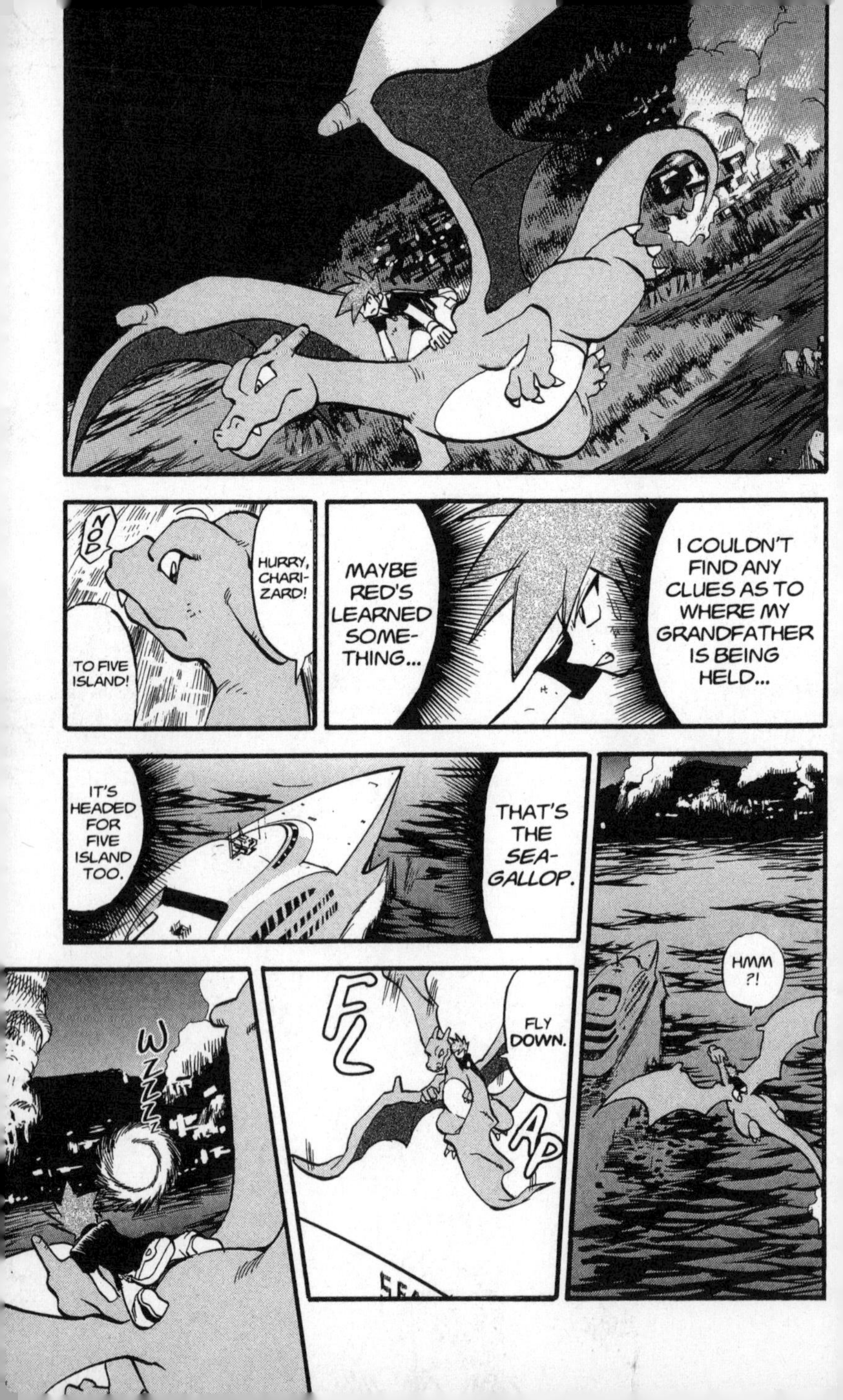
I COULDN'T FIND ANY CLUES AS TO WHERE MY GRANDFATHER IS BEING HELD...
MAYBE RED'S LEARNED SOME-THING...
HURRY, CHARI-ZARD!
TO FIVE ISLAND!
NOD
HMM ?!
THAT'S THE SEA-GALLOP.
IT'S HEADED FOR FIVE ISLAND TOO.
FLY DOWN.
FLAP
WZZZ

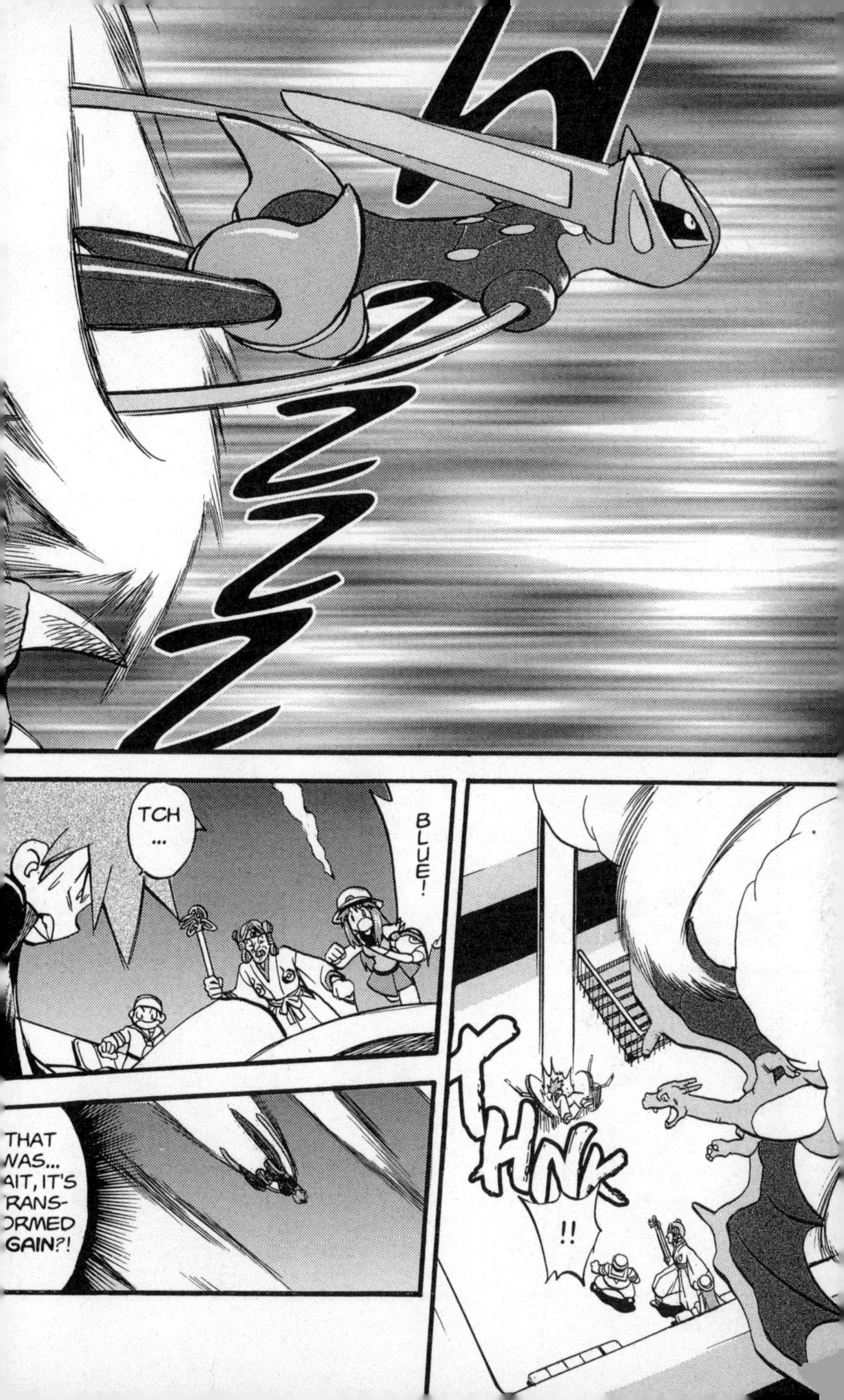
HNK
!!
BLUE!
TCH ...
THAT
WAS...
AIT, IT'S
RANS-
ORMED
GAIN?!

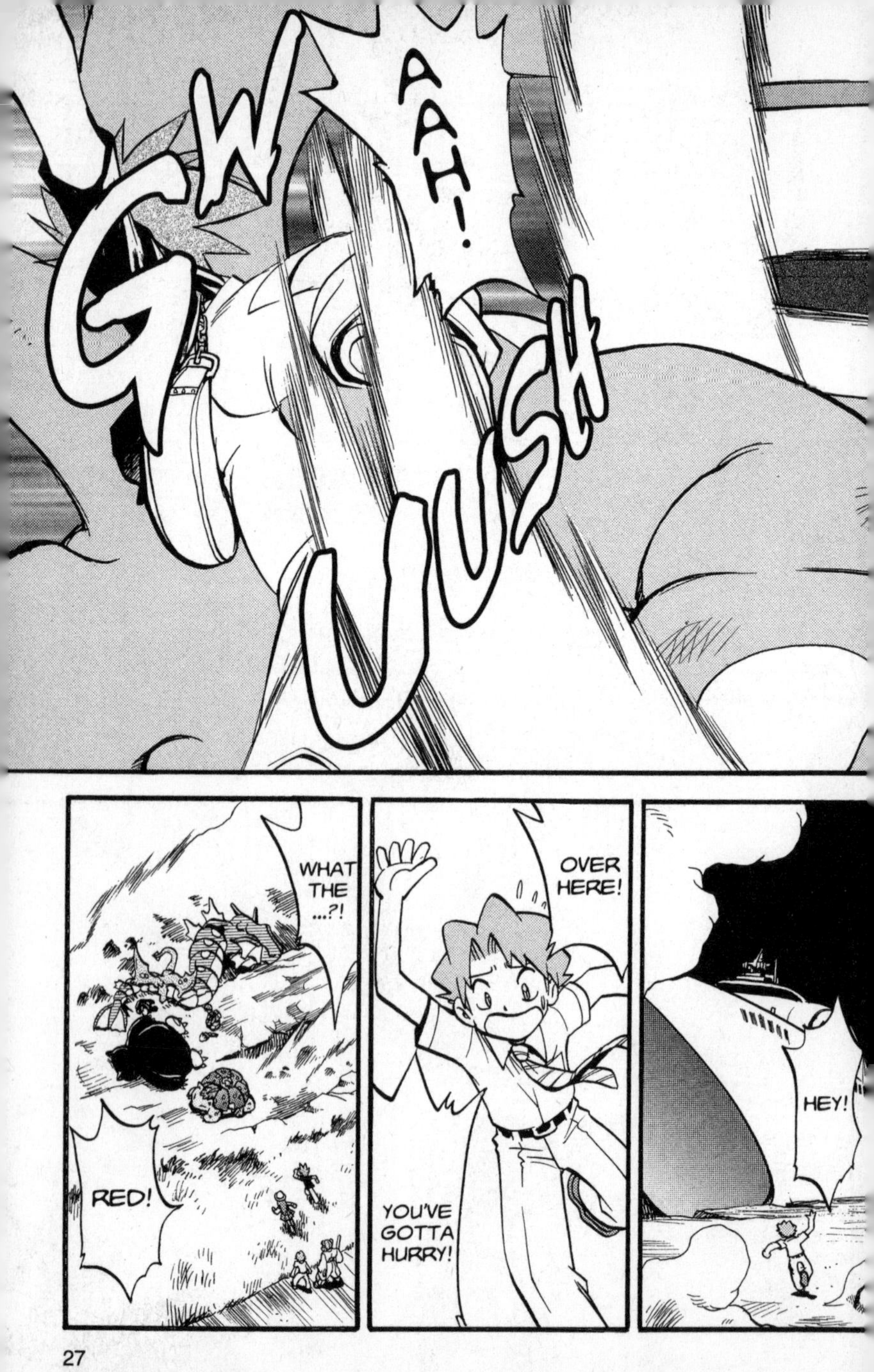
AAH!
GWUSH
HEY!
OVER HERE!
YOU'VE GOTTA HURRY!
WHAT THE ...?!
RED!

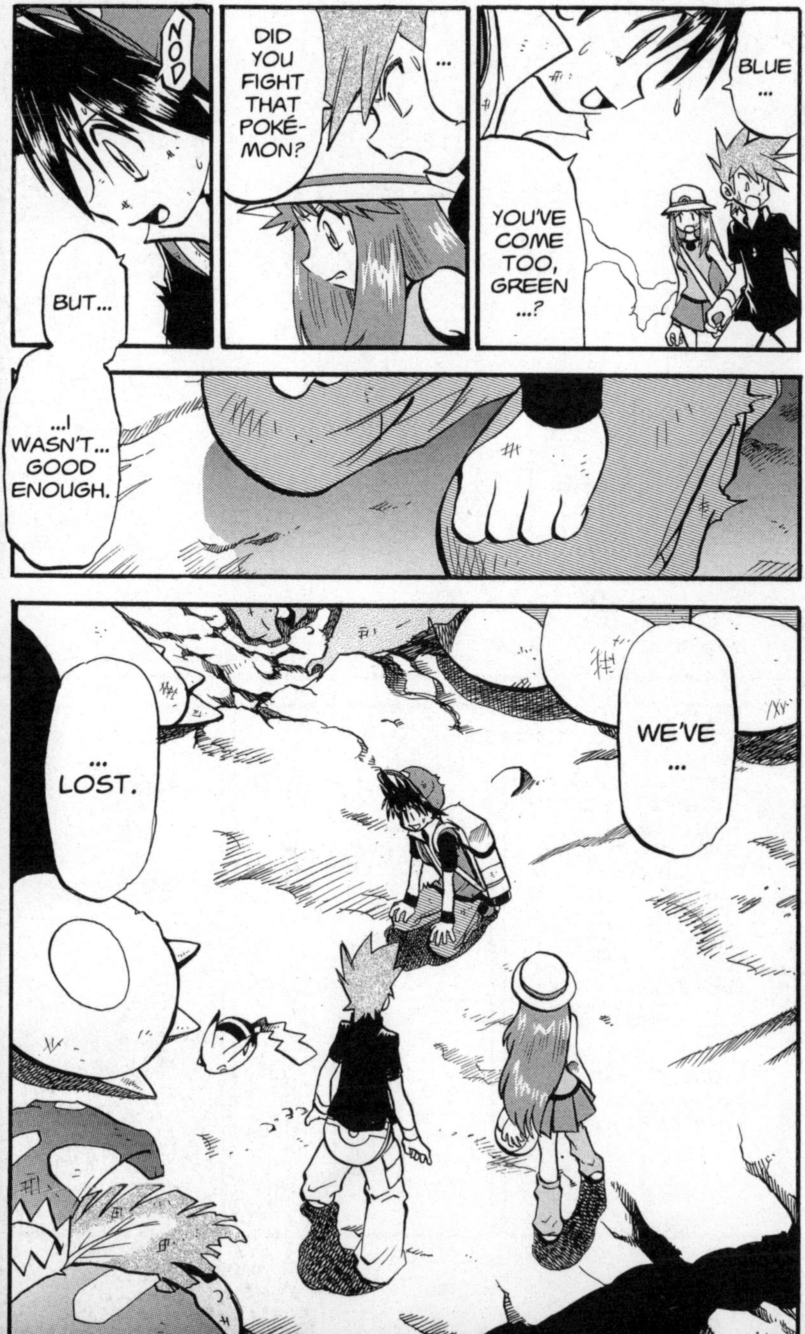
BLUE ...
YOU'VE COME TOO, GREEN ...?
...
DID YOU FIGHT THAT POKÉ-MON?
NOD
BUT...
...I WASN'T... GOOD ENOUGH.
WE'VE ...
... LOST.

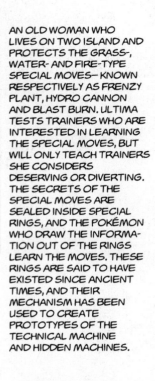
AN OLD WOMAN WHO LIVES ON TWO ISLAND AND PROTECTS THE GRASS-, WATER- AND FIRE-TYPE SPECIAL MOVES— KNOWN RESPECTIVELY AS FRENZY PLANT, HYDRO CANNON AND BLAST BURN. ULTIMA TESTS TRAINERS WHO ARE INTERESTED IN LEARNING THE SPECIAL MOVES, BUT WILL ONLY TEACH TRAINERS SHE CONSIDERS DESERVING OR DIVERTING. THE SECRETS OF THE SPECIAL MOVES ARE SEALED INSIDE SPECIAL RINGS, AND THE POKÉMON WHO DRAW THE INFORMATION OUT OF THE RINGS LEARN THE MOVES. THESE RINGS ARE SAID TO HAVE EXISTED SINCE ANCIENT TIMES, AND THEIR MECHANISM HAS BEEN USED TO CREATE PROTOTYPES OF THE TECHNICAL MACHINE AND HIDDEN MACHINES.

ULTIMA

- Birthplace: Cape Brink, Two Island
- Birthday: February 2nd
- Blood Type: B
- Job: Move Tutor
- Hobby: Coming up with new gimmicks for the training corridor. Sightseeing.
- Family: She was married once...

● Adventure 281 ●
Not Exactly Normal

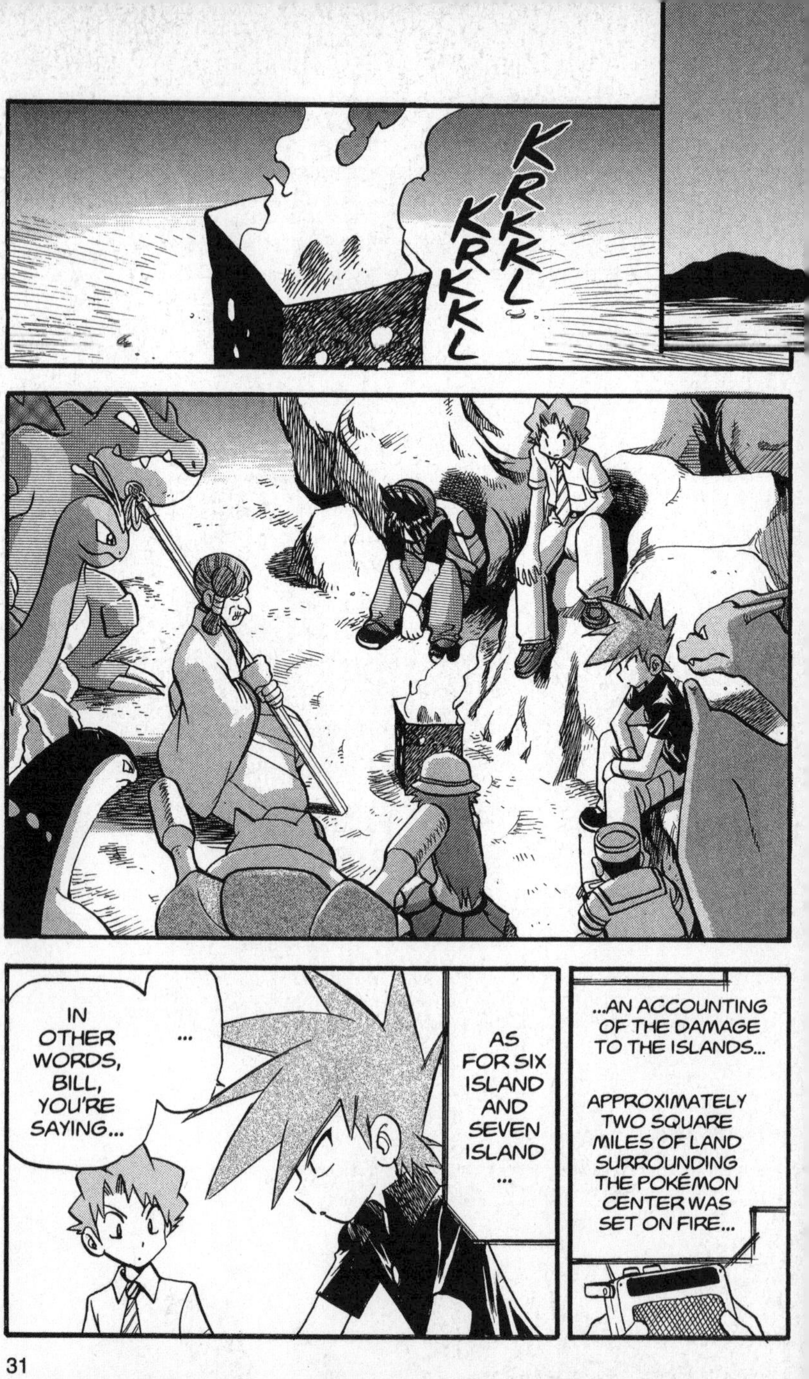
KRKKL KRKKL
...AN ACCOUNTING OF THE DAMAGE TO THE ISLANDS...
APPROXIMATELY TWO SQUARE MILES OF LAND SURROUNDING THE POKÉMON CENTER WAS SET ON FIRE...
AS FOR SIX ISLAND AND SEVEN ISLAND ...
...
IN OTHER WORDS, BILL, YOU'RE SAYING...

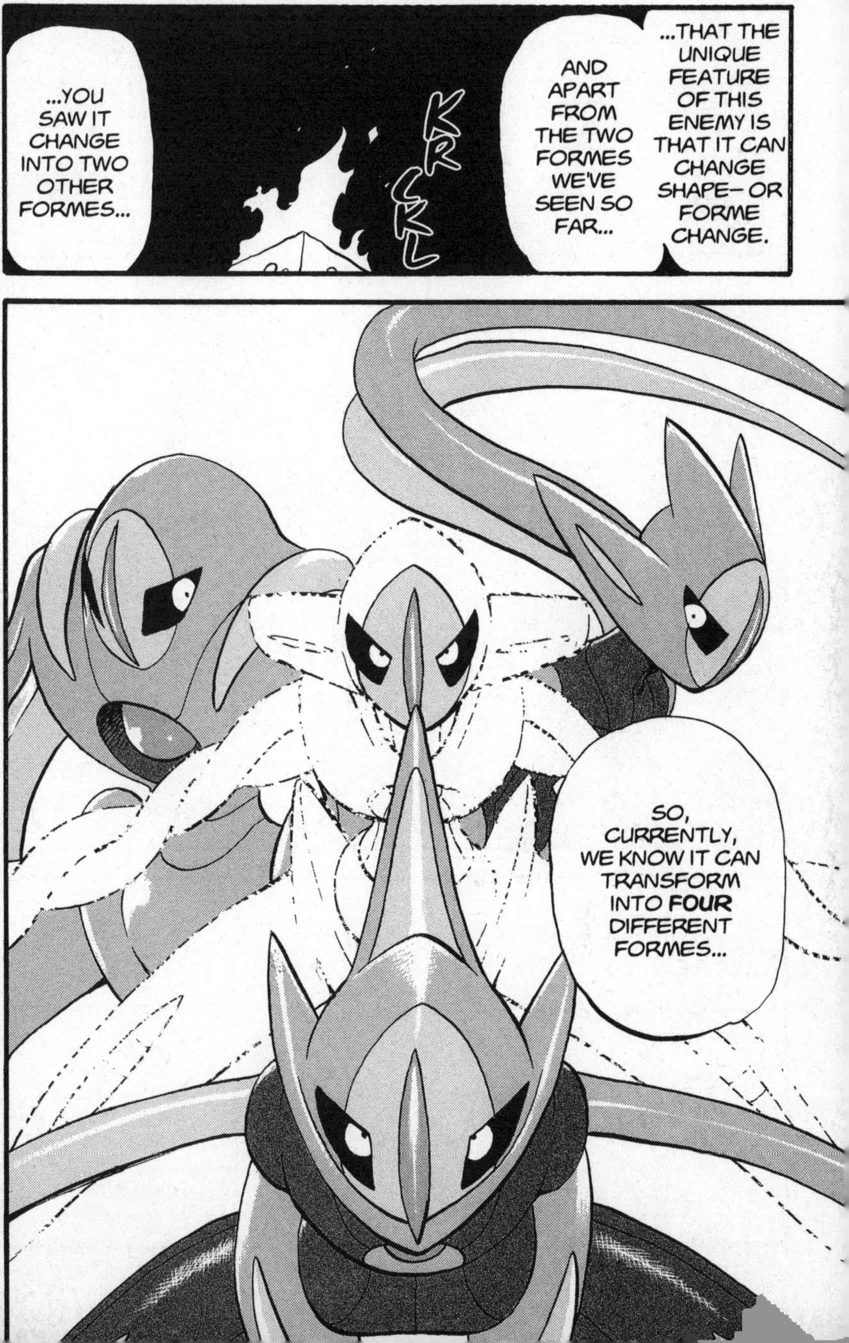
...THAT THE UNIQUE FEATURE OF THIS ENEMY IS THAT IT CAN CHANGE SHAPE—OR FORME CHANGE.
AND APART FROM THE TWO FORMES WE'VE SEEN SO FAR...
KRKL
...YOU SAW IT CHANGE INTO TWO OTHER FORMES...
SO, CURRENTLY, WE KNOW IT CAN TRANSFORM INTO **FOUR** DIFFERENT FORMES...

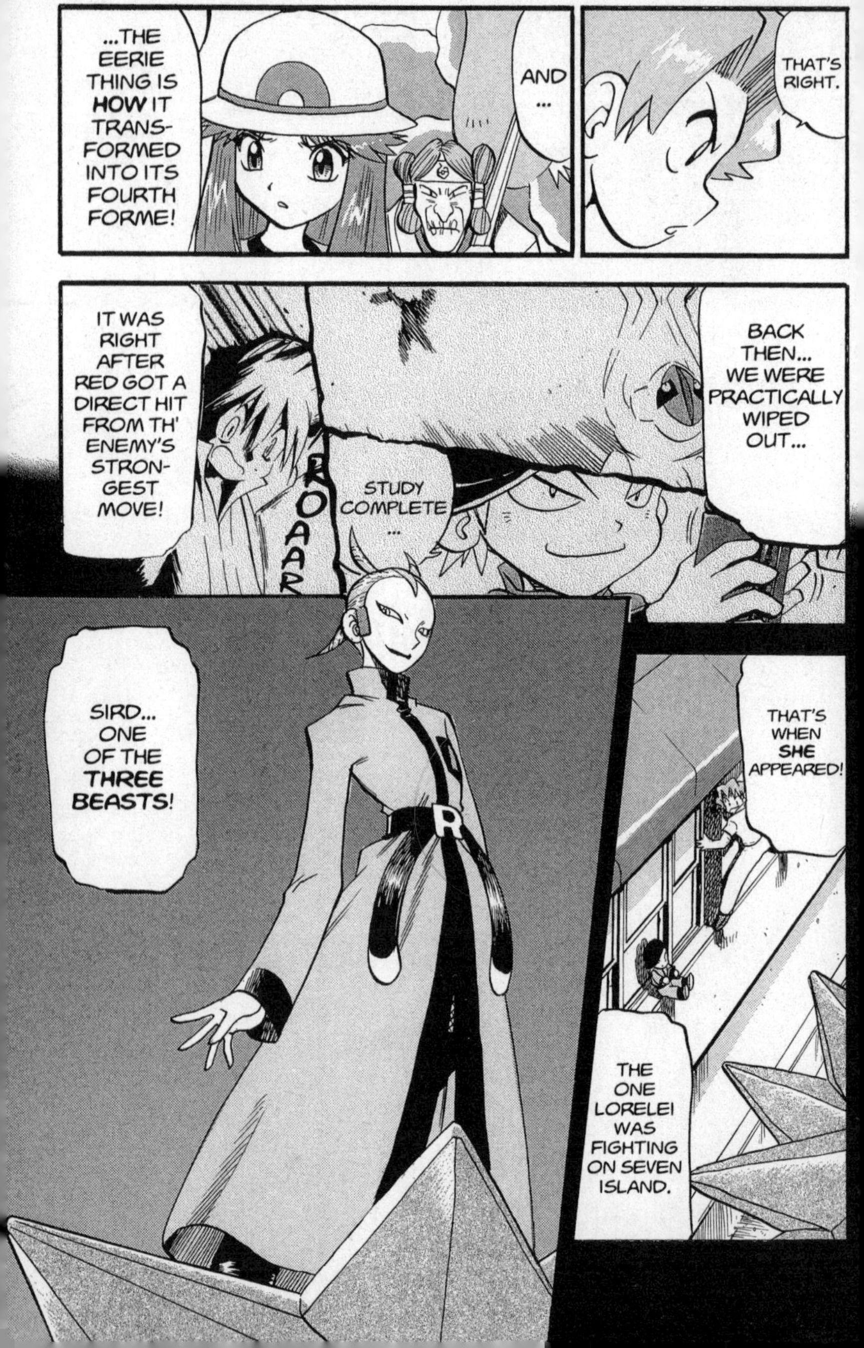
THAT'S RIGHT.
AND ...
...THE EERIE THING IS **HOW** IT TRANS-FORMED INTO ITS FOURTH FORME!
BACK THEN... WE WERE PRACTICALLY WIPED OUT...
IT WAS RIGHT AFTER RED GOT A DIRECT HIT FROM TH' ENEMY'S STRON-GEST MOVE!
ROAAR
STUDY COMPLETE ...
THAT'S WHEN **SHE** APPEARED!
THE ONE LORELEI WAS FIGHTING ON SEVEN ISLAND.
SIRD... ONE OF THE **THREE BEASTS**!

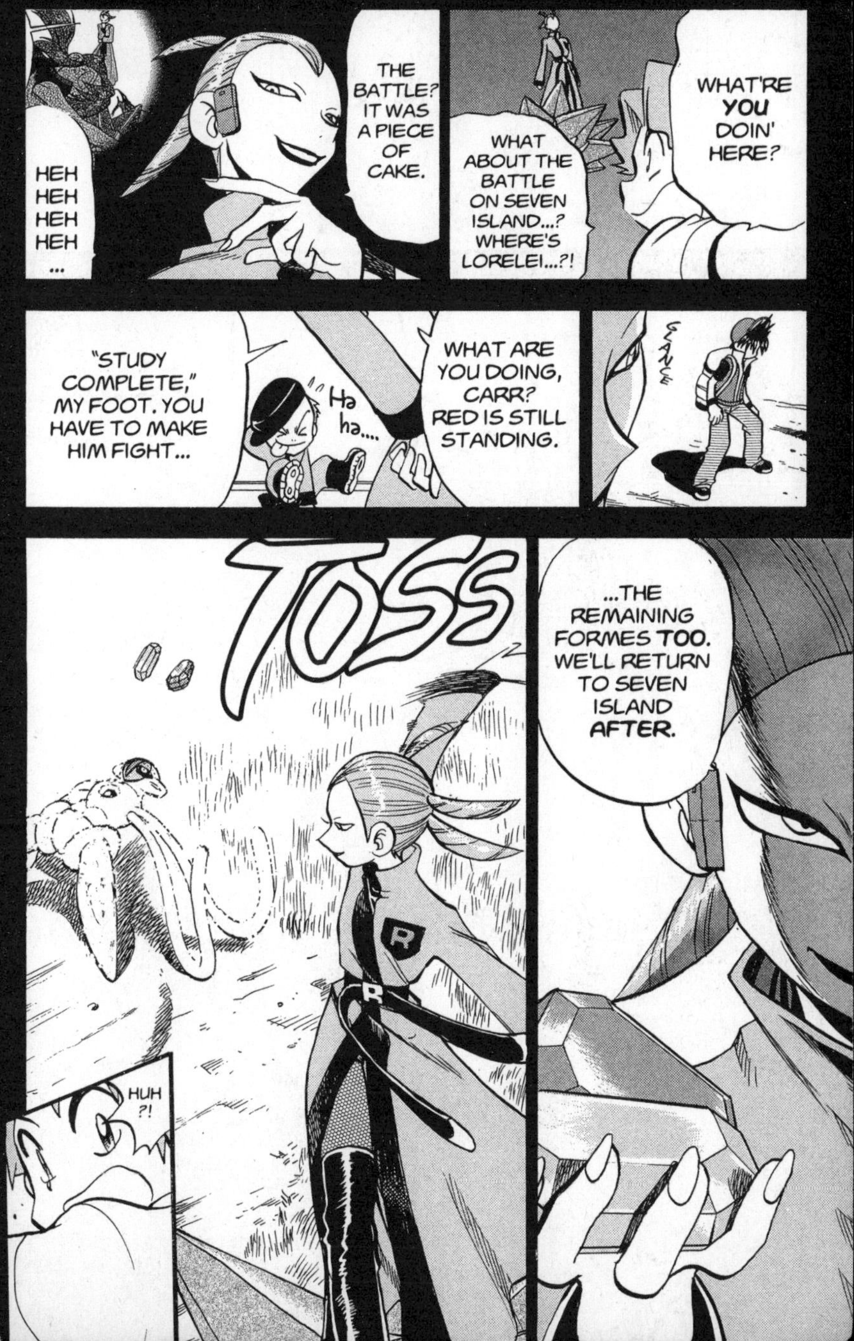
WHAT'RE YOU DOIN' HERE?
WHAT ABOUT THE BATTLE ON SEVEN ISLAND...? WHERE'S LORELEI...?!
THE BATTLE? IT WAS A PIECE OF CAKE.
HEH HEH HEH HEH ...
GLANCE
WHAT ARE YOU DOING, CARR? RED IS STILL STANDING.
Ha ha....
"STUDY COMPLETE," MY FOOT. YOU HAVE TO MAKE HIM FIGHT...
...THE REMAINING FORMES TOO. WE'LL RETURN TO SEVEN ISLAND AFTER.
TOSS
HUH ?!

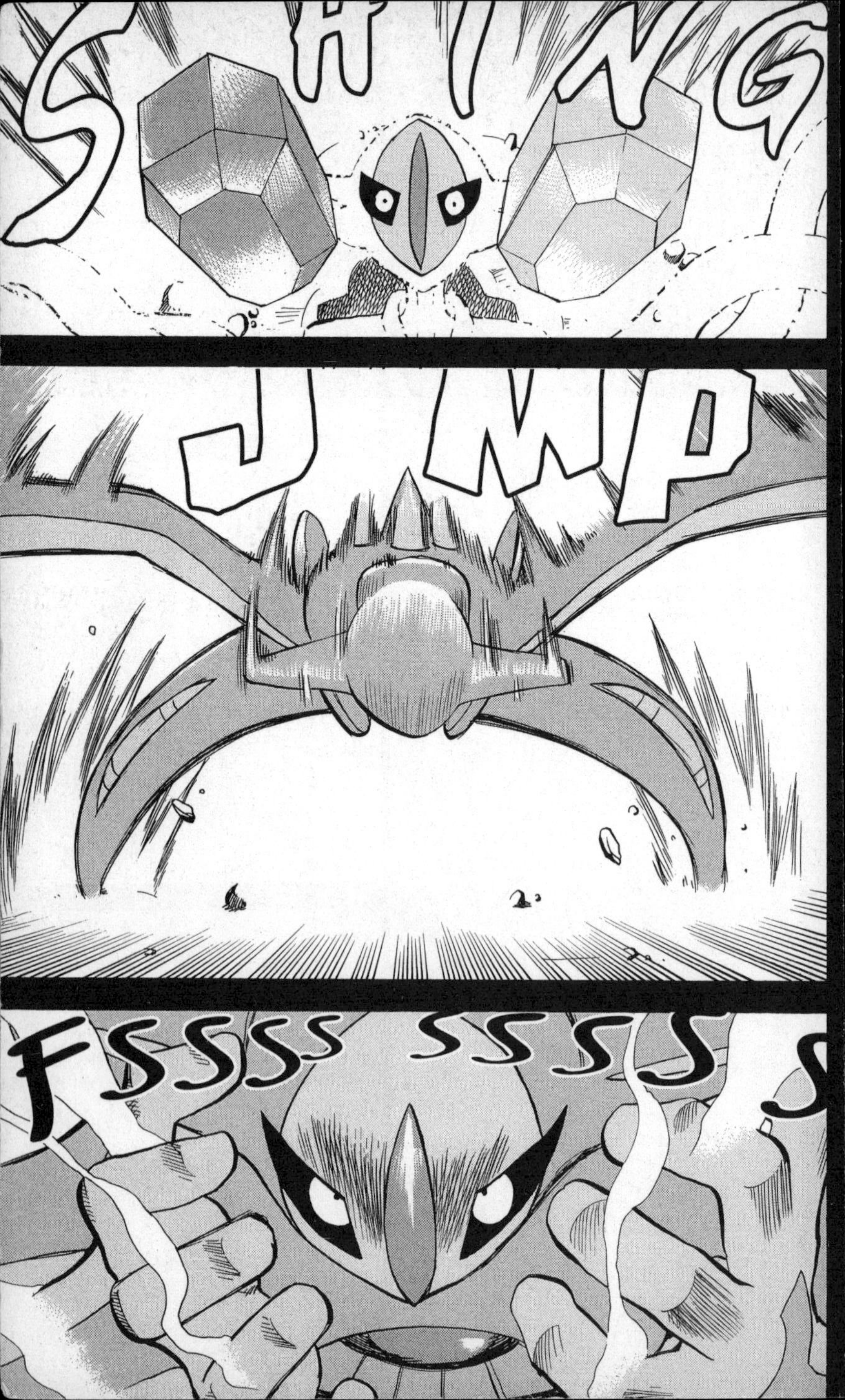
SHING
JMP
FSSSS SSSSS

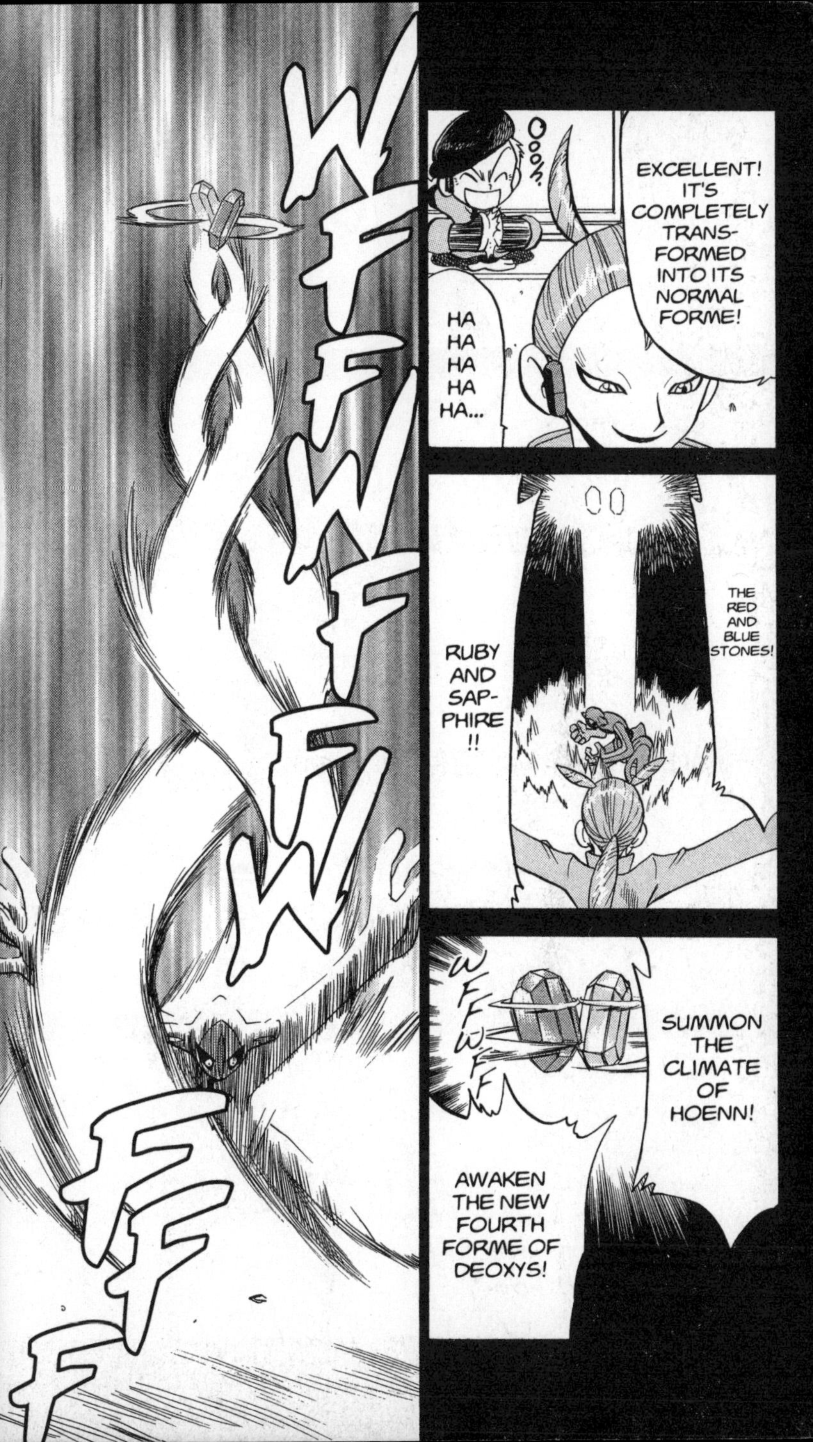
EXCELLENT! IT'S COMPLETELY TRANS-FORMED INTO ITS NORMAL FORME!
Oooh.
HA HA HA HA HA...
THE RED AND BLUE STONES!
RUBY AND SAP-PHIRE!!
WFFWFF
SUMMON THE CLIMATE OF HOENN!
AWAKEN THE NEW FOURTH FORME OF DEOXYS!

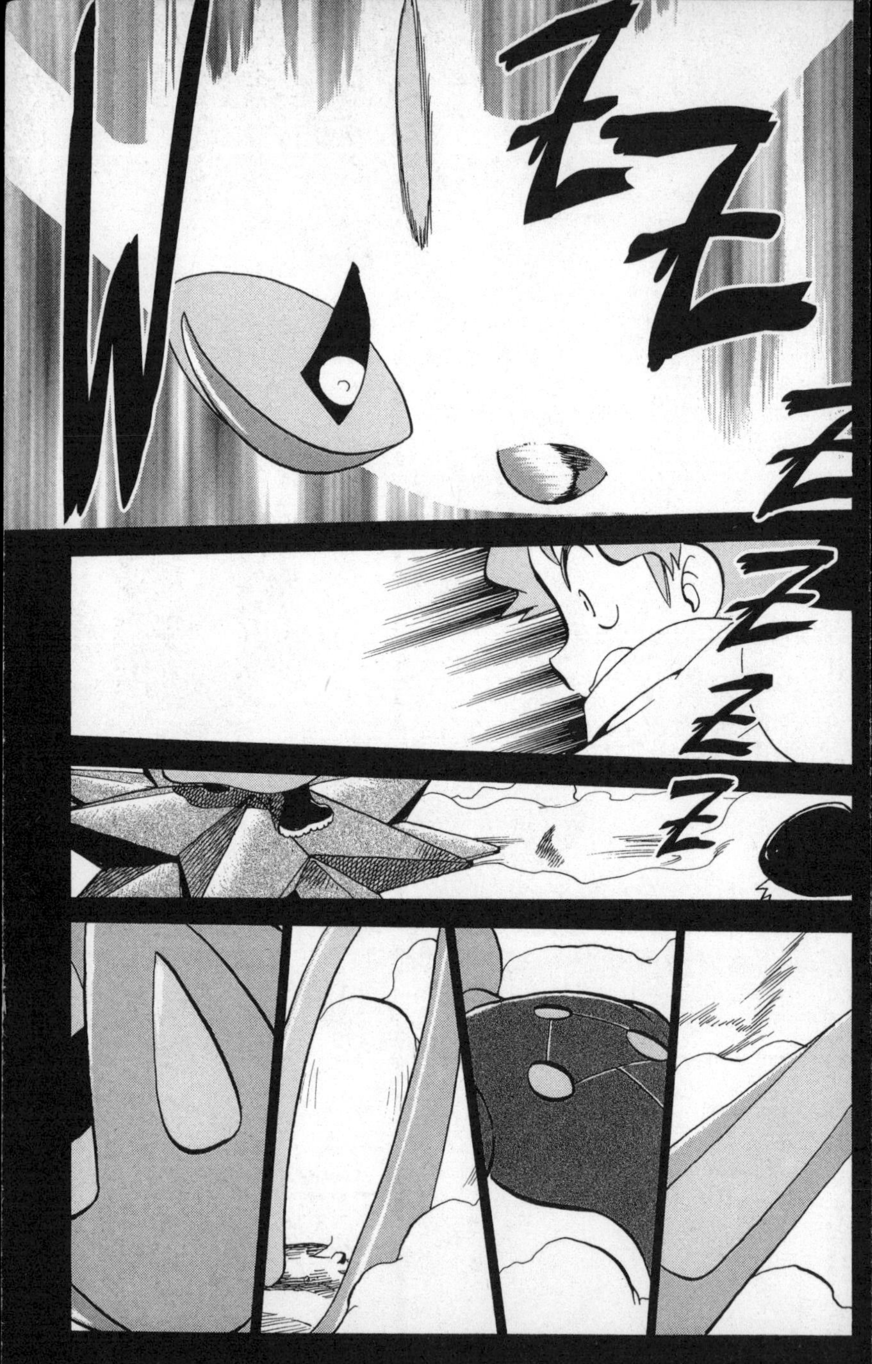

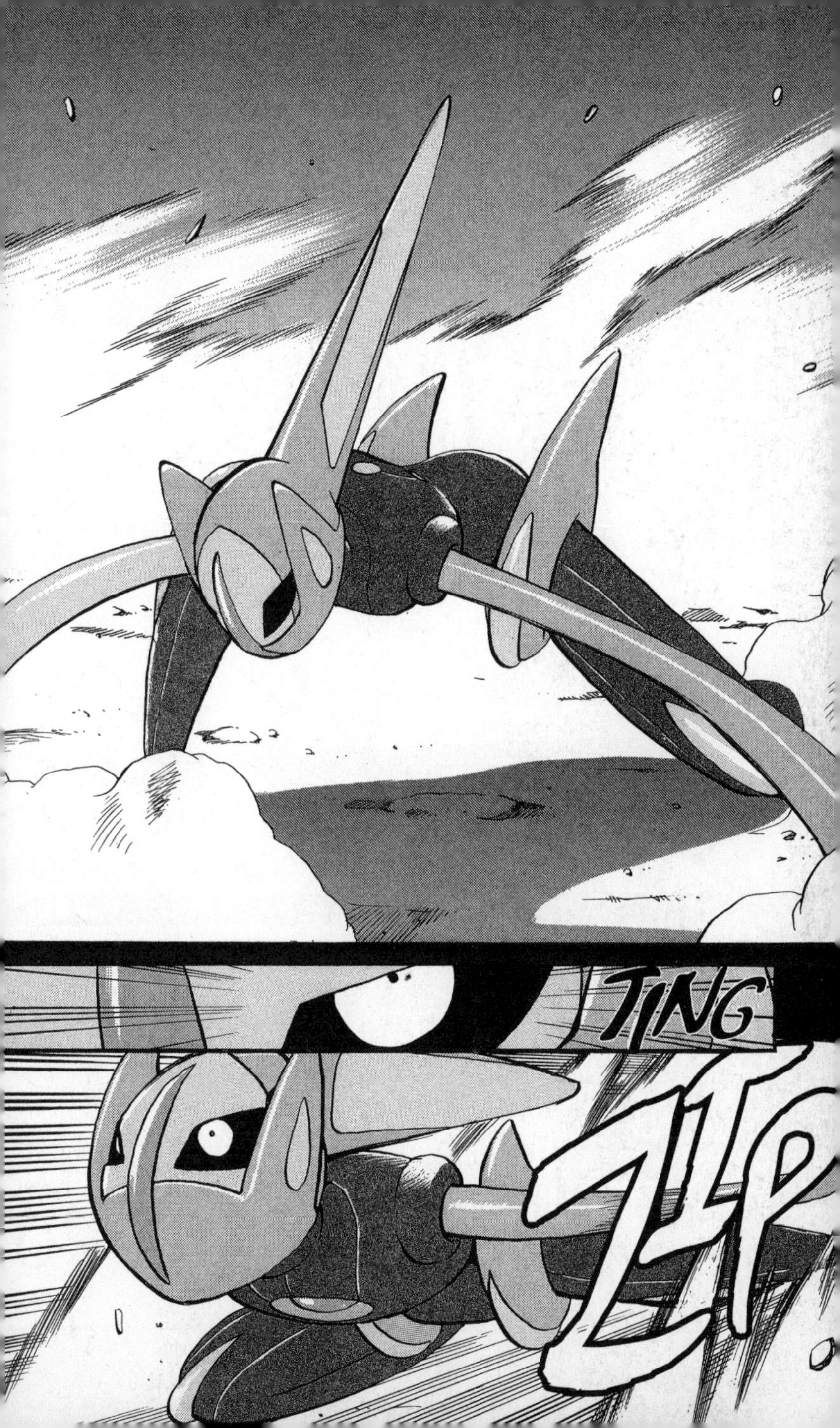
TING
ZIP

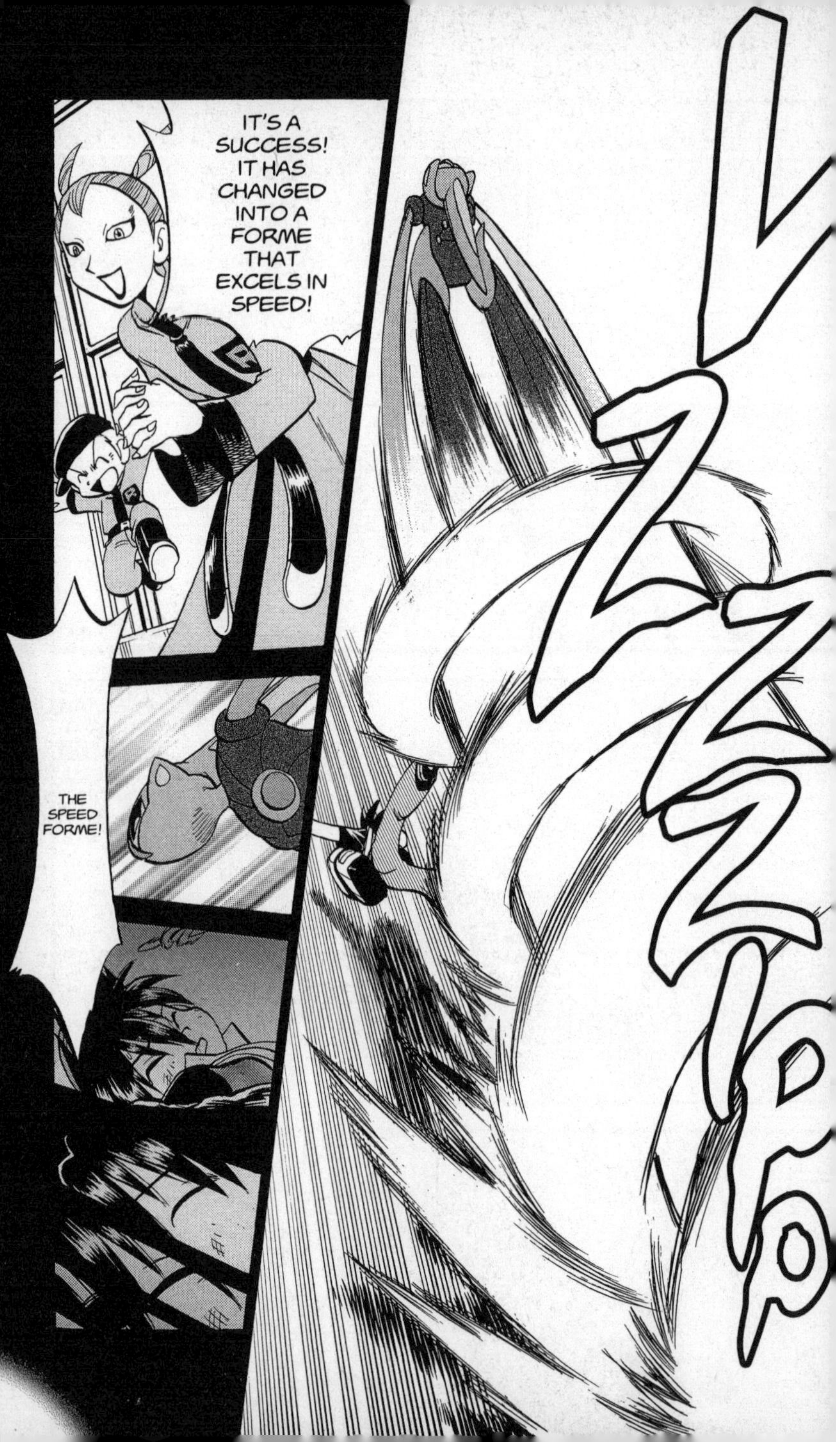
IT'S A SUCCESS! IT HAS CHANGED INTO A FORME THAT EXCELS IN SPEED!
THE SPEED FORME!

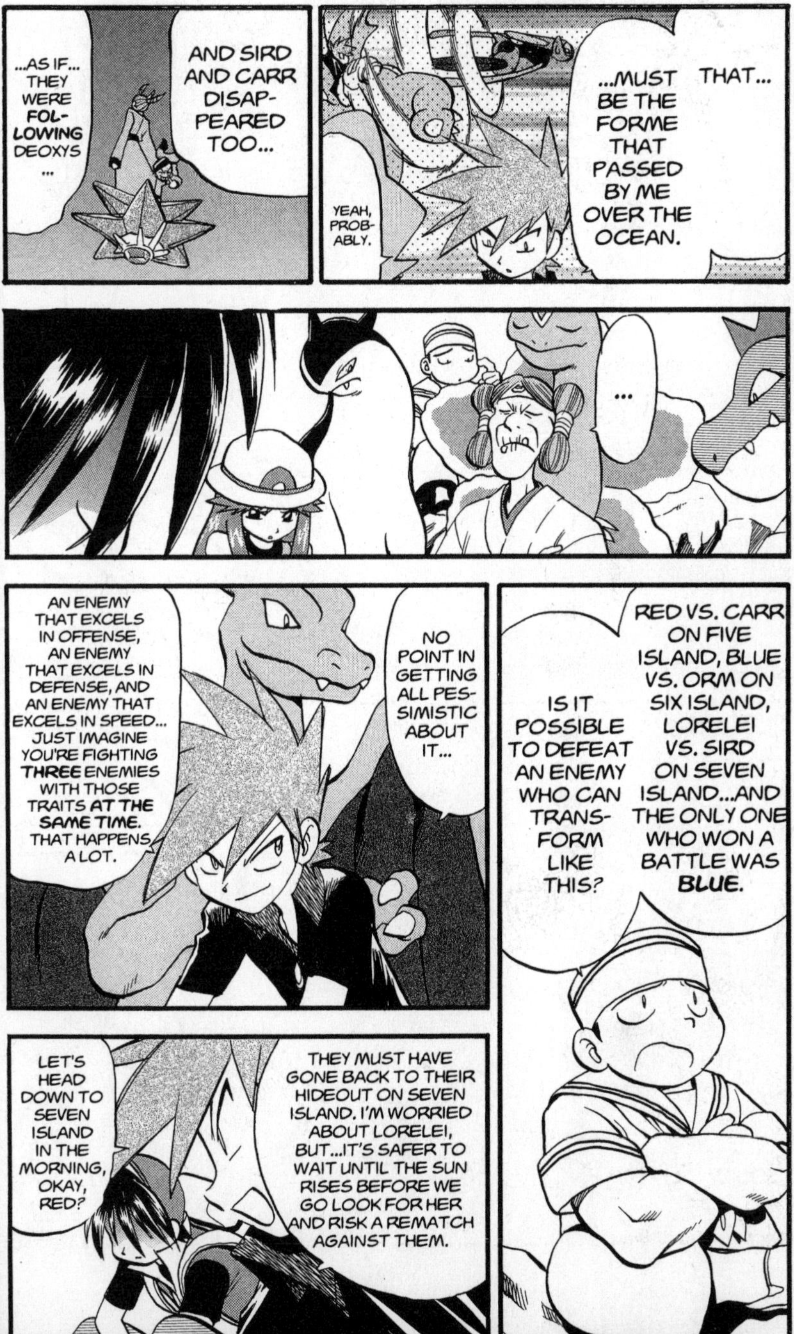
THAT...
...MUST BE THE FORME THAT PASSED BY ME OVER THE OCEAN.
YEAH, PROBABLY.
AND SIRD AND CARR DISAP-PEARED TOO...
...AS IF... THEY WERE FOL-LOWING DEOXYS...
...
RED VS. CARR ON FIVE ISLAND, BLUE VS. ORM ON SIX ISLAND, LORELEI VS. SIRD ON SEVEN ISLAND...AND THE ONLY ONE WHO WON A BATTLE WAS BLUE.
IS IT POSSIBLE TO DEFEAT AN ENEMY WHO CAN TRANS-FORM LIKE THIS?
NO POINT IN GETTING ALL PES-SIMISTIC ABOUT IT...
AN ENEMY THAT EXCELS IN OFFENSE, AN ENEMY THAT EXCELS IN DEFENSE, AND AN ENEMY THAT EXCELS IN SPEED... JUST IMAGINE YOU'RE FIGHTING THREE ENEMIES WITH THOSE TRAITS AT THE SAME TIME. THAT HAPPENS A LOT.
THEY MUST HAVE GONE BACK TO THEIR HIDEOUT ON SEVEN ISLAND. I'M WORRIED ABOUT LORELEI, BUT...IT'S SAFER TO WAIT UNTIL THE SUN RISES BEFORE WE GO LOOK FOR HER AND RISK A REMATCH AGAINST THEM.
LET'S HEAD DOWN TO SEVEN ISLAND IN THE MORNING, OKAY, RED?

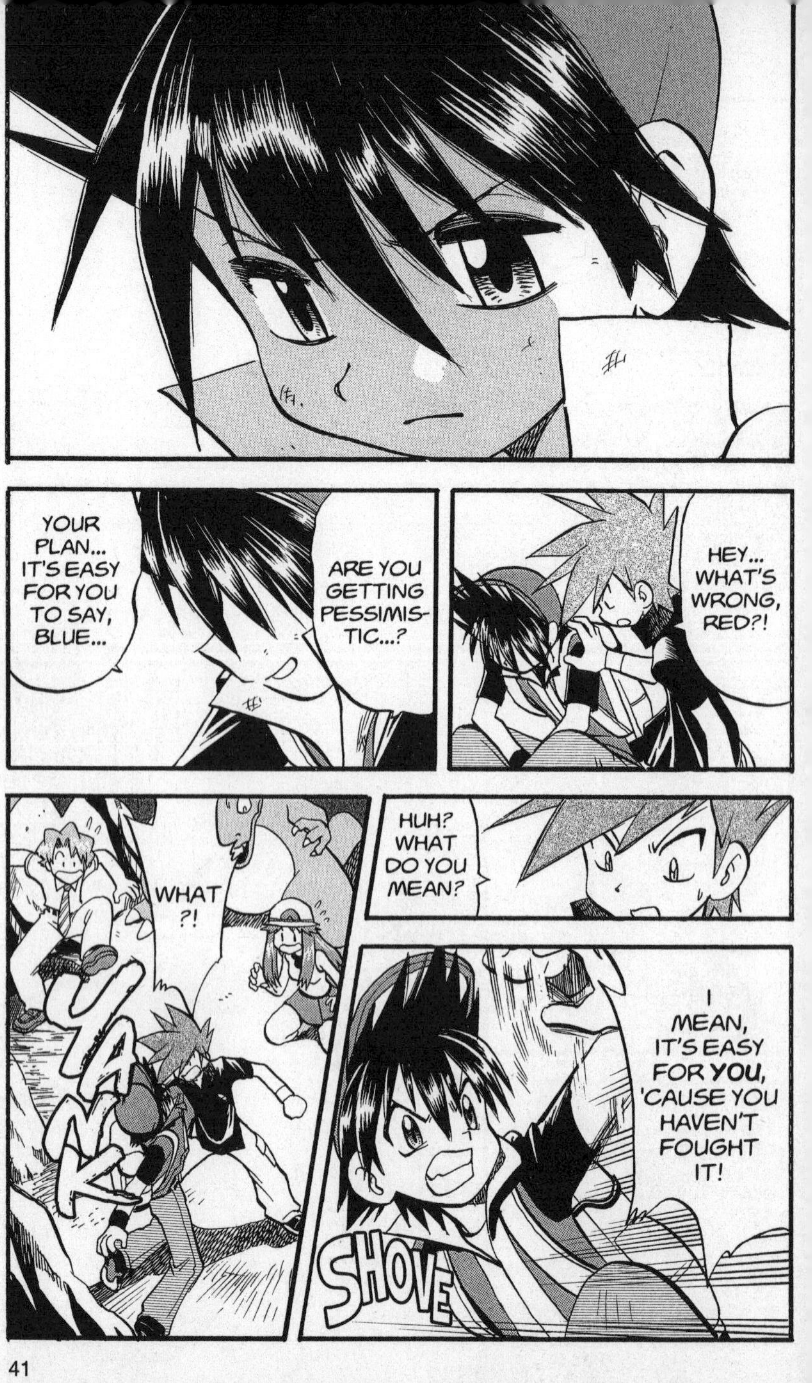
HEY... WHAT'S WRONG, RED?!
ARE YOU GETTING PESSIMIS-TIC...?
YOUR PLAN... IT'S EASY FOR YOU TO SAY, BLUE...
HUH? WHAT DO YOU MEAN?
I MEAN, IT'S EASY FOR **YOU**, 'CAUSE YOU HAVEN'T FOUGHT IT!
SHOVE
WHAT ?!

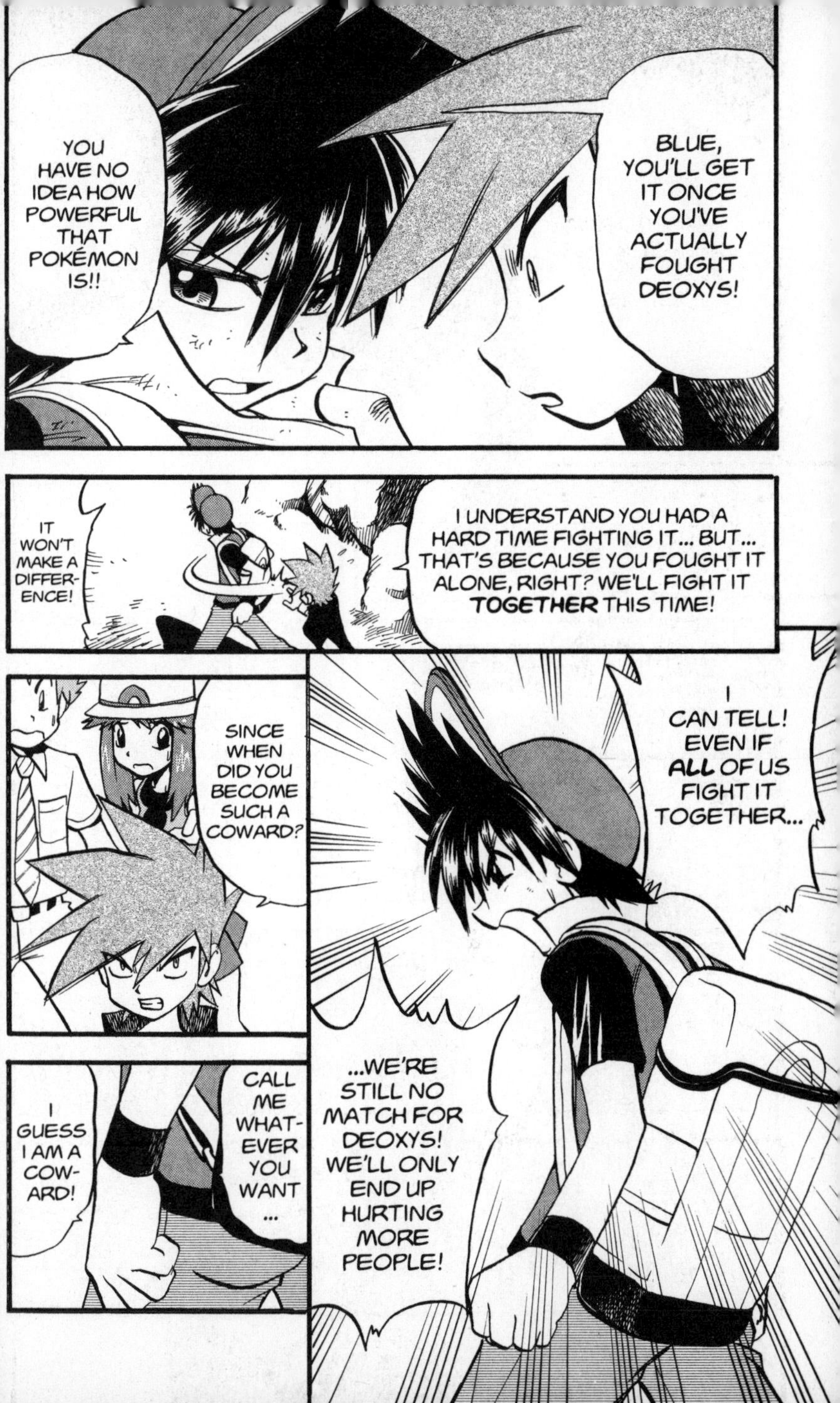
BLUE, YOU'LL GET IT ONCE YOU'VE ACTUALLY FOUGHT DEOXYS!
YOU HAVE NO IDEA HOW POWERFUL THAT POKÉMON IS!!
I UNDERSTAND YOU HAD A HARD TIME FIGHTING IT... BUT... THAT'S BECAUSE YOU FOUGHT IT ALONE, RIGHT? WE'LL FIGHT IT **TOGETHER** THIS TIME!
IT WON'T MAKE A DIFFERENCE!
I CAN TELL! EVEN IF **ALL** OF US FIGHT IT TOGETHER...
...WE'RE STILL NO MATCH FOR DEOXYS! WE'LL ONLY END UP HURTING MORE PEOPLE!
SINCE WHEN DID YOU BECOME SUCH A COWARD?
CALL ME WHATEVER YOU WANT...
I GUESS I AM A COWARD!

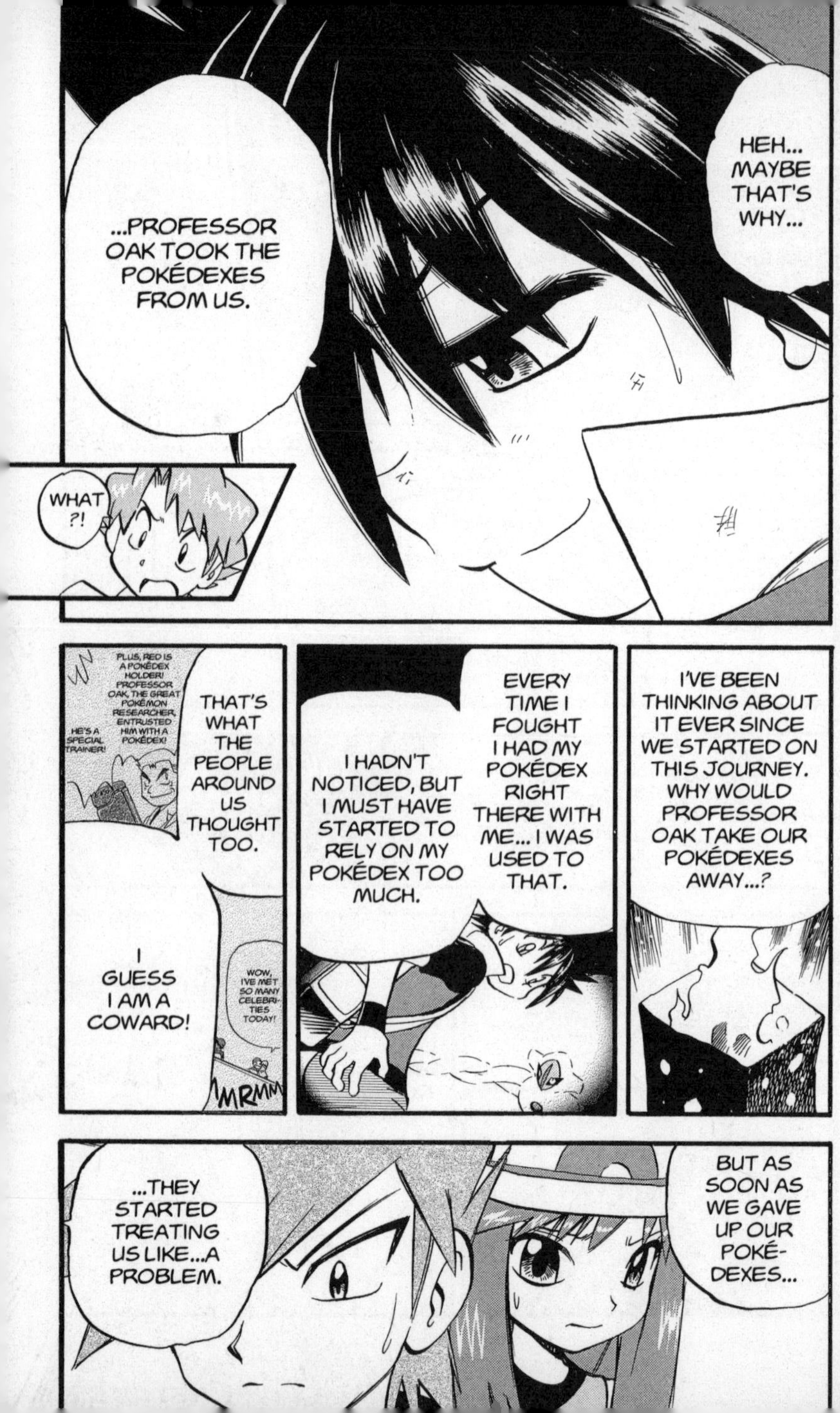
HEH... MAYBE THAT'S WHY...
...PROFESSOR OAK TOOK THE POKÉDEXES FROM US.
WHAT?!
I'VE BEEN THINKING ABOUT IT EVER SINCE WE STARTED ON THIS JOURNEY. WHY WOULD PROFESSOR OAK TAKE OUR POKÉDEXES AWAY...?
EVERY TIME I FOUGHT I HAD MY POKÉDEX RIGHT THERE WITH ME... I WAS USED TO THAT.
I HADN'T NOTICED, BUT I MUST HAVE STARTED TO RELY ON MY POKÉDEX TOO MUCH.
THAT'S WHAT THE PEOPLE AROUND US THOUGHT TOO.
PLUS, RED IS A POKÉDEX HOLDER! PROFESSOR OAK, THE GREAT POKÉMON RESEARCHER, ENTRUSTED HIM WITH A POKÉDEX!
HE'S A SPECIAL TRAINER!
I GUESS I AM A COWARD!
WOW, I'VE MET SO MANY CELEBRITIES TODAY!
MRMM
BUT AS SOON AS WE GAVE UP OUR POKÉDEXES...
...THEY STARTED TREATING US LIKE...A PROBLEM.

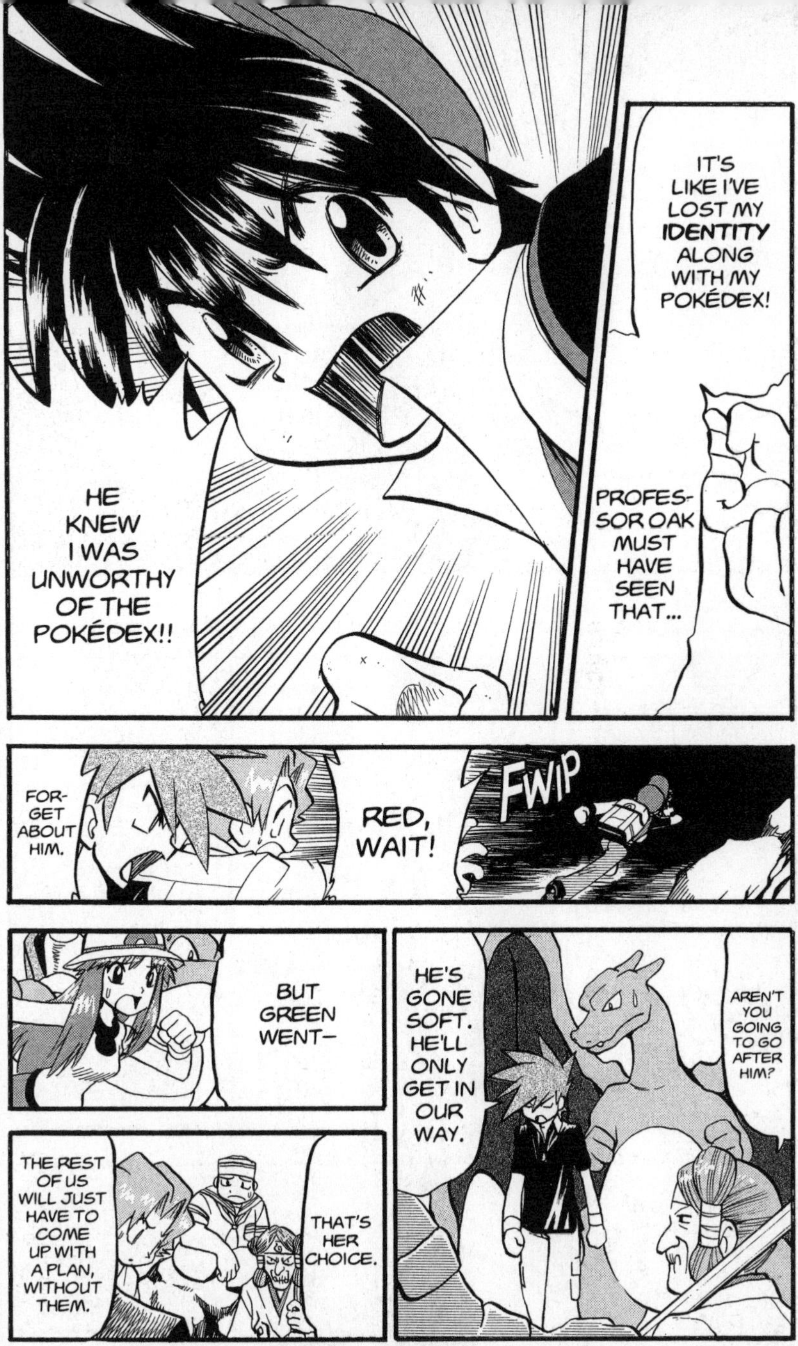
IT'S LIKE I'VE LOST MY **IDENTITY** ALONG WITH MY POKÉDEX!
PROFES-SOR OAK MUST HAVE SEEN THAT...
HE KNEW I WAS UNWORTHY OF THE POKÉDEX!!
FWIP
RED, WAIT!
FOR-GET ABOUT HIM.
AREN'T YOU GOING TO GO AFTER HIM?
HE'S GONE SOFT. HE'LL ONLY GET IN OUR WAY.
BUT GREEN WENT—
THAT'S HER CHOICE.
THE REST OF US WILL JUST HAVE TO COME UP WITH A PLAN, WITHOUT THEM.

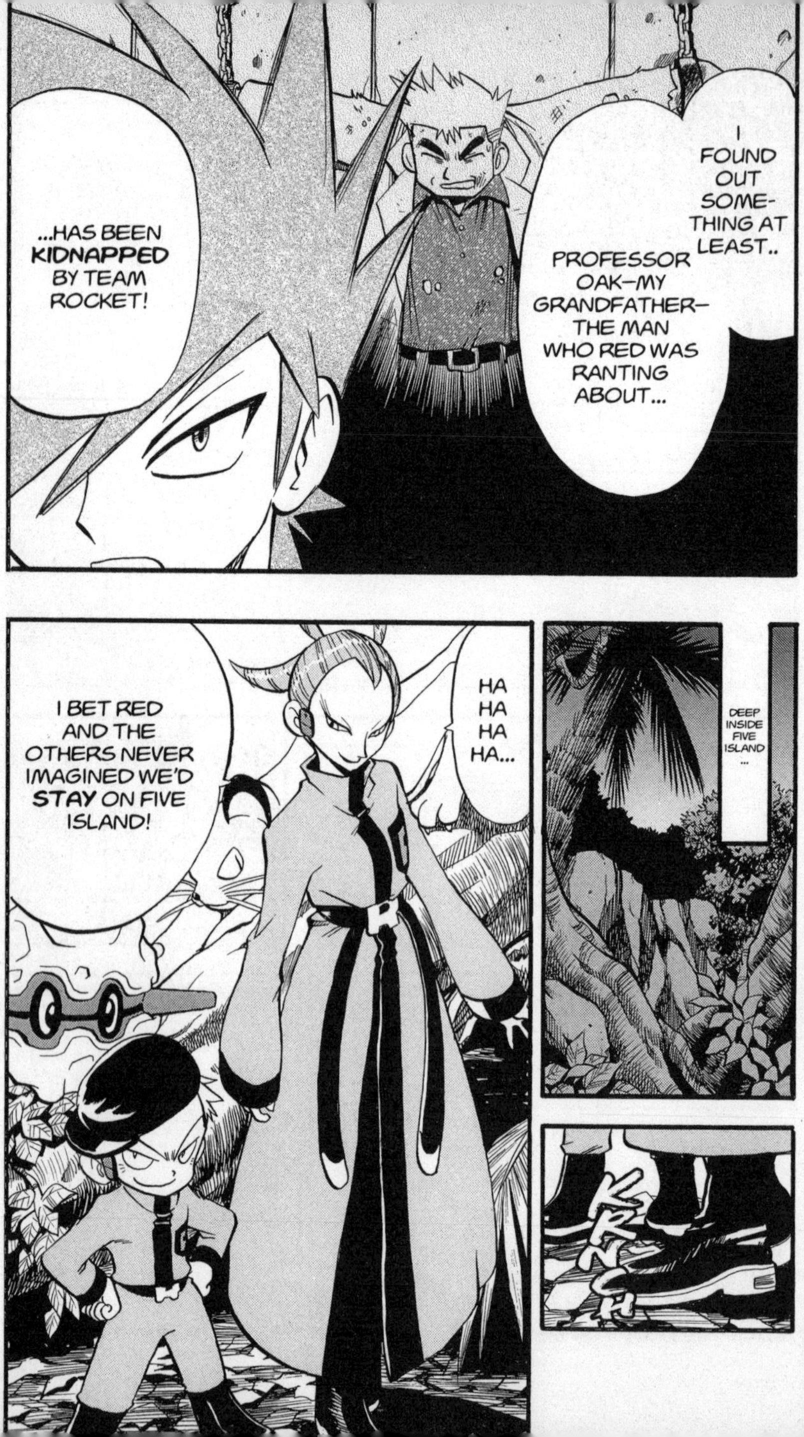
I FOUND OUT SOMETHING AT LEAST..
PROFESSOR OAK—MY GRANDFATHER—THE MAN WHO RED WAS RANTING ABOUT...
...HAS BEEN **KIDNAPPED** BY TEAM ROCKET!
DEEP INSIDE FIVE ISLAND ...
HA HA HA HA...
I BET RED AND THE OTHERS NEVER IMAGINED WE'D **STAY** ON FIVE ISLAND!

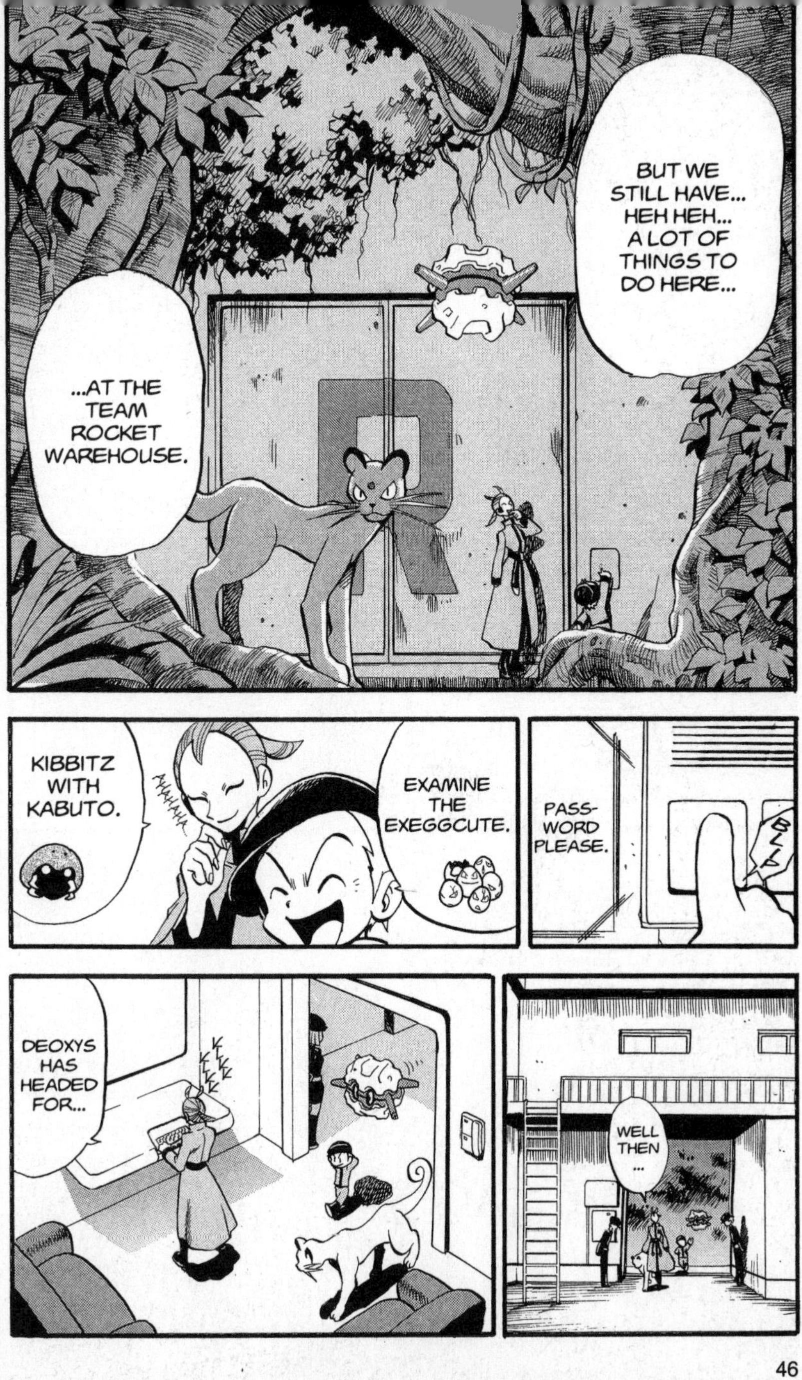
BUT WE STILL HAVE... HEH HEH... A LOT OF THINGS TO DO HERE...
...AT THE TEAM ROCKET WAREHOUSE.
PASS-WORD PLEASE.
EXAMINE THE EXEGGCUTE.
AHAHAHA
KIBBITZ WITH KABUTO.
WELL THEN ...
DEOXYS HAS HEADED FOR...

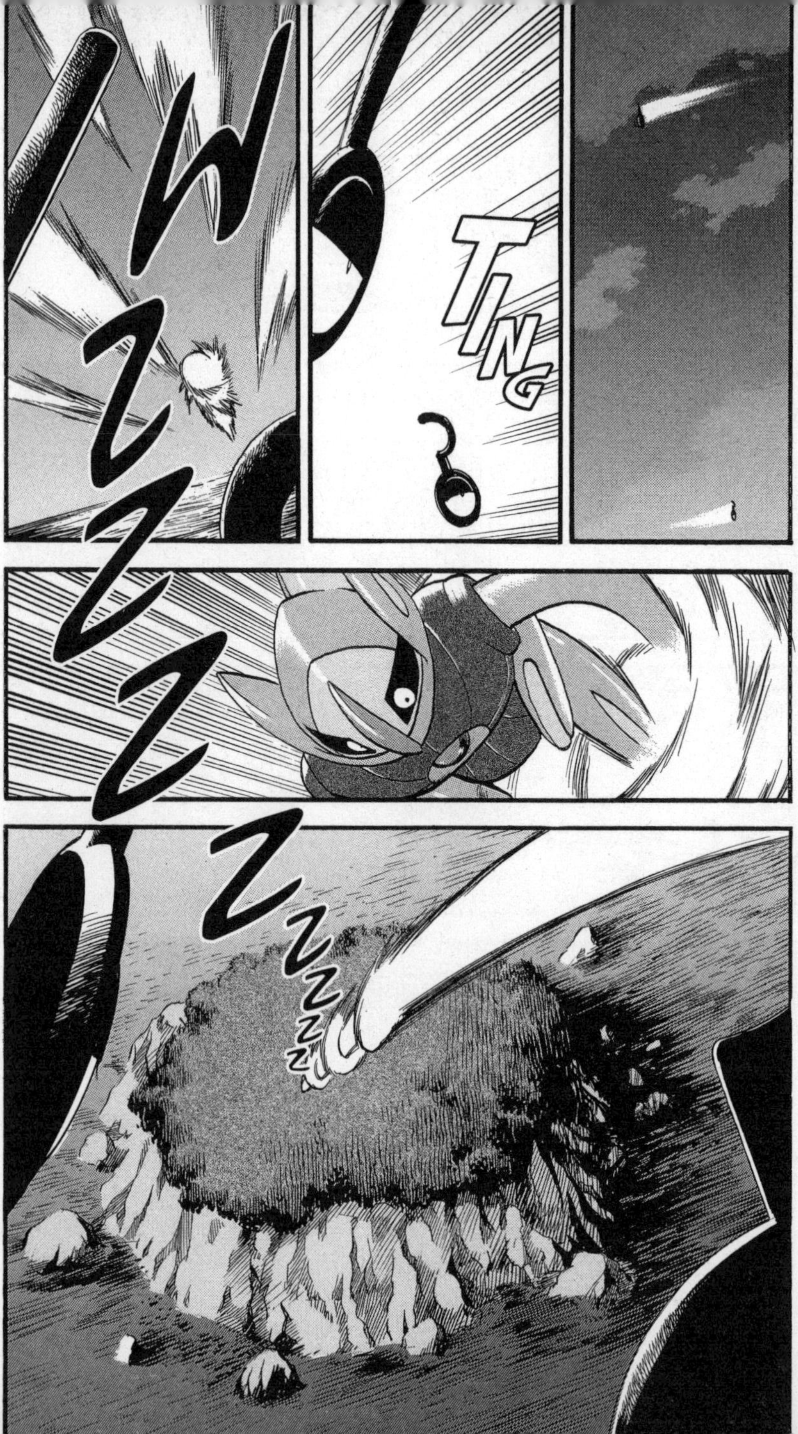
TING

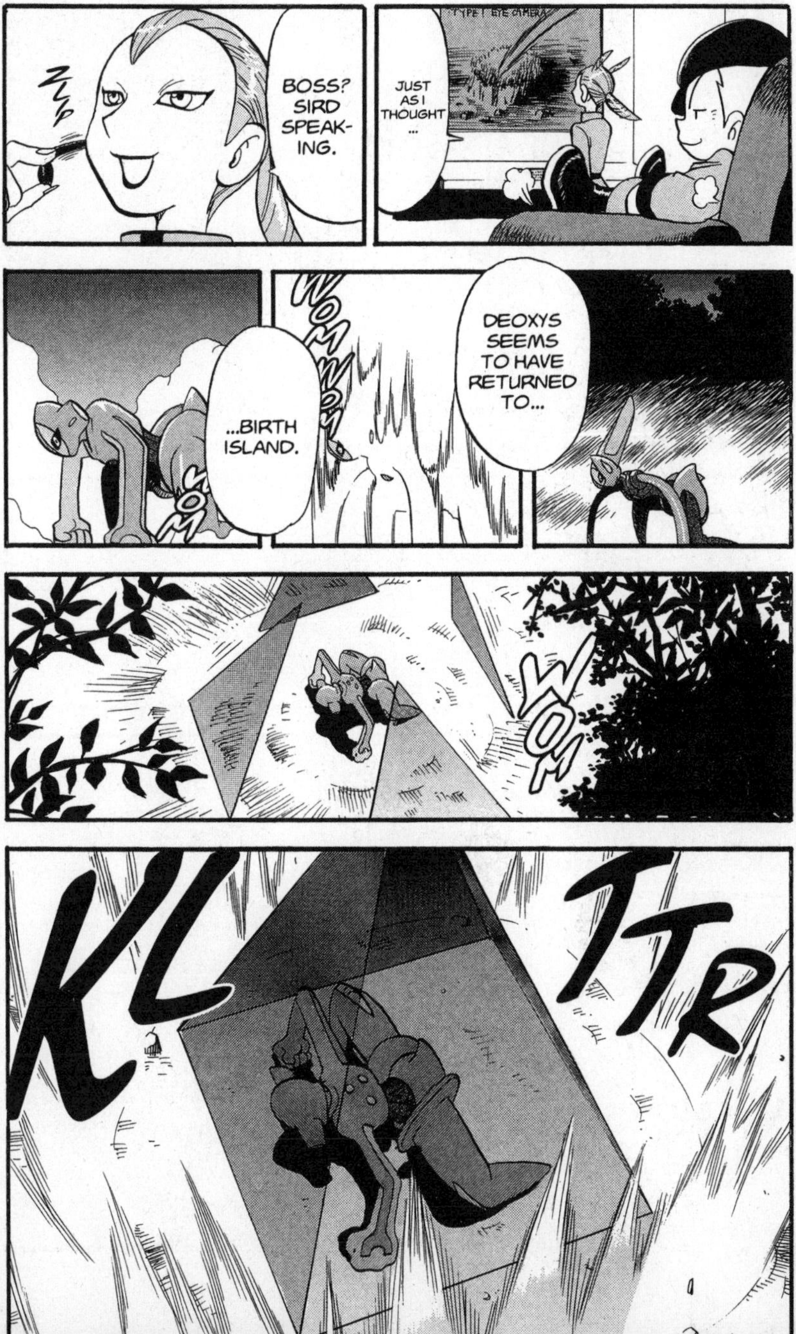
TYPE 1 EYE CAMERA
JUST AS I THOUGHT...
BOSS? SIRD SPEAKING.
DEOXYS SEEMS TO HAVE RETURNED TO...
...BIRTH ISLAND.
WOM
WOM
KL TTR

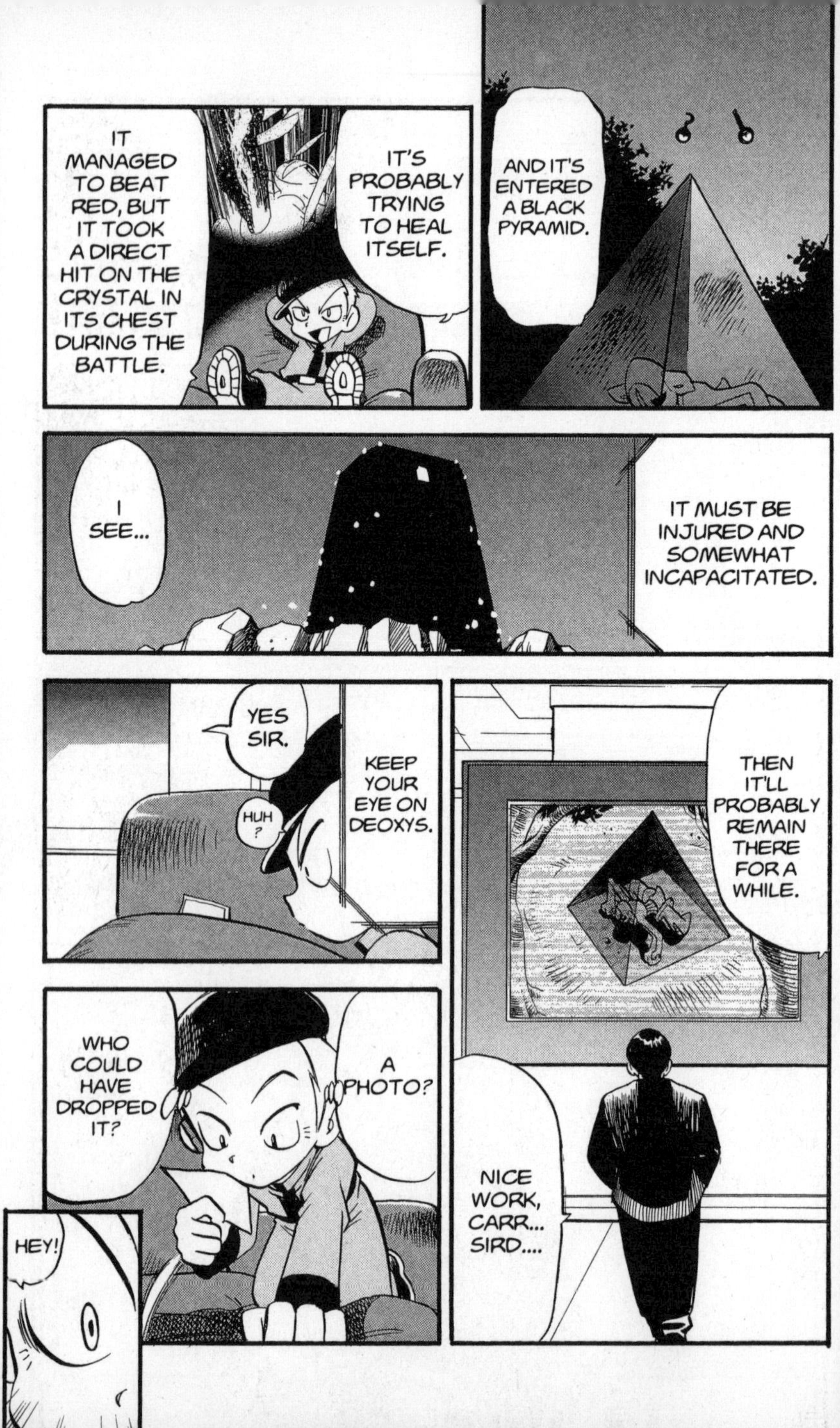
AND IT'S ENTERED A BLACK PYRAMID.
IT'S PROBABLY TRYING TO HEAL ITSELF.
IT MANAGED TO BEAT RED, BUT IT TOOK A DIRECT HIT ON THE CRYSTAL IN ITS CHEST DURING THE BATTLE.
IT MUST BE INJURED AND SOMEWHAT INCAPACITATED.
I SEE...
THEN IT'LL PROBABLY REMAIN THERE FOR A WHILE.
NICE WORK, CARR... SIRD....
KEEP YOUR EYE ON DEOXYS.
YES SIR.
HUH?
A PHOTO?
WHO COULD HAVE DROPPED IT?
HEY!

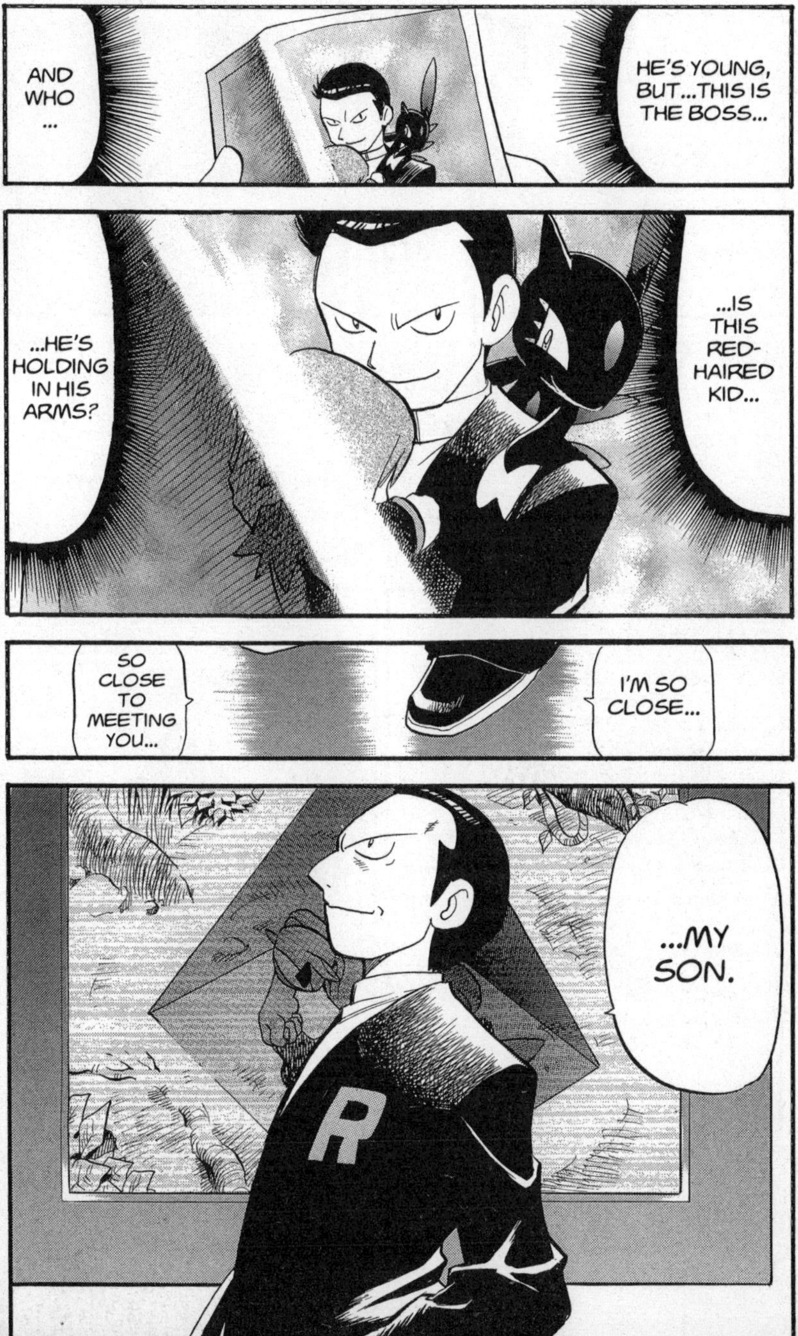
HE'S YOUNG, BUT...THIS IS THE BOSS...
AND WHO ...
...IS THIS RED-HAIRED KID...
...HE'S HOLDING IN HIS ARMS?
I'M SO CLOSE...
SO CLOSE TO MEETING YOU...
...MY SON.

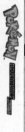

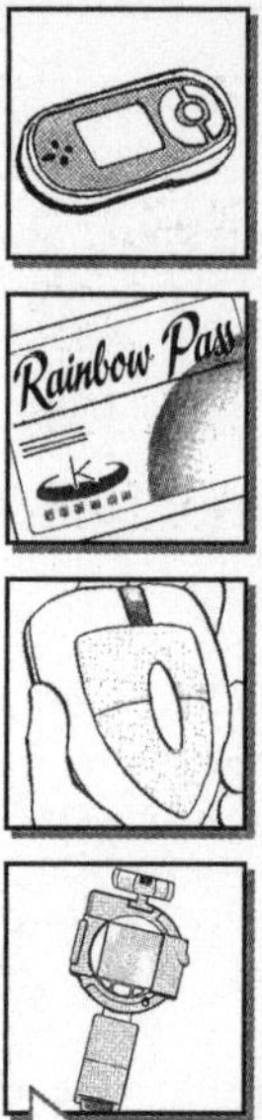
Rainbow Pass

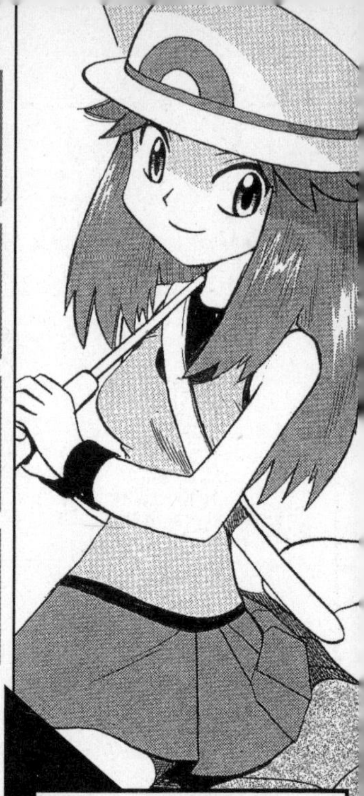

GREEN

- Birthplace: Pallet Town
- Birthday: June 1st
- Blood Type: B
- Age: 16 (As of the 5th Arc)
- Prizes Won: 3rd Place at the 9th Pokémon League
- Skills: Disguise, inventing and renovating machines
- Knowledge: She has a deep knowledge of Pokémon Evolution.
- Hobby: Collecting accessories (especially earrings) and cute shoes

GREEN WAS KIDNAPPED BY THE MASK OF ICE AND RAISED AS ONE OF HIS MASKED CHILDREN. AFTER ESCAPING FROM HIS TRAINING FACILITY, SHE MET RED AND BLUE AND HAD ADVENTURES WITH THEM. SHE HAS A VERY STRONG BOND WITH SILVER, ANOTHER OF THE CAPTIVE CHILDREN, WHOM SHE ESCAPED WITH. SHE PERFORMS METICULOUS RESEARCH BEFORE A BATTLE AND CREATES TRICKY PLANS TO OVERWHELM HER OPPONENT. SHE IS CHEERFUL AND SHREWD, BUT CURRENTLY DEVASTATED AFTER SEEING HER PARENTS GET ABDUCTED BY DEOXYS.

● Adventure 282 ●
Going Green

Pokémon Adventures
FireRed & LeafGreen
The Fifth Chapter

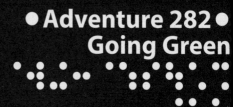

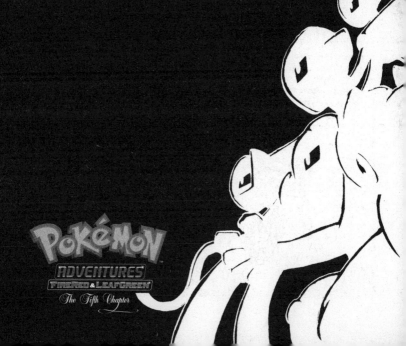

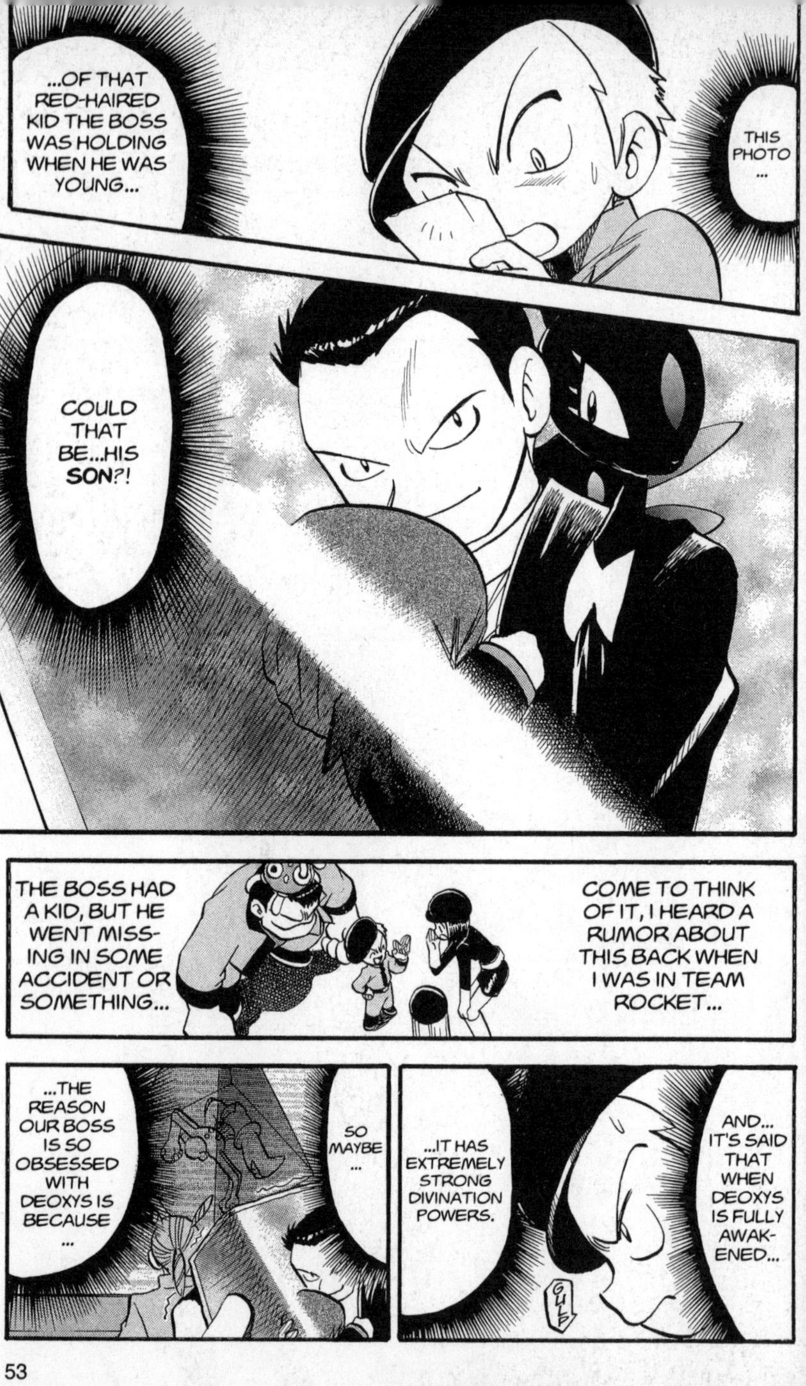

THIS PHOTO ...
...OF THAT RED-HAIRED KID THE BOSS WAS HOLDING WHEN HE WAS YOUNG...
COULD THAT BE...HIS SON?!
COME TO THINK OF IT, I HEARD A RUMOR ABOUT THIS BACK WHEN I WAS IN TEAM ROCKET...
THE BOSS HAD A KID, BUT HE WENT MISSING IN SOME ACCIDENT OR SOMETHING...
AND... IT'S SAID THAT WHEN DEOXYS IS FULLY AWAKENED...
...IT HAS EXTREMELY STRONG DIVINATION POWERS.
GULP
SO MAYBE ...
...THE REASON OUR BOSS IS SO OBSESSED WITH DEOXYS IS BECAUSE ...

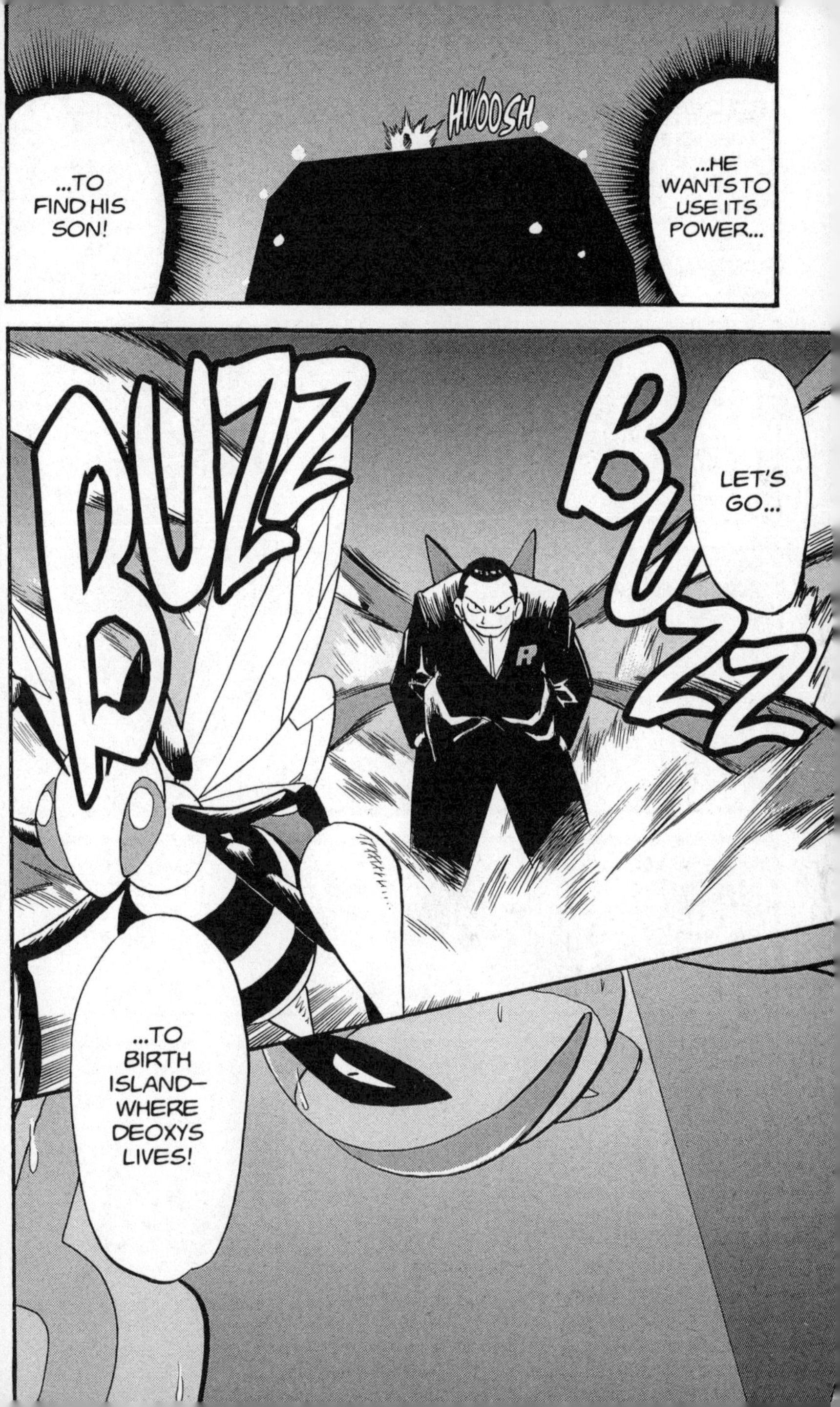
...HE WANTS TO USE ITS POWER...
HWOOSH
...TO FIND HIS SON!
LET'S GO...
BUZZ
BUZZ
...TO BIRTH ISLAND—WHERE DEOXYS LIVES!

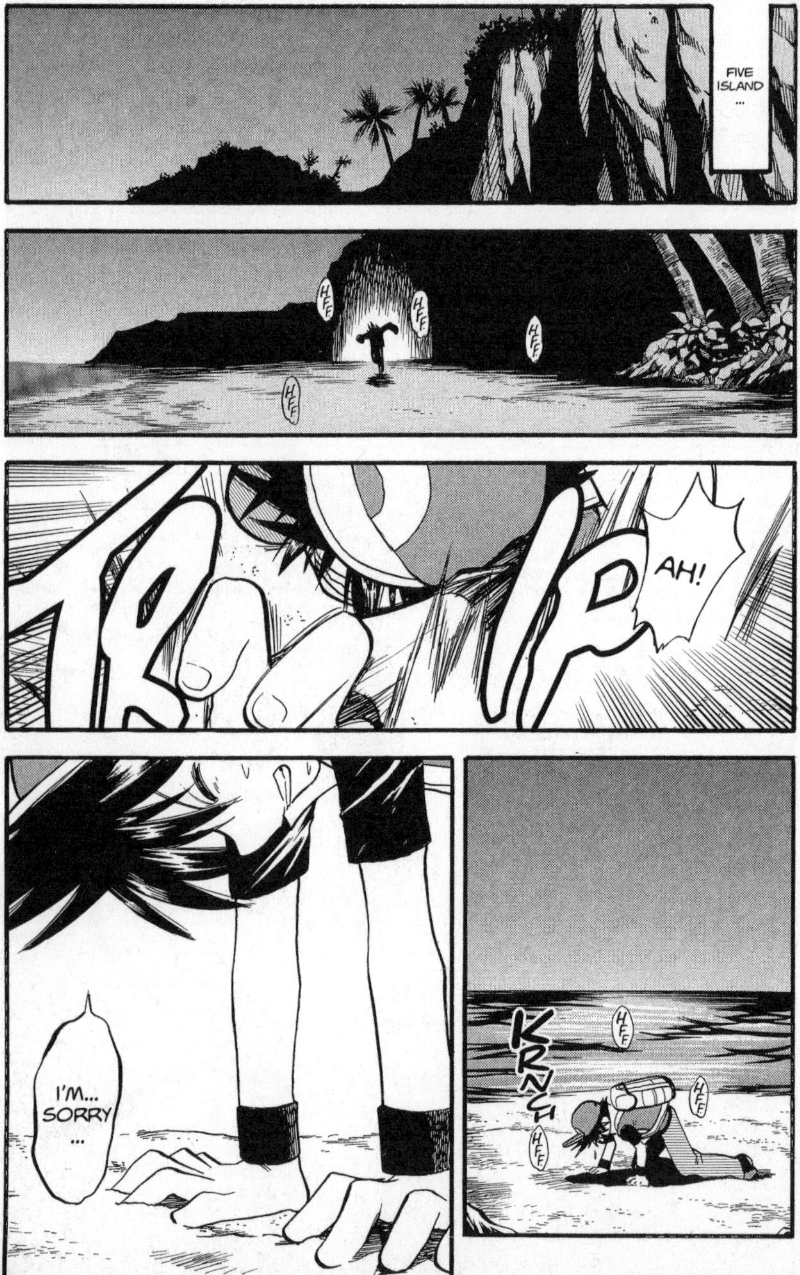

FIVE ISLAND ...
HFF
HFF
HFF
HFF
AH!
TRIP
HFF
HFF
KRNCH
HFF
I'M... SORRY ...

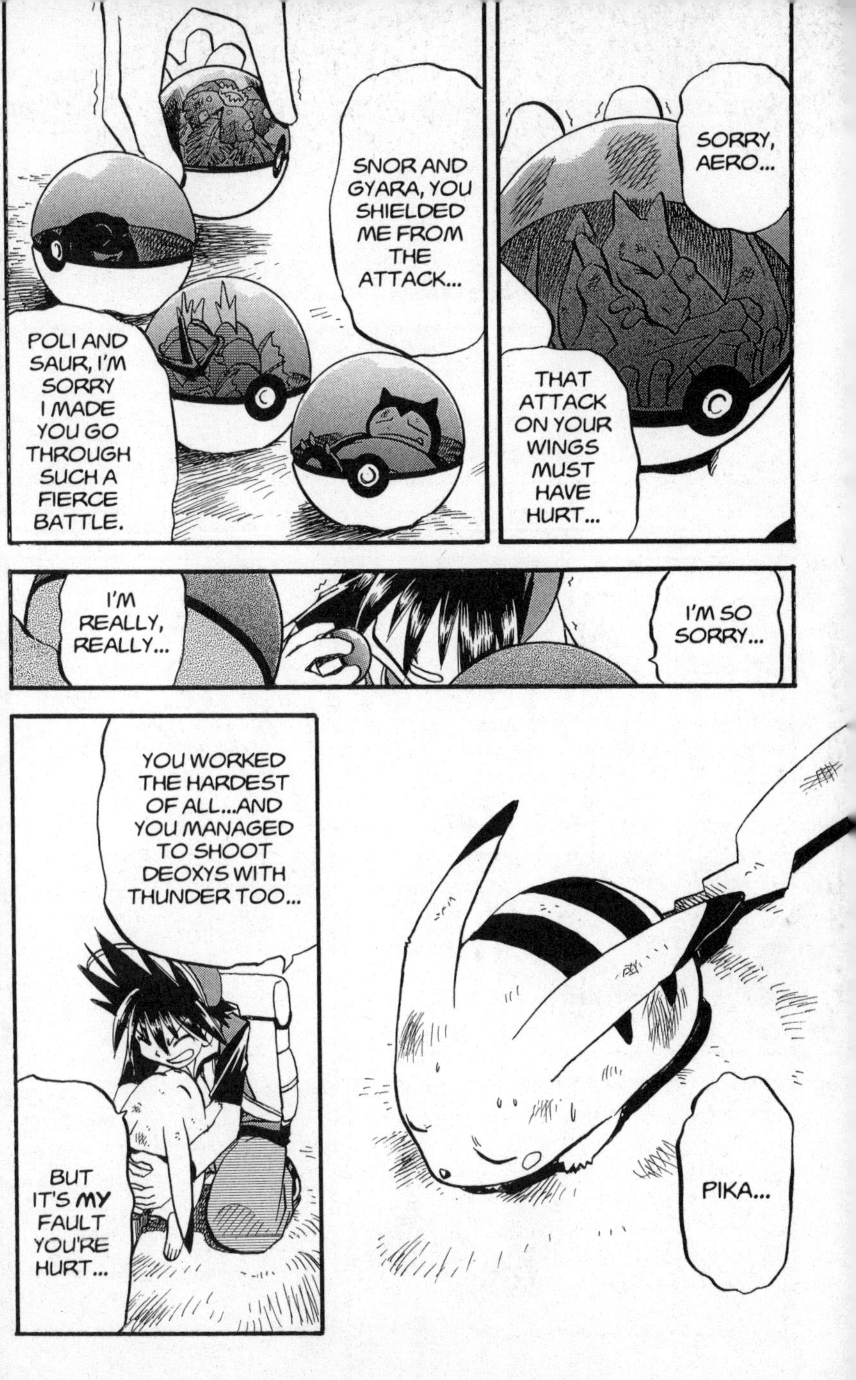
SORRY, AERO...
THAT ATTACK ON YOUR WINGS MUST HAVE HURT...
SNOR AND GYARA, YOU SHIELDED ME FROM THE ATTACK...
POLI AND SAUR, I'M SORRY I MADE YOU GO THROUGH SUCH A FIERCE BATTLE.
I'M SO SORRY...
I'M REALLY, REALLY...
YOU WORKED THE HARDEST OF ALL...AND YOU MANAGED TO SHOOT DEOXYS WITH THUNDER TOO...
PIKA...
BUT IT'S MY FAULT YOU'RE HURT...

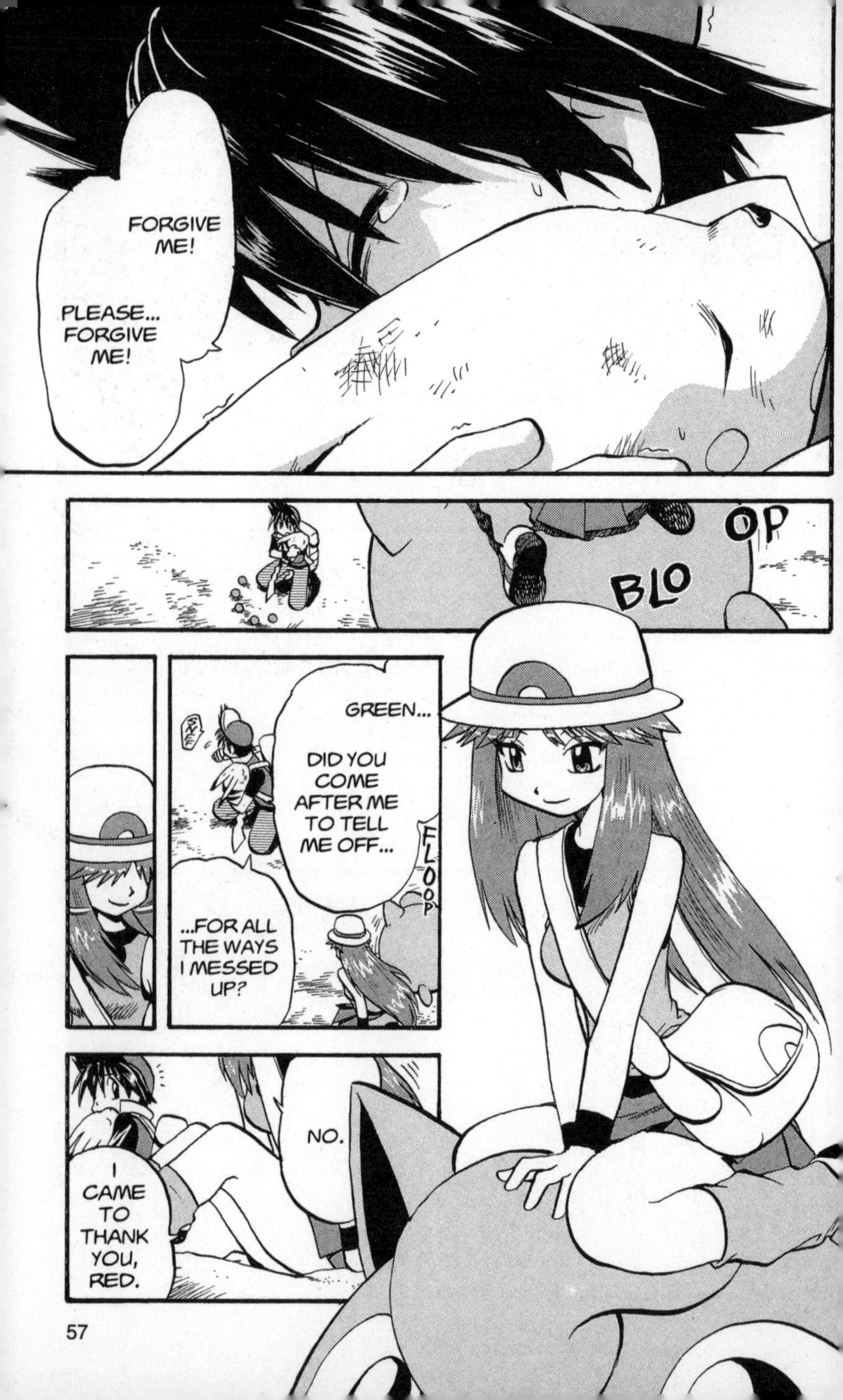
FORGIVE ME!
PLEASE... FORGIVE ME!
BLOOP
FLOOP
GREEN...
DID YOU COME AFTER ME TO TELL ME OFF...
...FOR ALL THE WAYS I MESSED UP?
NO.
I CAME TO THANK YOU, RED.

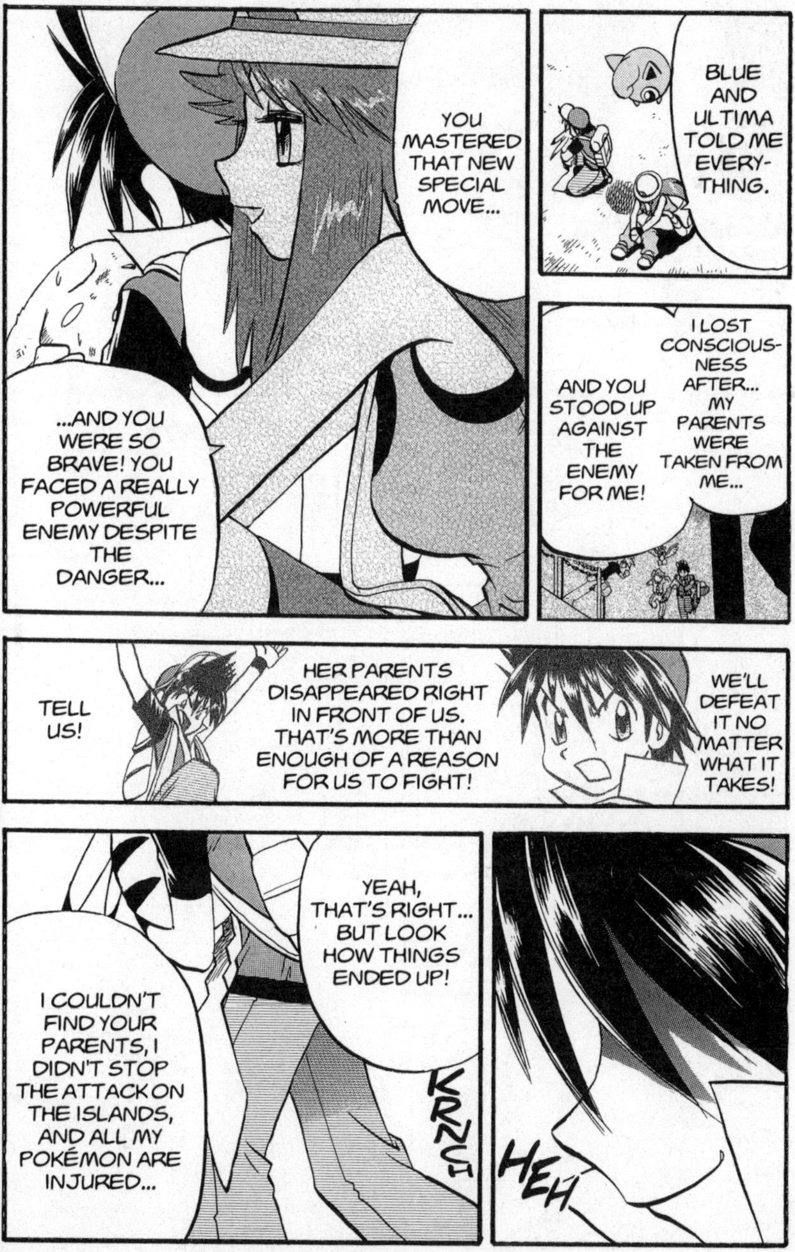

BLUE AND ULTIMA TOLD ME EVERYTHING.
I LOST CONSCIOUSNESS AFTER... MY PARENTS WERE TAKEN FROM ME...
AND YOU STOOD UP AGAINST THE ENEMY FOR ME!
YOU MASTERED THAT NEW SPECIAL MOVE...
...AND YOU WERE SO BRAVE! YOU FACED A REALLY POWERFUL ENEMY DESPITE THE DANGER...
WE'LL DEFEAT IT NO MATTER WHAT IT TAKES!
HER PARENTS DISAPPEARED RIGHT IN FRONT OF US. THAT'S MORE THAN ENOUGH OF A REASON FOR US TO FIGHT!
TELL US!
HEH
YEAH, THAT'S RIGHT... BUT LOOK HOW THINGS ENDED UP!
KRNCH
I COULDN'T FIND YOUR PARENTS, I DIDN'T STOP THE ATTACK ON THE ISLANDS, AND ALL MY POKÉMON ARE INJURED...

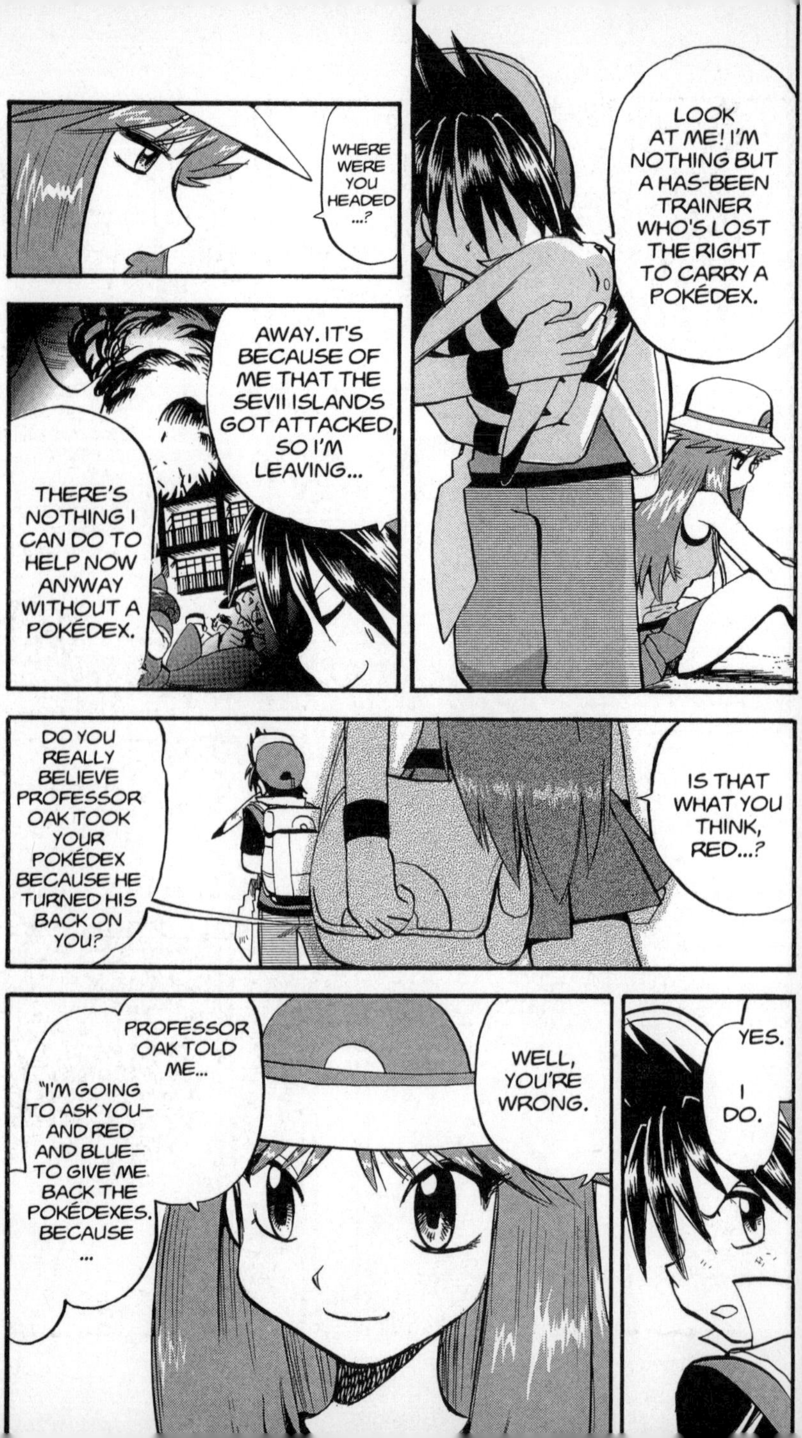
LOOK AT ME! I'M NOTHING BUT A HAS-BEEN TRAINER WHO'S LOST THE RIGHT TO CARRY A POKÉDEX.
WHERE WERE YOU HEADED ...?
AWAY. IT'S BECAUSE OF ME THAT THE SEVII ISLANDS GOT ATTACKED, SO I'M LEAVING...
THERE'S NOTHING I CAN DO TO HELP NOW ANYWAY WITHOUT A POKÉDEX.
IS THAT WHAT YOU THINK, RED...?
DO YOU REALLY BELIEVE PROFESSOR OAK TOOK YOUR POKÉDEX BECAUSE HE TURNED HIS BACK ON YOU?
YES.
I DO.
WELL, YOU'RE WRONG.
PROFESSOR OAK TOLD ME...
"I'M GOING TO ASK YOU—AND RED AND BLUE—TO GIVE ME BACK THE POKÉDEXES. BECAUSE ...

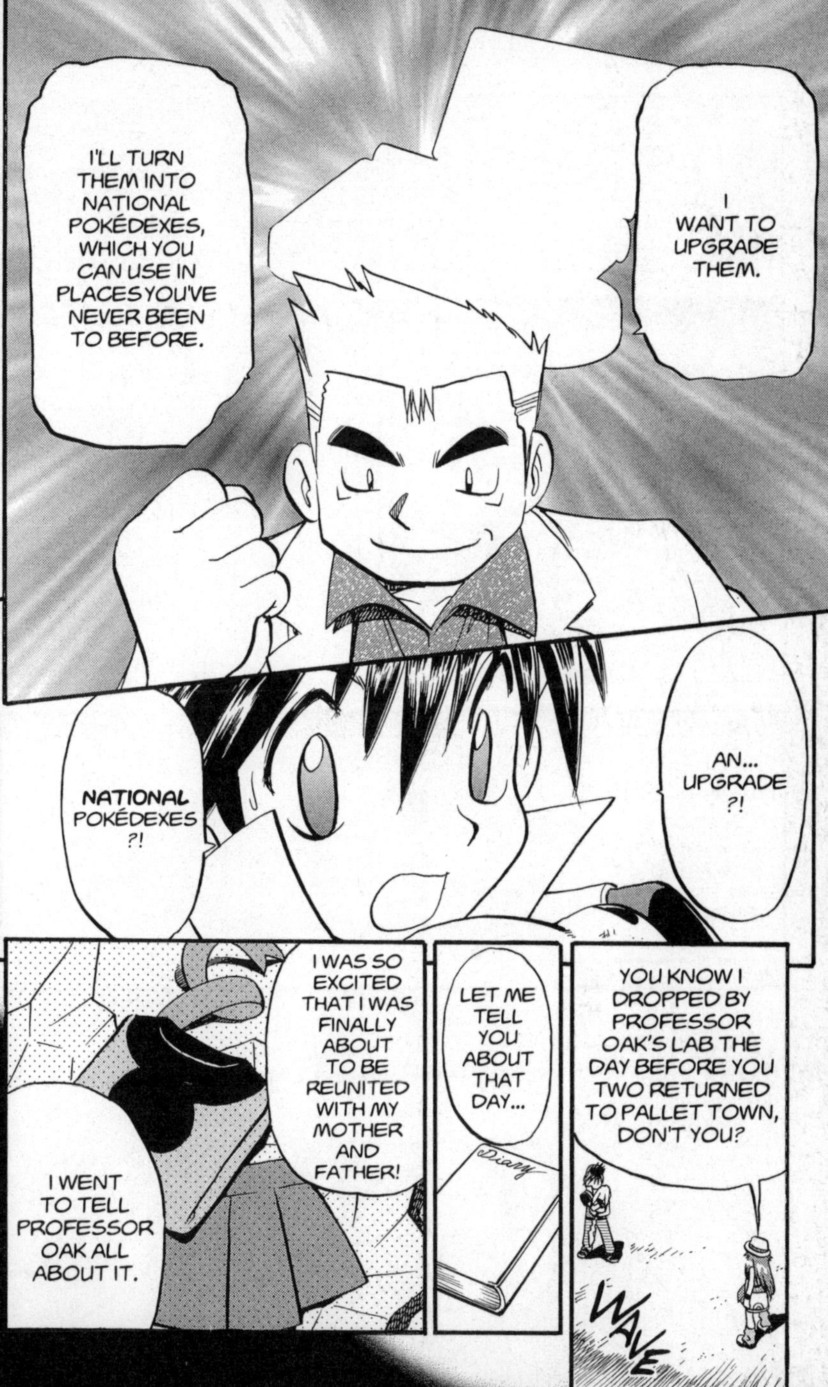
I WANT TO UPGRADE THEM.
I'LL TURN THEM INTO NATIONAL POKÉDEXES, WHICH YOU CAN USE IN PLACES YOU'VE NEVER BEEN TO BEFORE.
AN... UPGRADE ?!
NATIONAL POKÉDEXES ?!
YOU KNOW I DROPPED BY PROFESSOR OAK'S LAB THE DAY BEFORE YOU TWO RETURNED TO PALLET TOWN, DON'T YOU?
WAVE
LET ME TELL YOU ABOUT THAT DAY...
Diary
I WAS SO EXCITED THAT I WAS FINALLY ABOUT TO BE REUNITED WITH MY MOTHER AND FATHER!
I WENT TO TELL PROFESSOR OAK ALL ABOUT IT.

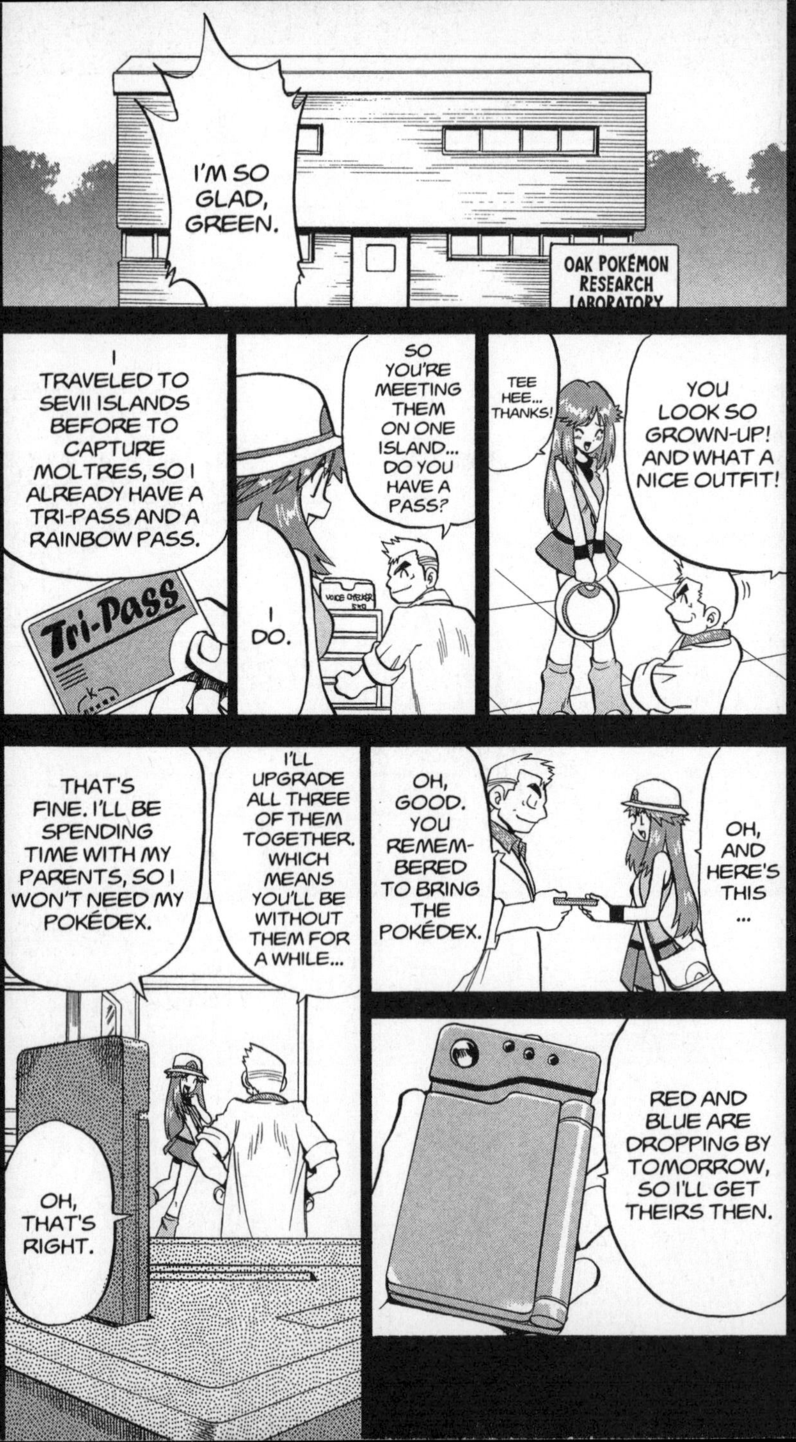
I'M SO GLAD, GREEN.
OAK POKÉMON RESEARCH LABORATORY
YOU LOOK SO GROWN-UP! AND WHAT A NICE OUTFIT!
TEE HEE... THANKS!
SO YOU'RE MEETING THEM ON ONE ISLAND... DO YOU HAVE A PASS?
I DO.
I TRAVELED TO SEVII ISLANDS BEFORE TO CAPTURE MOLTRES, SO I ALREADY HAVE A TRI-PASS AND A RAINBOW PASS.
Tri-Pass
OH, AND HERE'S THIS ...
OH, GOOD. YOU REMEMBERED TO BRING THE POKÉDEX.
RED AND BLUE ARE DROPPING BY TOMORROW, SO I'LL GET THEIRS THEN.
I'LL UPGRADE ALL THREE OF THEM TOGETHER. WHICH MEANS YOU'LL BE WITHOUT THEM FOR A WHILE...
THAT'S FINE. I'LL BE SPENDING TIME WITH MY PARENTS, SO I WON'T NEED MY POKÉDEX.
OH, THAT'S RIGHT.

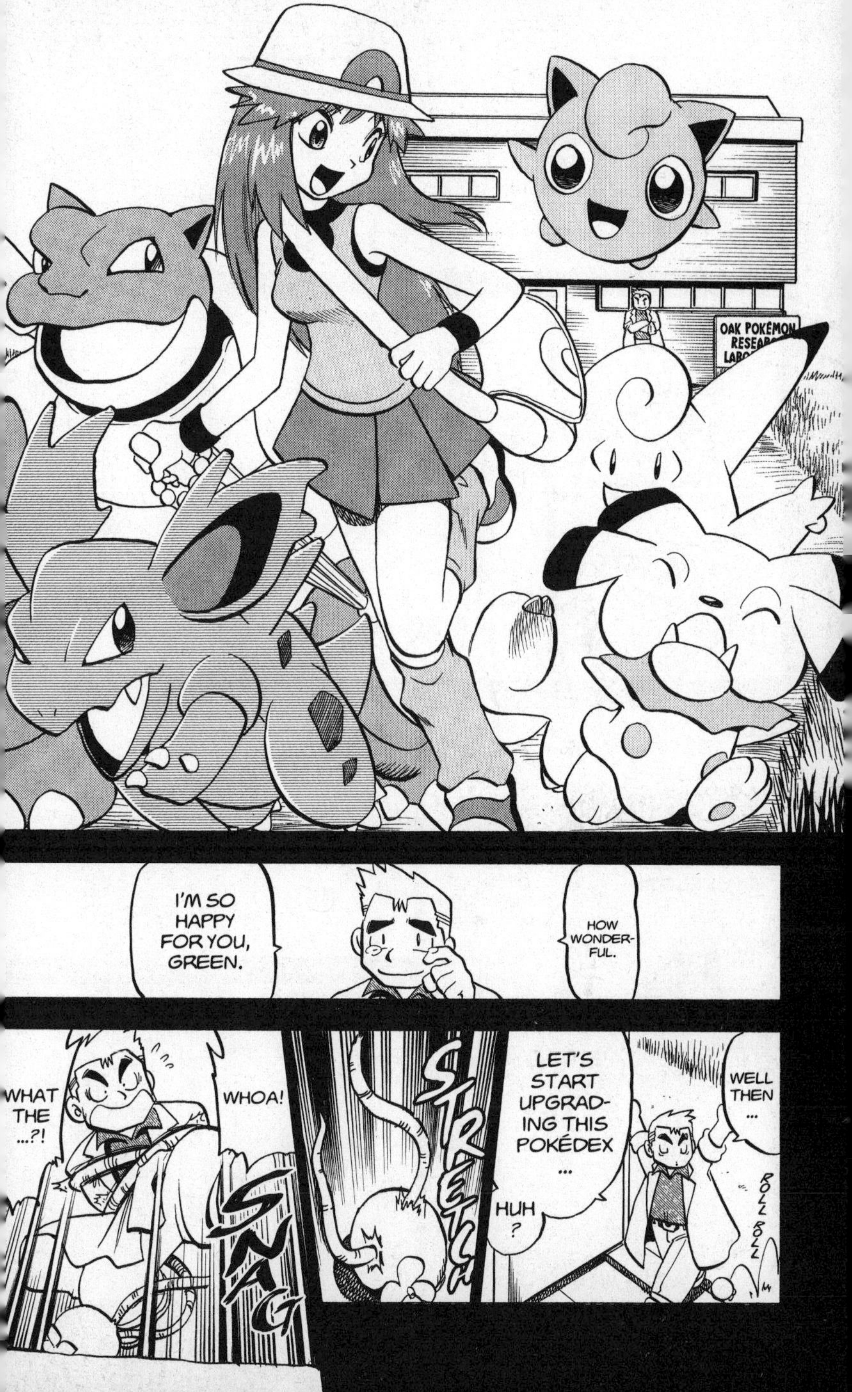
OAK POKÉMON
HOW WONDER-FUL.
I'M SO HAPPY FOR YOU, GREEN.
WELL THEN ...
ROLL ROLL
LET'S START UPGRAD-ING THIS POKÉDEX ...
HUH ?
STRETCH
WHOA!
SNAG
WHAT THE ...?!

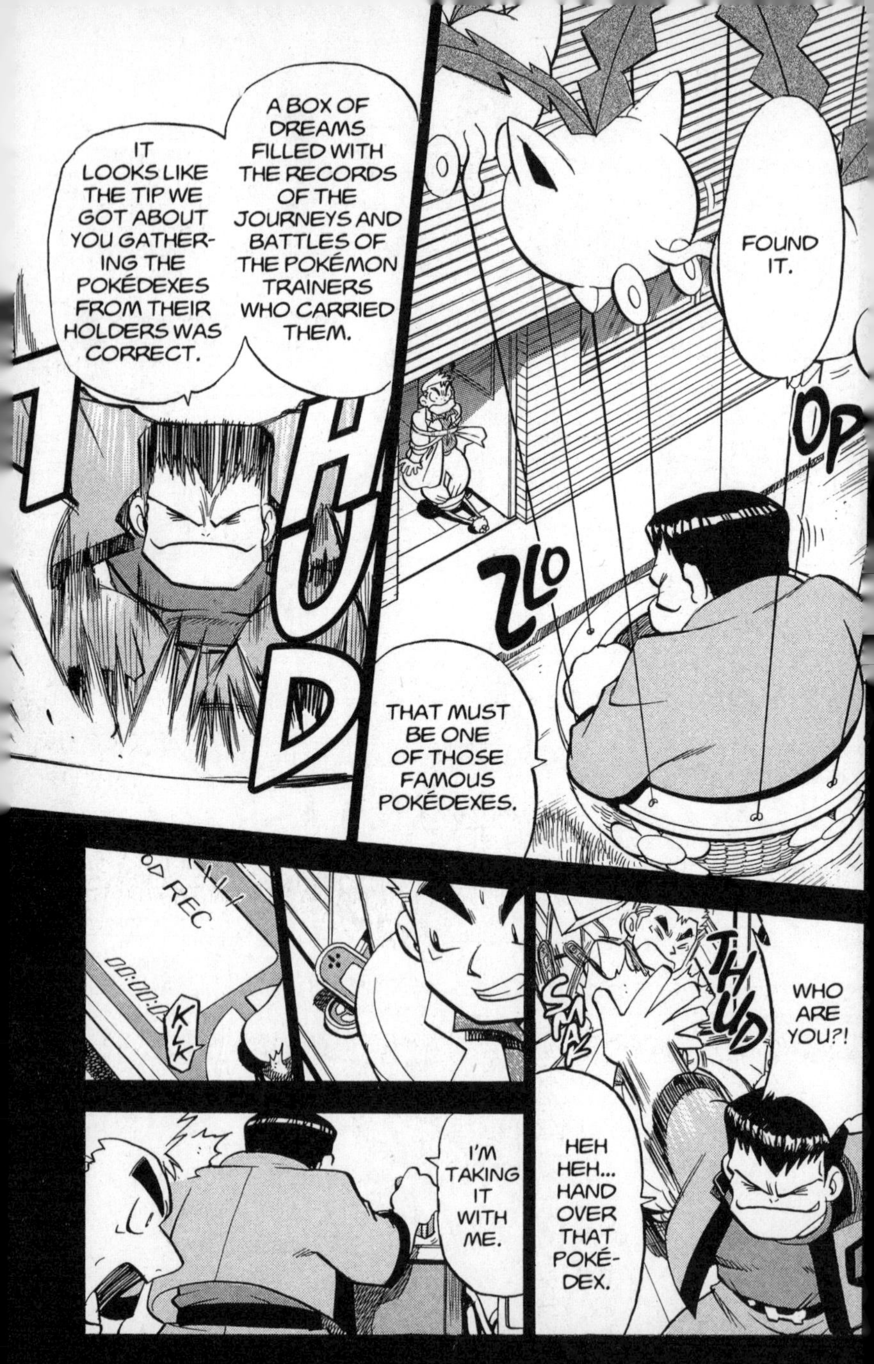
FOUND IT.
OP
ZLO
THAT MUST BE ONE OF THOSE FAMOUS POKÉDEXES.
A BOX OF DREAMS FILLED WITH THE RECORDS OF THE JOURNEYS AND BATTLES OF THE POKÉMON TRAINERS WHO CARRIED THEM.
IT LOOKS LIKE THE TIP WE GOT ABOUT YOU GATHERING THE POKÉDEXES FROM THEIR HOLDERS WAS CORRECT.
THUD
WHO ARE YOU?!
THUD
SMAK
REC
00:00:0
KLIK
HEH HEH... HAND OVER THAT POKÉDEX.
I'M TAKING IT WITH ME.

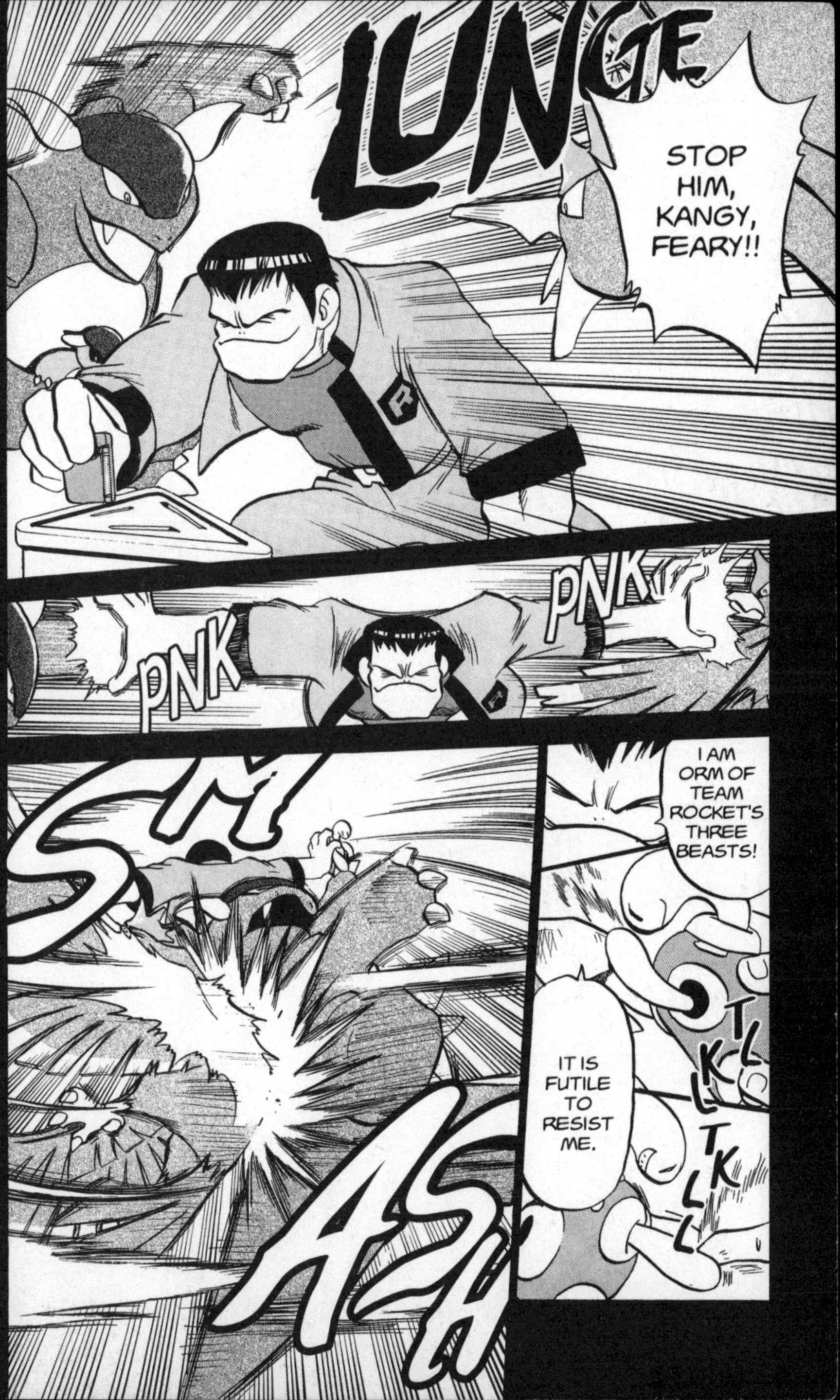
LUNGE
STOP HIM, KANGY, FEARY!!
PNK
PNK
I AM ORM OF TEAM ROCKET'S THREE BEASTS!
IT IS FUTILE TO RESIST ME.
TKLL
TKLLL
SMASH

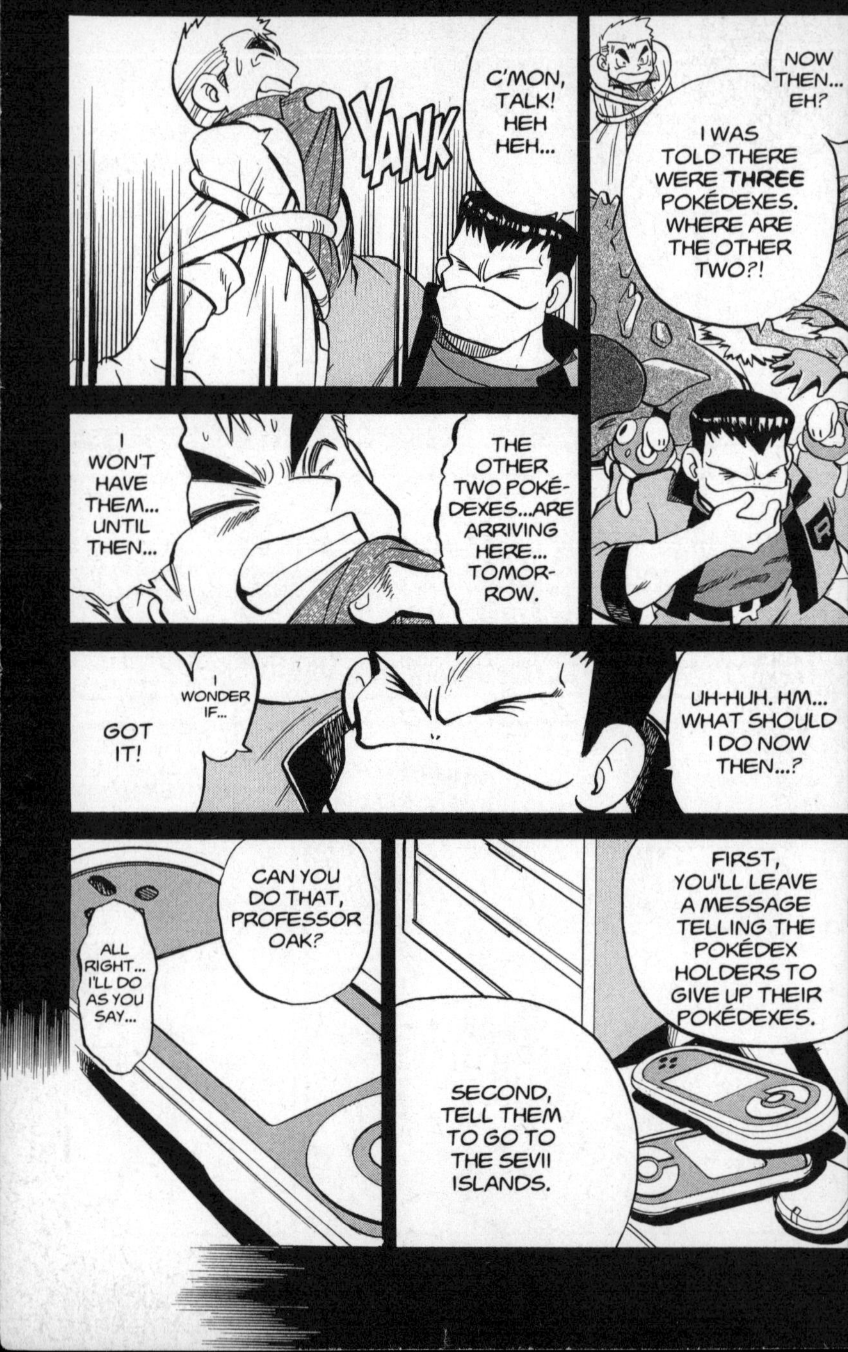
NOW THEN... EH?
I WAS TOLD THERE WERE **THREE** POKÉDEXES. WHERE ARE THE OTHER TWO?!
YANK
C'MON, TALK! HEH HEH...
THE OTHER TWO POKÉ-DEXES...ARE ARRIVING HERE... TOMOR-ROW.
I WON'T HAVE THEM... UNTIL THEN...
UH-HUH. HM... WHAT SHOULD I DO NOW THEN...?
I WONDER IF...
GOT IT!
FIRST, YOU'LL LEAVE A MESSAGE TELLING THE POKÉDEX HOLDERS TO GIVE UP THEIR POKÉDEXES.
SECOND, TELL THEM TO GO TO THE SEVII ISLANDS.
CAN YOU DO THAT, PROFESSOR OAK?
ALL RIGHT... I'LL DO AS YOU SAY...

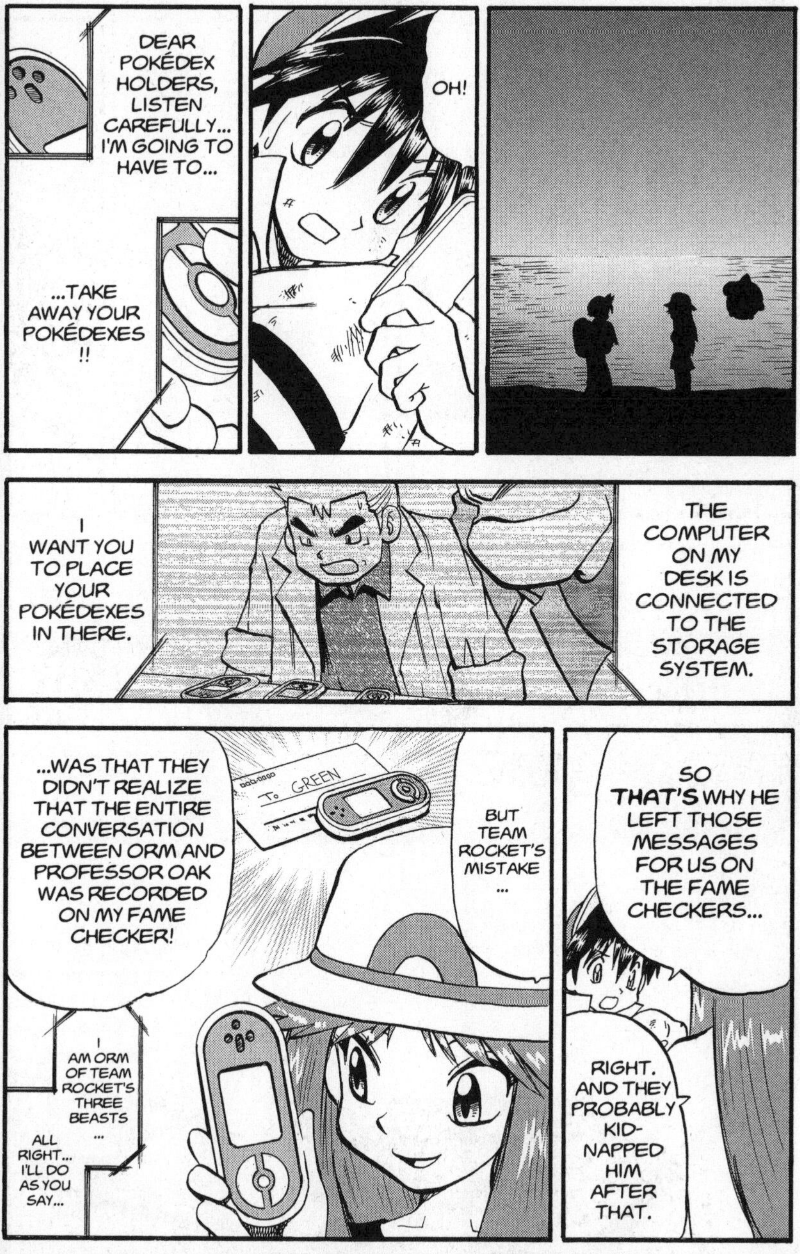
OH!
DEAR POKÉDEX HOLDERS, LISTEN CAREFULLY... I'M GOING TO HAVE TO...
...TAKE AWAY YOUR POKÉDEXES !!
THE COMPUTER ON MY DESK IS CONNECTED TO THE STORAGE SYSTEM.
I WANT YOU TO PLACE YOUR POKÉDEXES IN THERE.
SO **THAT'S** WHY HE LEFT THOSE MESSAGES FOR US ON THE FAME CHECKERS...
RIGHT. AND THEY PROBABLY KID-NAPPED HIM AFTER THAT.
BUT TEAM ROCKET'S MISTAKE ...
...WAS THAT THEY DIDN'T REALIZE THAT THE ENTIRE CONVERSATION BETWEEN ORM AND PROFESSOR OAK WAS RECORDED ON MY FAME CHECKER!
To GREEN
I AM ORM OF TEAM ROCKET'S THREE BEASTS ...
ALL RIGHT... I'LL DO AS YOU SAY...

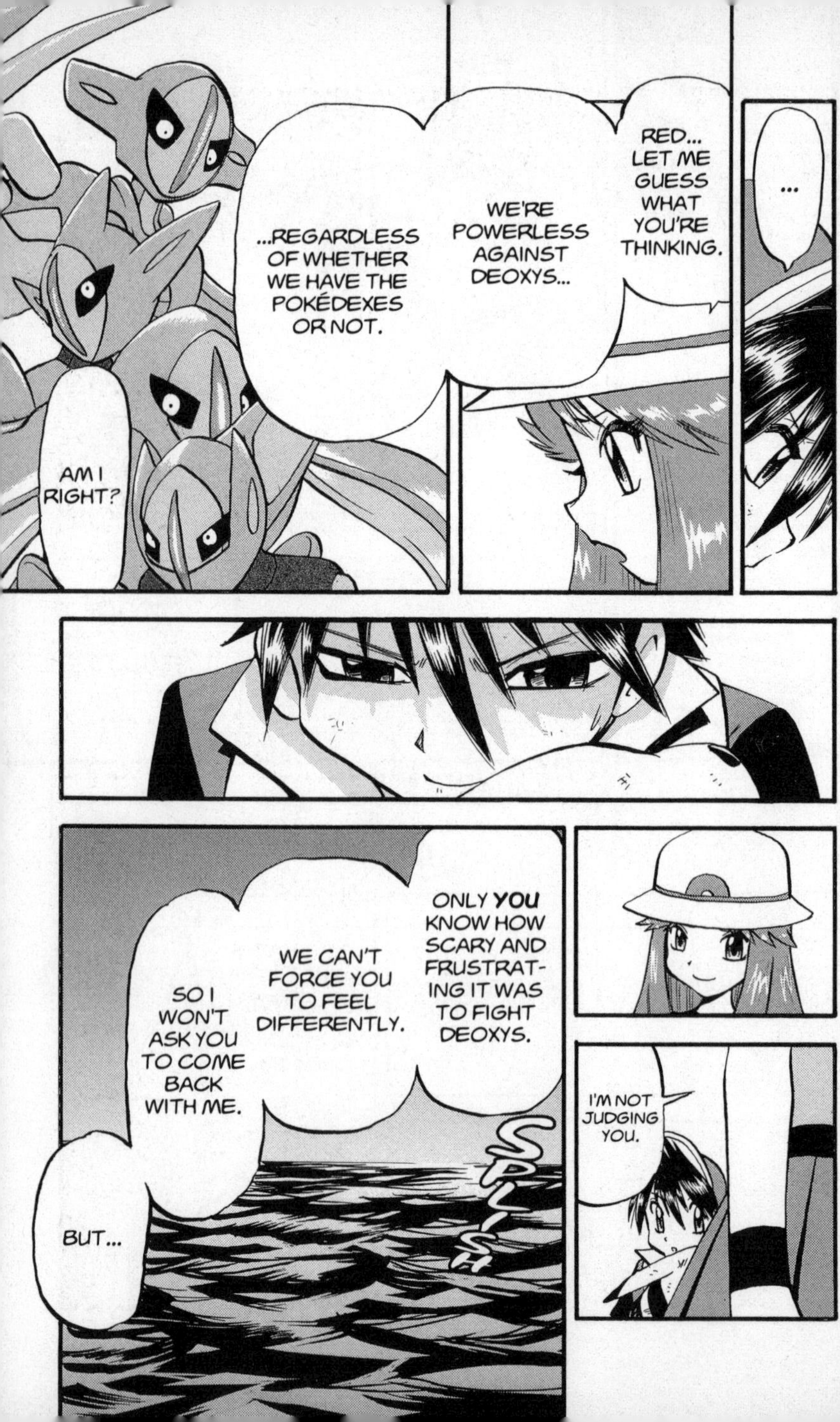
...
RED... LET ME GUESS WHAT YOU'RE THINKING.
WE'RE POWERLESS AGAINST DEOXYS...
...REGARDLESS OF WHETHER WE HAVE THE POKÉDEXES OR NOT.
AM I RIGHT?
I'M NOT JUDGING YOU.
ONLY **YOU** KNOW HOW SCARY AND FRUSTRATING IT WAS TO FIGHT DEOXYS.
WE CAN'T FORCE YOU TO FEEL DIFFERENTLY.
SO I WON'T ASK YOU TO COME BACK WITH ME.
BUT...
SPLISH

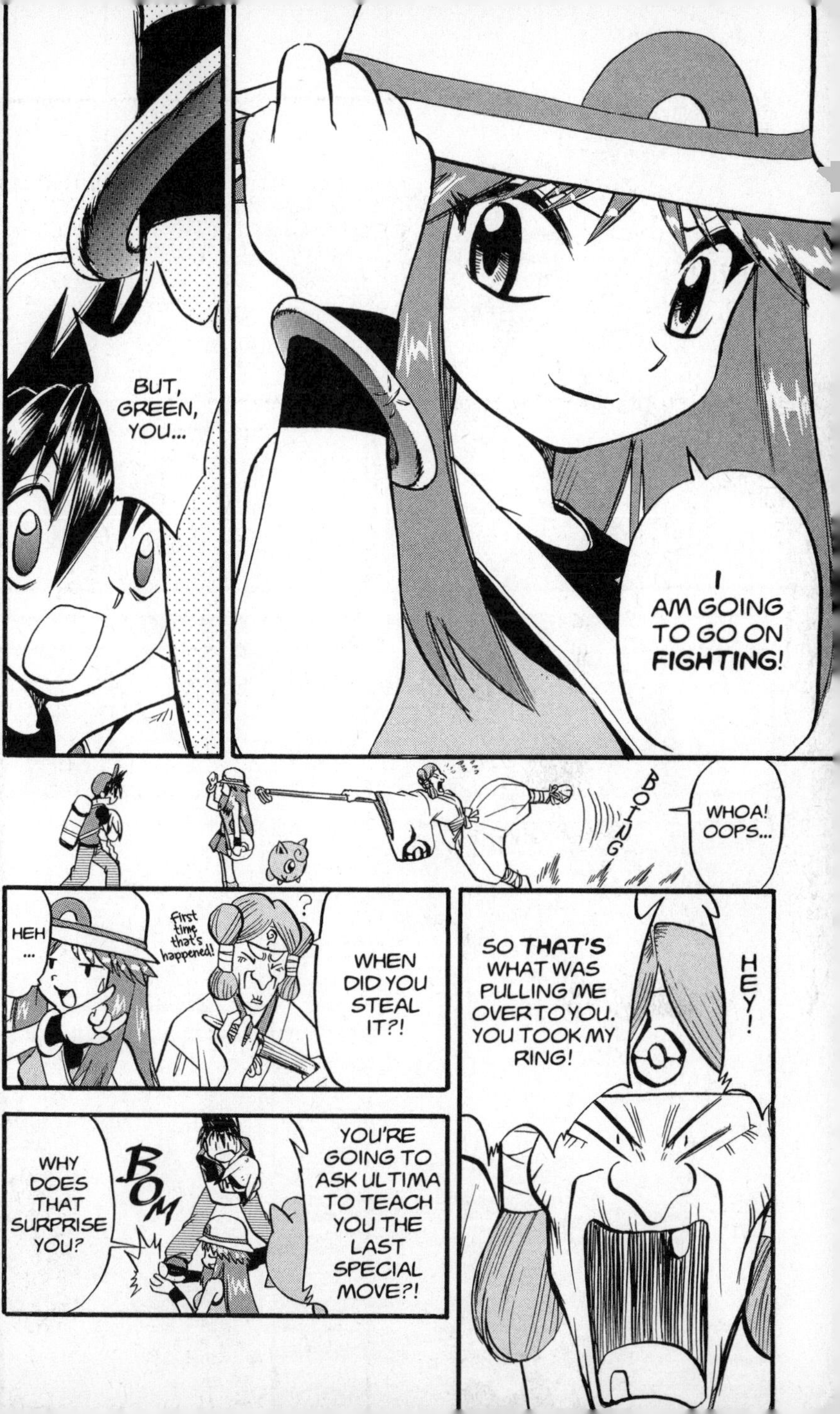

I AM GOING TO GO ON FIGHTING!
BUT, GREEN, YOU...
WHOA! OOPS...
BOING
HEY!
SO THAT'S WHAT WAS PULLING ME OVER TO YOU. YOU TOOK MY RING!
WHEN DID YOU STEAL IT?!
?
First time that's happened!
HEH ...
YOU'RE GOING TO ASK ULTIMA TO TEACH YOU THE LAST SPECIAL MOVE?!
BOM
WHY DOES THAT SURPRISE YOU?

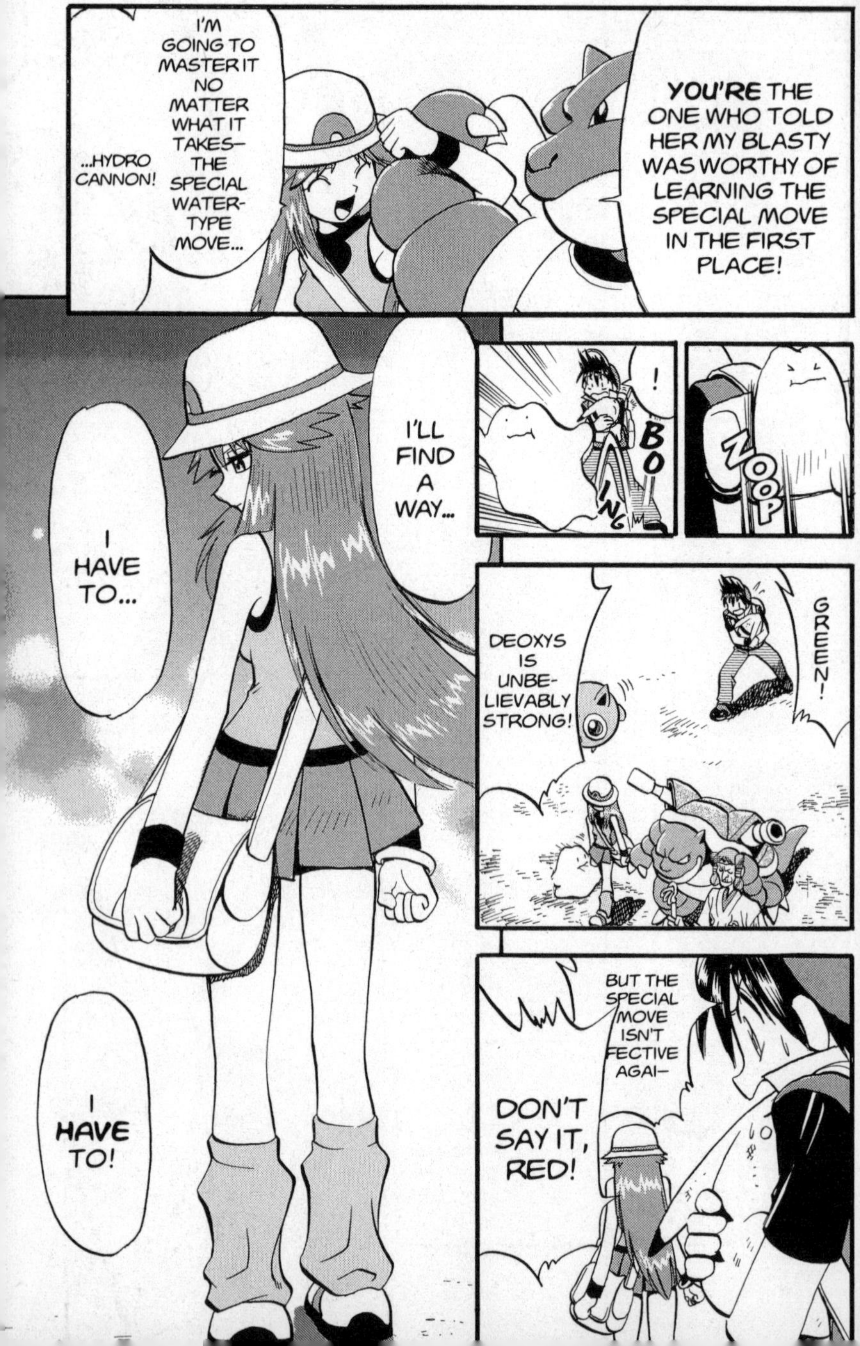
YOU'RE THE ONE WHO TOLD HER MY BLASTY WAS WORTHY OF LEARNING THE SPECIAL MOVE IN THE FIRST PLACE!
I'M GOING TO MASTER IT NO MATTER WHAT IT TAKES— THE SPECIAL WATER-TYPE MOVE...
...HYDRO CANNON!
NOOP
!
BOING
GREEN!
DEOXYS IS UNBELIEVABLY STRONG!
BUT THE SPECIAL MOVE ISN'T FECTIVE AGAI—
DON'T SAY IT, RED!
I'LL FIND A WAY...
I HAVE TO...
I HAVE TO!

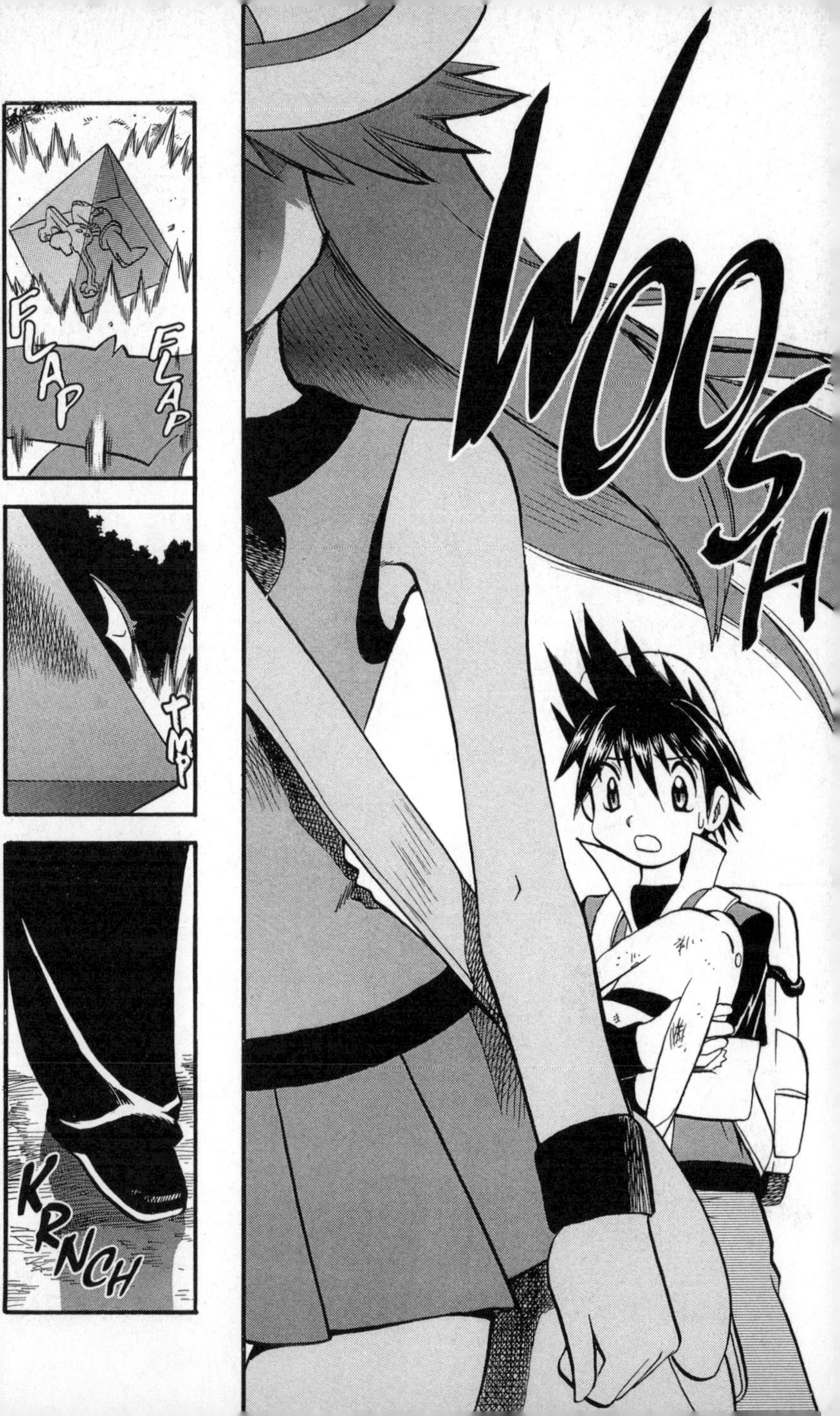
WOOSH
FLAP FLAP
TMP
KRNCH

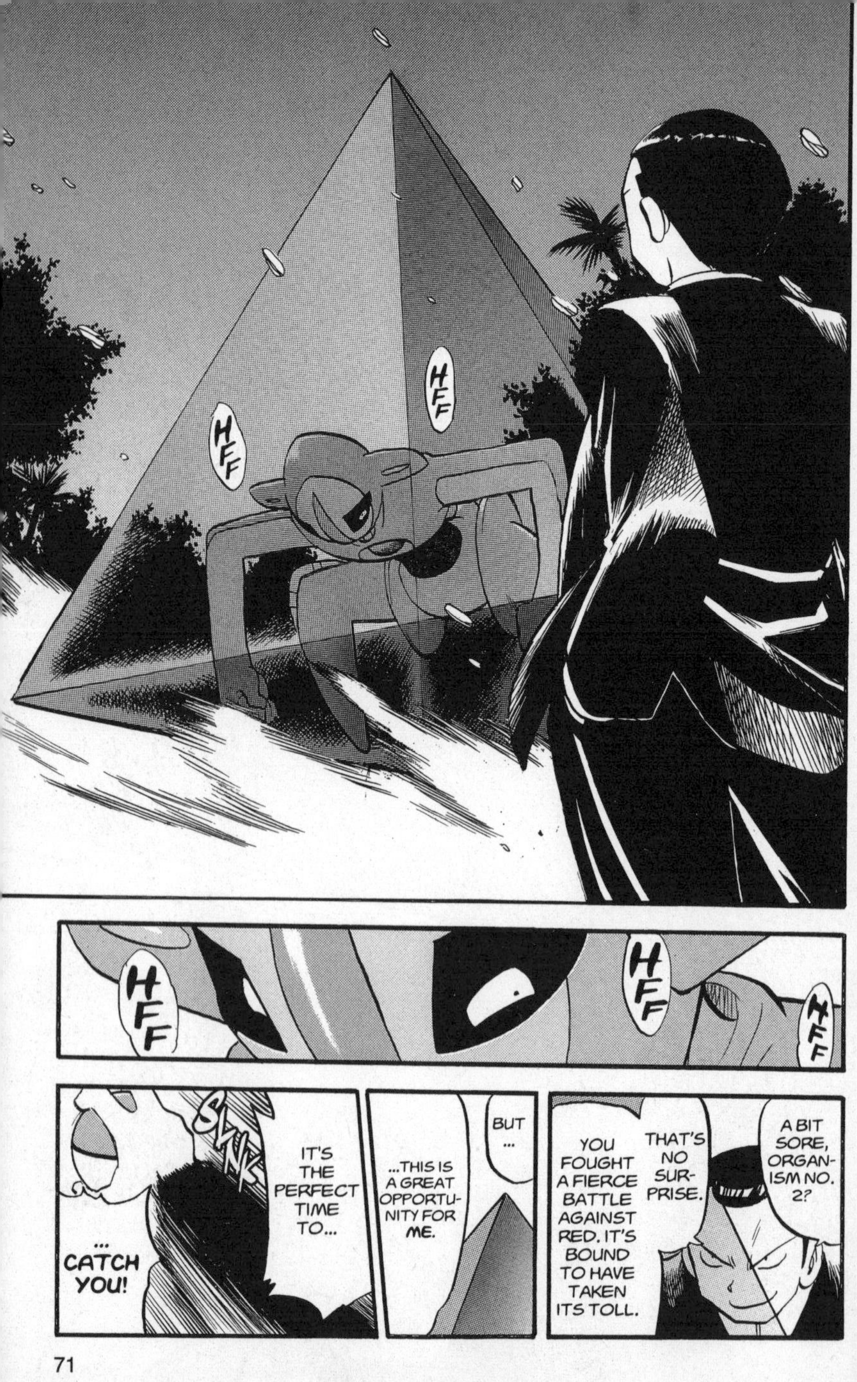
HFF
HFF
HFF
HFF
HFF
A BIT SORE, ORGANISM NO. 2?
THAT'S NO SURPRISE.
YOU FOUGHT A FIERCE BATTLE AGAINST RED. IT'S BOUND TO HAVE TAKEN ITS TOLL.
BUT ...
...THIS IS A GREAT OPPORTUNITY FOR ME.
SLNK
IT'S THE PERFECT TIME TO...
... CATCH YOU!

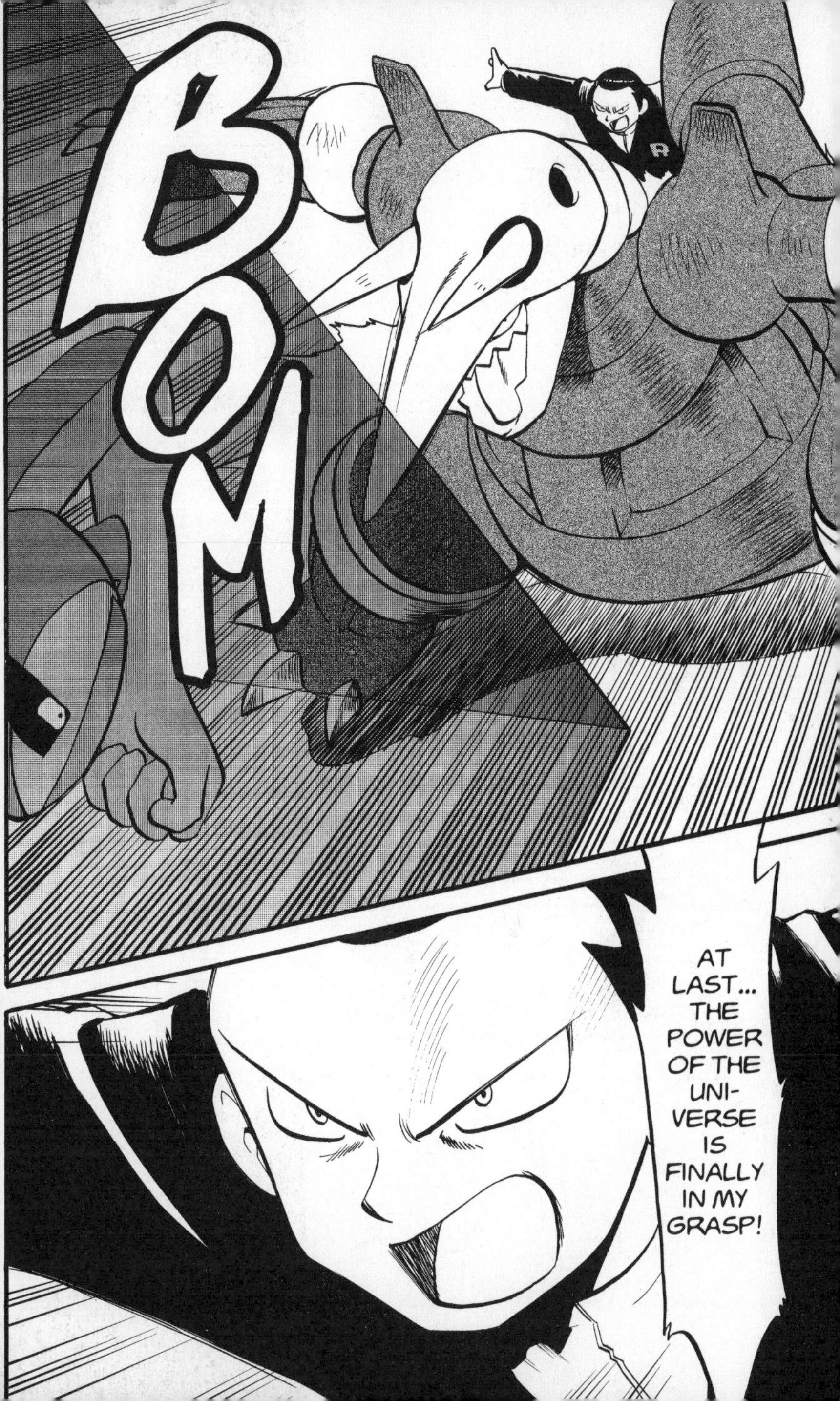
BOOM
AT LAST... THE POWER OF THE UNI-VERSE IS FINALLY IN MY GRASP!

Blasty/Blastoise ♂

LV. 80 (As of Adventure 282)

Ability: Torrent

Jolly Nature

Green received her main Pokémon, Blasty, from Professor Oak. A powerful and reliable Pokémon, it can use water as a weapon or a means of transportation.

Jiggly/Jigglypuff ♀

LV. 67 (As of Adventure 282)

Ability: Cute Charm

Lax Nature

Green has had Jiggly ever since she was a child. But because of the Masked Man, she was unable to truly befriend it until recently.

Ditty/Ditto

LV. 50 (As of Adventure 282)

Ability: Limber

Rash Nature

Ditty can change its shape into all sorts of things. It became friends with Ultima at the Sevii Islands and surprised Red and Blue with its transformation into Deoxys.

POKÉMON ON TEAM GREEN 1

POKÉMON STATS

TEAM GREEN

TEAM GREEN

1

• Adventure 283 •

Takes Patience, Knowledge, and a Really Quick Beedrill

Pokémon Adventures FireRed & LeafGreen The Fifth Chapter

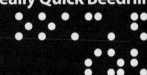

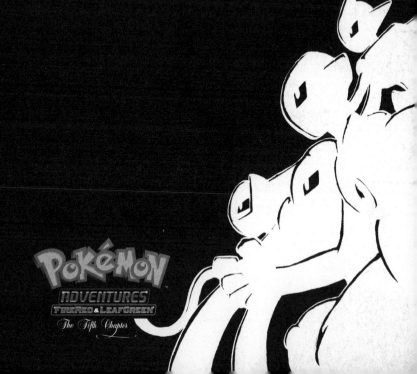

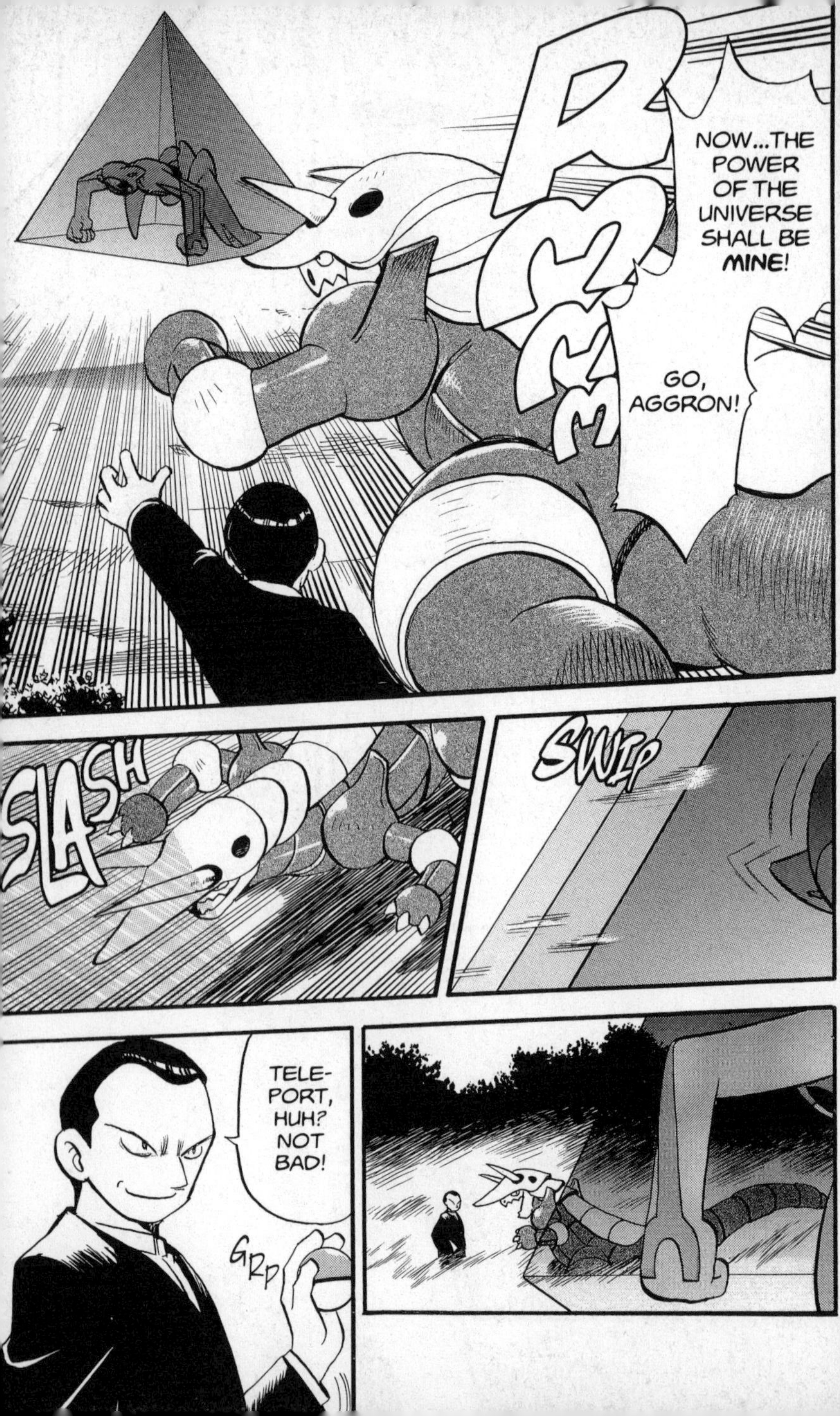
NOW...THE POWER OF THE UNIVERSE SHALL BE MINE!
GO, AGGRON!
SWIP
SLASH
TELE-PORT, HUH? NOT BAD!
GRP

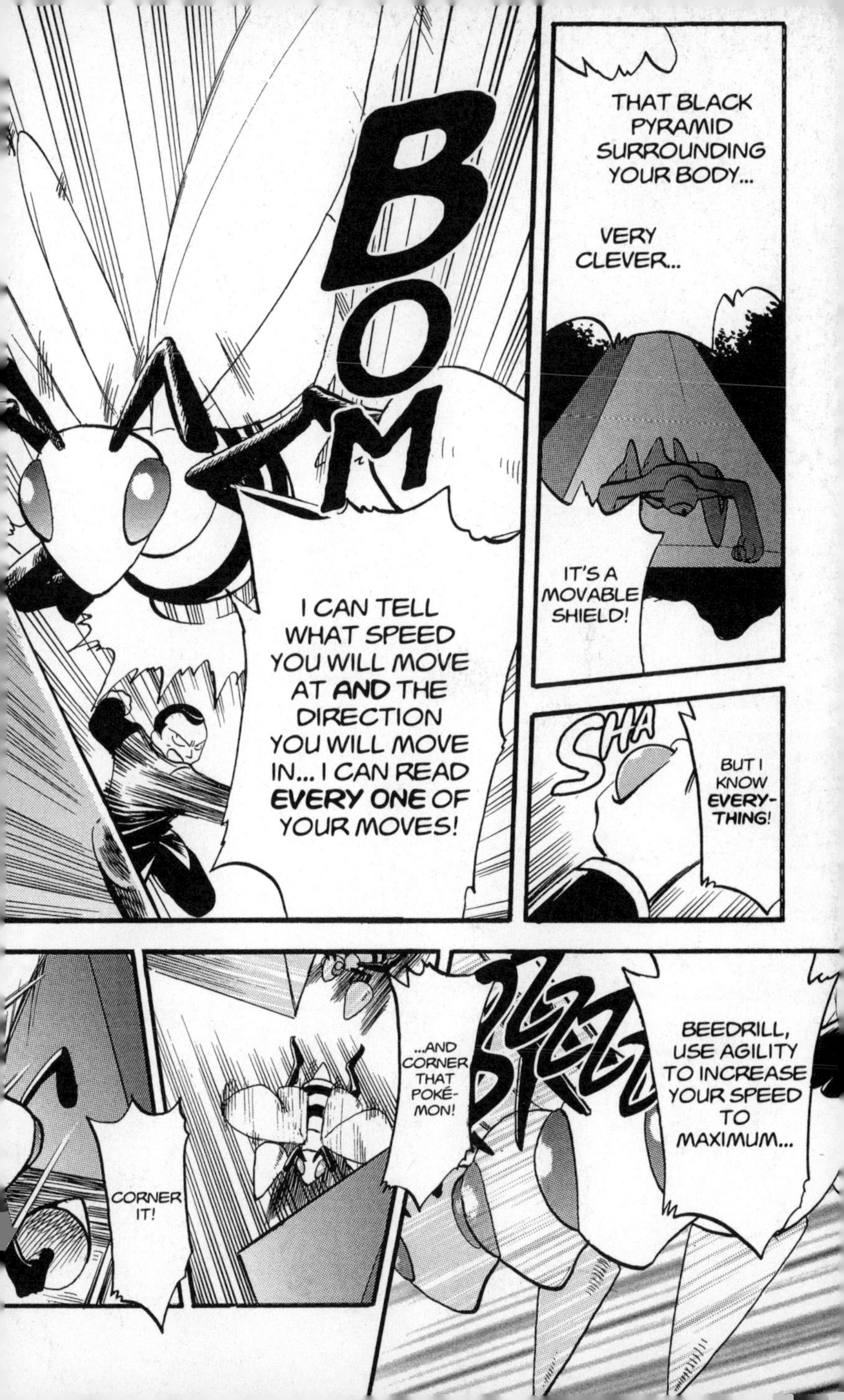
THAT BLACK PYRAMID SURROUNDING YOUR BODY...
VERY CLEVER...
IT'S A MOVABLE SHIELD!
SHA
BUT I KNOW **EVERYTHING**!
BOM
I CAN TELL WHAT SPEED YOU WILL MOVE AT **AND** THE DIRECTION YOU WILL MOVE IN... I CAN READ **EVERY ONE** OF YOUR MOVES!
BEEDRILL, USE AGILITY TO INCREASE YOUR SPEED TO MAXIMUM...
...AND CORNER THAT POKÉMON!
CORNER IT!

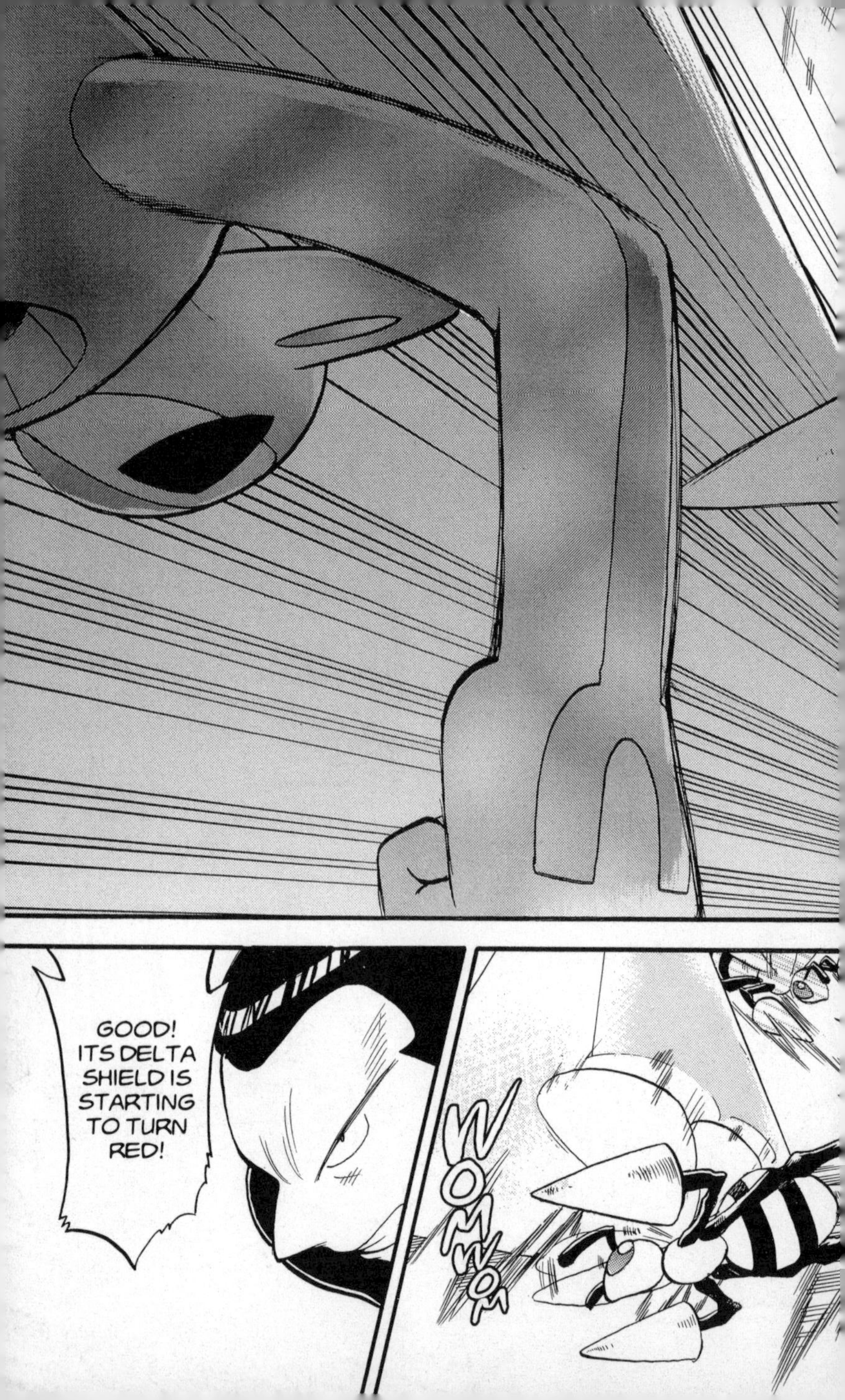
WOMWOM
GOOD! ITS DELTA SHIELD IS STARTING TO TURN RED!

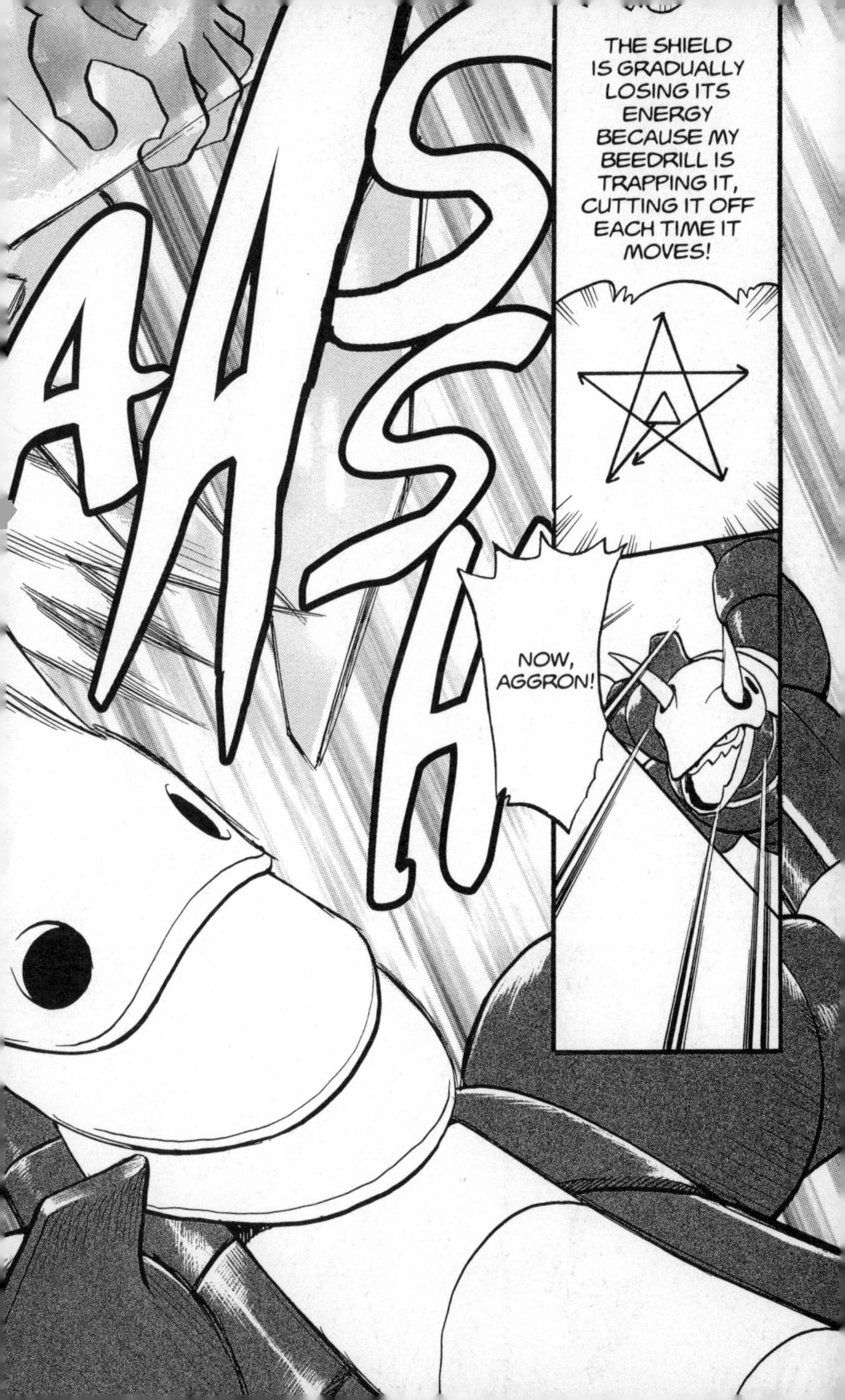
THE SHIELD IS GRADUALLY LOSING ITS ENERGY BECAUSE MY BEEDRILL IS TRAPPING IT, CUTTING IT OFF EACH TIME IT MOVES!
NOW, AGGRON!

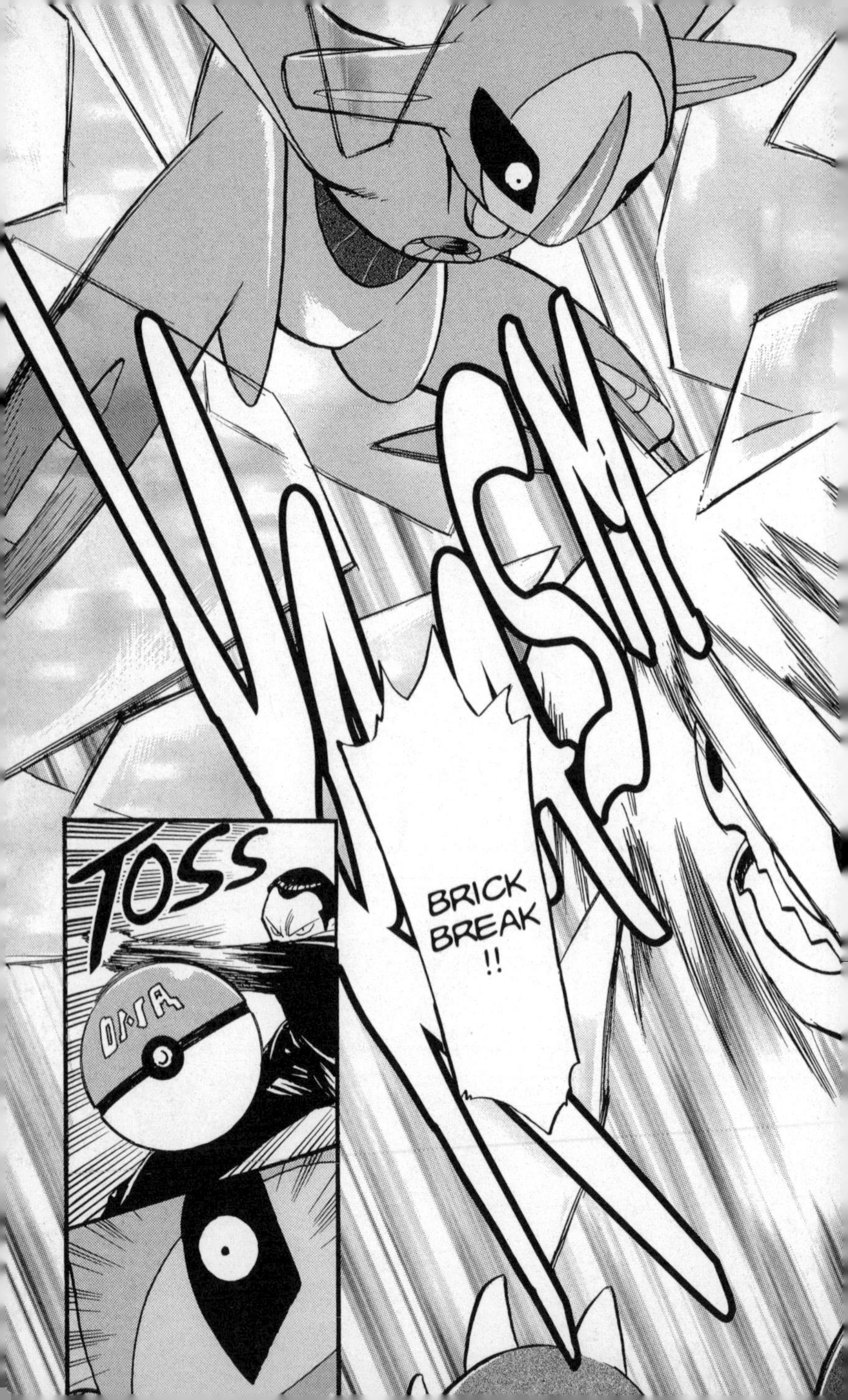
BRICK BREAK !!
TOSS

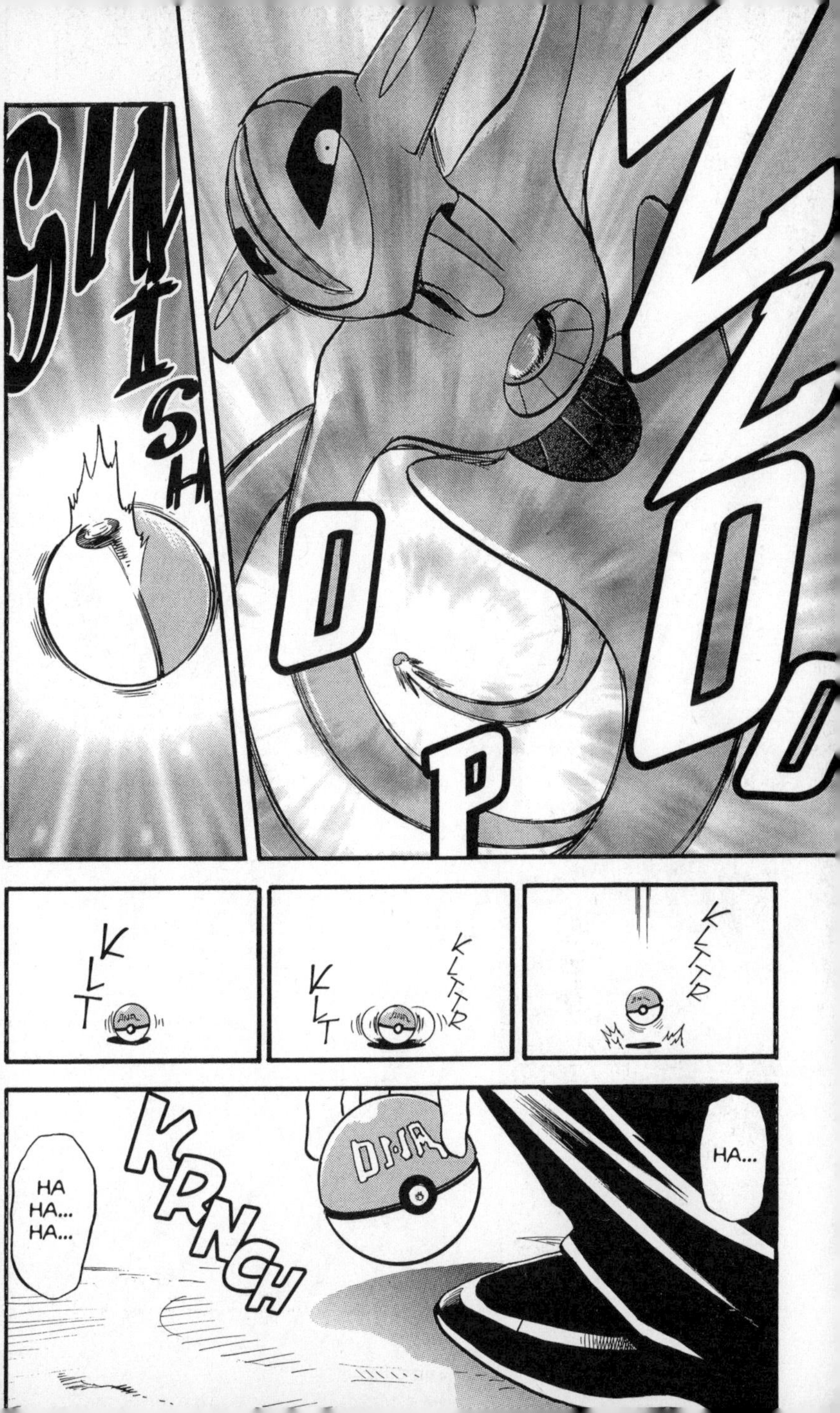
SWISH
KLTTR
KLT
KLTTR
KLT
HA...
KRNCH
HA HA... HA...

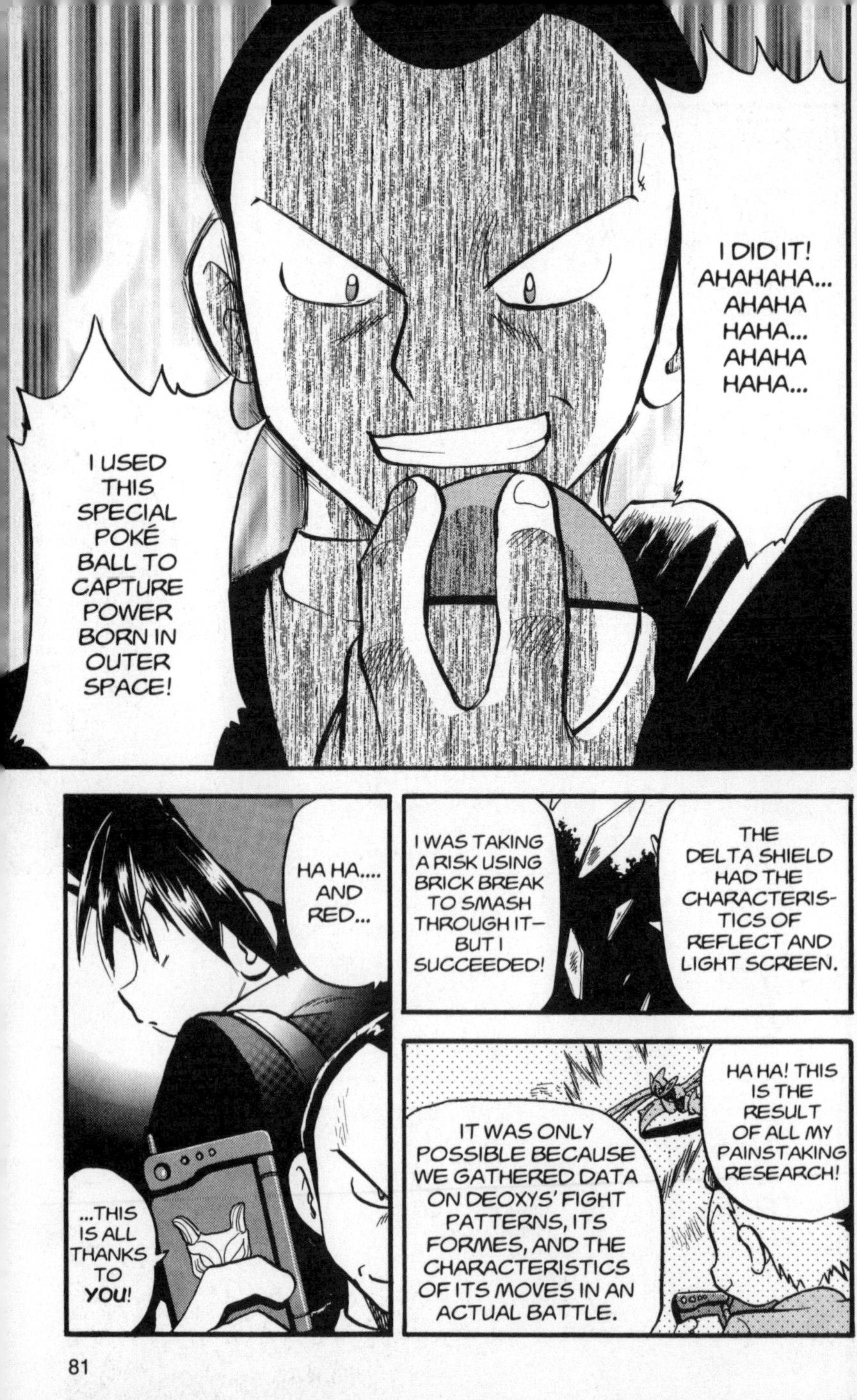
I DID IT! AHAHAHA... AHAHA HAHA... AHAHA HAHA...
I USED THIS SPECIAL POKÉ BALL TO CAPTURE POWER BORN IN OUTER SPACE!
THE DELTA SHIELD HAD THE CHARACTERISTICS OF REFLECT AND LIGHT SCREEN.
I WAS TAKING A RISK USING BRICK BREAK TO SMASH THROUGH IT—BUT I SUCCEEDED!
HA HA! THIS IS THE RESULT OF ALL MY PAINSTAKING RESEARCH!
IT WAS ONLY POSSIBLE BECAUSE WE GATHERED DATA ON DEOXYS' FIGHT PATTERNS, ITS FORMES, AND THE CHARACTERISTICS OF ITS MOVES IN AN ACTUAL BATTLE.
HA HA.... AND RED...
...THIS IS ALL THANKS TO YOU!

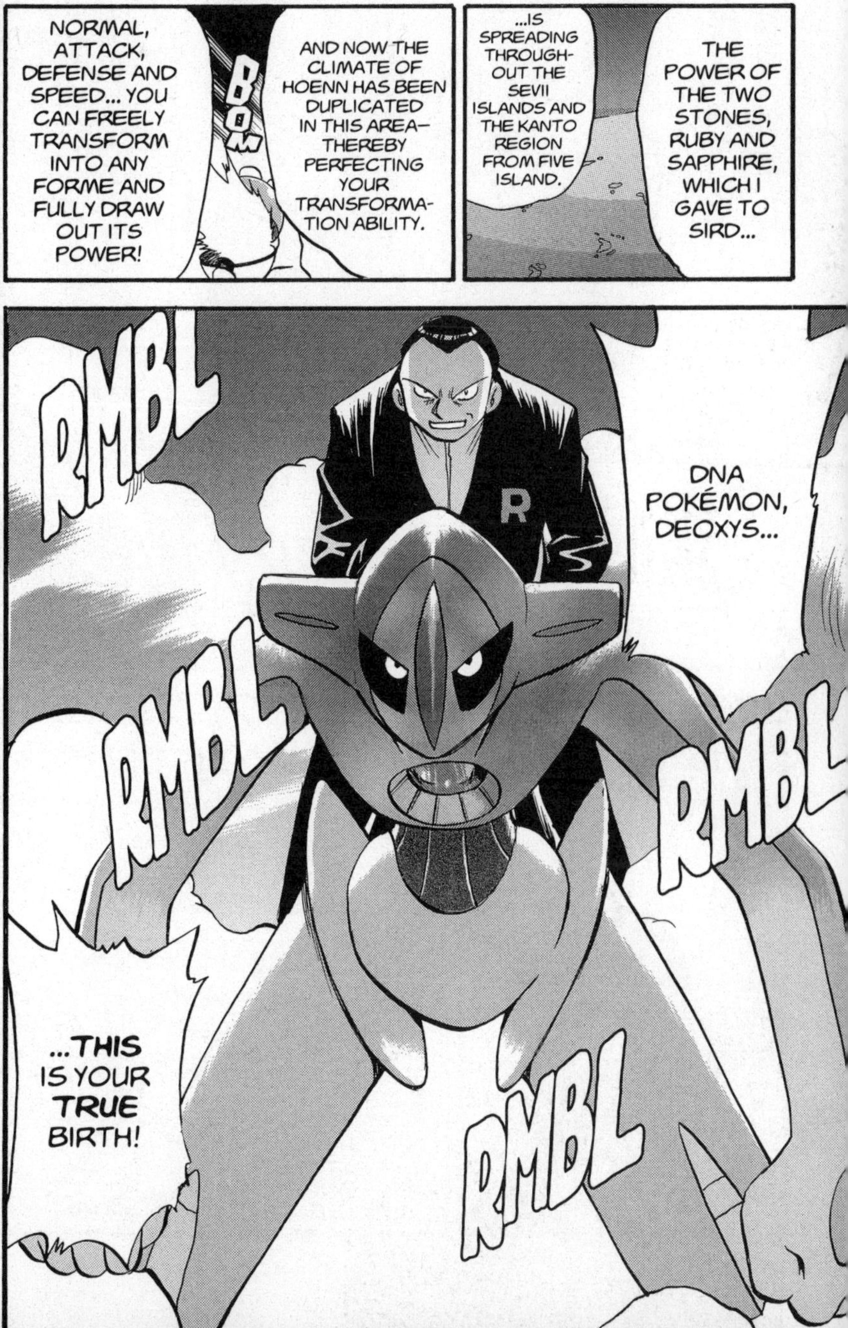
THE POWER OF THE TWO STONES, RUBY AND SAPPHIRE, WHICH I GAVE TO SIRD...
...IS SPREADING THROUGH-OUT THE SEVII ISLANDS AND THE KANTO REGION FROM FIVE ISLAND.
AND NOW THE CLIMATE OF HOENN HAS BEEN DUPLICATED IN THIS AREA— THEREBY PERFECTING YOUR TRANSFORMATION ABILITY.
BOOM
NORMAL, ATTACK, DEFENSE AND SPEED... YOU CAN FREELY TRANSFORM INTO ANY FORME AND FULLY DRAW OUT ITS POWER!
DNA POKÉMON, DEOXYS...
RMBL
RMBL
RMBL
...THIS IS YOUR TRUE BIRTH!
RMBL

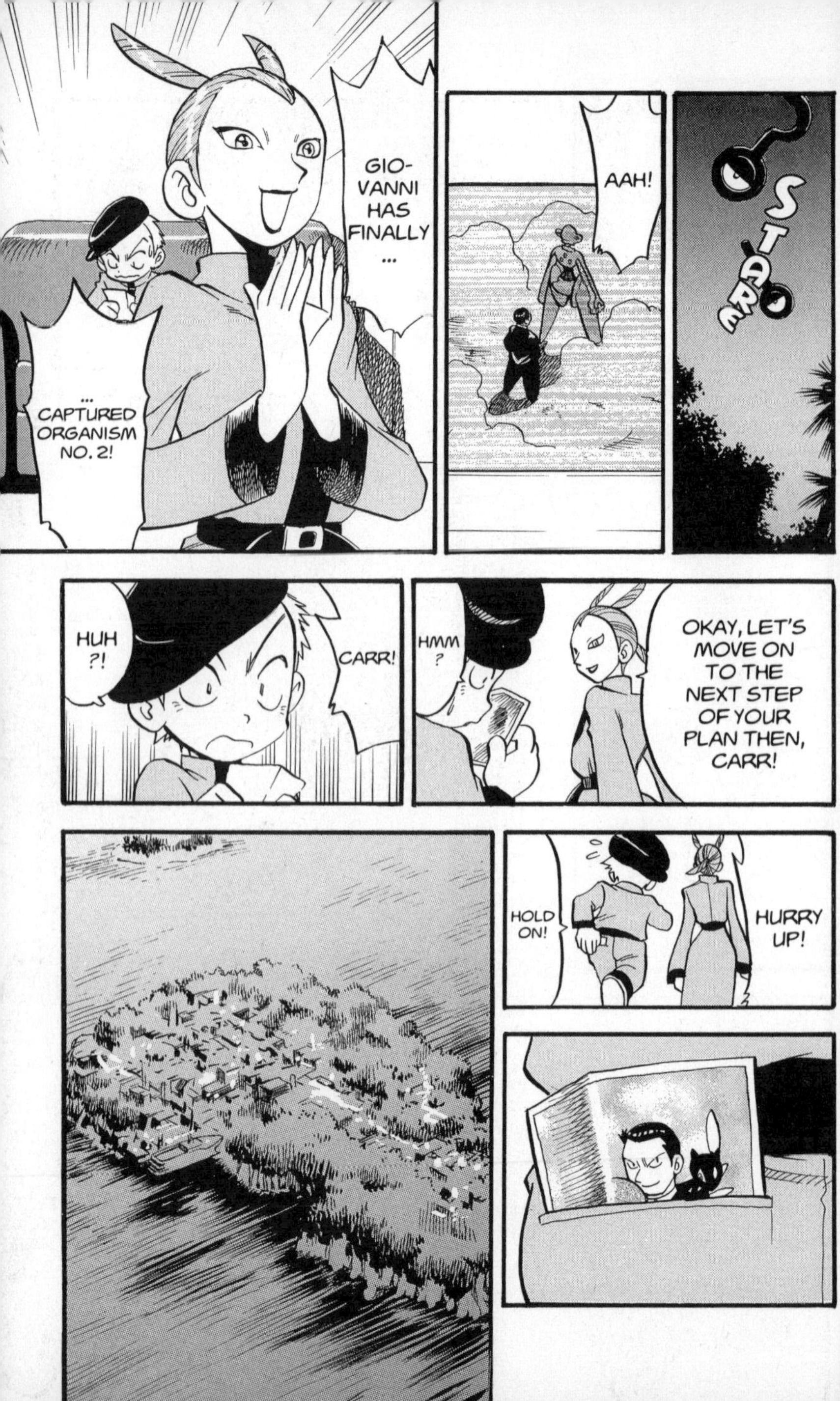
STARE
AAH!
GIO-VANNI HAS FINALLY...
...CAPTURED ORGANISM NO. 2!
OKAY, LET'S MOVE ON TO THE NEXT STEP OF YOUR PLAN THEN, CARR!
HMM?
CARR!
HUH?!
HURRY UP!
HOLD ON!

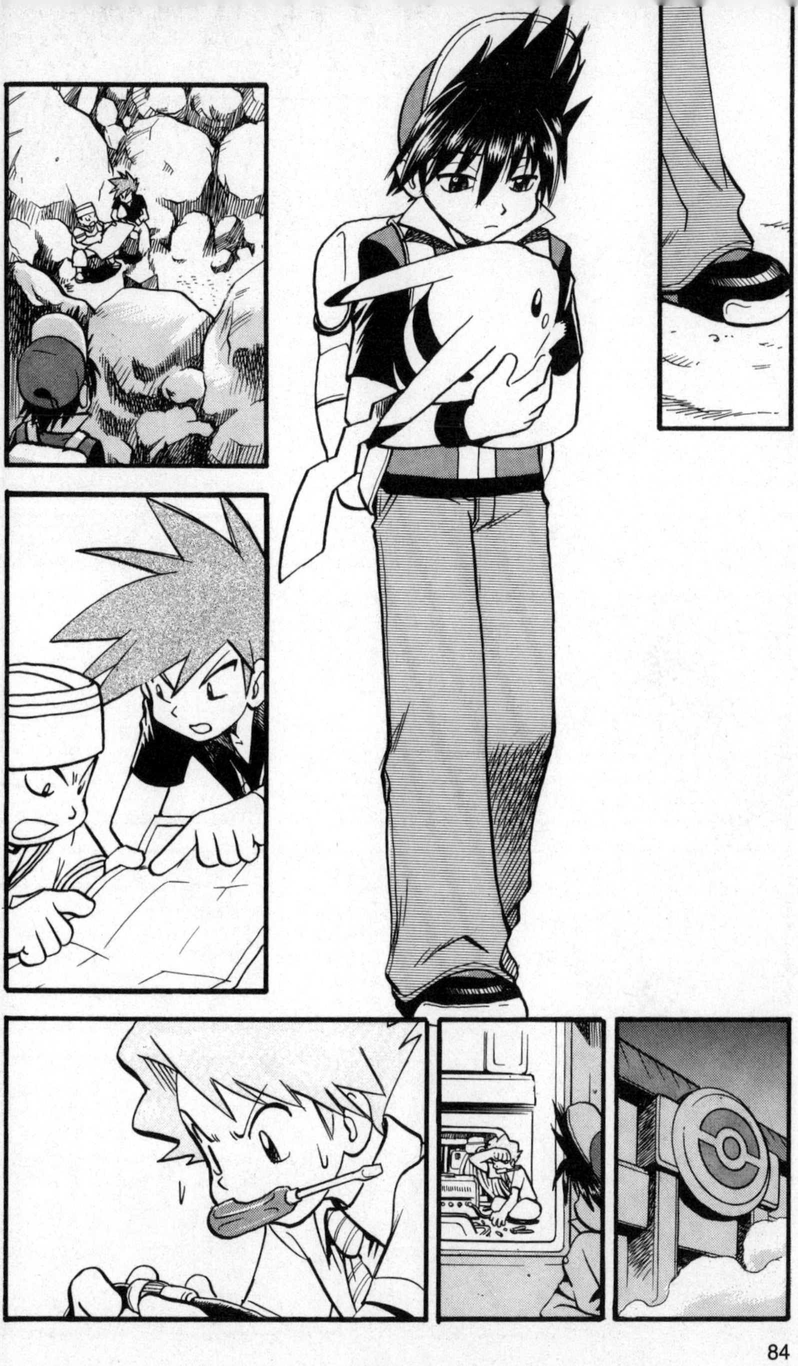

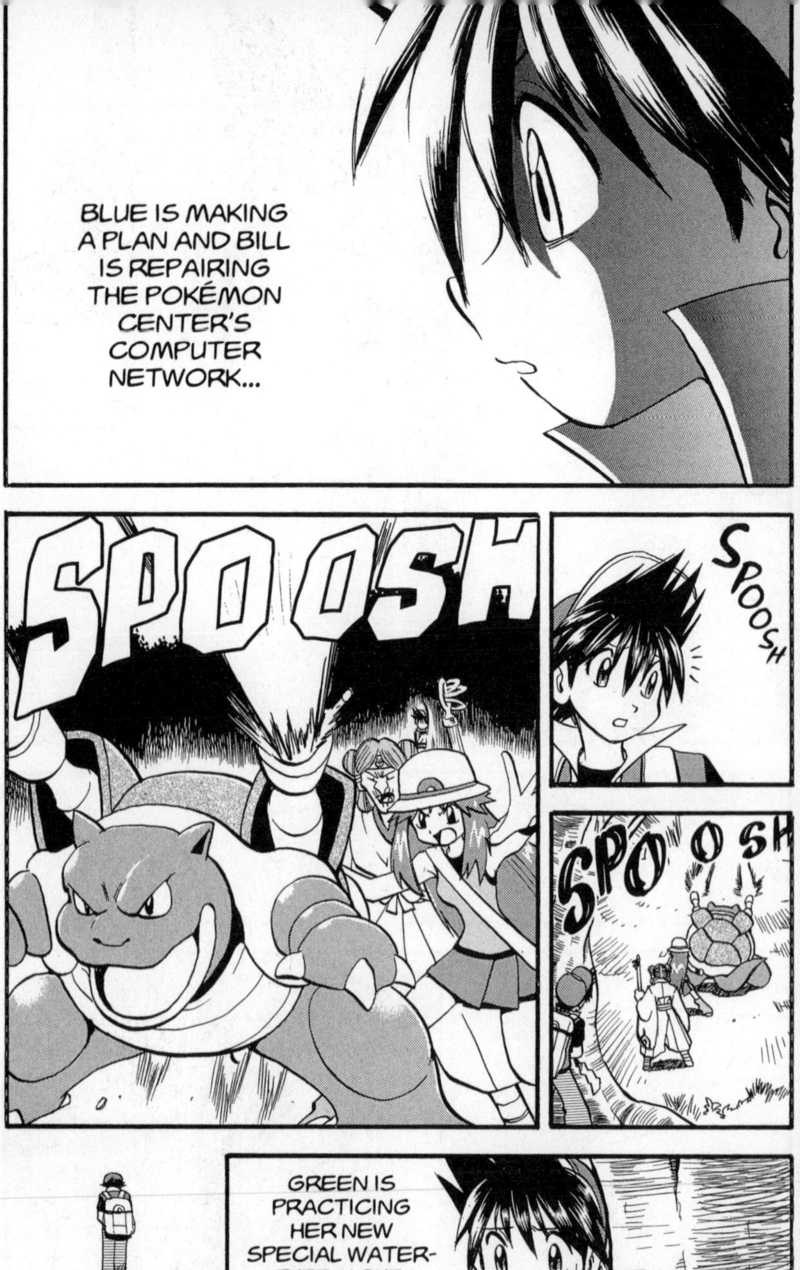
BLUE IS MAKING A PLAN AND BILL IS REPAIRING THE POKÉMON CENTER'S COMPUTER NETWORK...
SPOOSH
SPOOSH
SPOOSH
GREEN IS PRACTICING HER NEW SPECIAL WATER-TYPE MOVE, HYDRO CANNON...

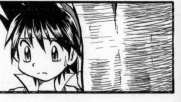

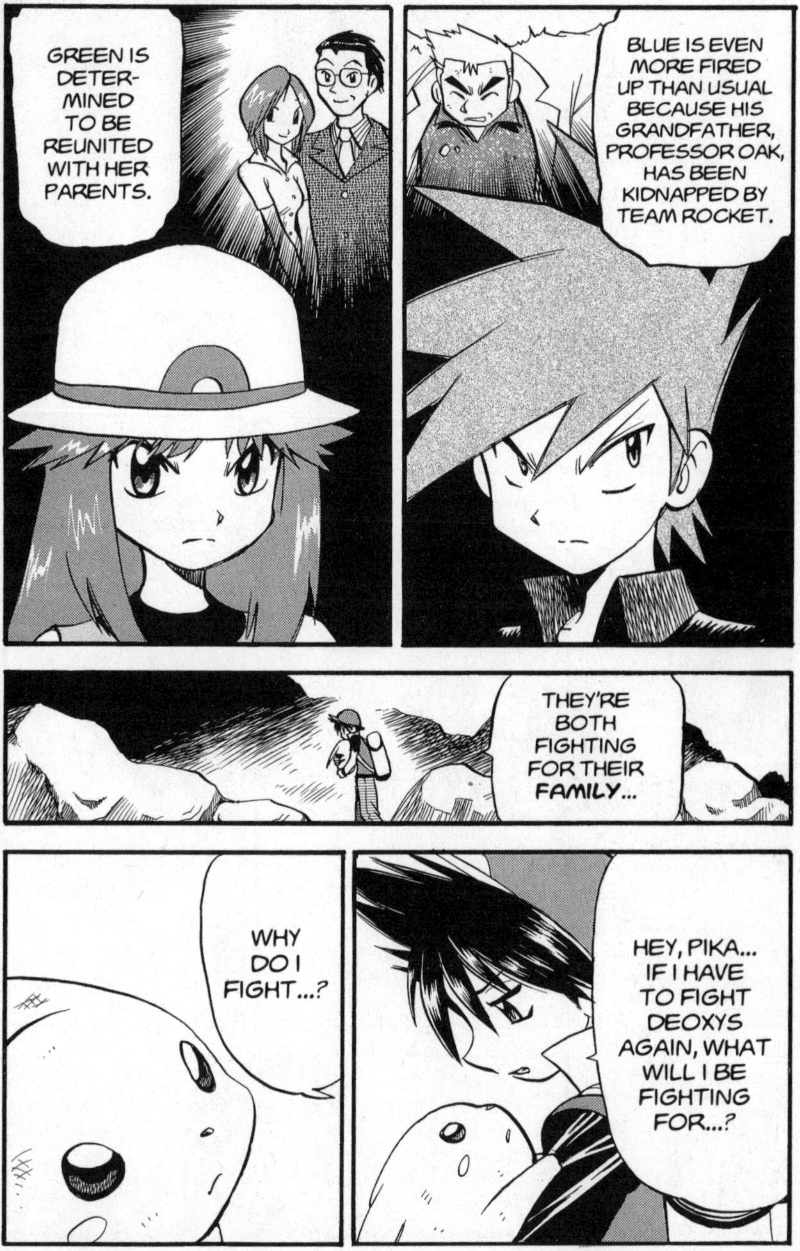
BLUE IS EVEN MORE FIRED UP THAN USUAL BECAUSE HIS GRANDFATHER, PROFESSOR OAK, HAS BEEN KIDNAPPED BY TEAM ROCKET.
GREEN IS DETER-MINED TO BE REUNITED WITH HER PARENTS.
THEY'RE BOTH FIGHTING FOR THEIR FAMILY...
HEY, PIKA... IF I HAVE TO FIGHT DEOXYS AGAIN, WHAT WILL I BE FIGHTING FOR...?
WHY DO I FIGHT...?

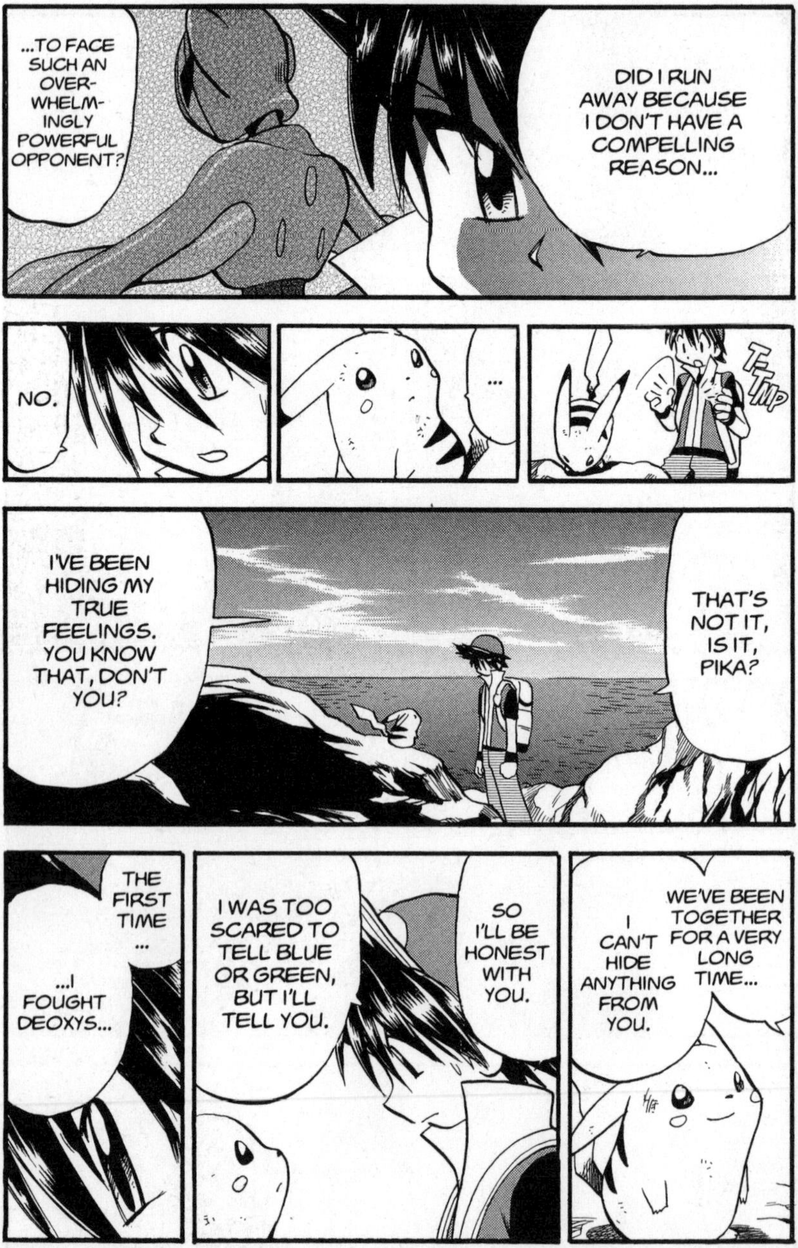
DID I RUN AWAY BECAUSE I DON'T HAVE A COMPELLING REASON...
...TO FACE SUCH AN OVER-WHELM-INGLY POWERFUL OPPONENT?
T-TMP
...
NO.
THAT'S NOT IT, IS IT, PIKA?
I'VE BEEN HIDING MY TRUE FEELINGS. YOU KNOW THAT, DON'T YOU?
WE'VE BEEN TOGETHER FOR A VERY LONG TIME...
I CAN'T HIDE ANYTHING FROM YOU.
SO I'LL BE HONEST WITH YOU.
I WAS TOO SCARED TO TELL BLUE OR GREEN, BUT I'LL TELL YOU.
THE FIRST TIME ...
...I FOUGHT DEOXYS...

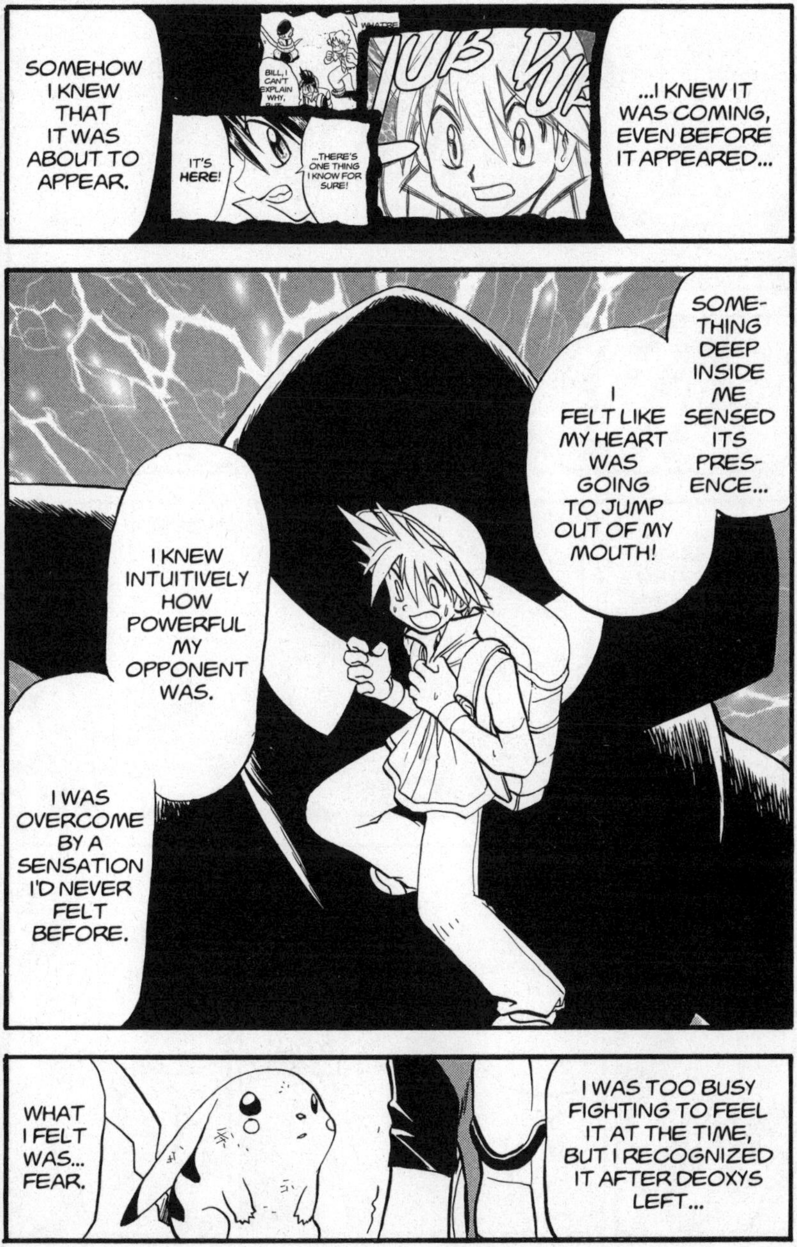
...I KNEW IT WAS COMING, EVEN BEFORE IT APPEARED...
BILL, I CAN'T EXPLAIN WHY,
...THERE'S ONE THING I KNOW FOR SURE!
IT'S HERE!
SOMEHOW I KNEW THAT IT WAS ABOUT TO APPEAR.
SOMETHING DEEP INSIDE ME SENSED ITS PRESENCE...
I FELT LIKE MY HEART WAS GOING TO JUMP OUT OF MY MOUTH!
I KNEW INTUITIVELY HOW POWERFUL MY OPPONENT WAS.
I WAS OVERCOME BY A SENSATION I'D NEVER FELT BEFORE.
I WAS TOO BUSY FIGHTING TO FEEL IT AT THE TIME, BUT I RECOGNIZED IT AFTER DEOXYS LEFT...
WHAT I FELT WAS... FEAR.

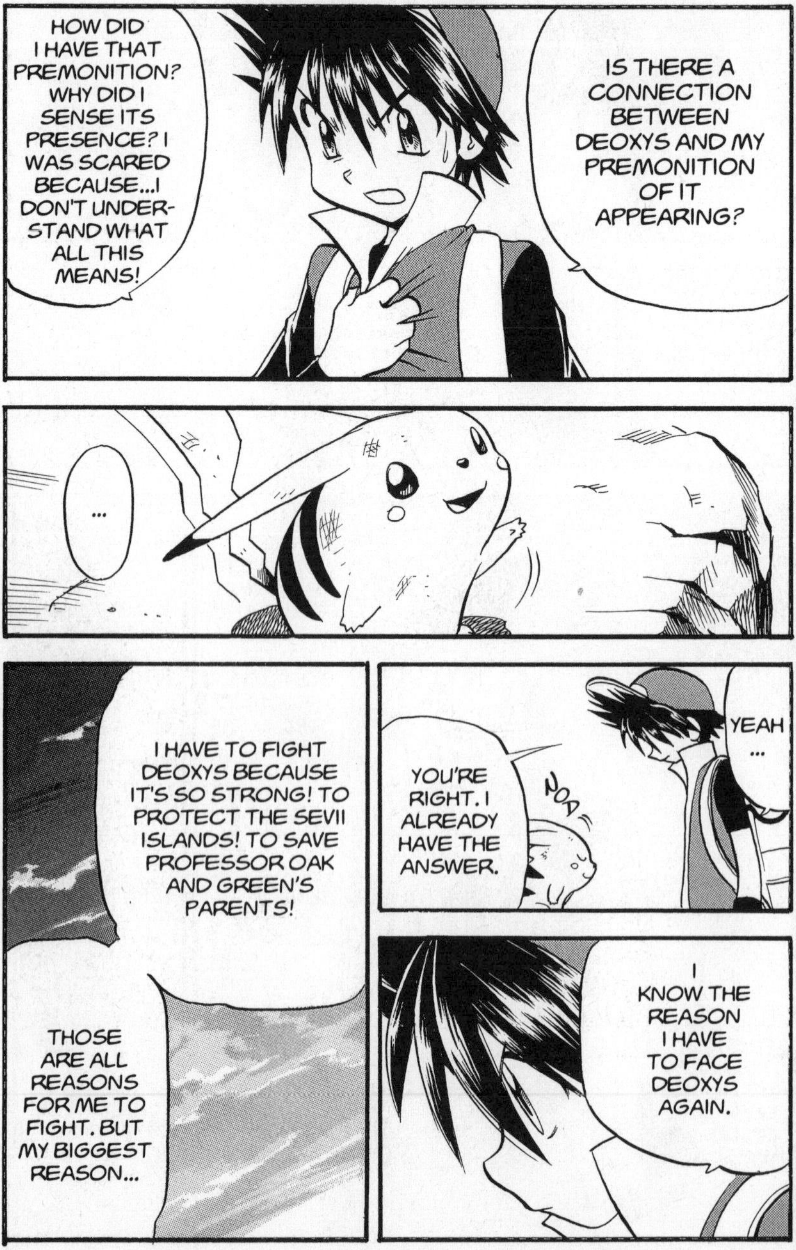
IS THERE A CONNECTION BETWEEN DEOXYS AND MY PREMONITION OF IT APPEARING?
HOW DID I HAVE THAT PREMONITION? WHY DID I SENSE ITS PRESENCE? I WAS SCARED BECAUSE...I DON'T UNDER-STAND WHAT ALL THIS MEANS!
...
YEAH ...
YOU'RE RIGHT. I ALREADY HAVE THE ANSWER.
NOD
I KNOW THE REASON I HAVE TO FACE DEOXYS AGAIN.
I HAVE TO FIGHT DEOXYS BECAUSE IT'S SO STRONG! TO PROTECT THE SEVII ISLANDS! TO SAVE PROFESSOR OAK AND GREEN'S PARENTS!
THOSE ARE ALL REASONS FOR ME TO FIGHT. BUT MY BIGGEST REASON...

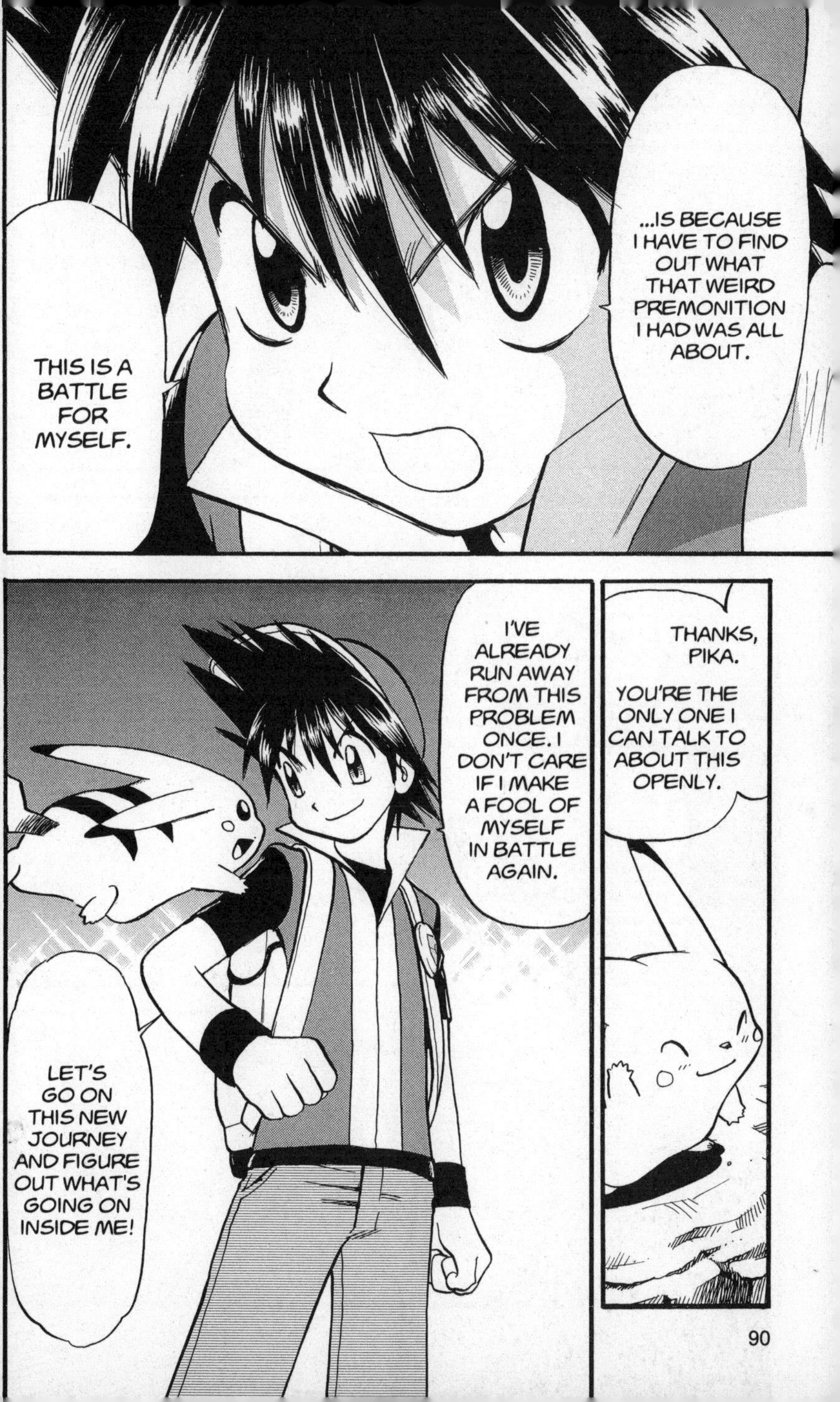
...IS BECAUSE I HAVE TO FIND OUT WHAT THAT WEIRD PREMONITION I HAD WAS ALL ABOUT.
THIS IS A BATTLE FOR MYSELF.
THANKS, PIKA.
YOU'RE THE ONLY ONE I CAN TALK TO ABOUT THIS OPENLY.
I'VE ALREADY RUN AWAY FROM THIS PROBLEM ONCE. I DON'T CARE IF I MAKE A FOOL OF MYSELF IN BATTLE AGAIN.
LET'S GO ON THIS NEW JOURNEY AND FIGURE OUT WHAT'S GOING ON INSIDE ME!

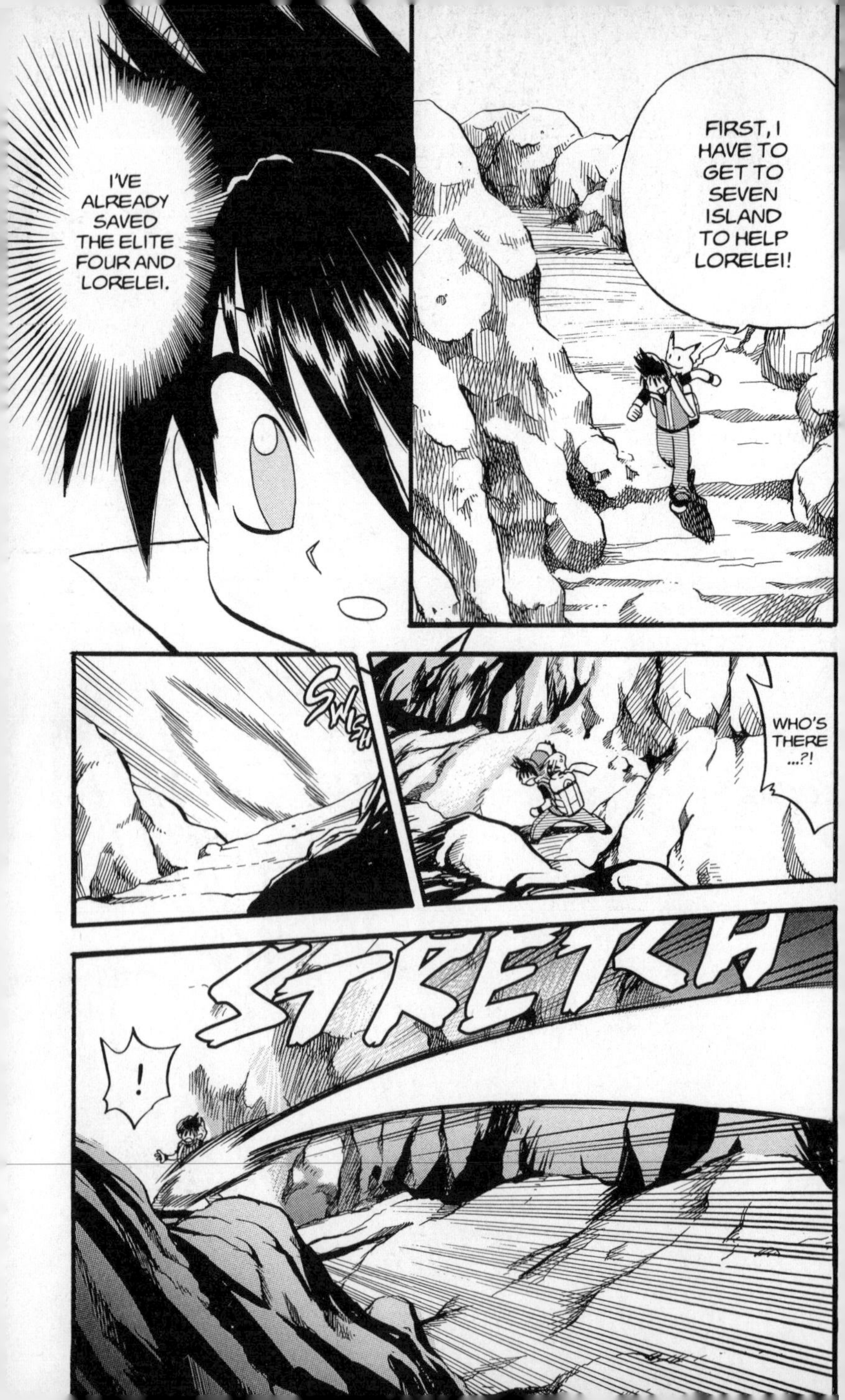
FIRST, I HAVE TO GET TO SEVEN ISLAND TO HELP LORELEI!
I'VE ALREADY SAVED THE ELITE FOUR AND LORELEI.
WHO'S THERE ...?!
SWISH
STRETCH
!

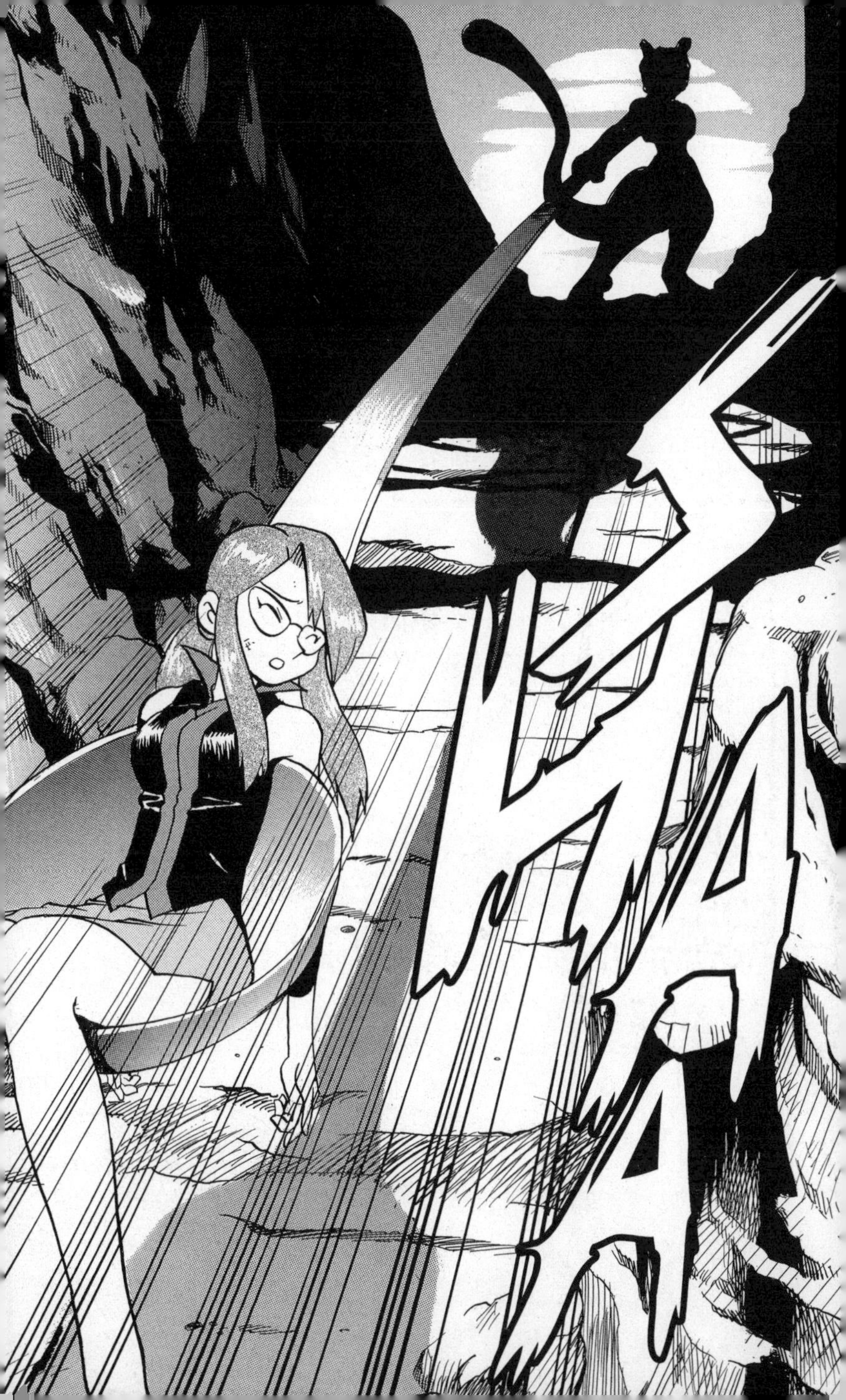

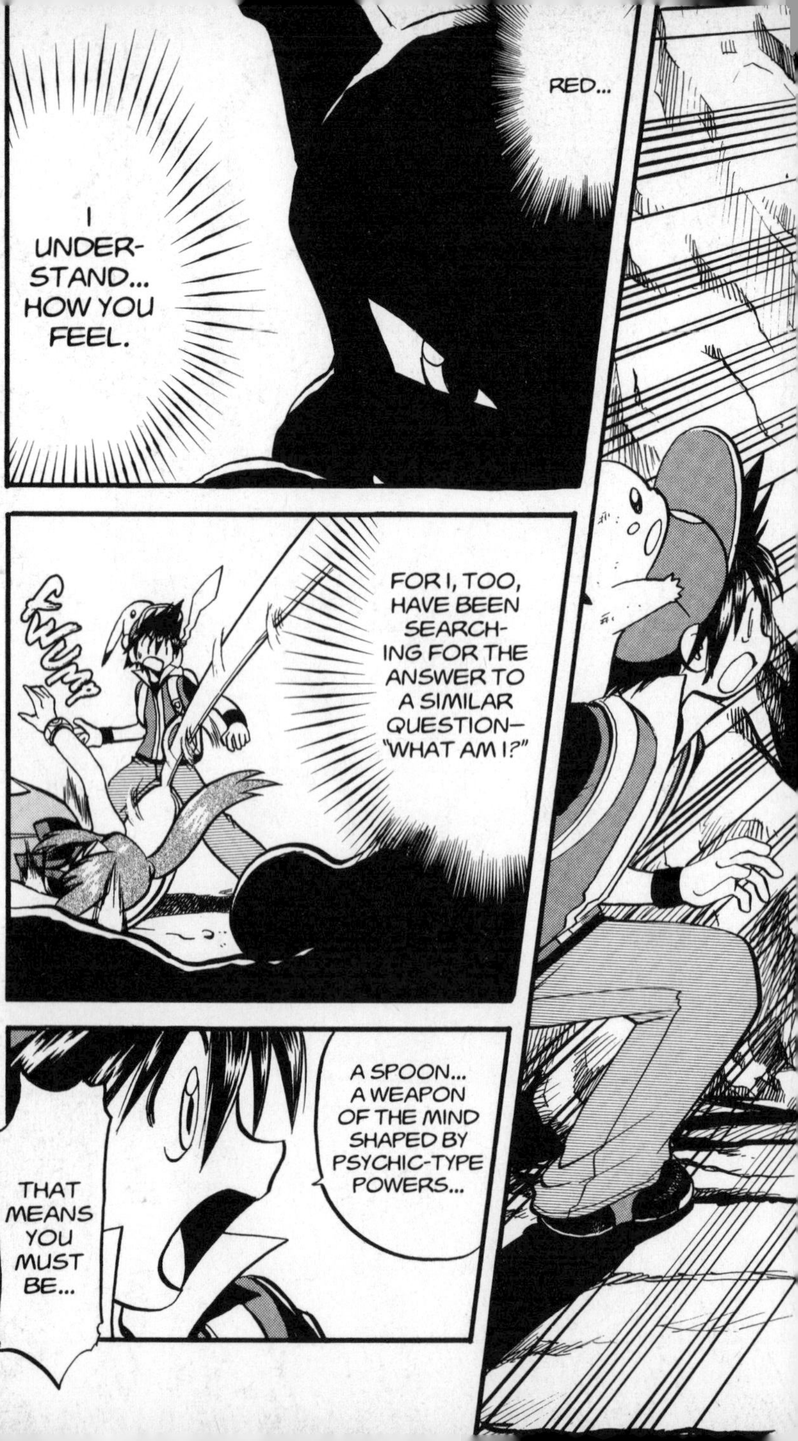
RED...
I UNDER-STAND... HOW YOU FEEL.
FOR I, TOO, HAVE BEEN SEARCHING FOR THE ANSWER TO A SIMILAR QUESTION—"WHAT AM I?"
FWUMP
A SPOON... A WEAPON OF THE MIND SHAPED BY PSYCHIC-TYPE POWERS...
THAT MEANS YOU MUST BE...

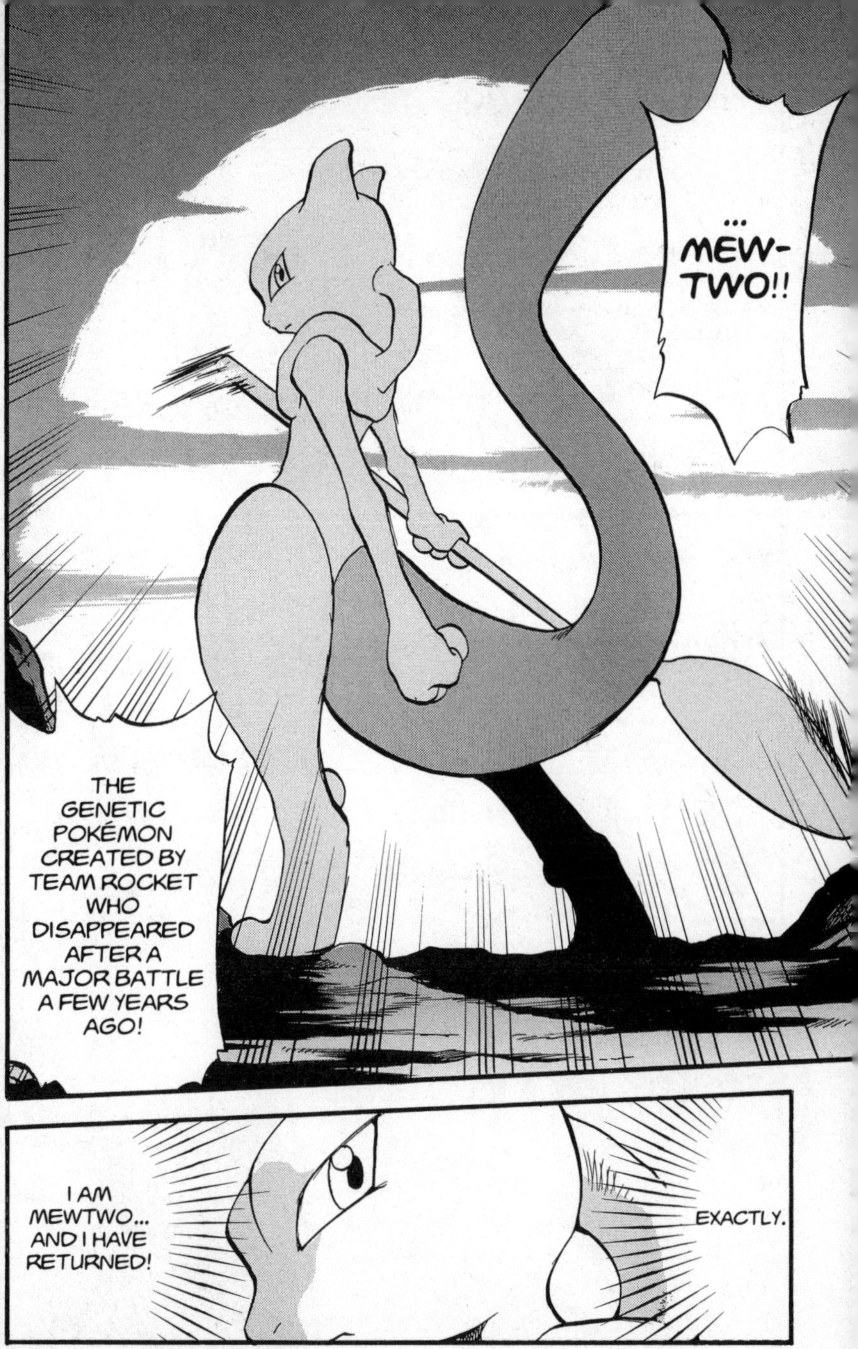
... MEW-TWO!!
THE GENETIC POKÉMON CREATED BY TEAM ROCKET WHO DISAPPEARED AFTER A MAJOR BATTLE A FEW YEARS AGO!
EXACTLY.
I AM MEWTWO... AND I HAVE RETURNED!

Clefy/Clefable ♂

Normal

LV. 68 (As of Adventure 283)

Ability: Cute Charm

Naughty Nature

Red evolved this Clefairy using his Moon Stone. It baffles its opponent with moves like Minimize and Metronome.

Nido/Nidorina ♀

Poison

LV. 69 (As of Adventure 283)

Ability: Poison Point

Quiet Nature

Nido is a powerful close-combat fighter who wields attacks using poison. Its ultrasonic cries befuddle its opponents.

Snubbull/Snubbull ♂

Normal

LV. 22 (As of Adventure 283)

Ability: Run Away

Timid Nature

Green added this Pokémon to her team for the battle against the Kanto Elite Four as her seventh trump card. Snubbull played an active role in the battle at Ilex Forest and is currently awaiting its turn to evolve.

• Adventure 284 •
Red, Green, Blue and Mewtwo Too

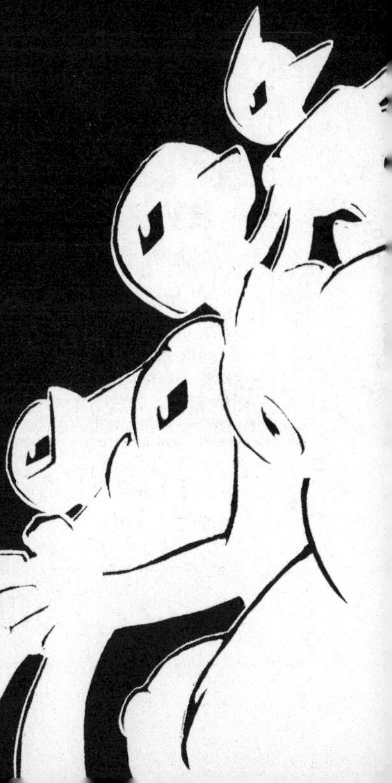

Pokémon Adventures
FireRed & LeafGreen
The Fifth Chapter

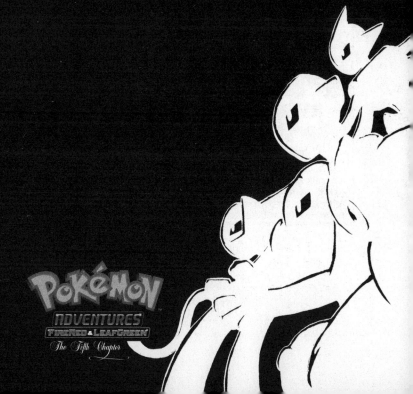

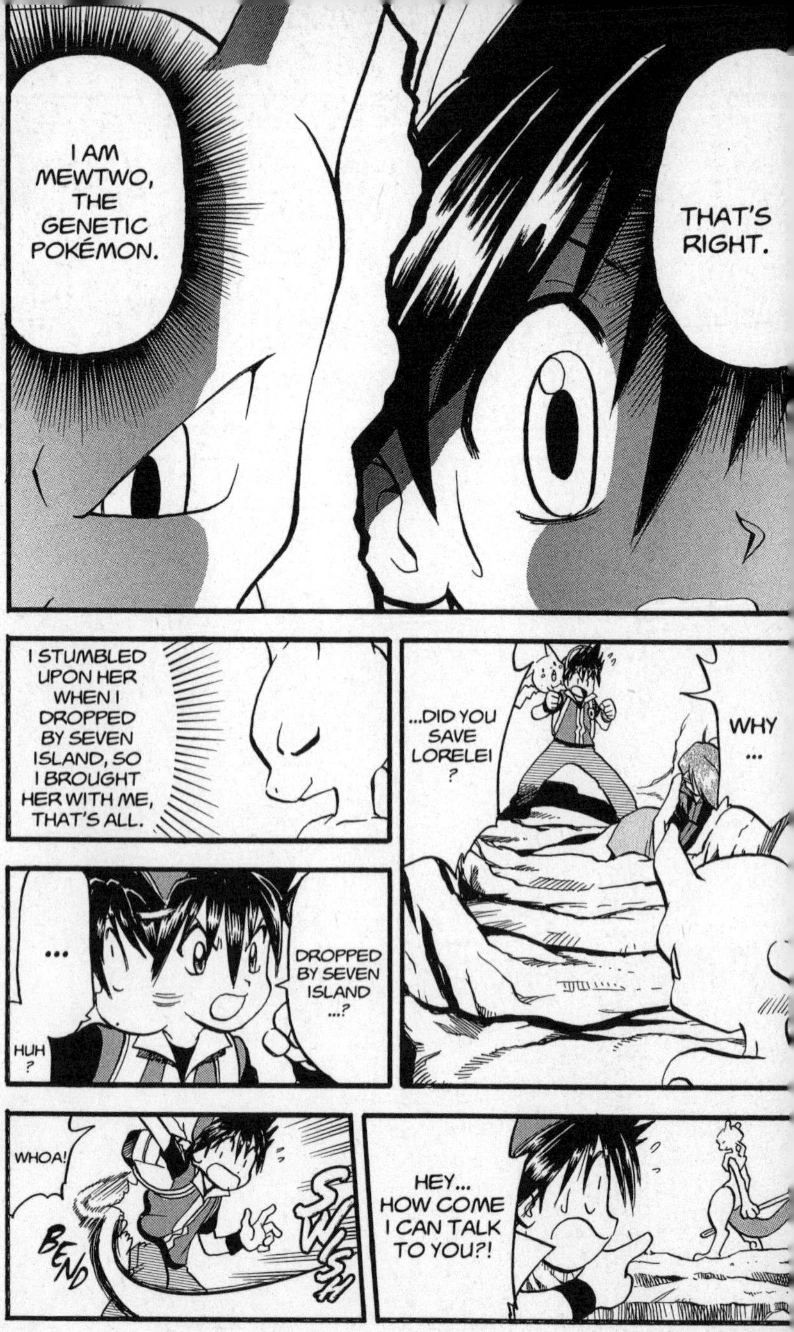
THAT'S RIGHT.
I AM MEWTWO, THE GENETIC POKÉMON.
WHY ...
...DID YOU SAVE LORELEI ?
I STUMBLED UPON HER WHEN I DROPPED BY SEVEN ISLAND, SO I BROUGHT HER WITH ME, THAT'S ALL.
DROPPED BY SEVEN ISLAND ...?
...
HUH ?
HEY... HOW COME I CAN TALK TO YOU?!
SWISH
WHOA!
BEND

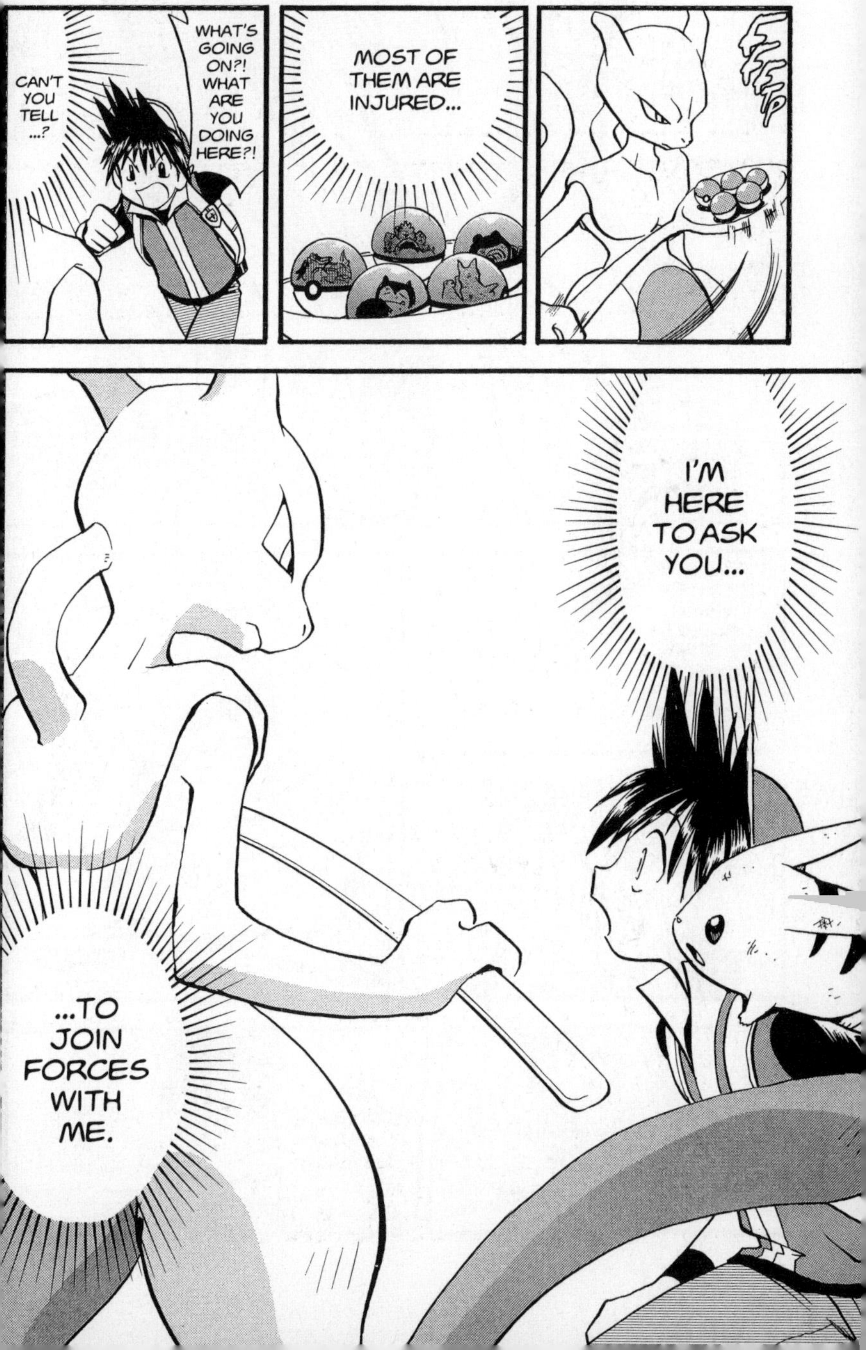
MOST OF THEM ARE INJURED...
WHAT'S GOING ON?! WHAT ARE YOU DOING HERE?!
CAN'T YOU TELL ...?
I'M HERE TO ASK YOU...
...TO JOIN FORCES WITH ME.

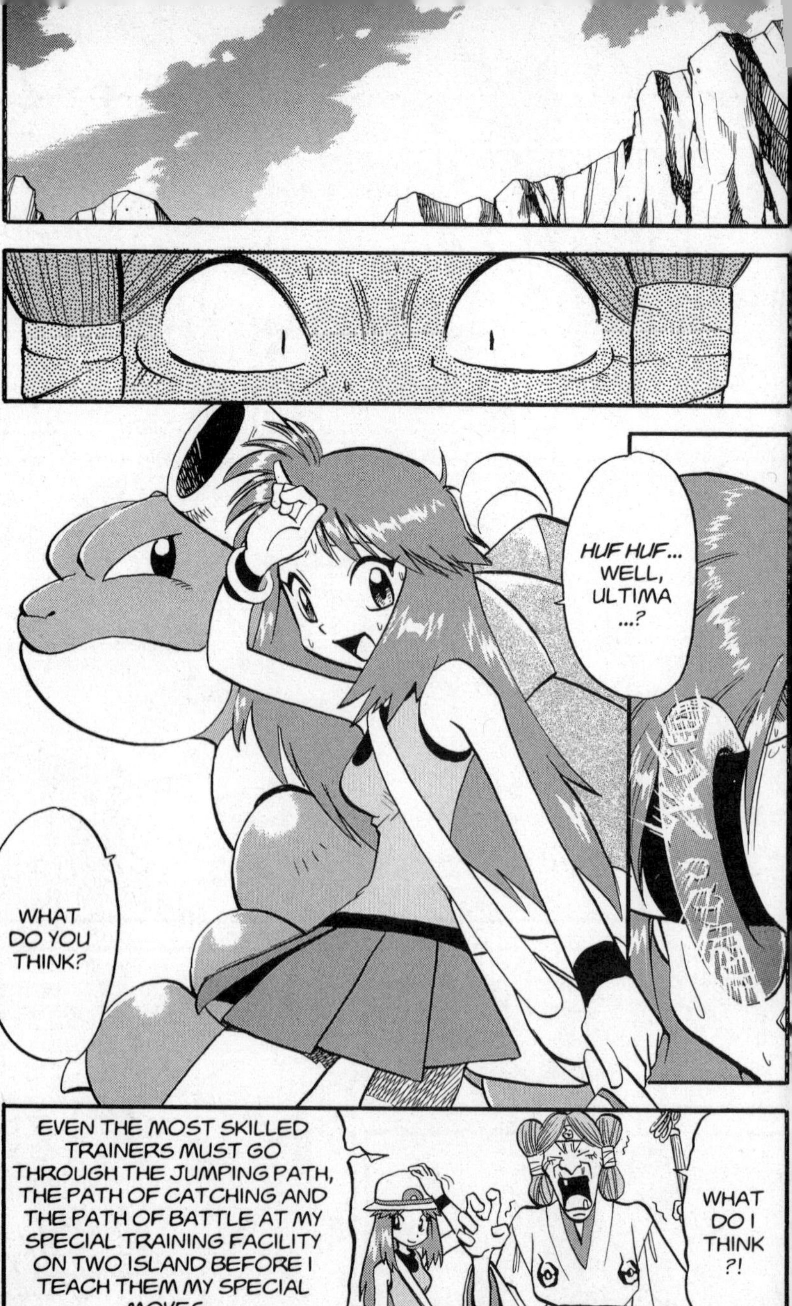
HUF HUF... WELL, ULTIMA ...?
WHAT DO YOU THINK?
WHAT DO I THINK ?!
EVEN THE MOST SKILLED TRAINERS MUST GO THROUGH THE JUMPING PATH, THE PATH OF CATCHING AND THE PATH OF BATTLE AT MY SPECIAL TRAINING FACILITY ON TWO ISLAND BEFORE I TEACH THEM MY SPECIAL MOVES...

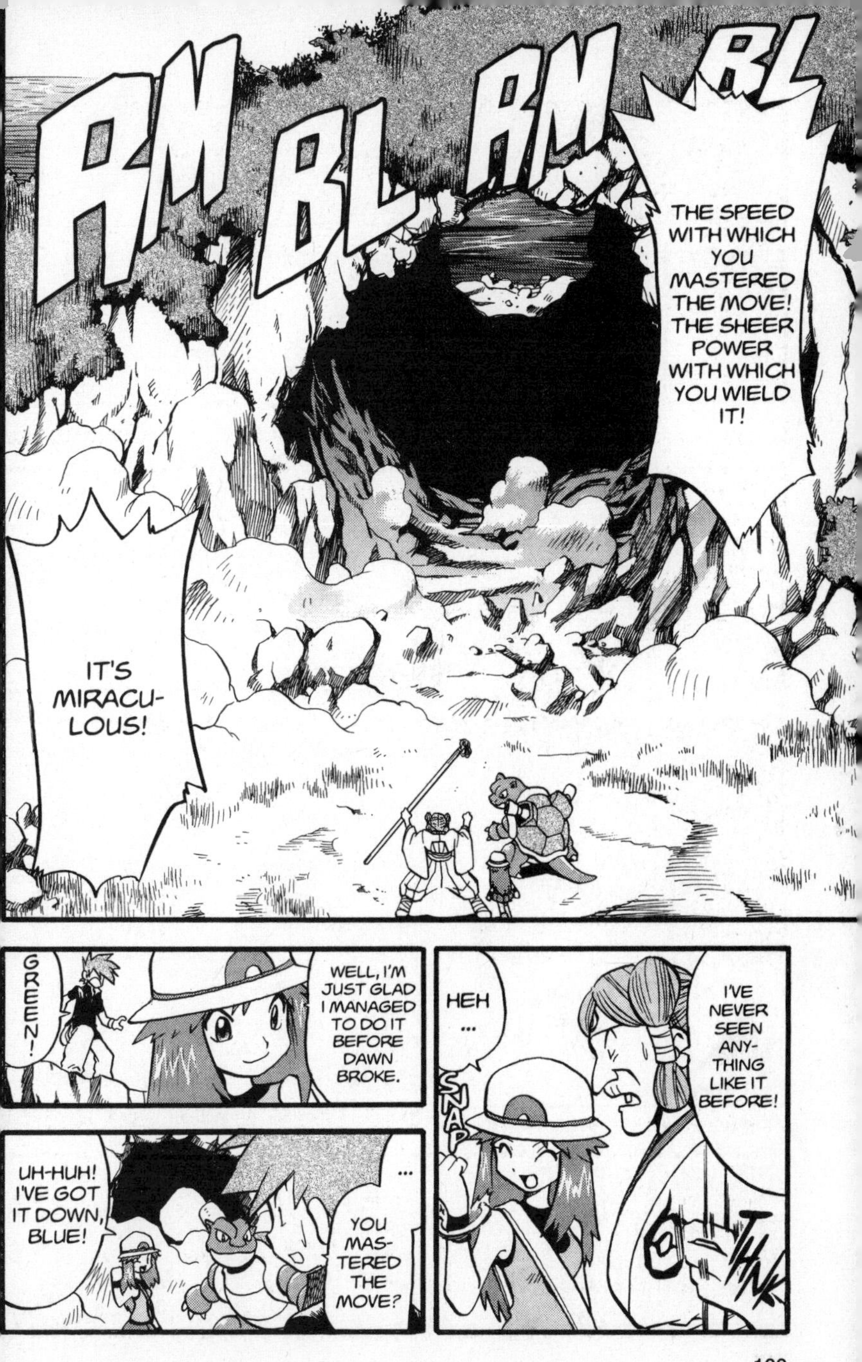
RM BL RM RL
THE SPEED WITH WHICH YOU MASTERED THE MOVE! THE SHEER POWER WITH WHICH YOU WIELD IT!
IT'S MIRACULOUS!
I'VE NEVER SEEN ANYTHING LIKE IT BEFORE!
HEH ...
SNAP
THNK
WELL, I'M JUST GLAD I MANAGED TO DO IT BEFORE DAWN BROKE.
GREEN!
... YOU MASTERED THE MOVE?
UH-HUH! I'VE GOT IT DOWN, BLUE!

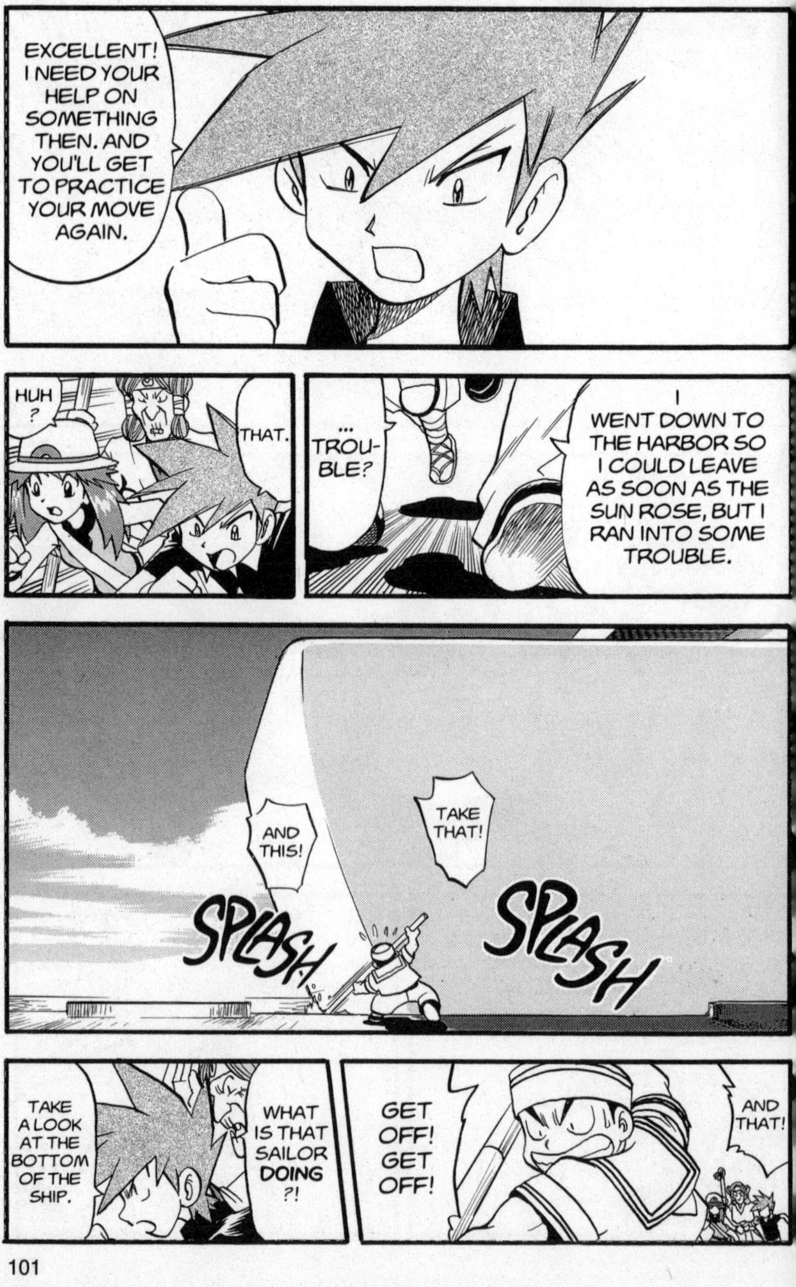
EXCELLENT! I NEED YOUR HELP ON SOMETHING THEN. AND YOU'LL GET TO PRACTICE YOUR MOVE AGAIN.
I WENT DOWN TO THE HARBOR SO I COULD LEAVE AS SOON AS THE SUN ROSE, BUT I RAN INTO SOME TROUBLE.
... TROUBLE?
THAT.
HUH?
TAKE THAT!
AND THIS!
SPLASH
SPLASH
AND THAT!
GET OFF! GET OFF!
WHAT IS THAT SAILOR DOING?!
TAKE A LOOK AT THE BOTTOM OF THE SHIP.

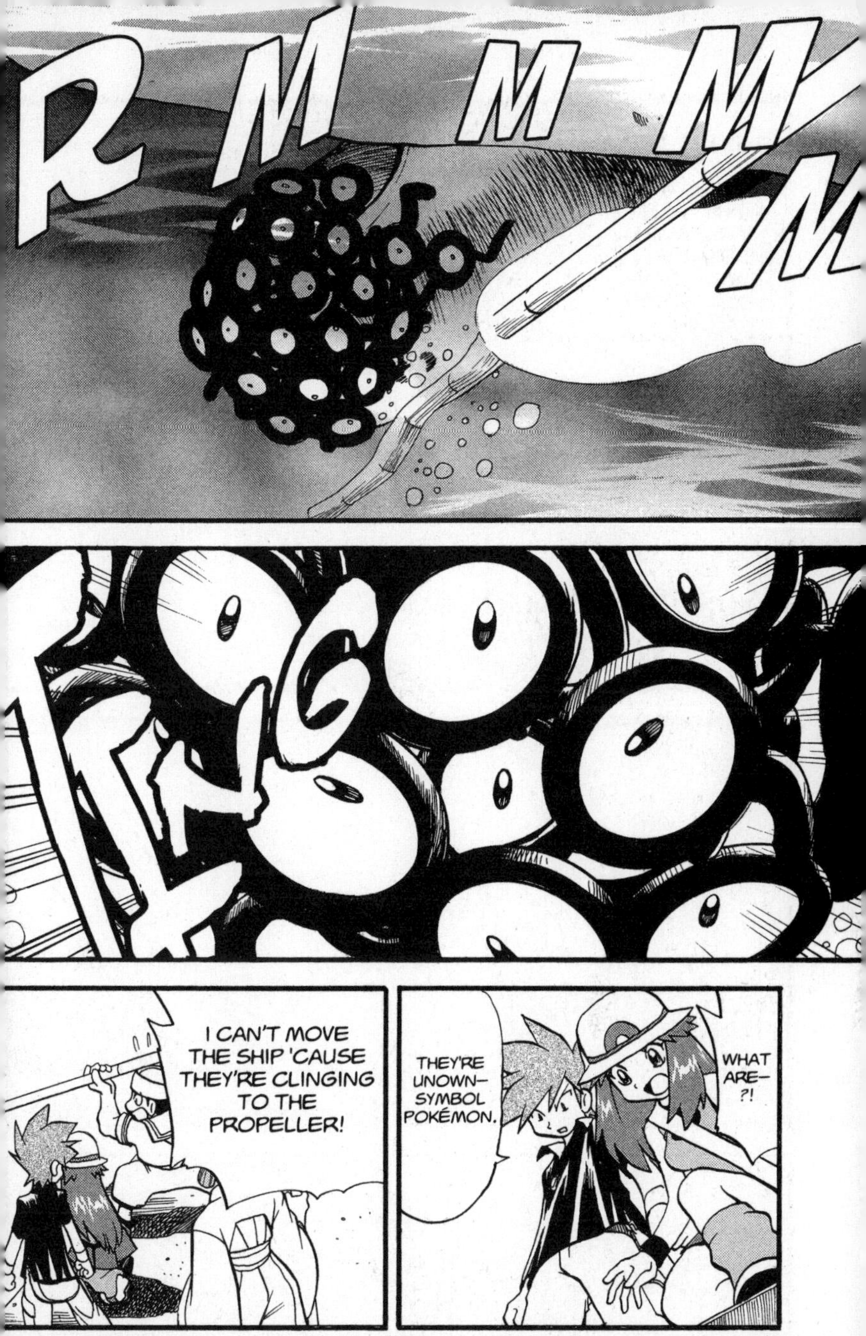
RMMMMM
WHAT ARE—?!
THEY'RE UNOWN—SYMBOL POKÉMON.
I CAN'T MOVE THE SHIP 'CAUSE THEY'RE CLINGING TO THE PROPELLER!

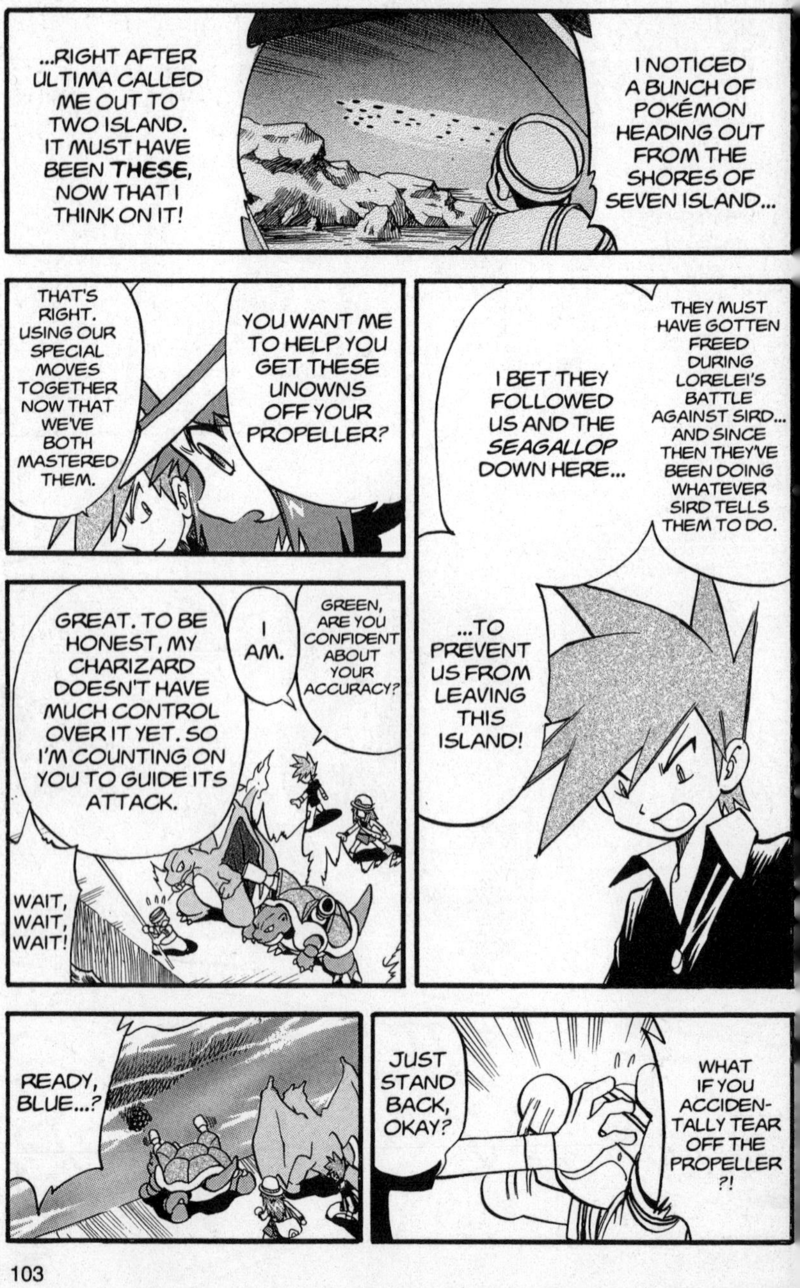
I NOTICED A BUNCH OF POKÉMON HEADING OUT FROM THE SHORES OF SEVEN ISLAND...
...RIGHT AFTER ULTIMA CALLED ME OUT TO TWO ISLAND. IT MUST HAVE BEEN **THESE**, NOW THAT I THINK ON IT!
THEY MUST HAVE GOTTEN FREED DURING LORELEI'S BATTLE AGAINST SIRD... AND SINCE THEN THEY'VE BEEN DOING WHATEVER SIRD TELLS THEM TO DO.
I BET THEY FOLLOWED US AND THE *SEAGALLOP* DOWN HERE...
...TO PREVENT US FROM LEAVING THIS ISLAND!
YOU WANT ME TO HELP YOU GET THESE UNOWNS OFF YOUR PROPELLER?
THAT'S RIGHT. USING OUR SPECIAL MOVES TOGETHER NOW THAT WE'VE BOTH MASTERED THEM.
GREEN, ARE YOU CONFIDENT ABOUT YOUR ACCURACY?
I AM.
GREAT. TO BE HONEST, MY CHARIZARD DOESN'T HAVE MUCH CONTROL OVER IT YET. SO I'M COUNTING ON YOU TO GUIDE ITS ATTACK.
WAIT, WAIT, WAIT!
WHAT IF YOU ACCIDEN-TALLY TEAR OFF THE PROPELLER ?!
JUST STAND BACK, OKAY?
READY, BLUE...?

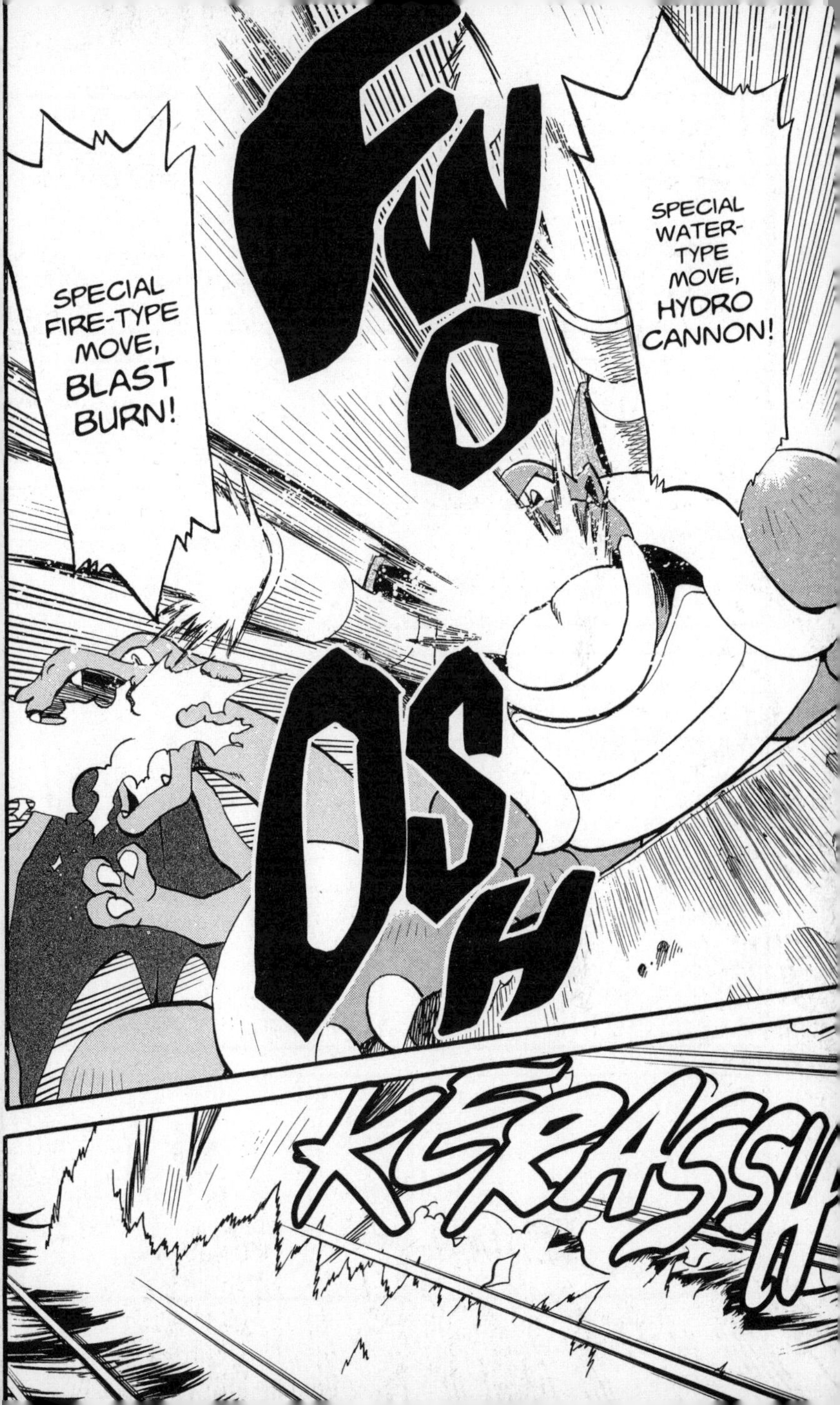
SPECIAL WATER-TYPE MOVE, HYDRO CANNON!
SPECIAL FIRE-TYPE MOVE, BLAST BURN!
FWOOSH
KRASSH

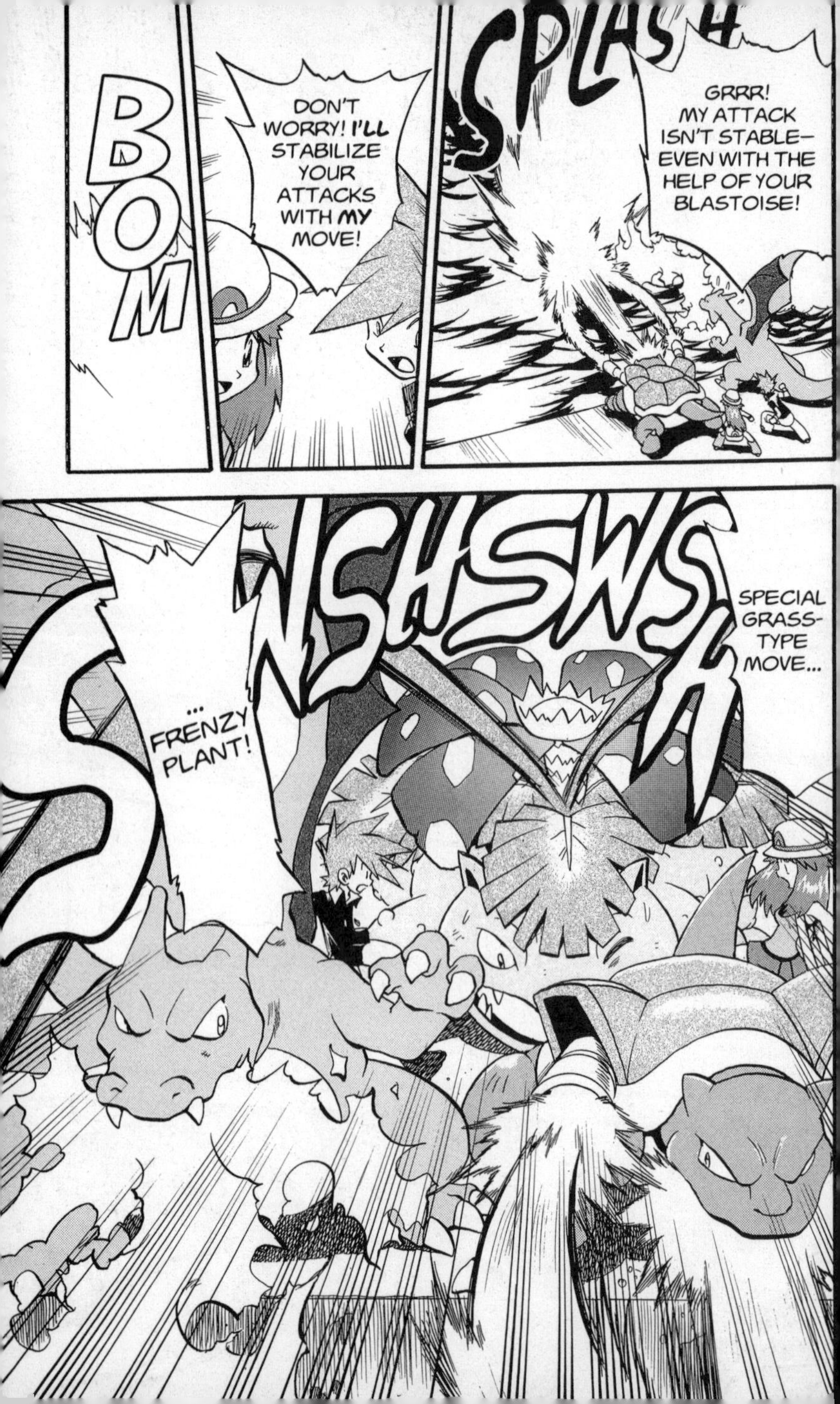
SPLASH
GRRR! MY ATTACK ISN'T STABLE— EVEN WITH THE HELP OF YOUR BLASTOISE!
DON'T WORRY! I'LL STABILIZE YOUR ATTACKS WITH MY MOVE!
BOOM
SPECIAL GRASS-TYPE MOVE...
...FRENZY PLANT!

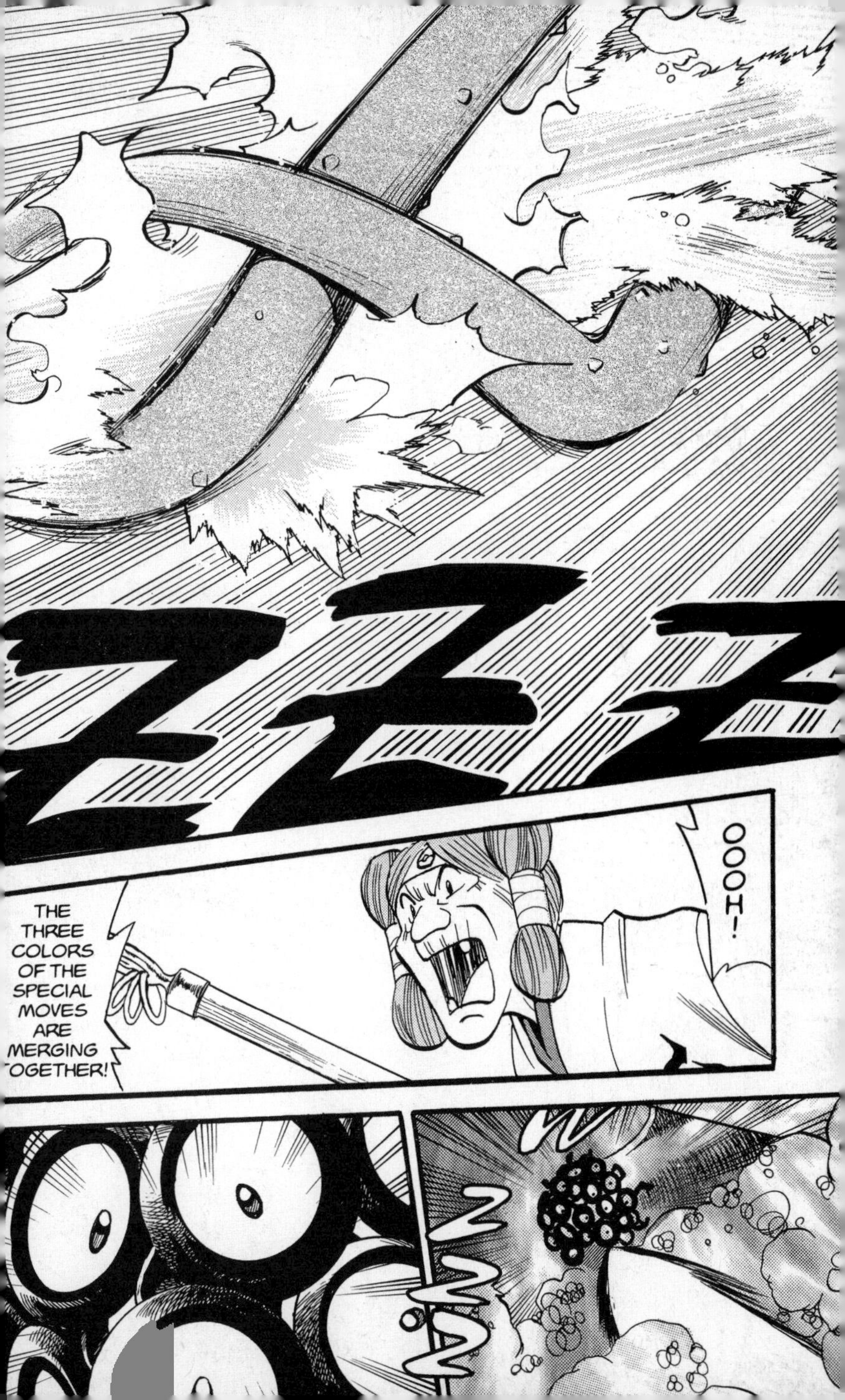
ZZZ
OOOOH!
THE THREE COLORS OF THE SPECIAL MOVES ARE MERGING TOGETHER!

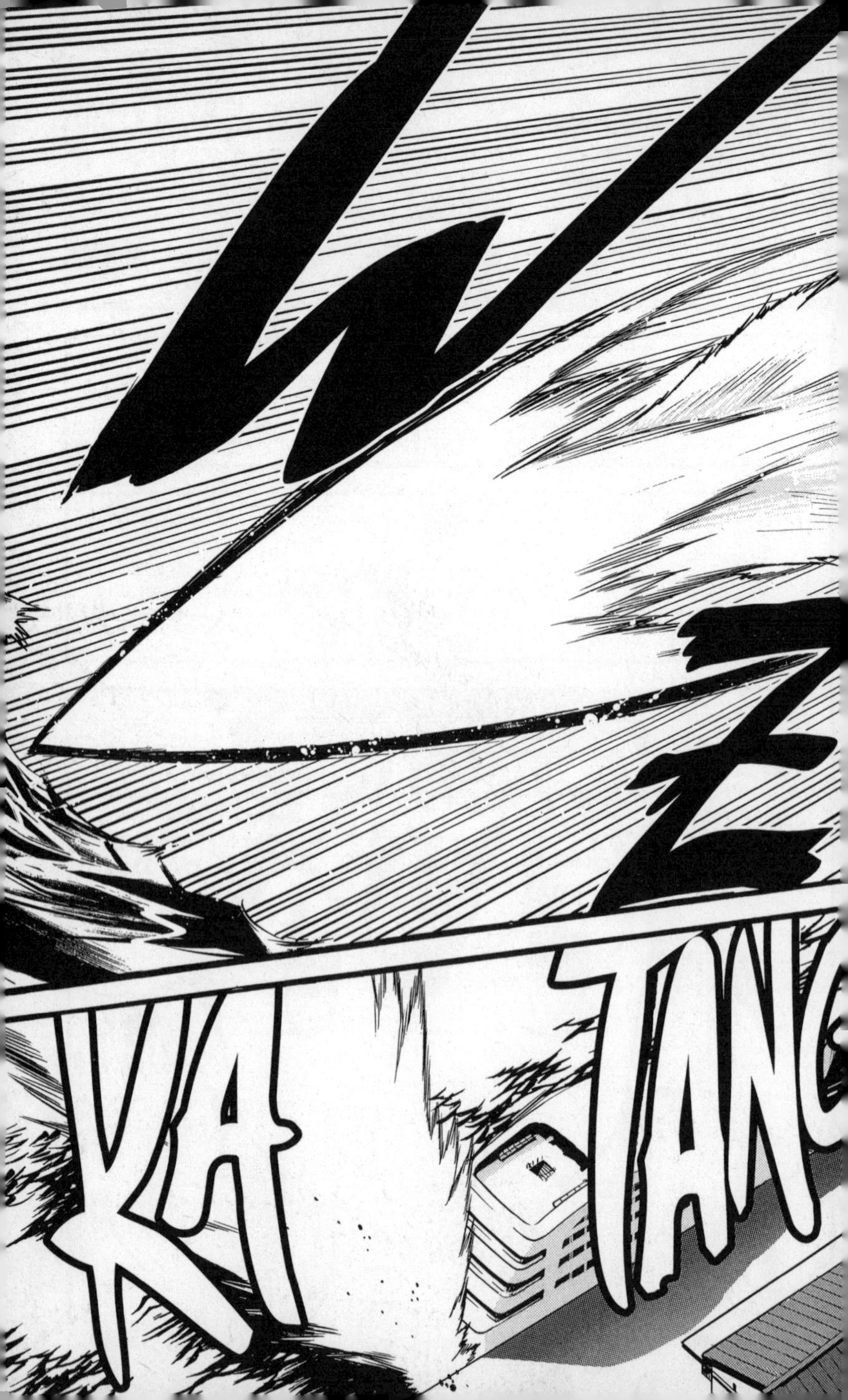
KA TANG

RED ...!

I WANT TO GO WITH YOU.

I'M SORRY I WORRIED YOU BOTH...

WHEN I REALIZED THAT, I KNEW I HAD TO COME BACK.

I HAVE TO SEE THIS THROUGH TO THE END.

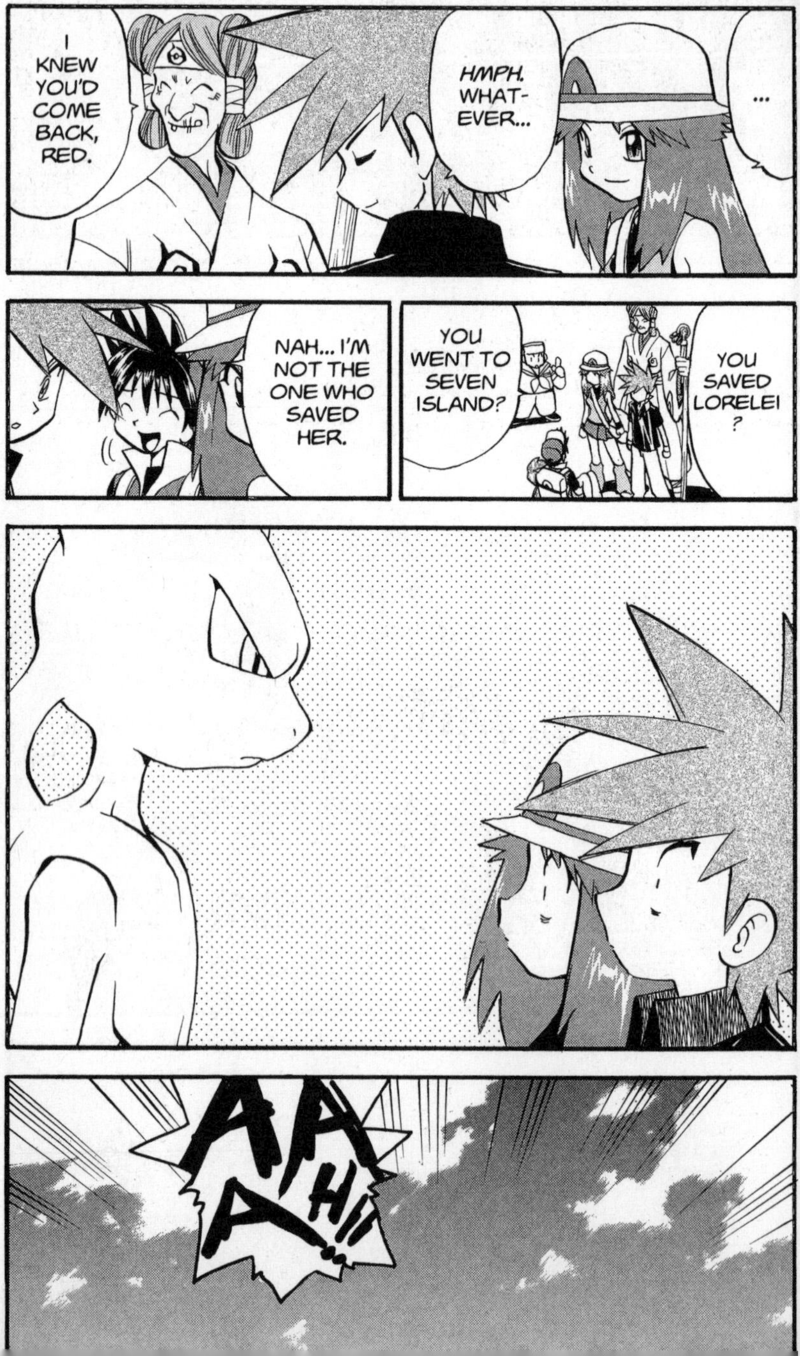
...
HMPH. WHAT-EVER...
I KNEW YOU'D COME BACK, RED.
YOU SAVED LORELEI?
YOU WENT TO SEVEN ISLAND?
NAH... I'M NOT THE ONE WHO SAVED HER.
AAAH!!

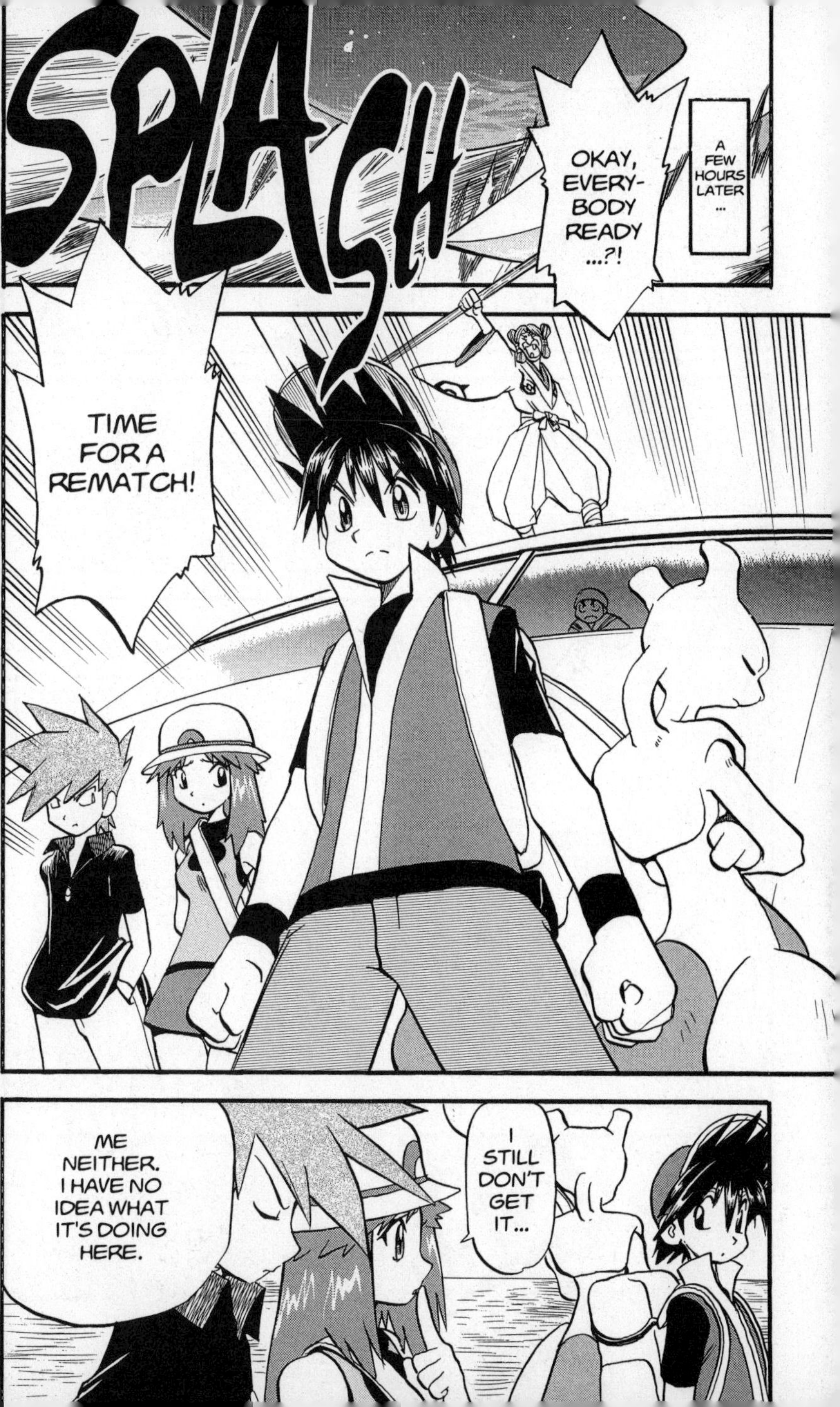

A FEW HOURS LATER...
OKAY, EVERY-BODY READY ...?!
SPLASH
TIME FOR A REMATCH!
I STILL DON'T GET IT...
ME NEITHER. I HAVE NO IDEA WHAT IT'S DOING HERE.

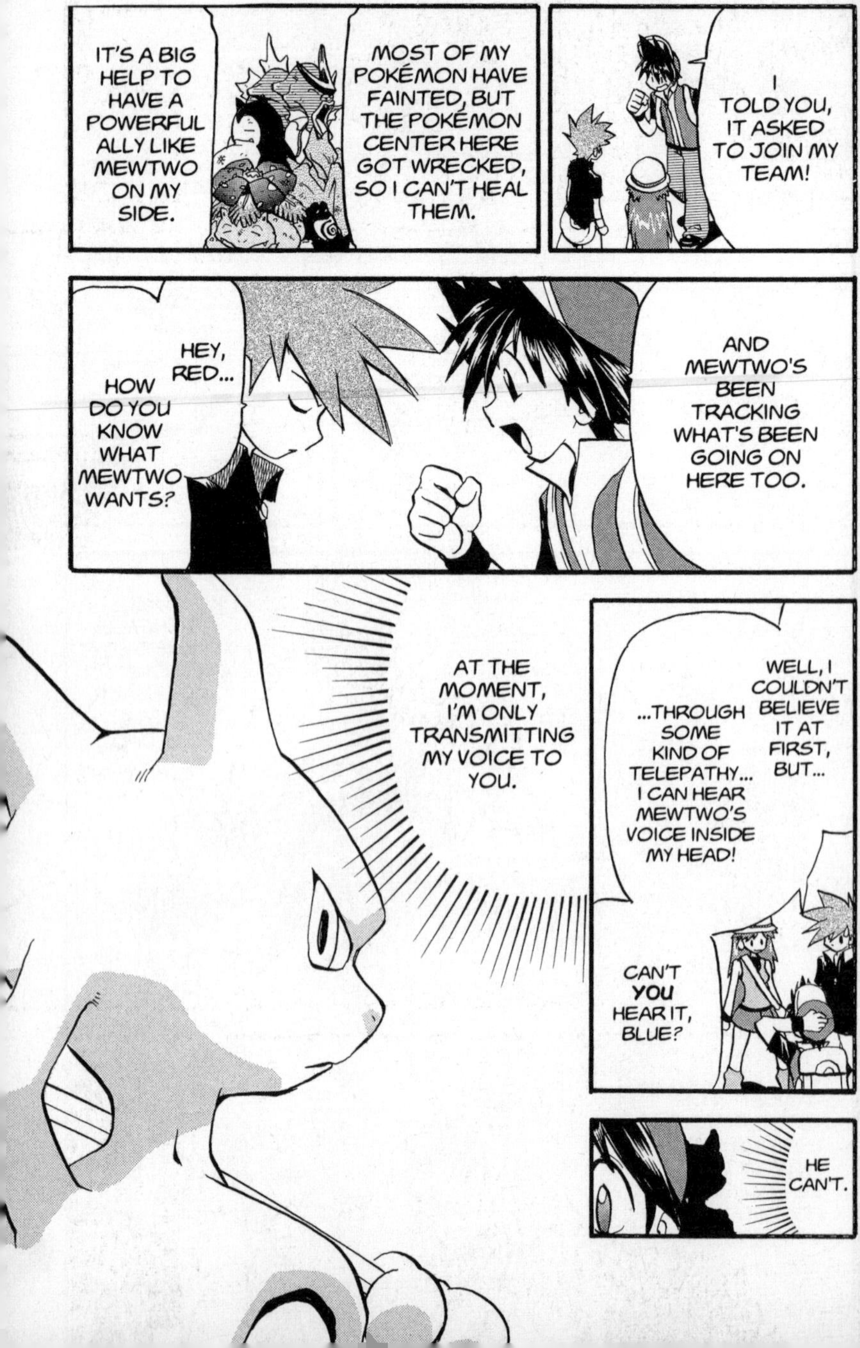
I TOLD YOU, IT ASKED TO JOIN MY TEAM!
MOST OF MY POKÉMON HAVE FAINTED, BUT THE POKÉMON CENTER HERE GOT WRECKED, SO I CAN'T HEAL THEM.
IT'S A BIG HELP TO HAVE A POWERFUL ALLY LIKE MEWTWO ON MY SIDE.
AND MEWTWO'S BEEN TRACKING WHAT'S BEEN GOING ON HERE TOO.
HEY, RED... HOW DO YOU KNOW WHAT MEWTWO WANTS?
WELL, I COULDN'T BELIEVE IT AT FIRST, BUT...
...THROUGH SOME KIND OF TELEPATHY... I CAN HEAR MEWTWO'S VOICE INSIDE MY HEAD!
CAN'T **YOU** HEAR IT, BLUE?
HE CAN'T.
AT THE MOMENT, I'M ONLY TRANSMITTING MY VOICE TO YOU.

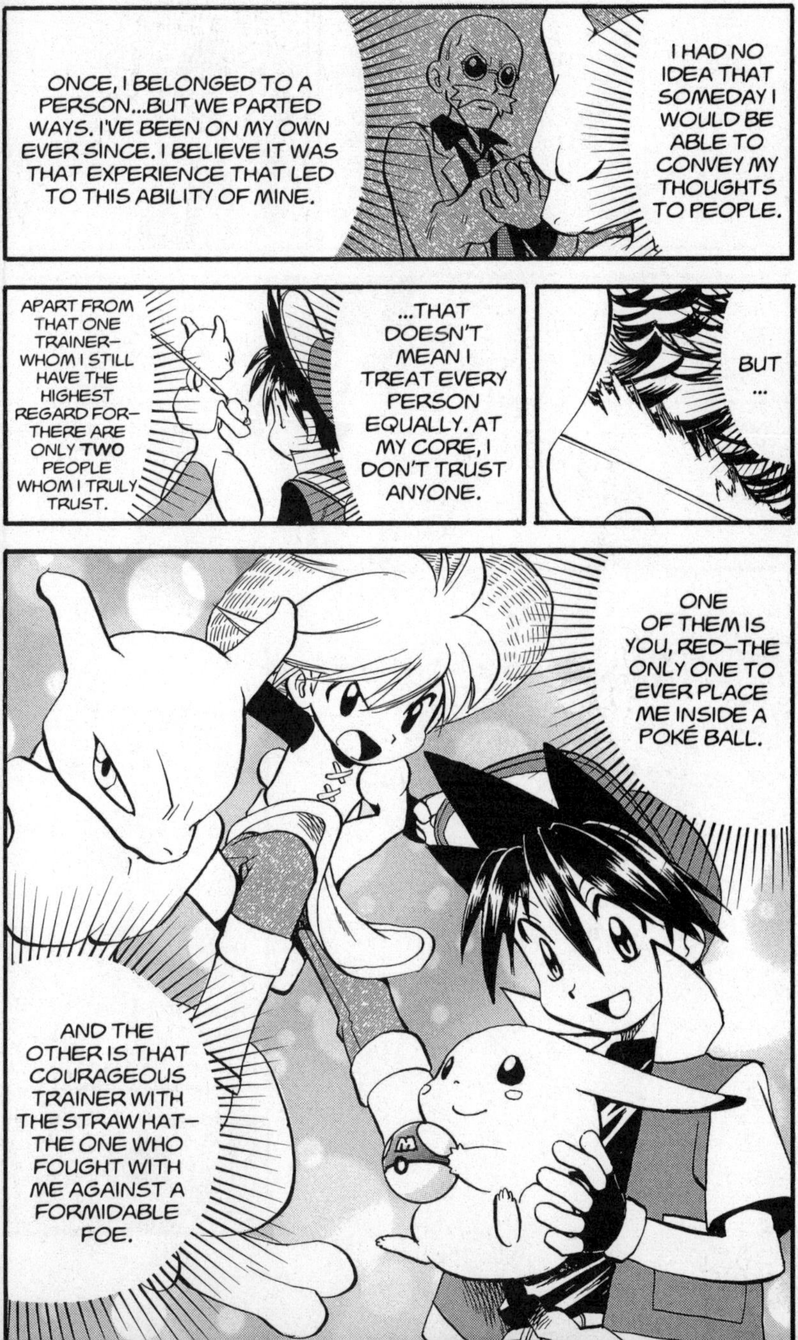
I HAD NO IDEA THAT SOMEDAY I WOULD BE ABLE TO CONVEY MY THOUGHTS TO PEOPLE.
ONCE, I BELONGED TO A PERSON...BUT WE PARTED WAYS. I'VE BEEN ON MY OWN EVER SINCE. I BELIEVE IT WAS THAT EXPERIENCE THAT LED TO THIS ABILITY OF MINE.
BUT ...
...THAT DOESN'T MEAN I TREAT EVERY PERSON EQUALLY. AT MY CORE, I DON'T TRUST ANYONE.
APART FROM THAT ONE TRAINER—WHOM I STILL HAVE THE HIGHEST REGARD FOR—THERE ARE ONLY **TWO** PEOPLE WHOM I TRULY TRUST.
ONE OF THEM IS YOU, RED—THE ONLY ONE TO EVER PLACE ME INSIDE A POKÉ BALL.
AND THE OTHER IS THAT COURAGEOUS TRAINER WITH THE STRAW HAT—THE ONE WHO FOUGHT WITH ME AGAINST A FORMIDABLE FOE.

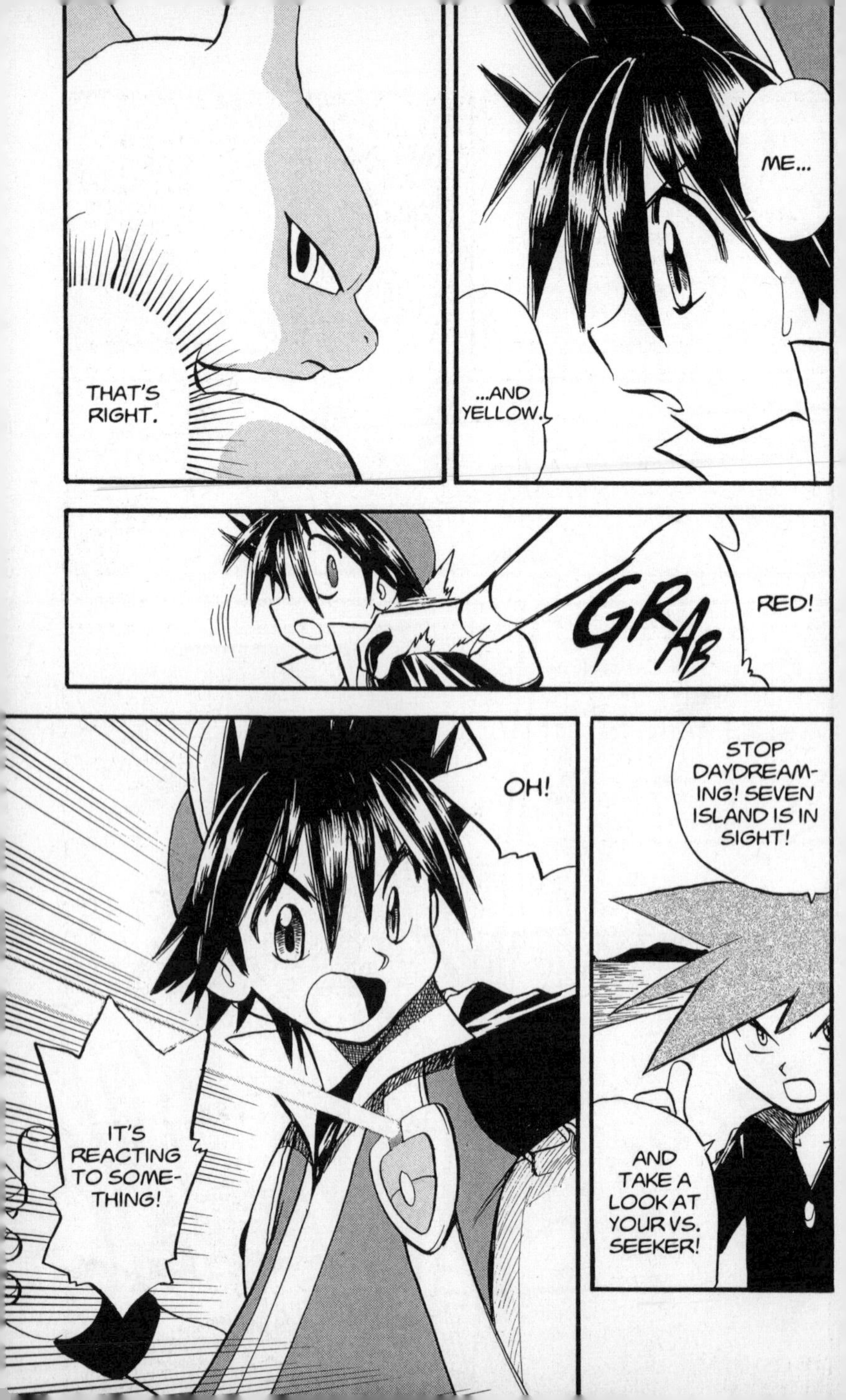
ME...
...AND YELLOW.
THAT'S RIGHT.
RED!
GRAB
STOP DAYDREAMING! SEVEN ISLAND IS IN SIGHT!
AND TAKE A LOOK AT YOUR VS. SEEKER!
OH!
IT'S REACTING TO SOMETHING!

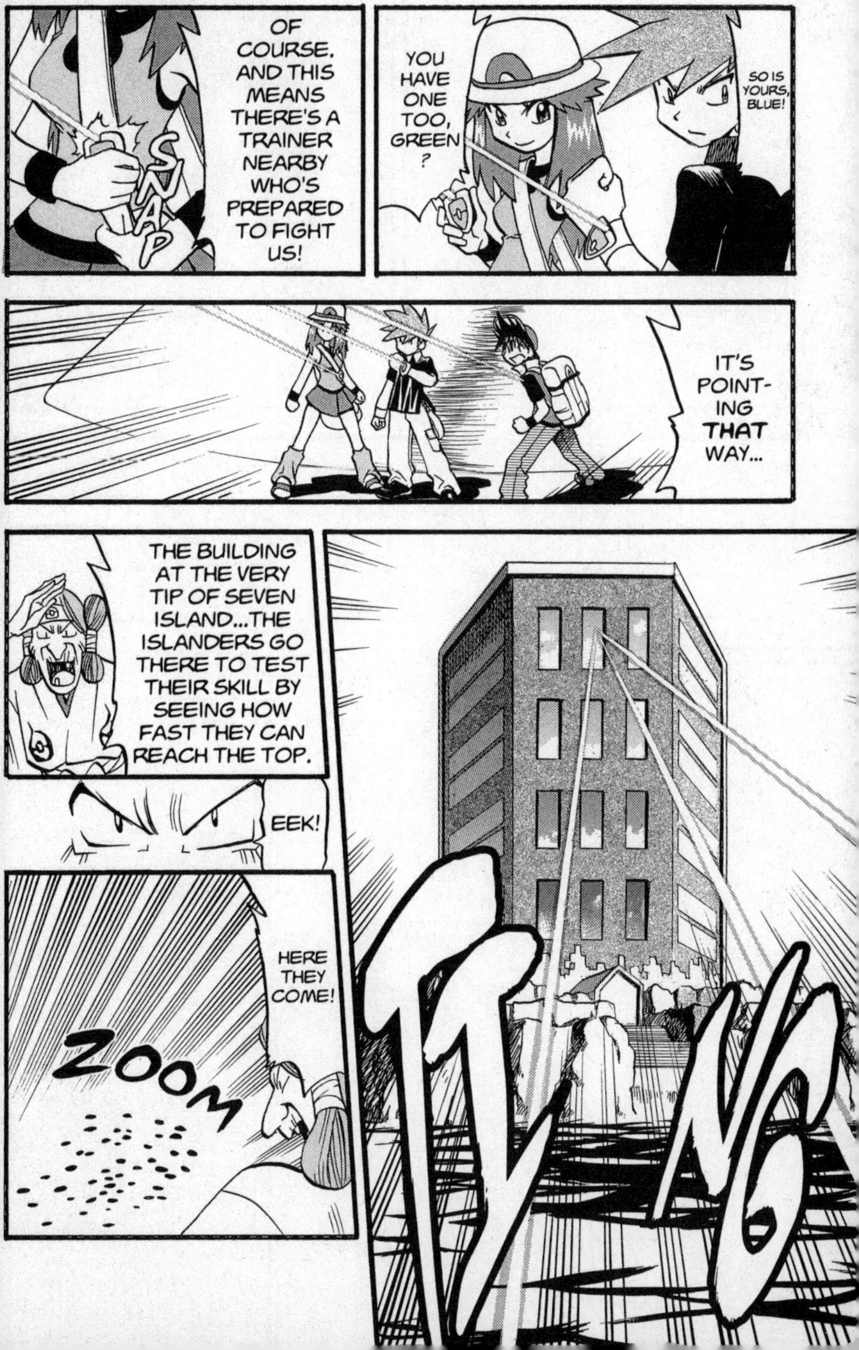

YOU HAVE ONE TOO, GREEN?
SO IS YOURS, BLUE!
OF COURSE. AND THIS MEANS THERE'S A TRAINER NEARBY WHO'S PREPARED TO FIGHT US!
SNAP
IT'S POINTING THAT WAY...
TWNG
THE BUILDING AT THE VERY TIP OF SEVEN ISLAND...THE ISLANDERS GO THERE TO TEST THEIR SKILL BY SEEING HOW FAST THEY CAN REACH THE TOP.
EEK!
HERE THEY COME!
ZOOM

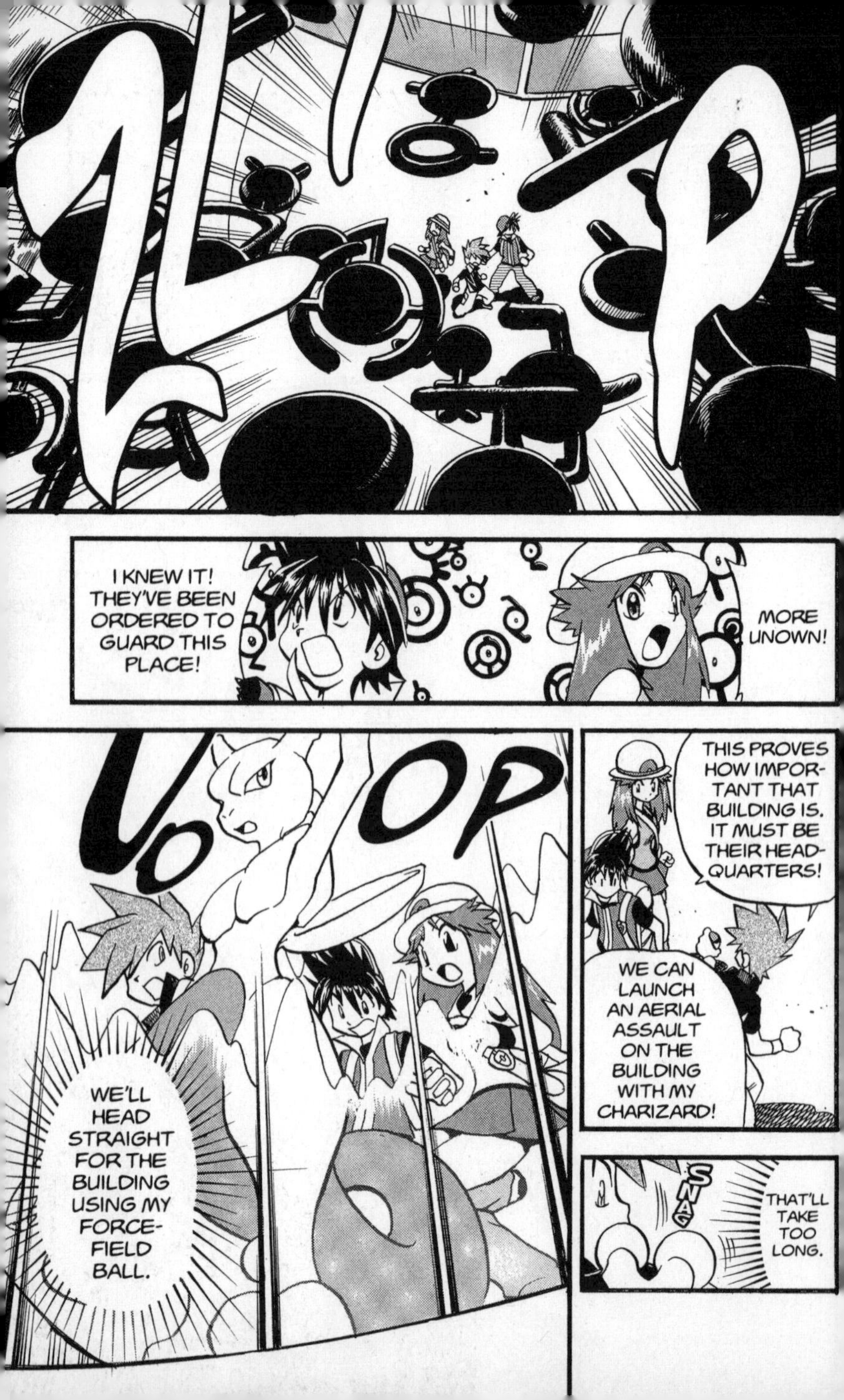
ZIP
MORE UNOWN!
I KNEW IT! THEY'VE BEEN ORDERED TO GUARD THIS PLACE!
THIS PROVES HOW IMPOR-TANT THAT BUILDING IS. IT MUST BE THEIR HEAD-QUARTERS!
WE CAN LAUNCH AN AERIAL ASSAULT ON THE BUILDING WITH MY CHARIZARD!
SNAG
THAT'LL TAKE TOO LONG.
VOOP
WE'LL HEAD STRAIGHT FOR THE BUILDING USING MY FORCE-FIELD BALL.

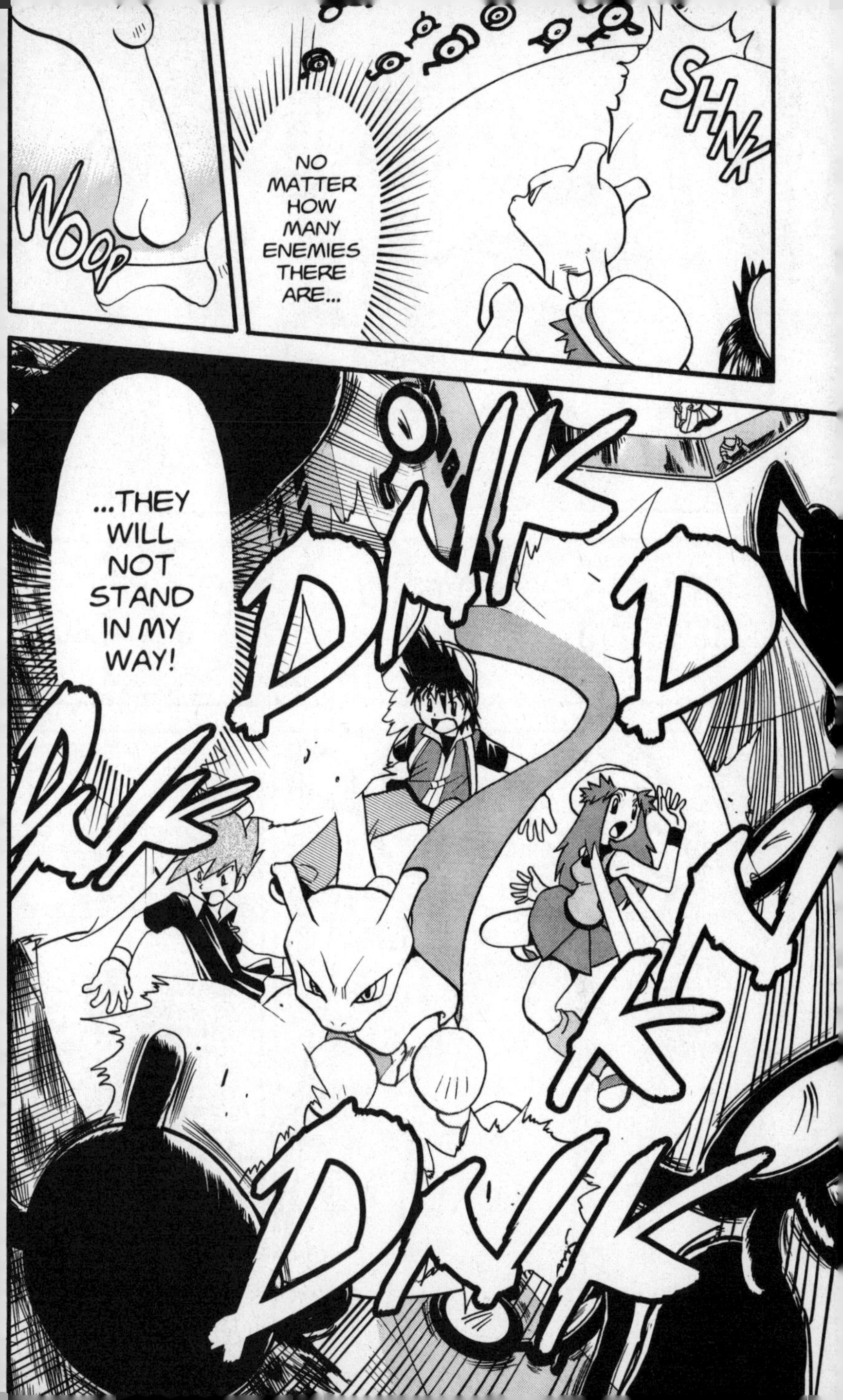
SHNK
NO MATTER HOW MANY ENEMIES THERE ARE...
WOOP
...THEY WILL NOT STAND IN MY WAY!
DINK
DINK
DINK
DINK
DINK

Character Profile

LORELEI

LORELEI

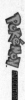

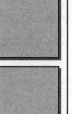

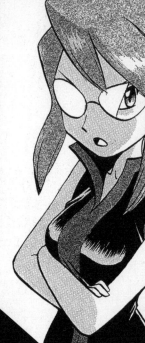

ONE OF THE KANTO ELITE FOUR AND AN EXPERT ON ICE-TYPE POKÉMON. SHE EXCELS IN BLOCKING HER OPPONENT'S MOVES WITH ICE-TYPE MOVES. IT WAS BEING RESCUED BY AGATHA AS A CHILD THAT LED TO HER TAKING PART IN LANCE'S NEFARIOUS SCHEMES. LORELEI SEEMS ALOOF AND DISTANT, BUT INSIDE SHE IS FILLED WITH AFFECTION FOR HER POKÉMON. SHE JOINED THIS BATTLE AFTER HEARING THAT TEAM ROCKET WAS CAUSING TROUBLE IN HER HOMETOWN, FOUR ISLAND, AND FOUGHT SIRD. SHE CAN USE ICE BEAM TO CREATE AN ICE-STATUE DOUBLE OF ANYONE.

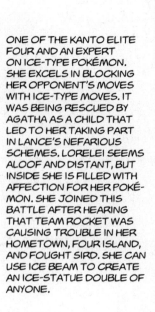

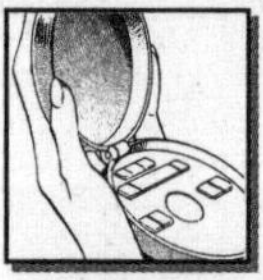

- **Birthplace: Four Island**
- **Birthday: March 15**
- **Blood Type: B**
- **Pokémon on her Team: Cloyster, Jynx, Slowking, Dewgong, Lapras**

• Adventure 285 •
Once More into the Unown

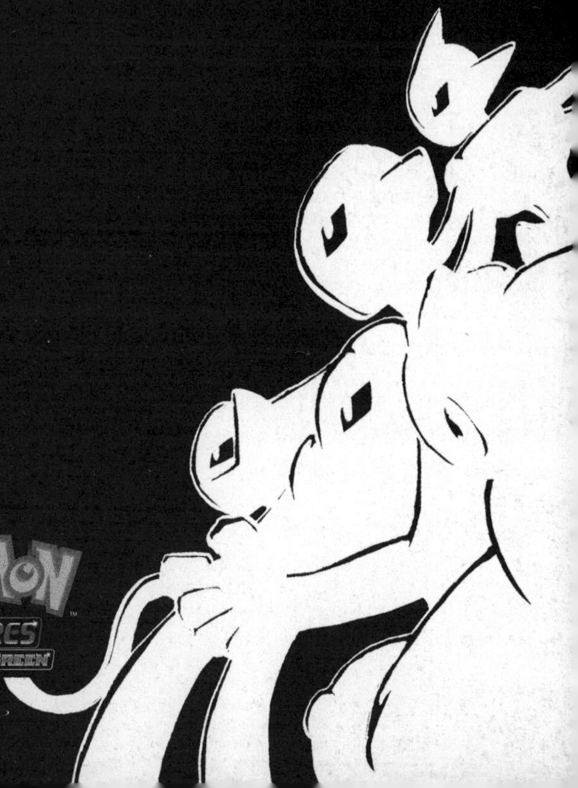

Pokémon Adventures
FireRed & LeafGreen
The Fifth Chapter

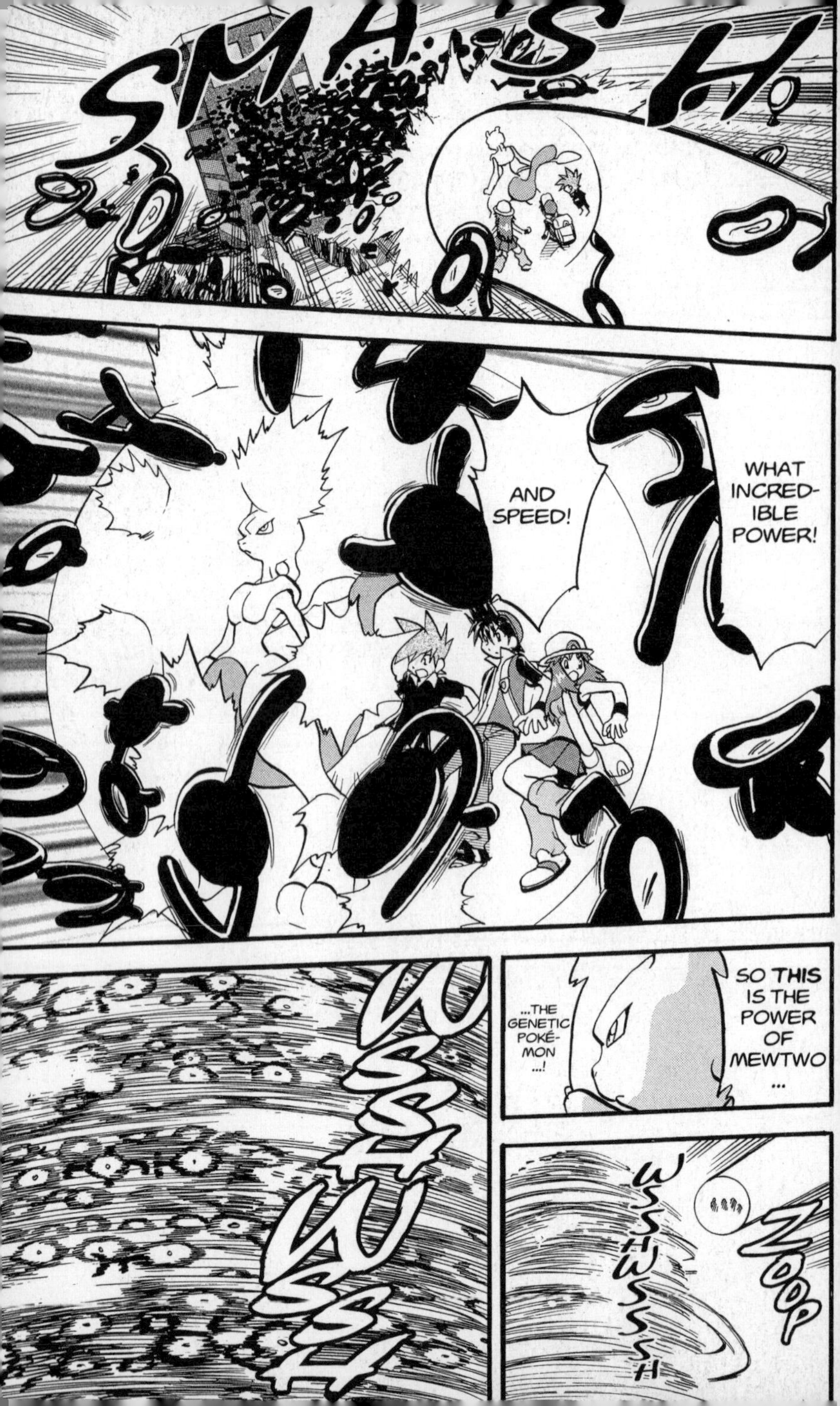
SMASH
WHAT INCREDIBLE POWER!
AND SPEED!
SO THIS IS THE POWER OF MEWTWO...
...THE GENETIC POKÉMON...!
ZOOP

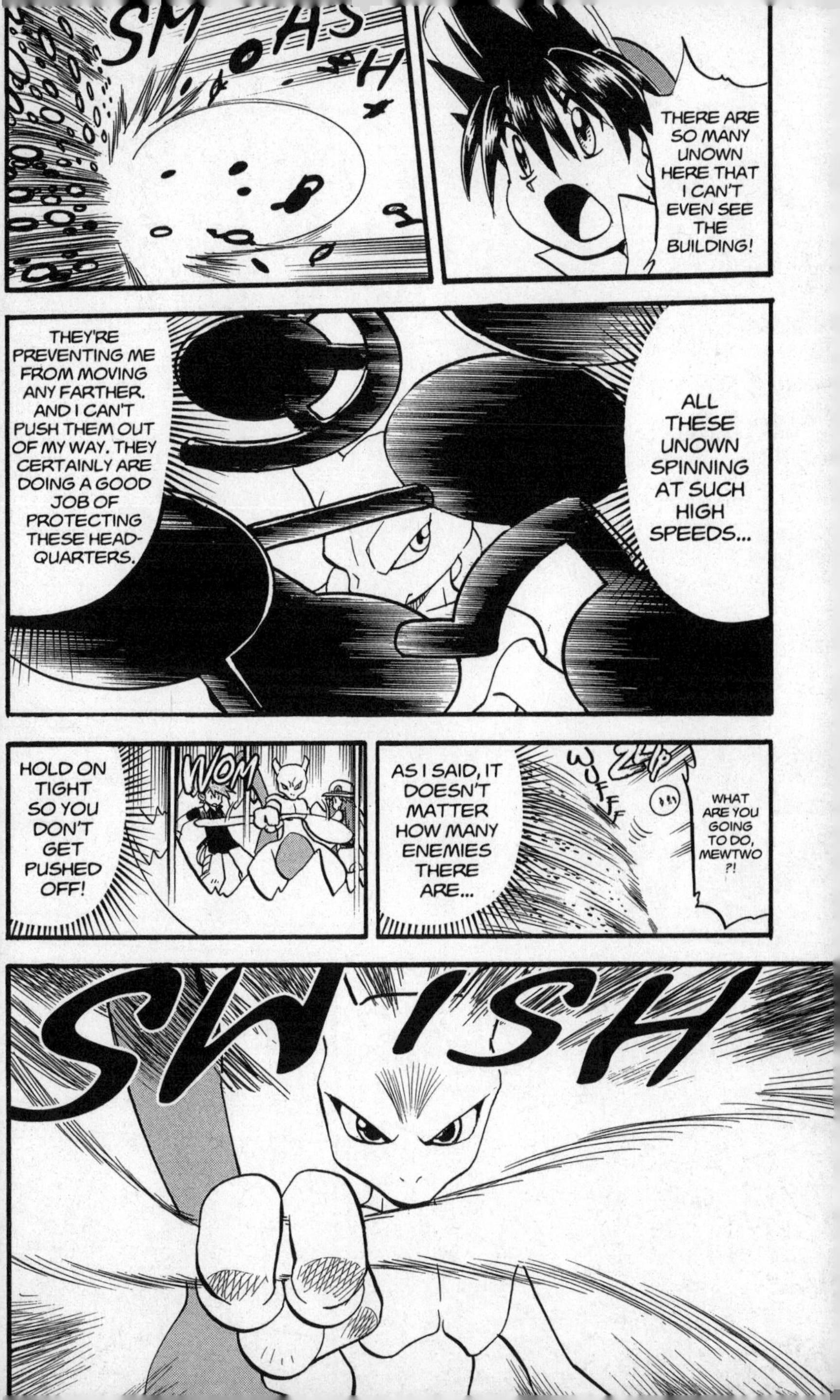
THERE ARE SO MANY UNOWN HERE THAT I CAN'T EVEN SEE THE BUILDING!
ALL THESE UNOWN SPINNING AT SUCH HIGH SPEEDS...
THEY'RE PREVENTING ME FROM MOVING ANY FARTHER. AND I CAN'T PUSH THEM OUT OF MY WAY. THEY CERTAINLY ARE DOING A GOOD JOB OF PROTECTING THESE HEAD-QUARTERS.
WHAT ARE YOU GOING TO DO, MEWTWO?!
AS I SAID, IT DOESN'T MATTER HOW MANY ENEMIES THERE ARE...
WOM
HOLD ON TIGHT SO YOU DON'T GET PUSHED OFF!
SWISH

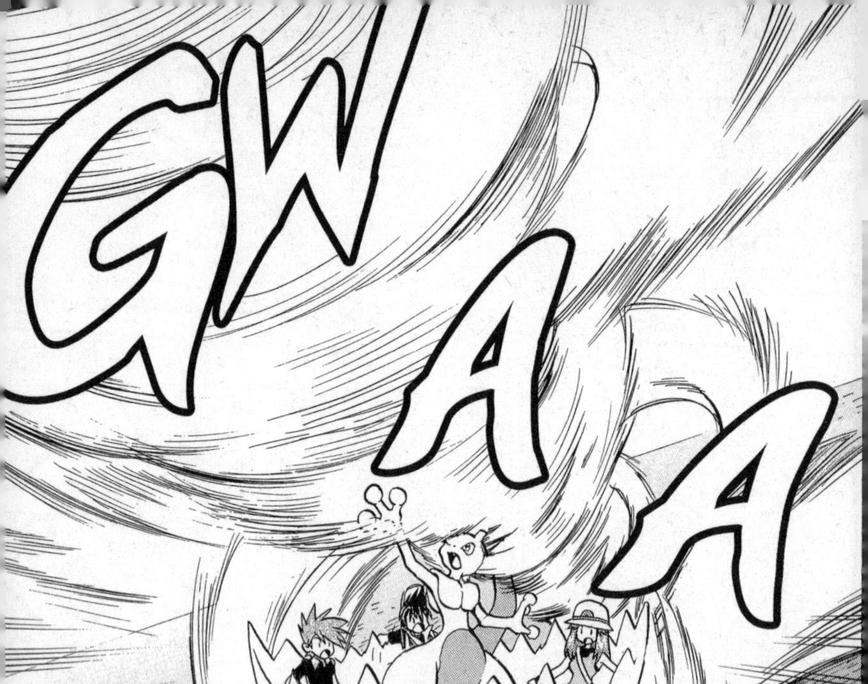
GWAAARR
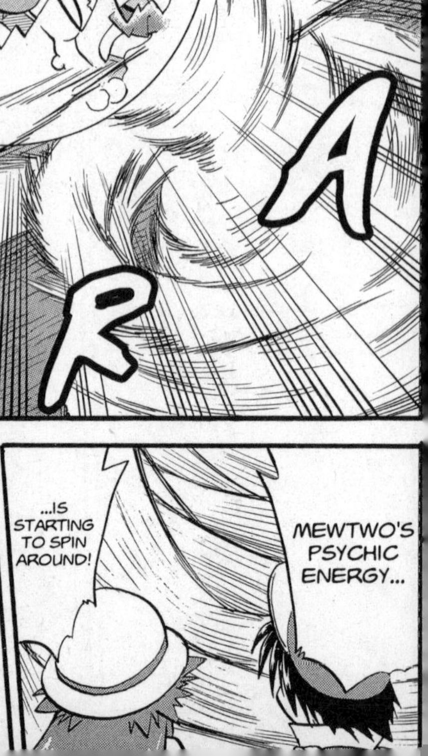
MEWTWO'S PSYCHIC ENERGY...
...IS STARTING TO SPIN AROUND!
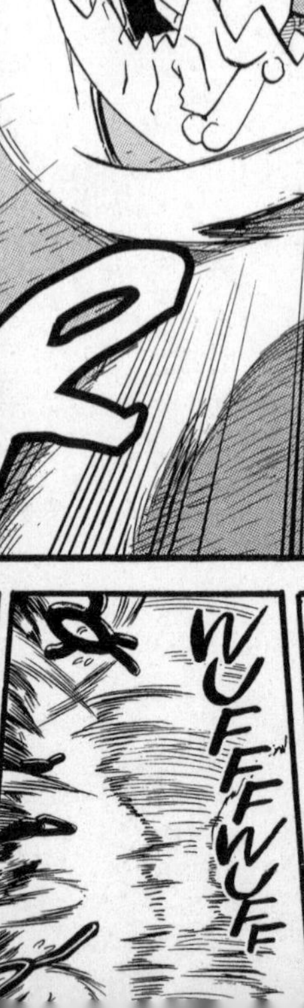
WUFFFWUFF
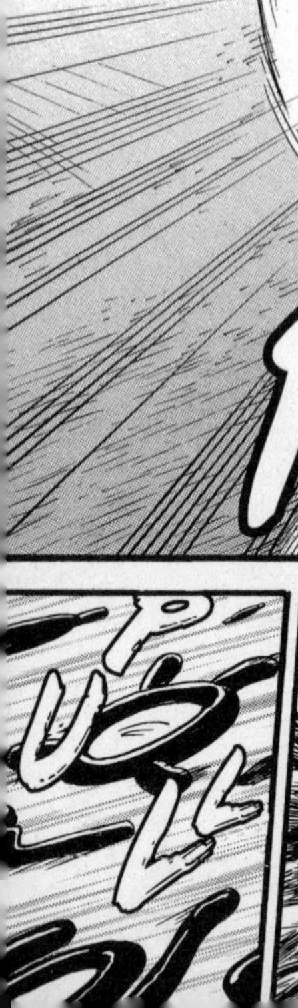
PULL

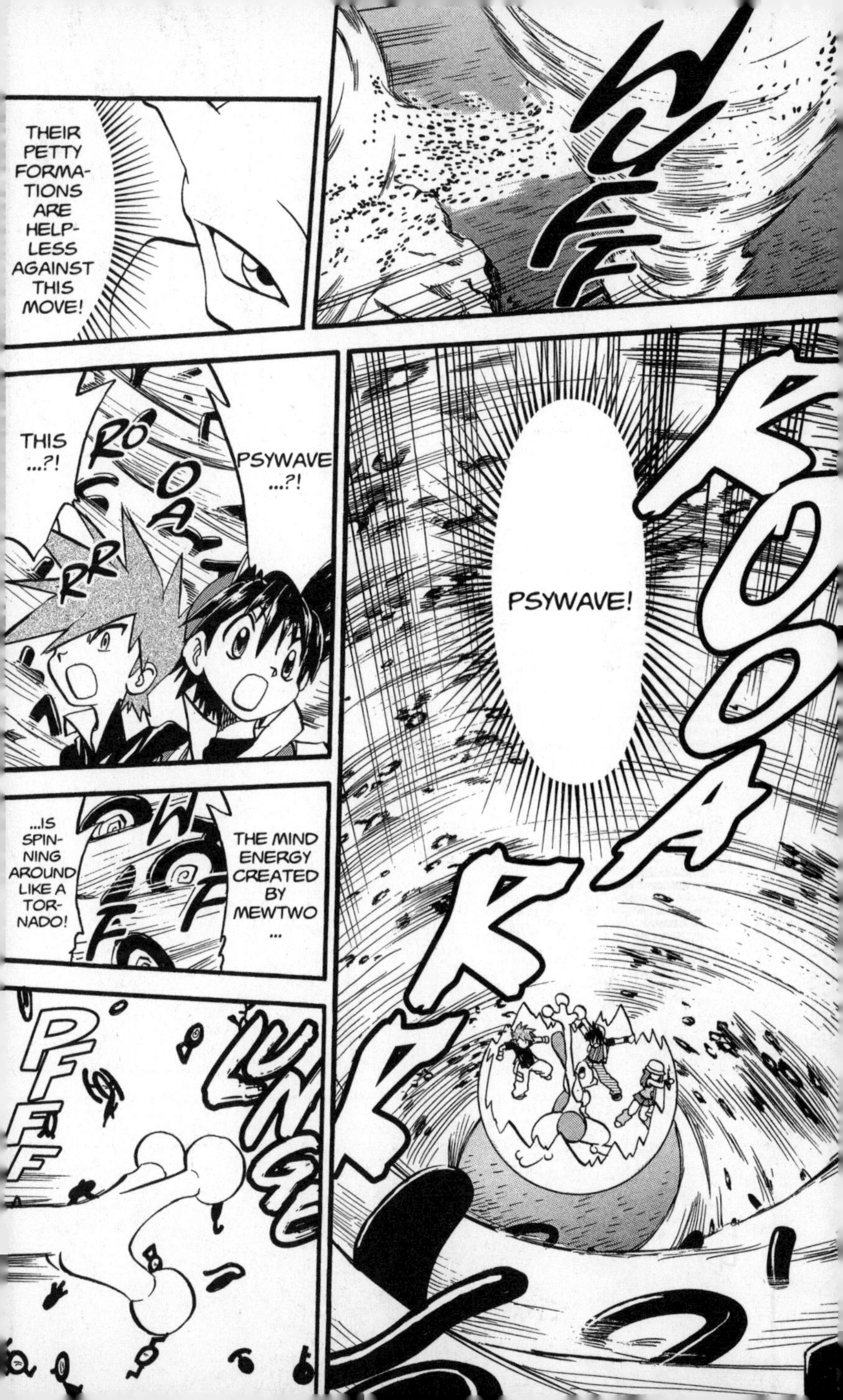

THEIR PETTY FORMATIONS ARE HELPLESS AGAINST THIS MOVE!
PSYWAVE!
PSYWAVE ...?!
THIS ...?!
THE MIND ENERGY CREATED BY MEWTWO ...
...IS SPINNING AROUND LIKE A TORNADO!
PFFFF

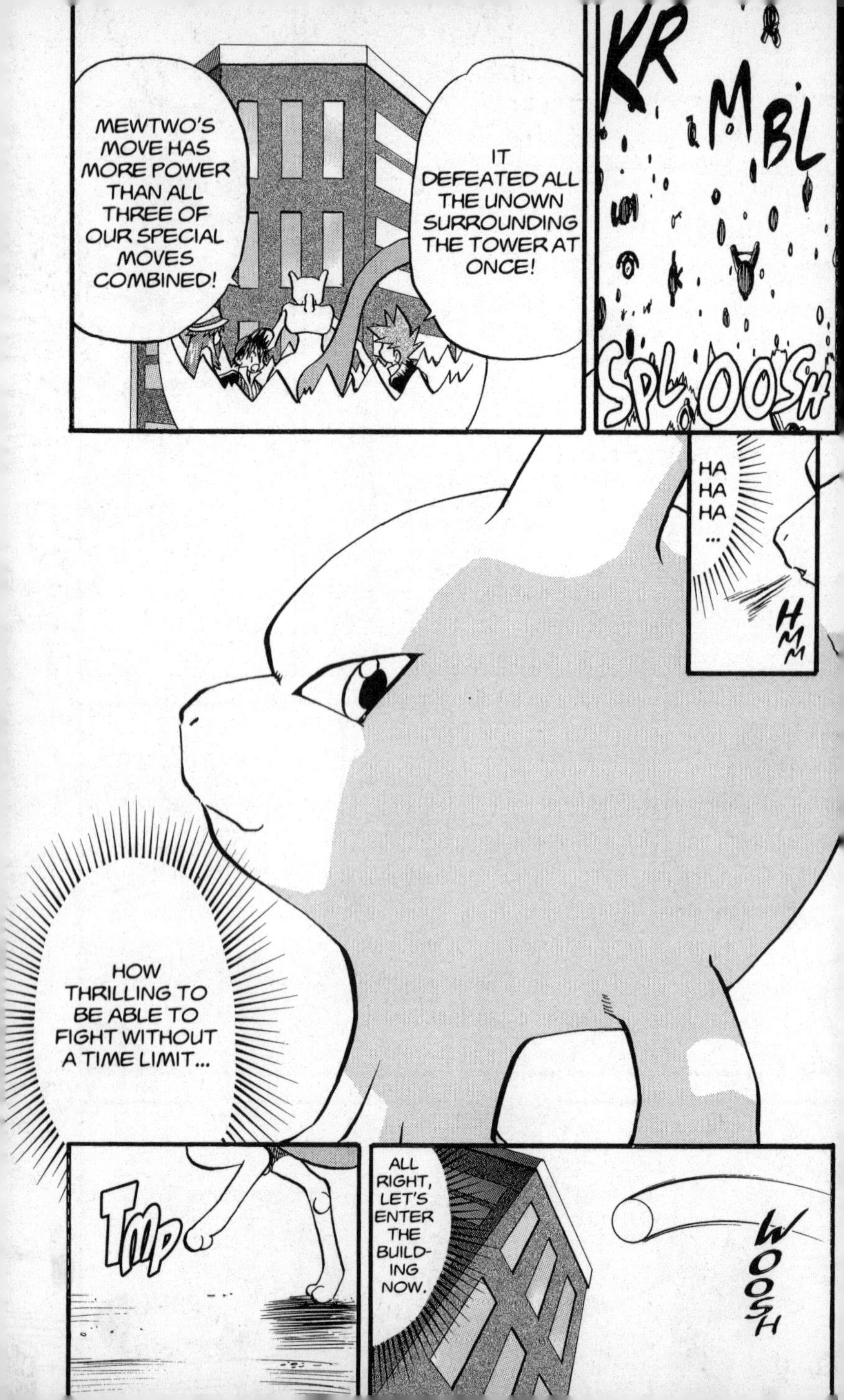
KRMBL
SPLOOSH
IT DEFEATED ALL THE UNOWN SURROUNDING THE TOWER AT ONCE!
MEWTWO'S MOVE HAS MORE POWER THAN ALL THREE OF OUR SPECIAL MOVES COMBINED!
HA HA HA...
HMM
HOW THRILLING TO BE ABLE TO FIGHT WITHOUT A TIME LIMIT...
ALL RIGHT, LET'S ENTER THE BUILD-ING NOW.
WOOSH
TMP

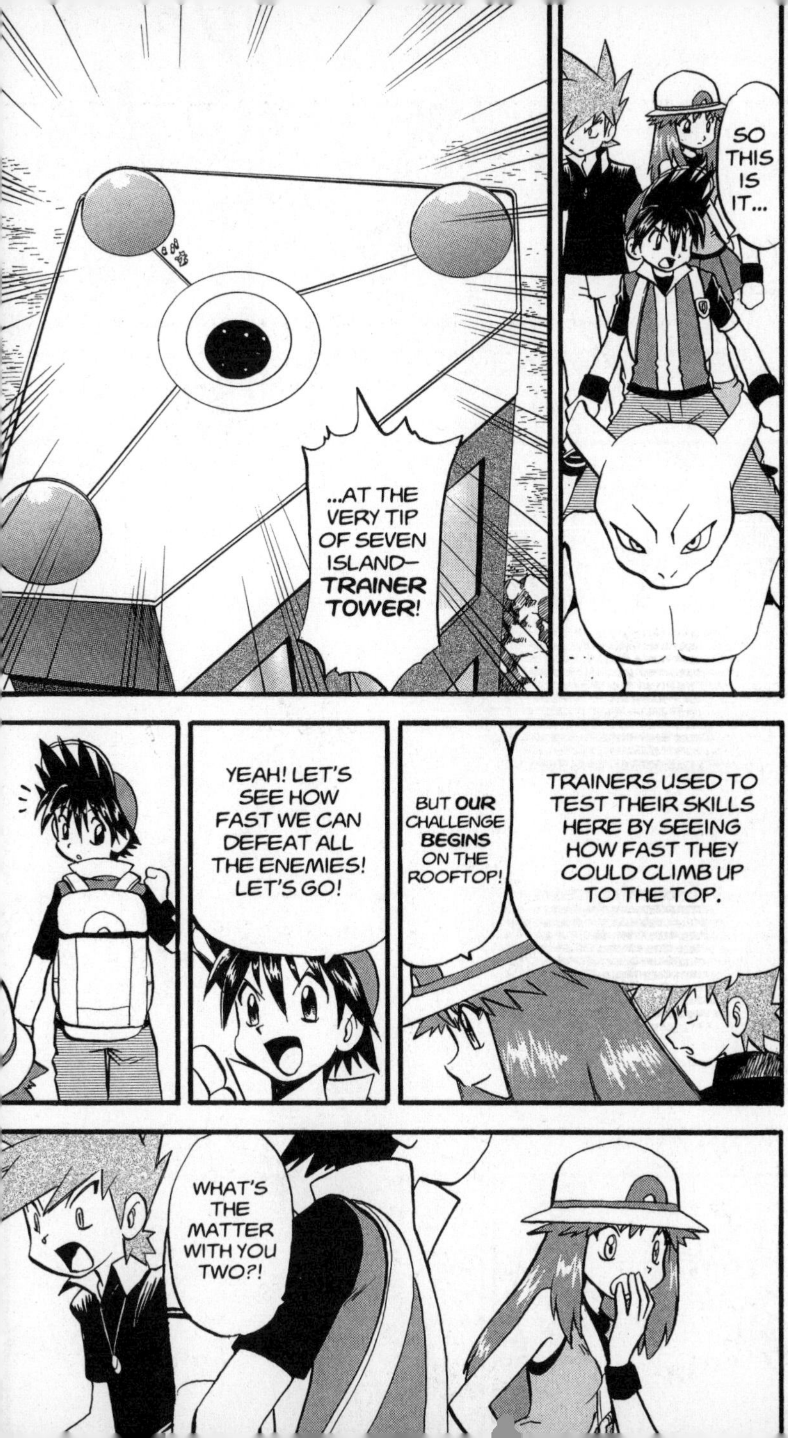
SO THIS IS IT...
...AT THE VERY TIP OF SEVEN ISLAND—**TRAINER TOWER!**
TRAINERS USED TO TEST THEIR SKILLS HERE BY SEEING HOW FAST THEY COULD CLIMB UP TO THE TOP.
BUT **OUR CHALLENGE BEGINS** ON THE ROOFTOP!
YEAH! LET'S SEE HOW FAST WE CAN DEFEAT ALL THE ENEMIES! LET'S GO!
WHAT'S THE MATTER WITH YOU TWO?!

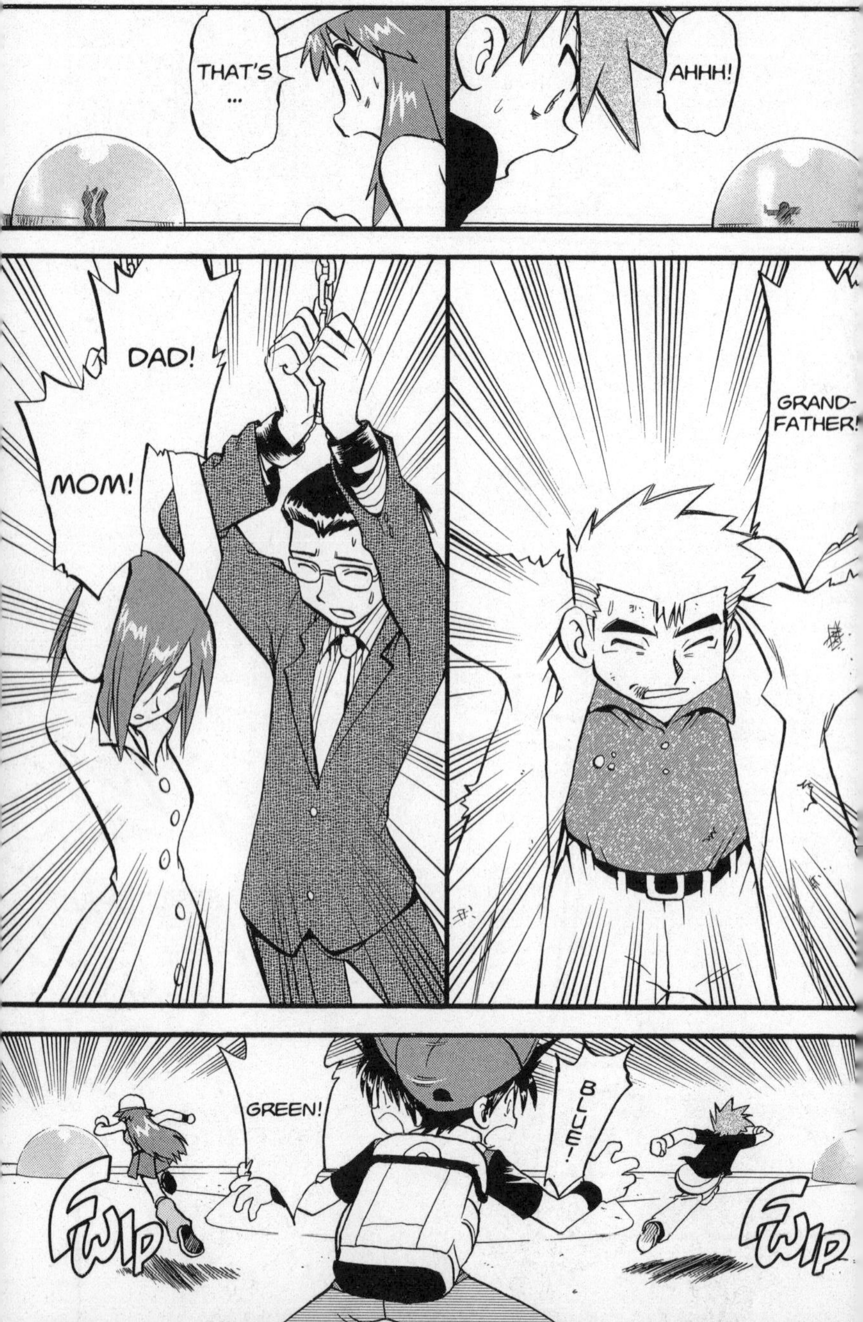
AHHH!
THAT'S ...
GRAND-FATHER!
DAD!
MOM!
BLUE!
GREEN!
FWIP
FWIP

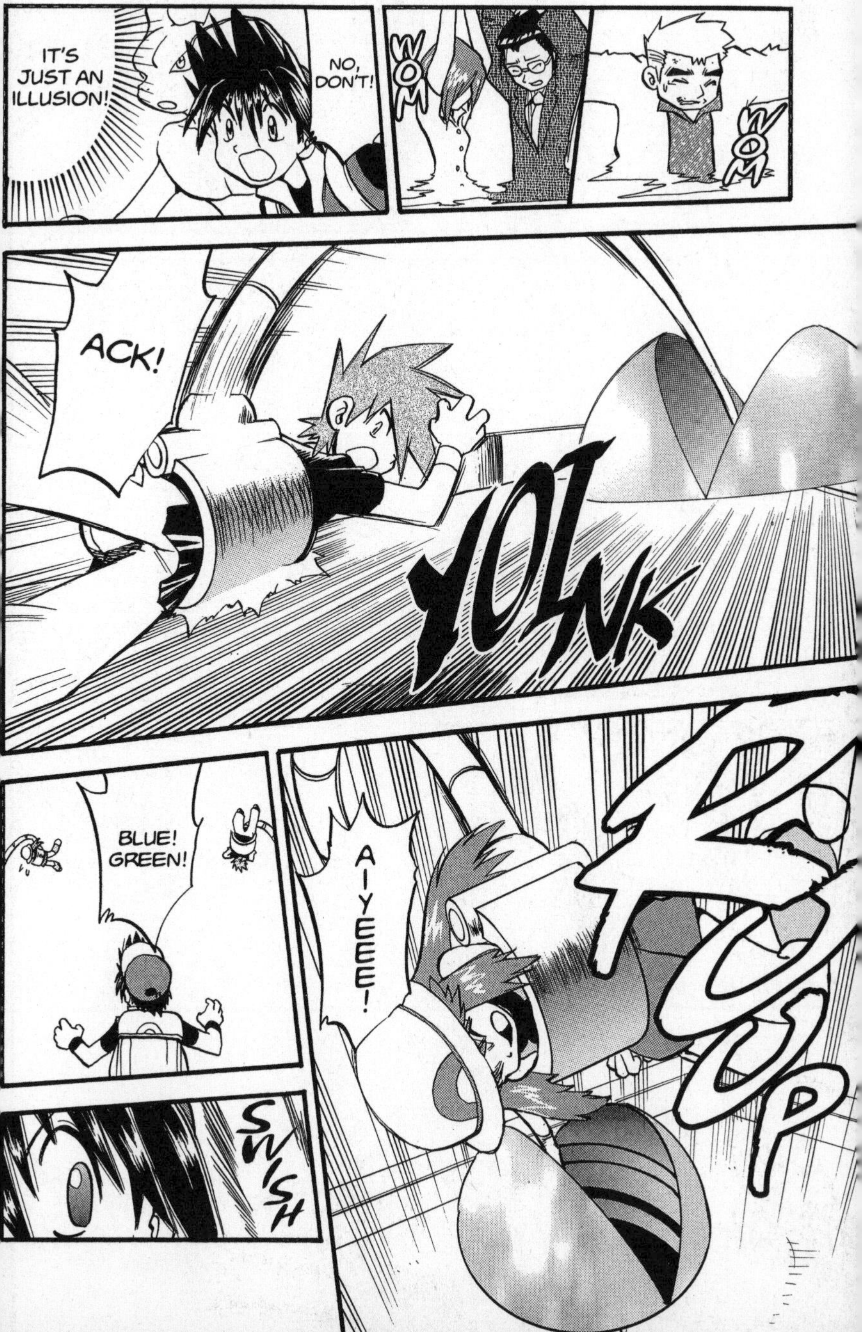
WOM
WOM
NO, DON'T!
IT'S JUST AN ILLUSION!
ACK!
YOINK
FOOP
AIYEEE!
BLUE! GREEN!
SWISH

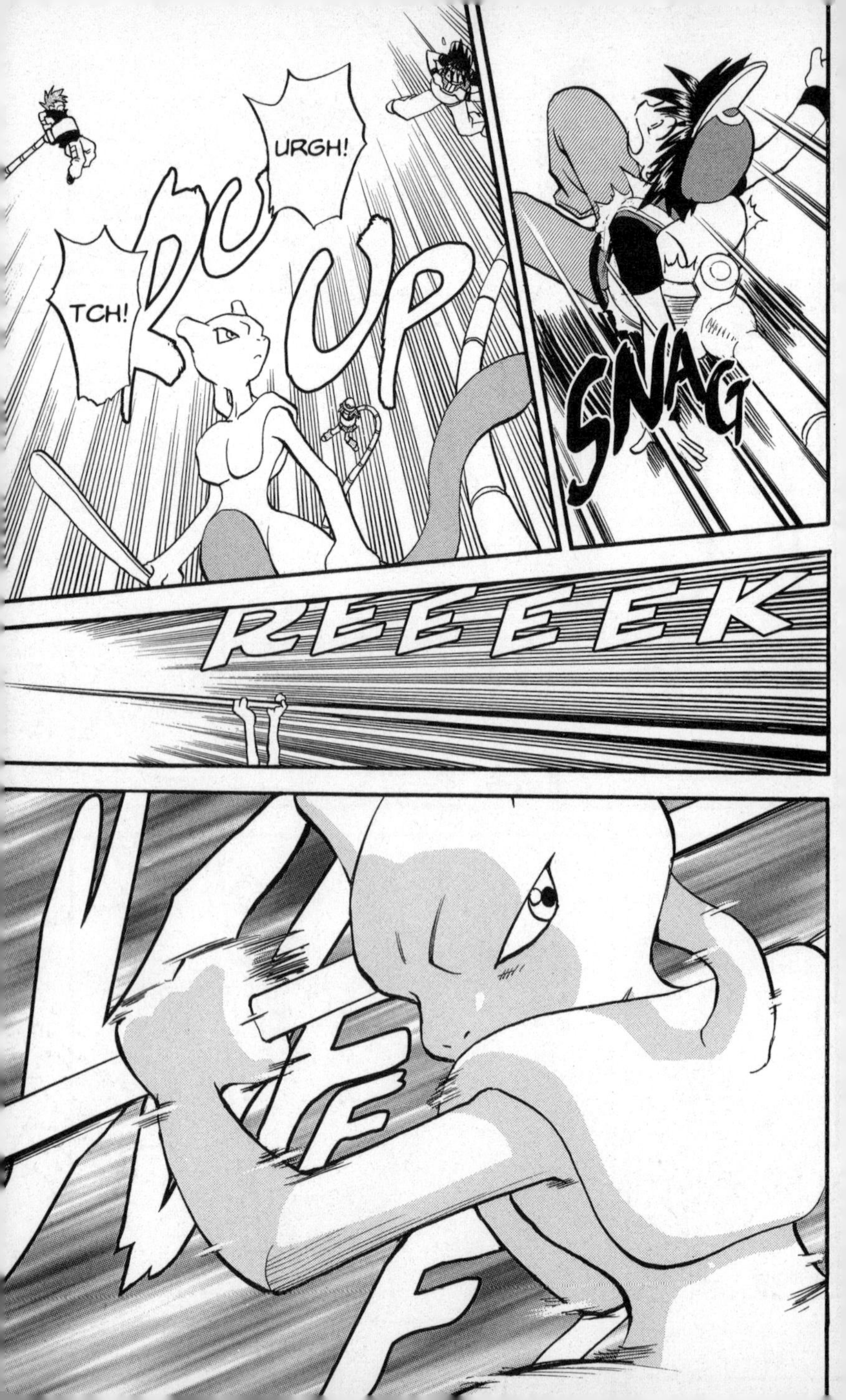
SNAG
URGH!
TCH!
REEEEEK

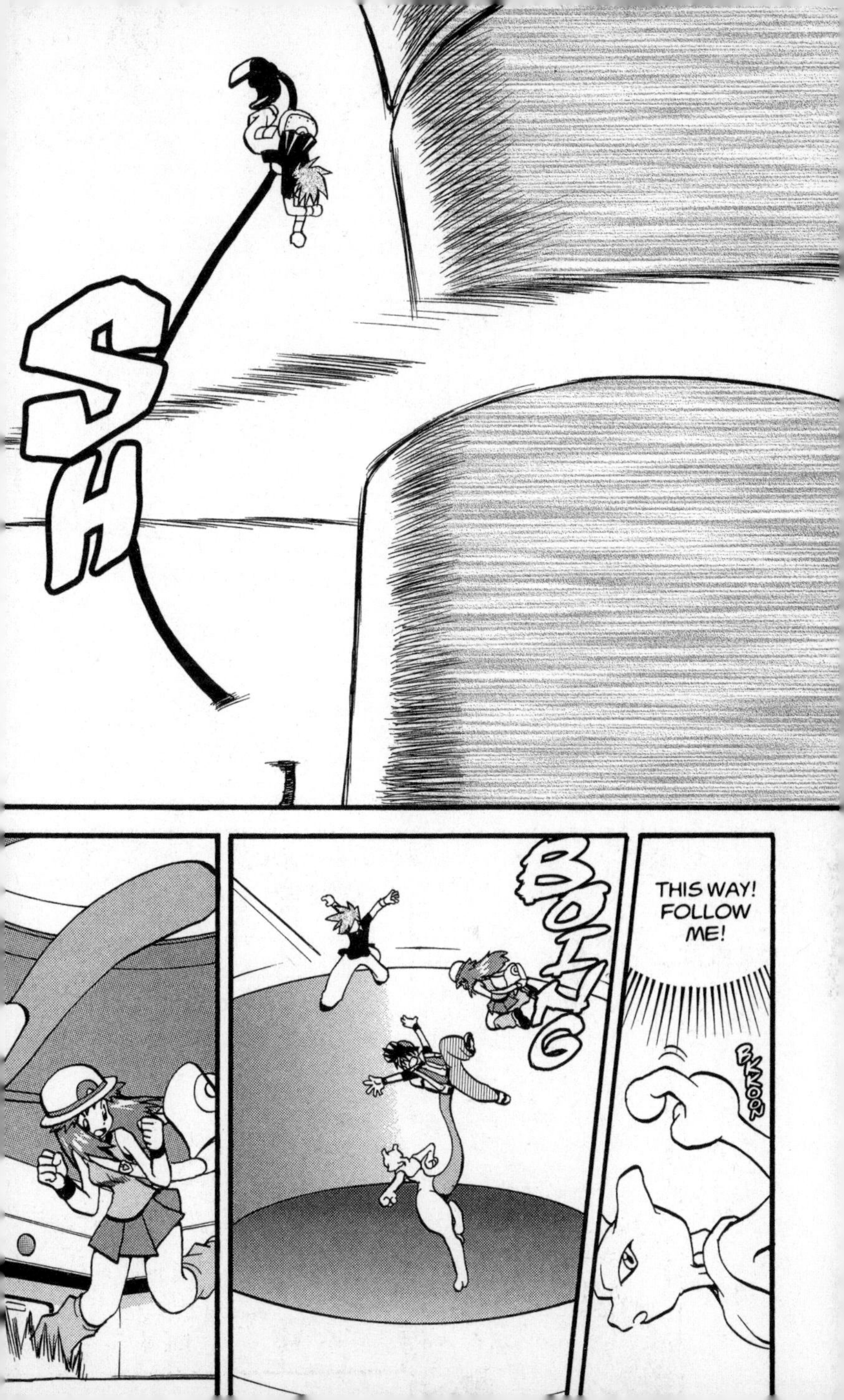
SH
THIS WAY! FOLLOW ME!
BWOON
BOING

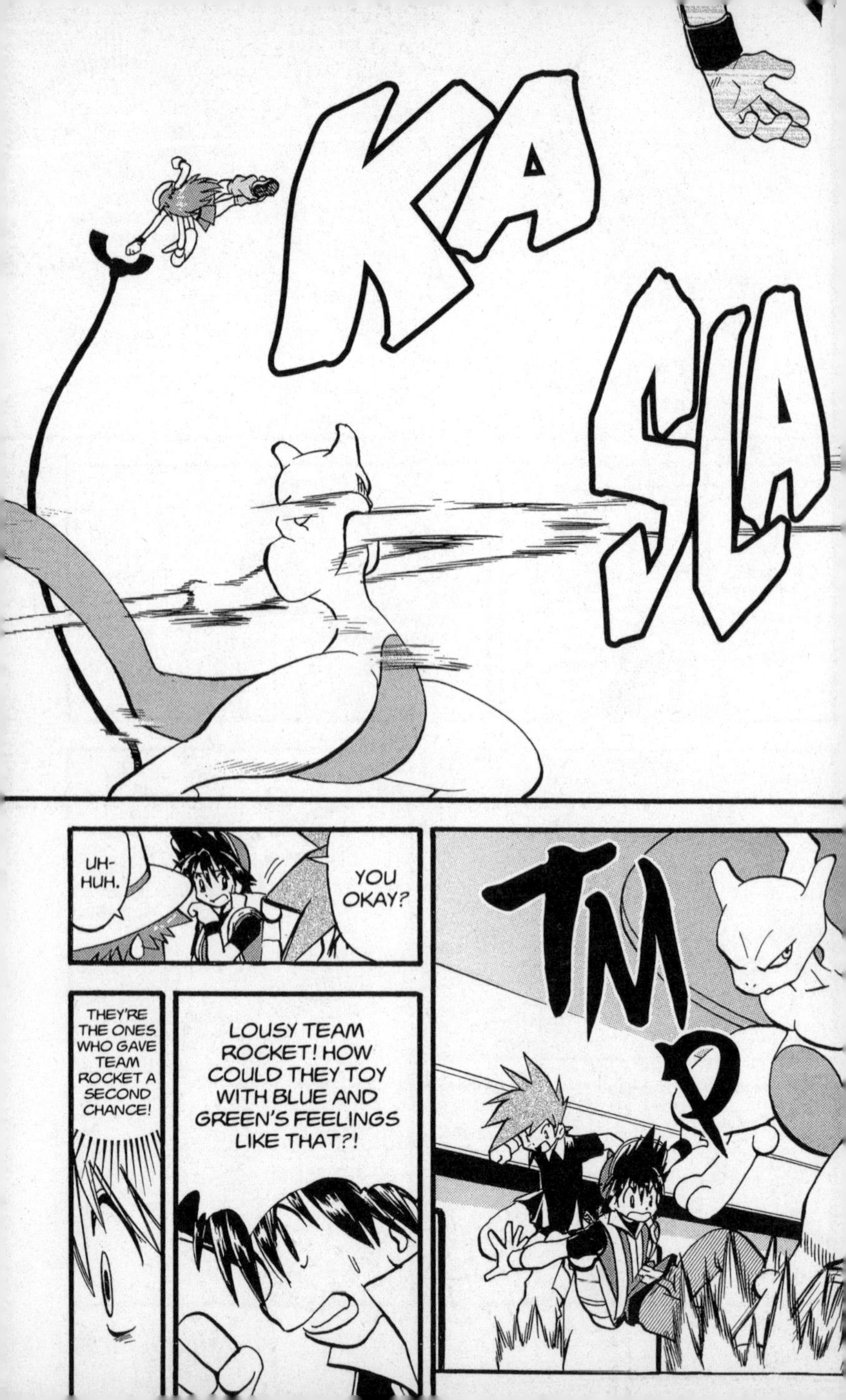
KA
SLA
TMP
YOU OKAY?
UH-HUH.
LOUSY TEAM ROCKET! HOW COULD THEY TOY WITH BLUE AND GREEN'S FEELINGS LIKE THAT?!
THEY'RE THE ONES WHO GAVE TEAM ROCKET A SECOND CHANCE!

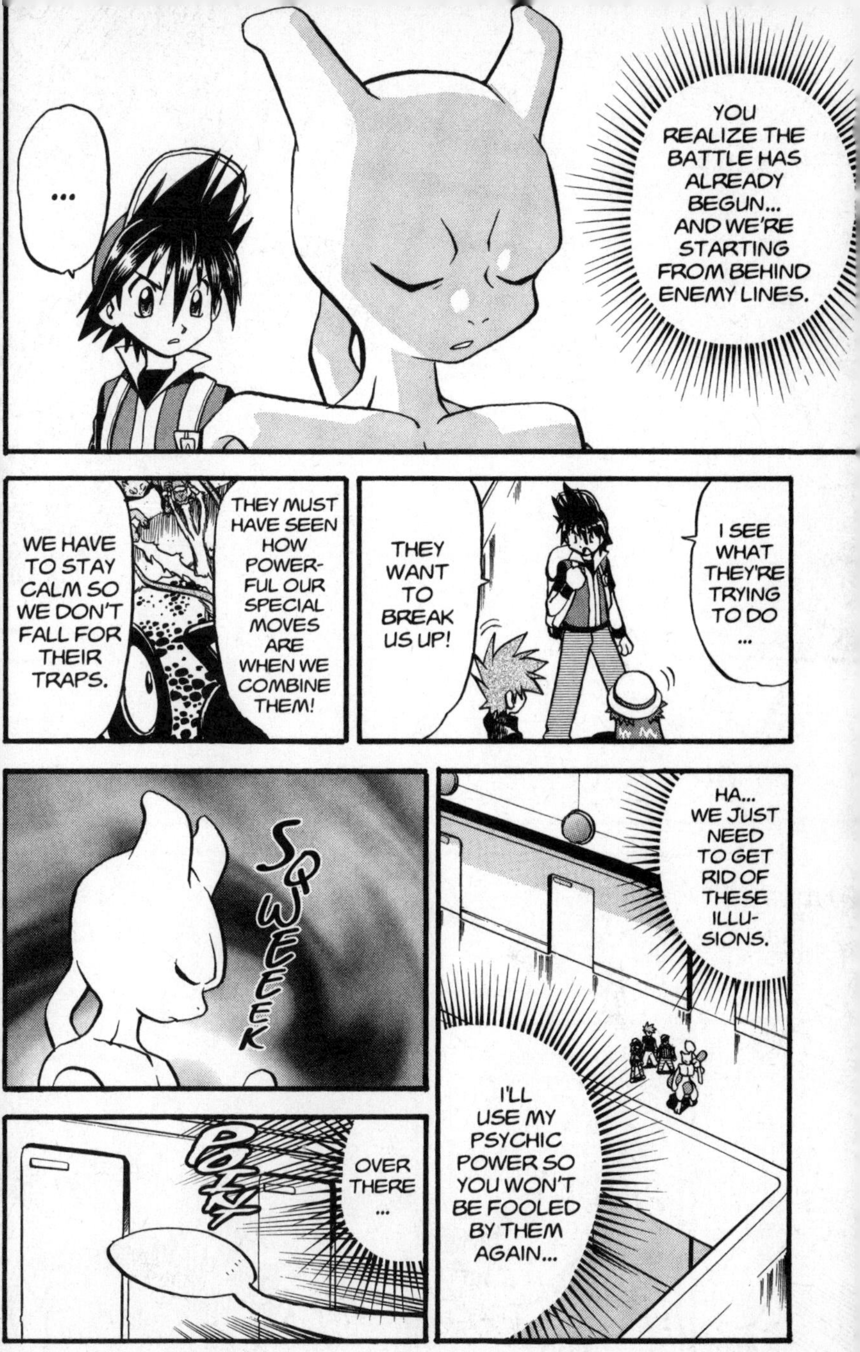
YOU REALIZE THE BATTLE HAS ALREADY BEGUN... AND WE'RE STARTING FROM BEHIND ENEMY LINES.
...
I SEE WHAT THEY'RE TRYING TO DO ...
THEY WANT TO BREAK US UP!
THEY MUST HAVE SEEN HOW POWER-FUL OUR SPECIAL MOVES ARE WHEN WE COMBINE THEM!
WE HAVE TO STAY CALM SO WE DON'T FALL FOR THEIR TRAPS.
HA... WE JUST NEED TO GET RID OF THESE ILLU-SIONS.
I'LL USE MY PSYCHIC POWER SO YOU WON'T BE FOOLED BY THEM AGAIN...
SQWEEEEK
POP
OVER THERE ...

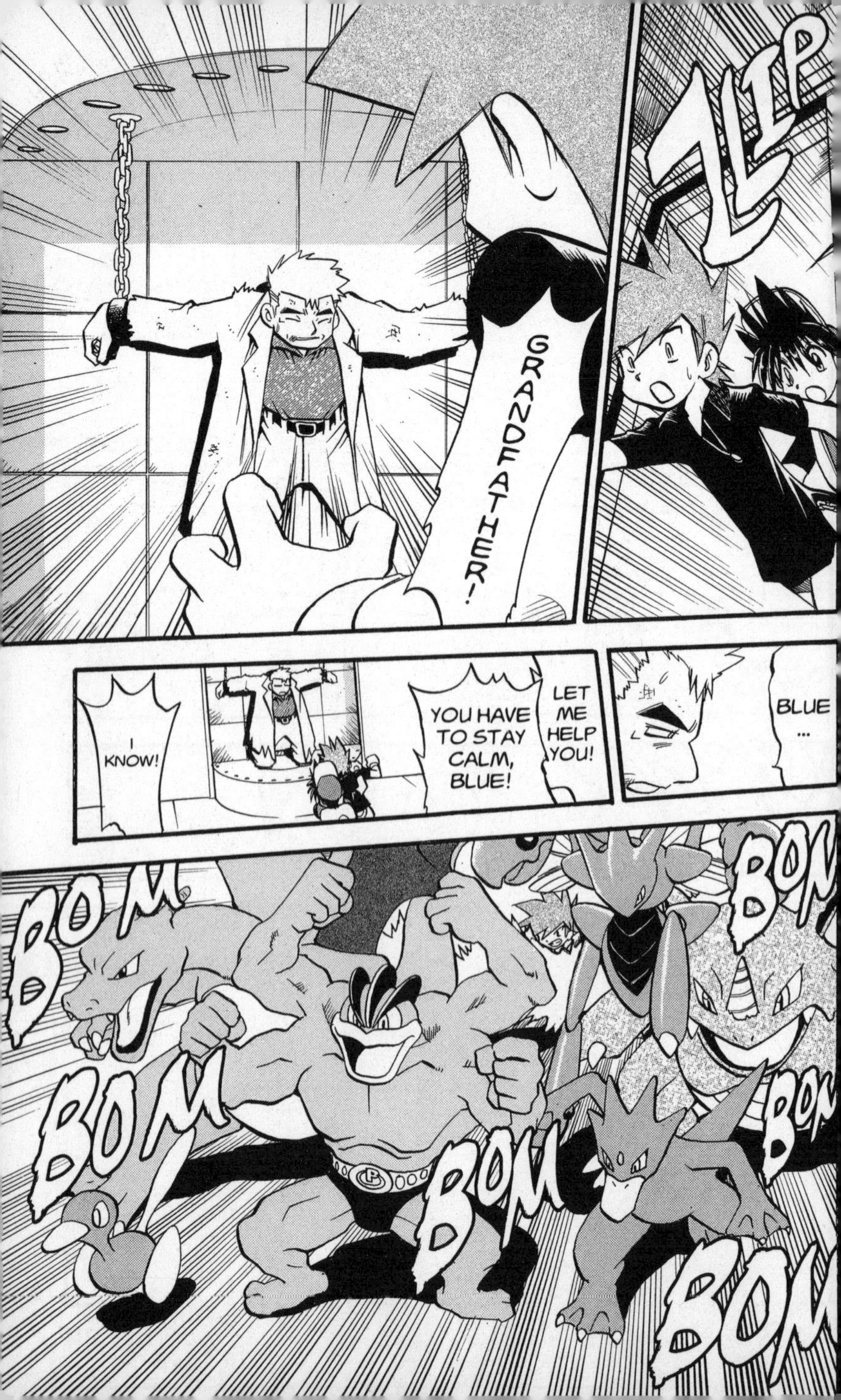
ZIP
GRANDFATHER!
BLUE ...
LET ME HELP YOU!
YOU HAVE TO STAY CALM, BLUE!
I KNOW!
BOM
BOM
BOM
BOM
BOM
BOM

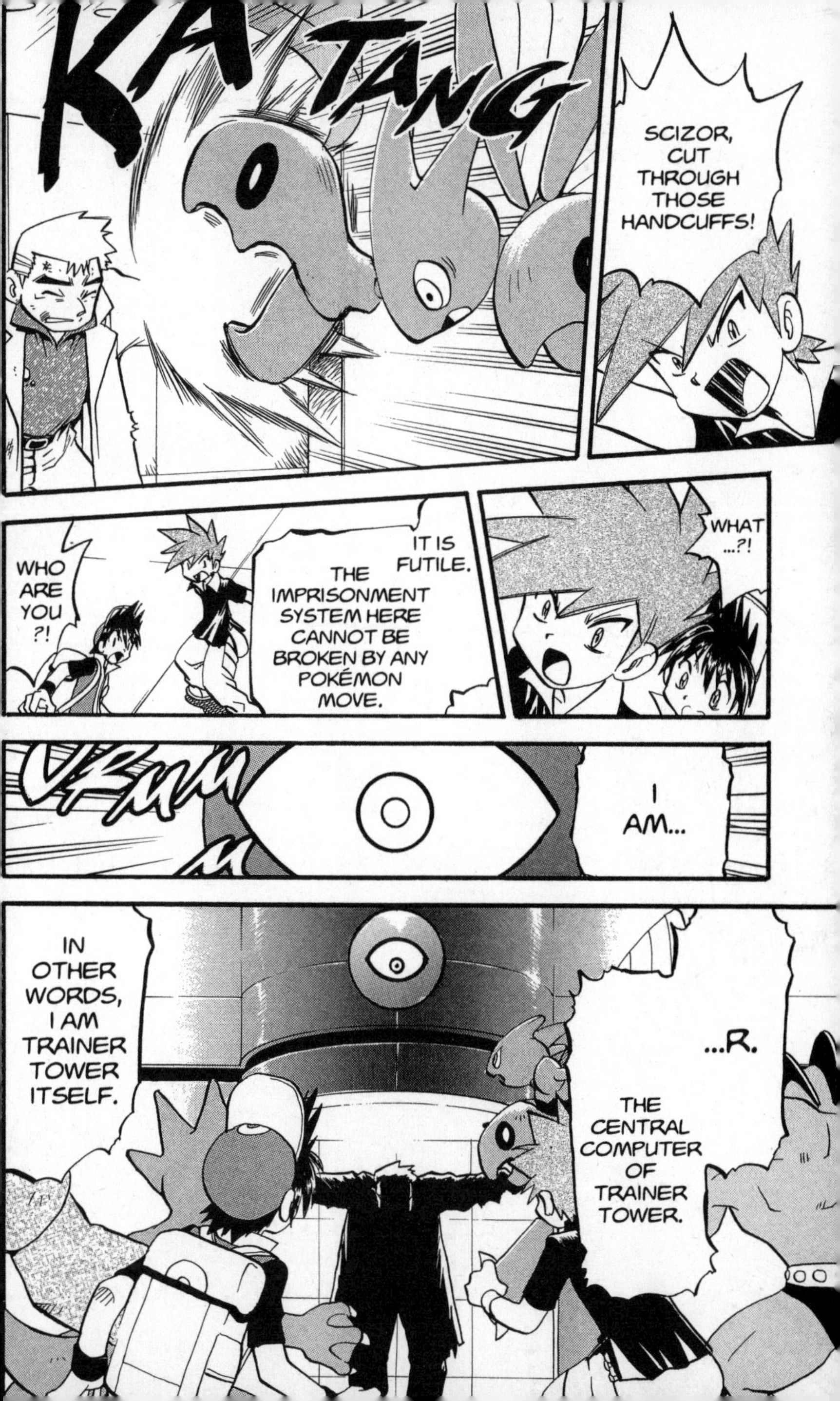
SCIZOR, CUT THROUGH THOSE HANDCUFFS!
KA TANG
WHAT ...?!
IT IS FUTILE.
THE IMPRISONMENT SYSTEM HERE CANNOT BE BROKEN BY ANY POKÉMON MOVE.
WHO ARE YOU ?!
I AM...
...R.
THE CENTRAL COMPUTER OF TRAINER TOWER.
IN OTHER WORDS, I AM TRAINER TOWER ITSELF.

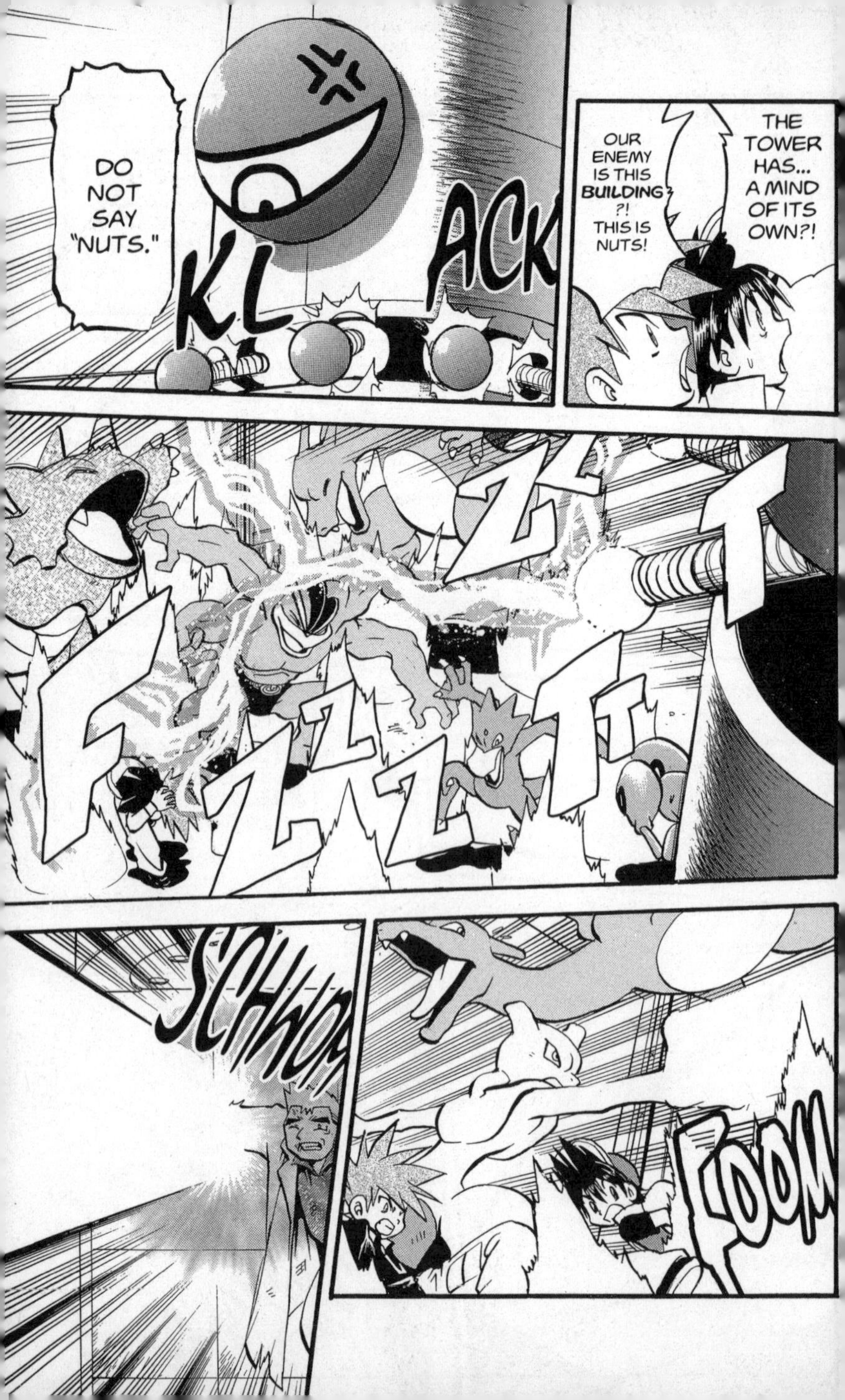
THE TOWER HAS... A MIND OF ITS OWN?!
OUR ENEMY IS THIS **BUILDING**?! THIS IS NUTS!
DO NOT SAY "NUTS."
KLACK

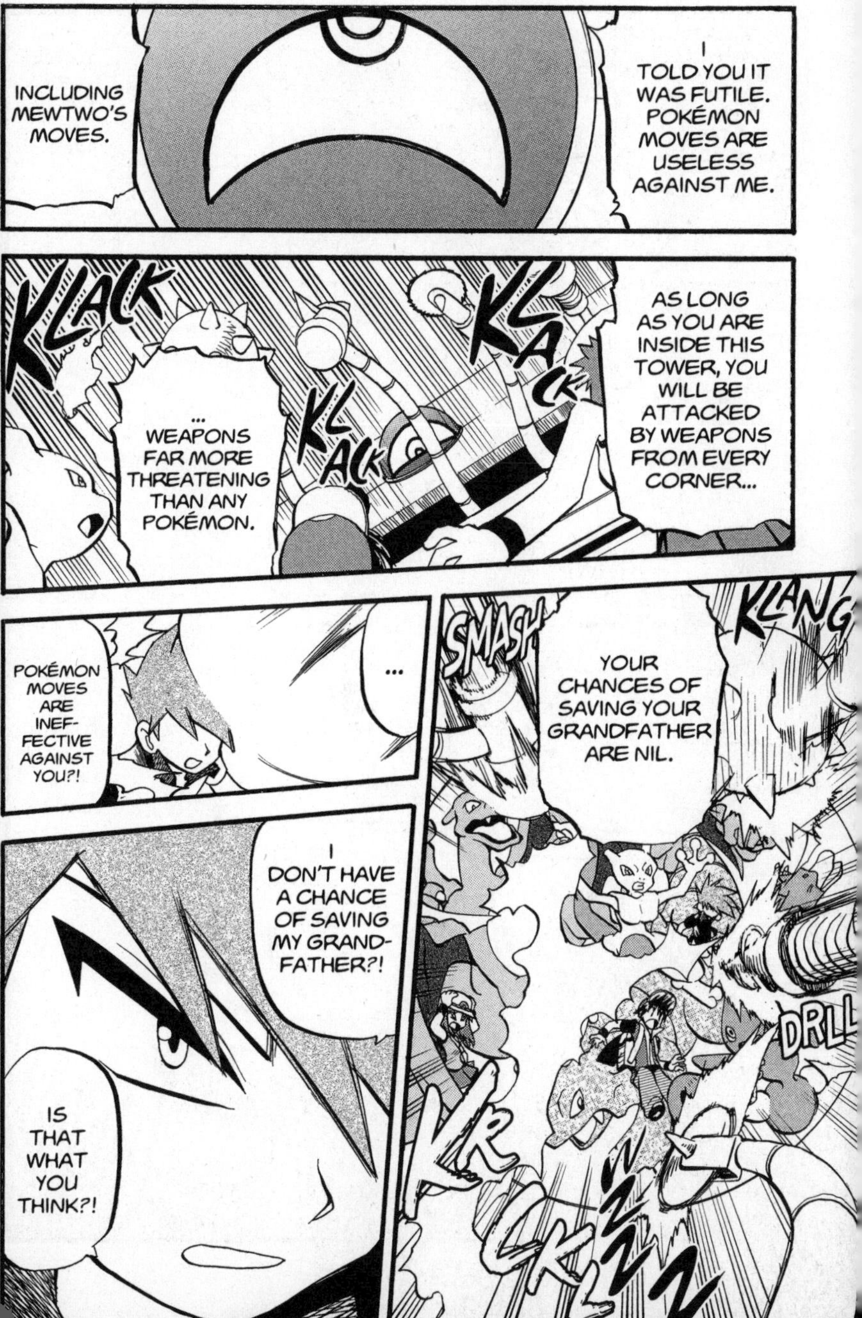
I TOLD YOU IT WAS FUTILE. POKÉMON MOVES ARE USELESS AGAINST ME.
INCLUDING MEWTWO'S MOVES.
KLACK
AS LONG AS YOU ARE INSIDE THIS TOWER, YOU WILL BE ATTACKED BY WEAPONS FROM EVERY CORNER...
KLACK
... WEAPONS FAR MORE THREATENING THAN ANY POKÉMON.
KLACK
KLANG
SMASH
YOUR CHANCES OF SAVING YOUR GRANDFATHER ARE NIL.
DRLL
WZZZZ
...
POKÉMON MOVES ARE INEF-FECTIVE AGAINST YOU?!
I DON'T HAVE A CHANCE OF SAVING MY GRAND-FATHER?!
IS THAT WHAT YOU THINK?!

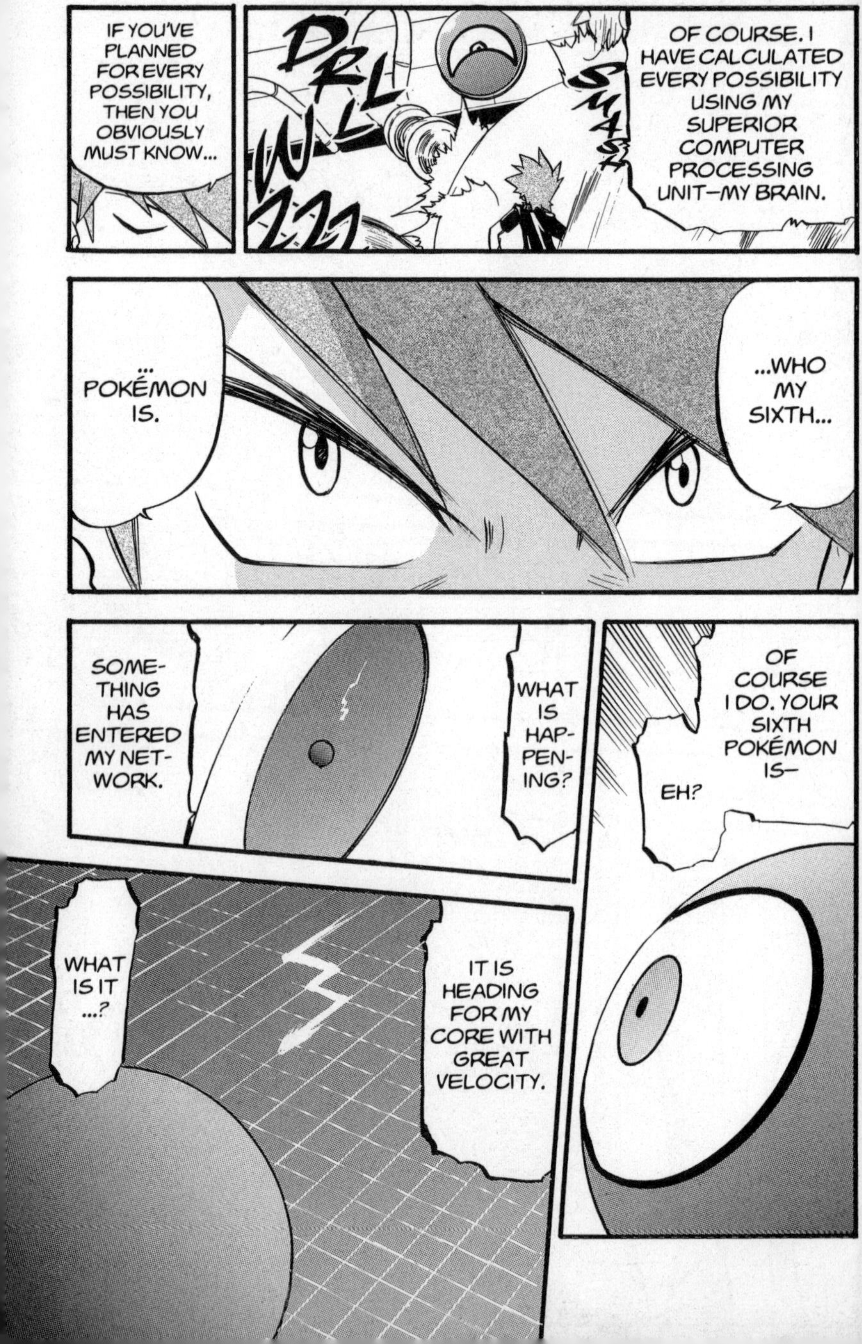
OF COURSE. I HAVE CALCULATED EVERY POSSIBILITY USING MY SUPERIOR COMPUTER PROCESSING UNIT—MY BRAIN.
SMASH
DRLL
IF YOU'VE PLANNED FOR EVERY POSSIBILITY, THEN YOU OBVIOUSLY MUST KNOW...
...WHO MY SIXTH...
... POKÉMON IS.
OF COURSE I DO. YOUR SIXTH POKÉMON IS—
EH?
WHAT IS HAPPENING?
SOMETHING HAS ENTERED MY NETWORK.
IT IS HEADING FOR MY CORE WITH GREAT VELOCITY.
WHAT IS IT ...?

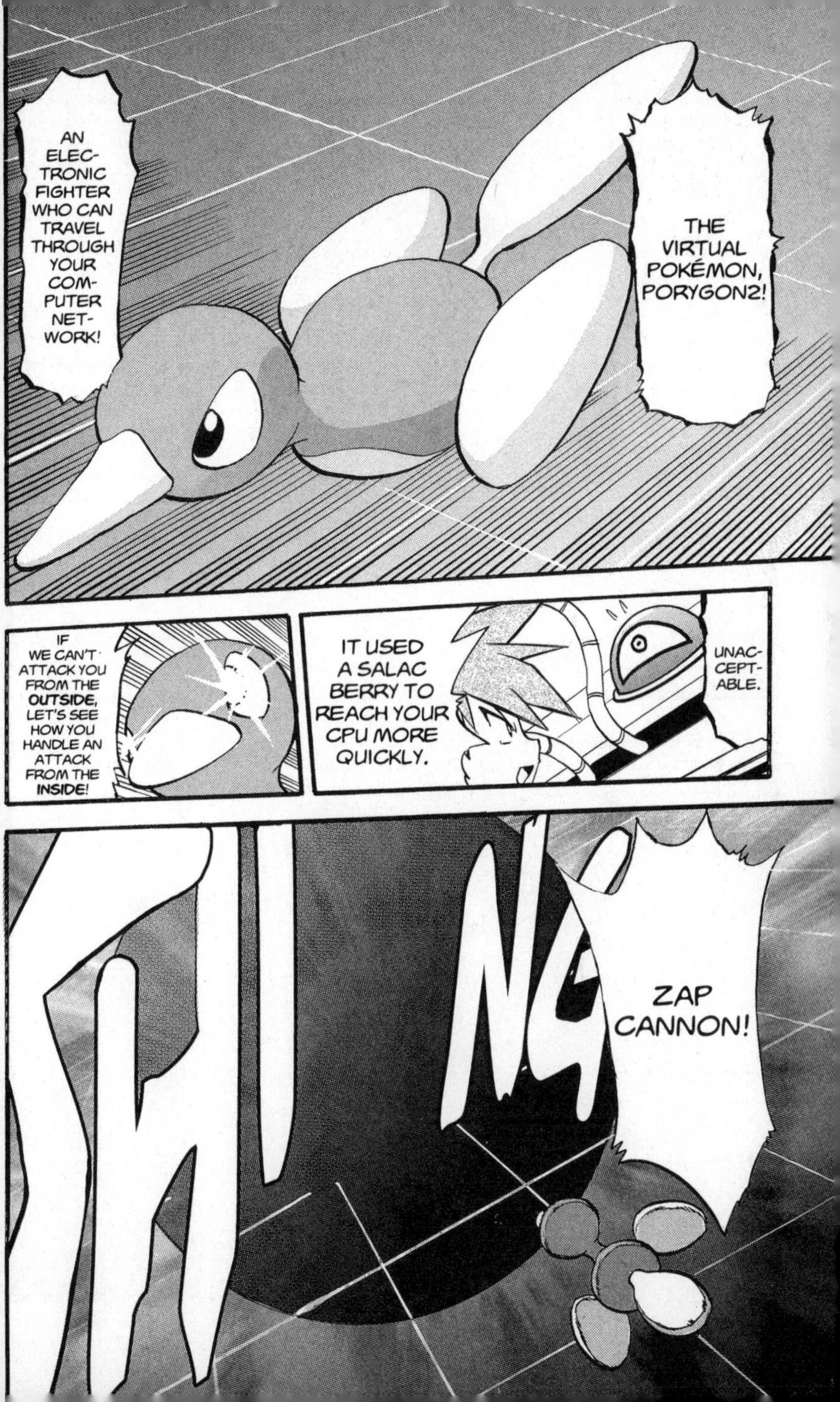
THE VIRTUAL POKÉMON, PORYGON2!
AN ELECTRONIC FIGHTER WHO CAN TRAVEL THROUGH YOUR COMPUTER NETWORK!
UNACCEPTABLE.
IT USED A SALAC BERRY TO REACH YOUR CPU MORE QUICKLY.
IF WE CAN'T ATTACK YOU FROM THE **OUTSIDE**, LET'S SEE HOW YOU HANDLE AN ATTACK FROM THE **INSIDE**!
ZAP CANNON!

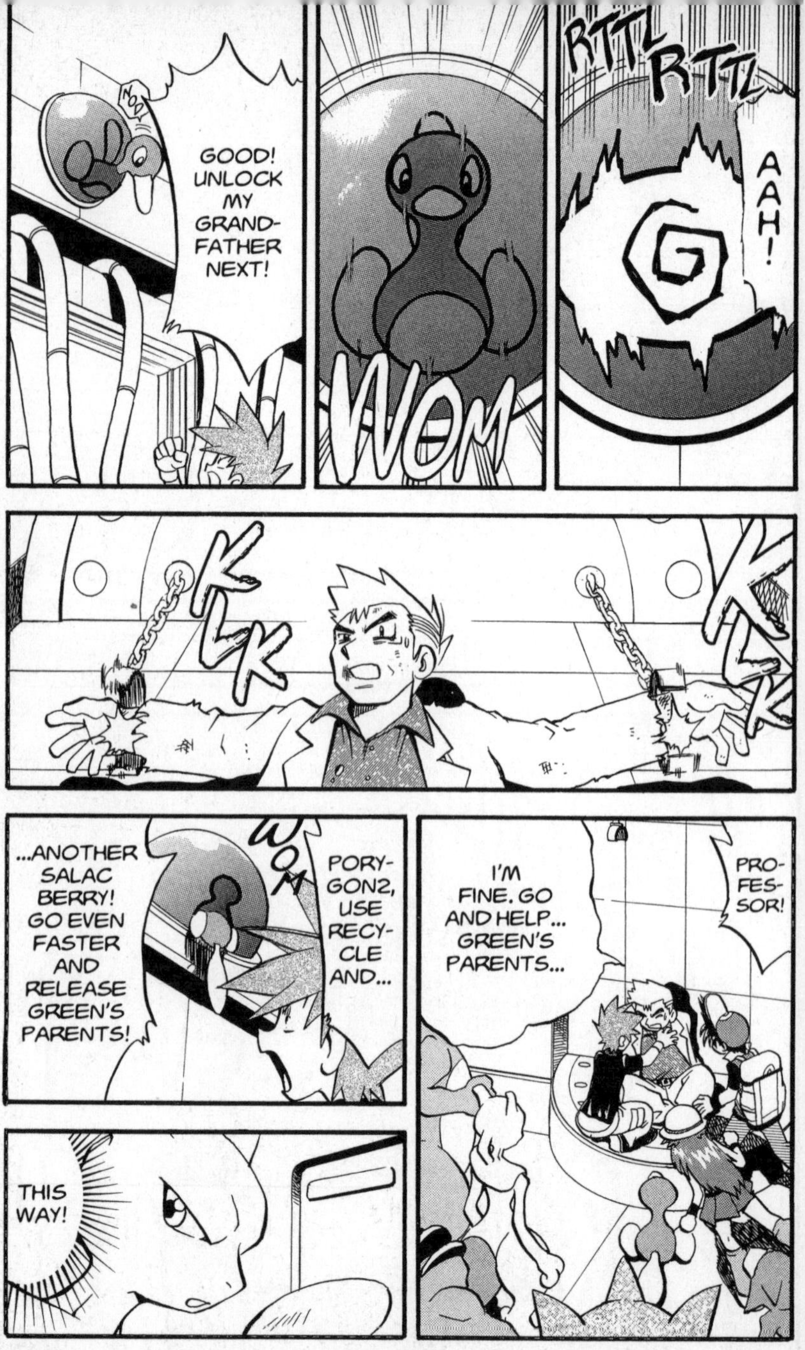
RTTL RTTL
AAH!
WOM
NOD
GOOD! UNLOCK MY GRAND-FATHER NEXT!
KLK
KLK
PRO-FES-SOR!
I'M FINE. GO AND HELP... GREEN'S PARENTS...
WOM
PORY-GON2, USE RECY-CLE AND...
...ANOTHER SALAC BERRY! GO EVEN FASTER AND RELEASE GREEN'S PARENTS!
THIS WAY!

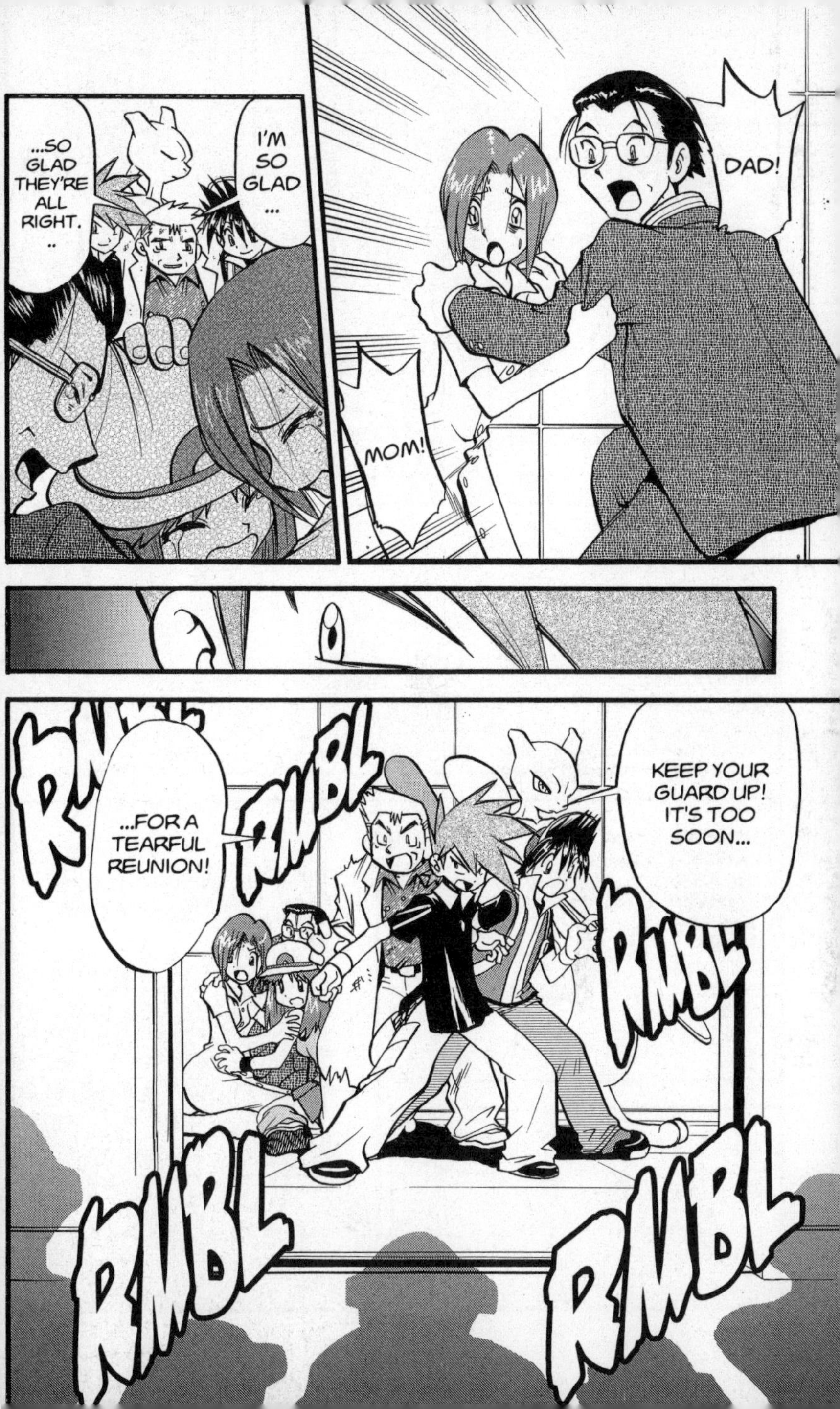
DAD!
MOM!
I'M SO GLAD...
...SO GLAD THEY'RE ALL RIGHT...
KEEP YOUR GUARD UP! IT'S TOO SOON...
RMBL
RMBL
...FOR A TEARFUL REUNION!
RMBL
RMBL

CHARACTER PROFILE

CELIO

CELIO DEVELOPED THE POKéMON TRANSPORTER SYSTEM WITH BILL AND IS CURRENTLY MANAGING IT. HE IS CALM AND QUIET, WITH A KEEN SENSE OF JUS-TICE. HE RESPECTS BILL, A SENIOR RESEARCHER, AND STRIVES TO EMULATE HIM. CELIO GOT CAUGHT UP IN THE TROUBLE WITH TEAM ROCKET AFTER THE TRANSPORTER AT SEVII ISLANDS BEGAN TO MALFUNCTION. HE HAS DECIDED TO SUPPORT RED AND HIS FRIENDS.

CELIO

- Birthplace: One Island
- Birthday: November 12
- Blood Type: A
- Job: Pokémon Transporter System Developer/Manager

• Adventure 286 •
Meet Deoxys, and Deoxys, and Deoxys, and…

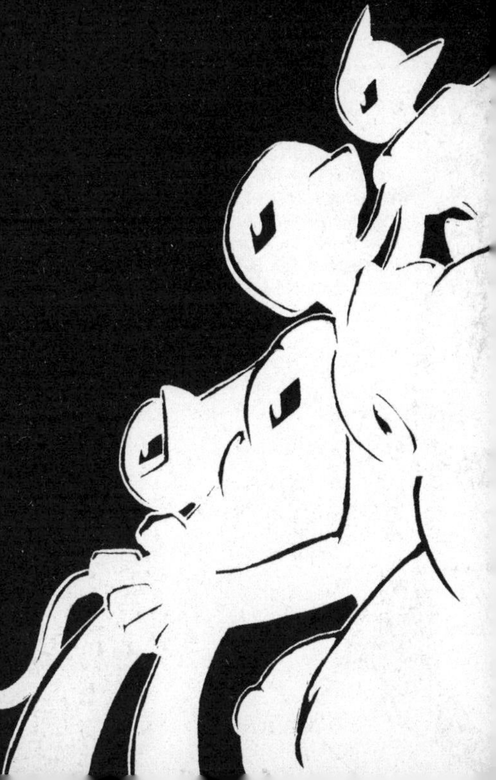

Pokémon Adventures
FireRed & LeafGreen
The Fifth Chapter

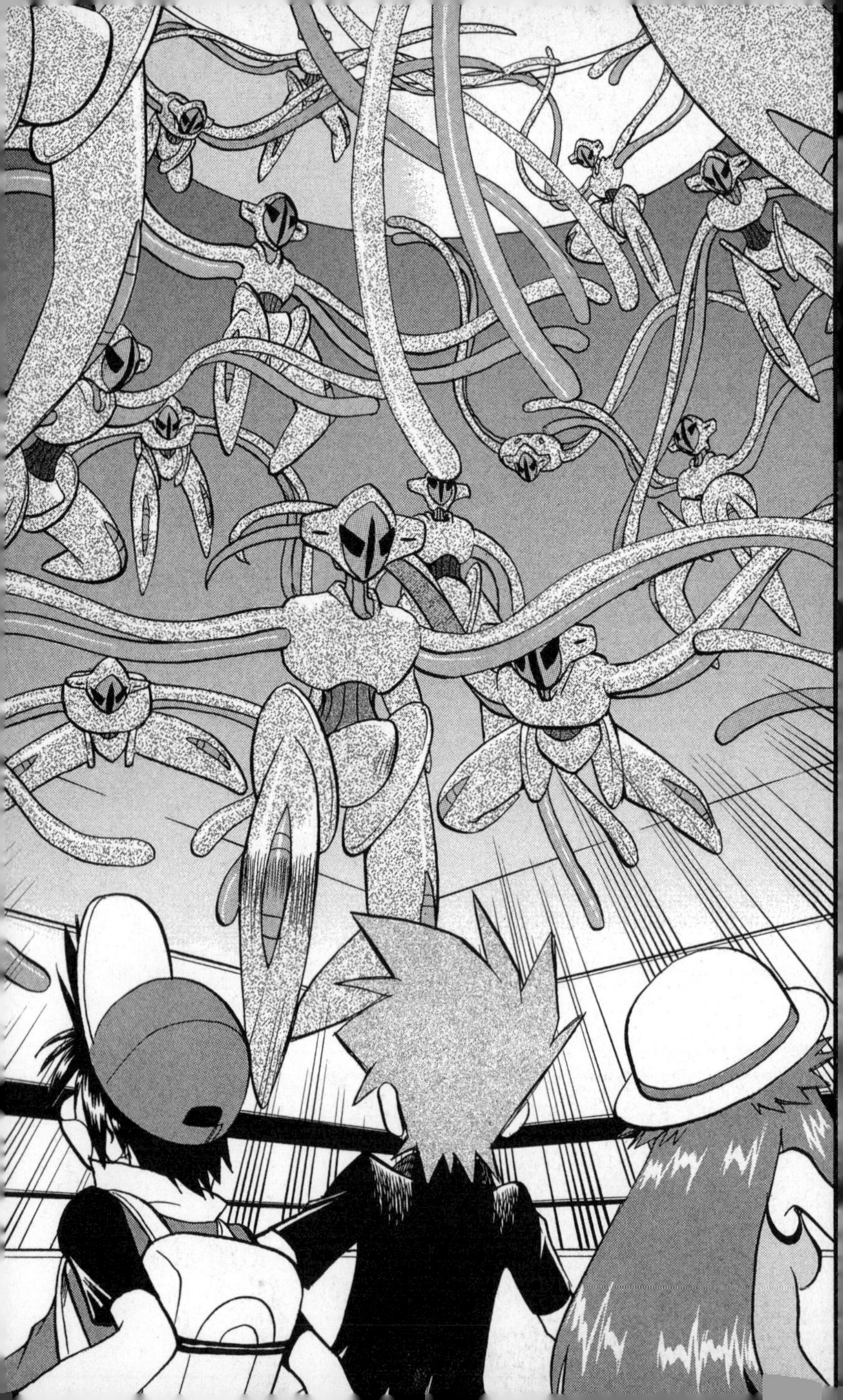

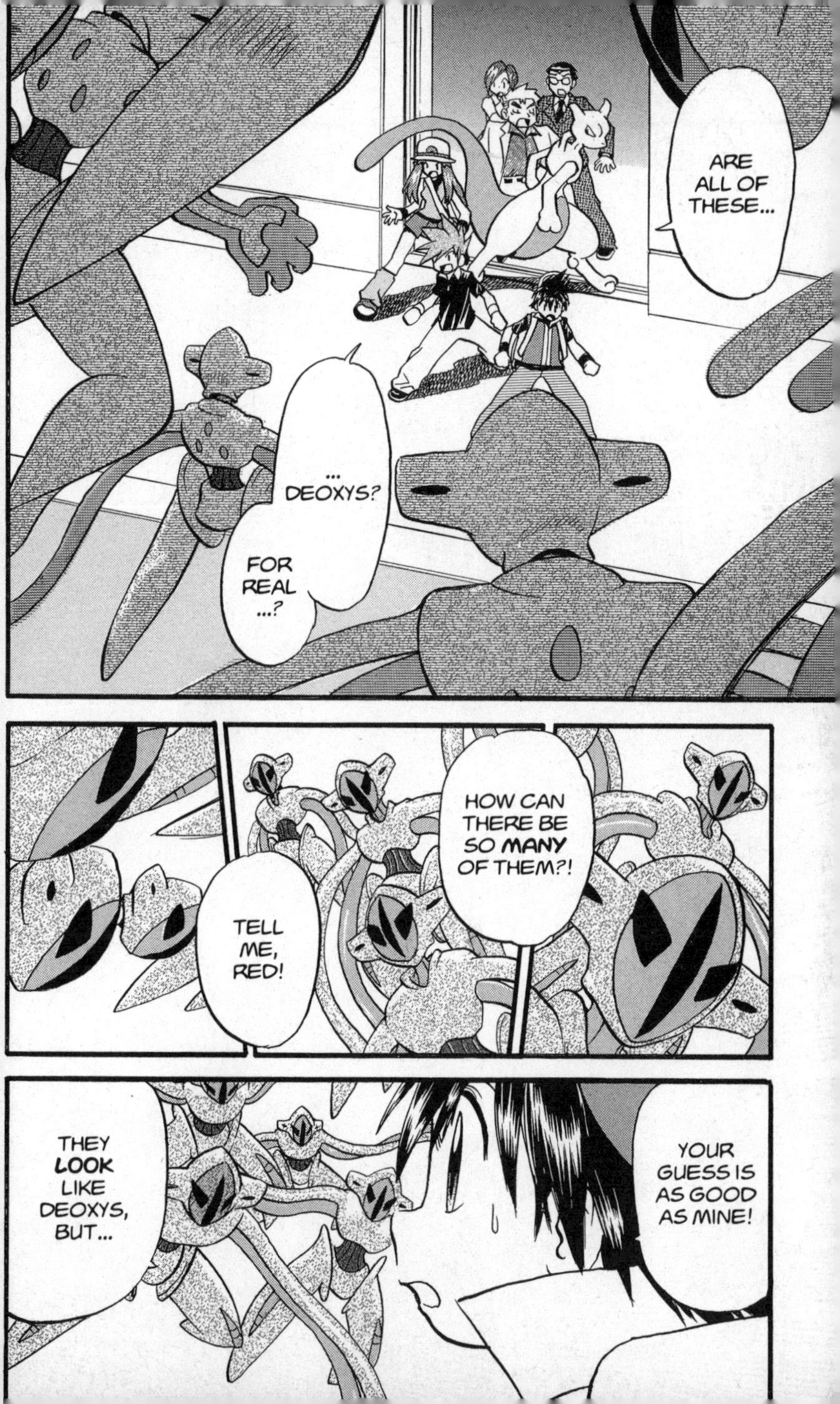
ARE ALL OF THESE...
... DEOXYS?
FOR REAL ...?
HOW CAN THERE BE SO **MANY** OF THEM?!
TELL ME, RED!
YOUR GUESS IS AS GOOD AS MINE!
THEY **LOOK** LIKE DEOXYS, BUT...

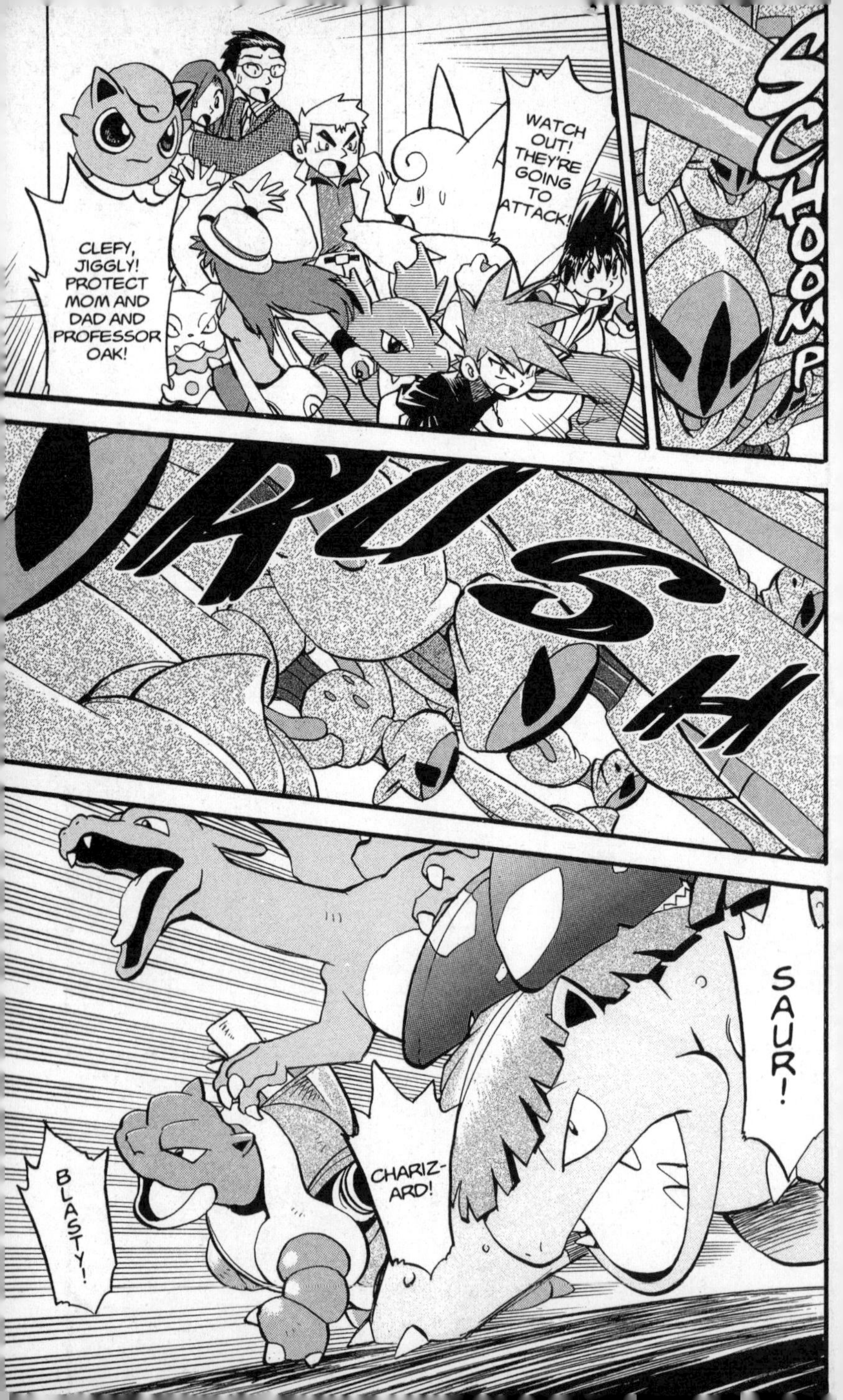
SCHOOMP
WATCH OUT! THEY'RE GOING TO ATTACK!
CLEFY, JIGGLY! PROTECT MOM AND DAD AND PROFESSOR OAK!
RUSH
SAUR!
CHARIZ-ARD!
BLASTY!

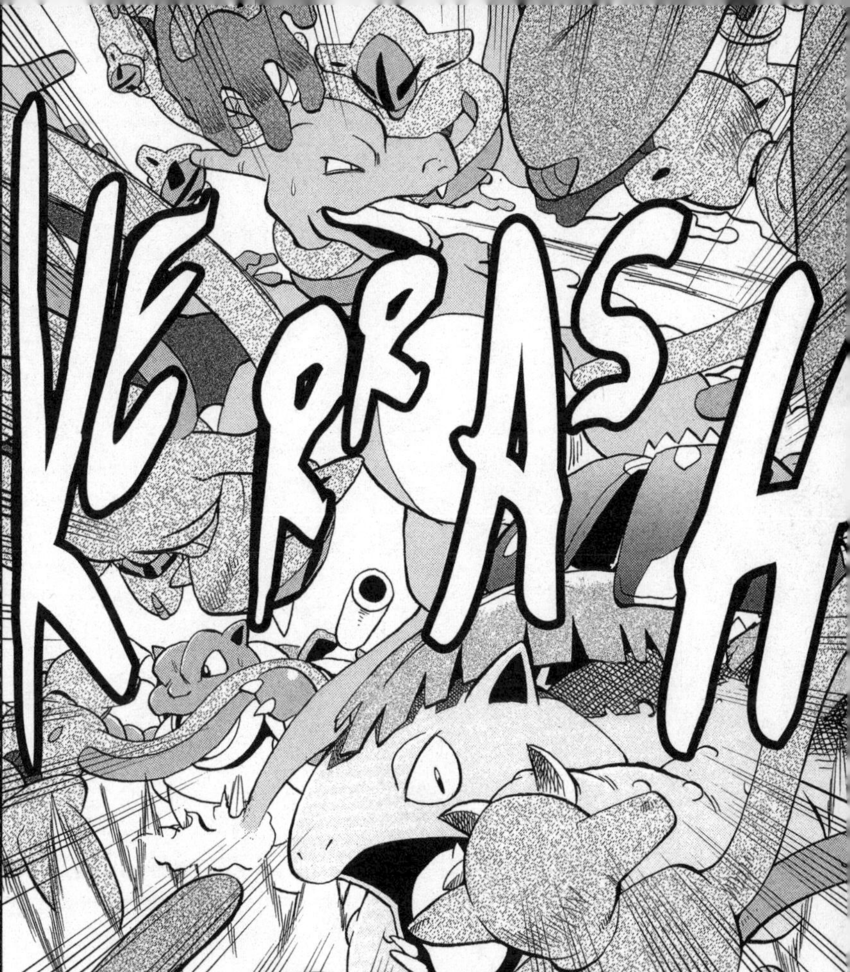
KRRASH
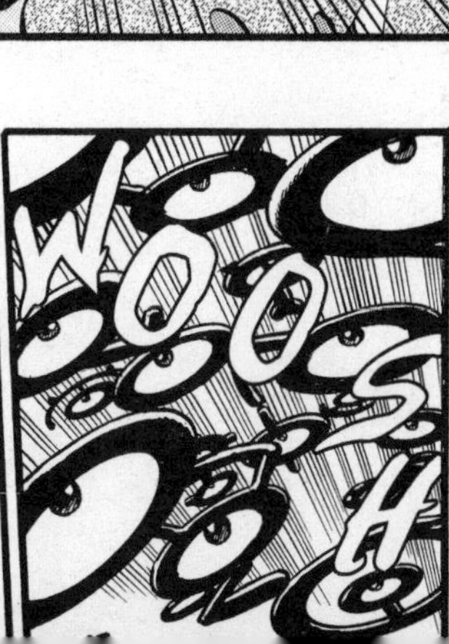
WOOOSH
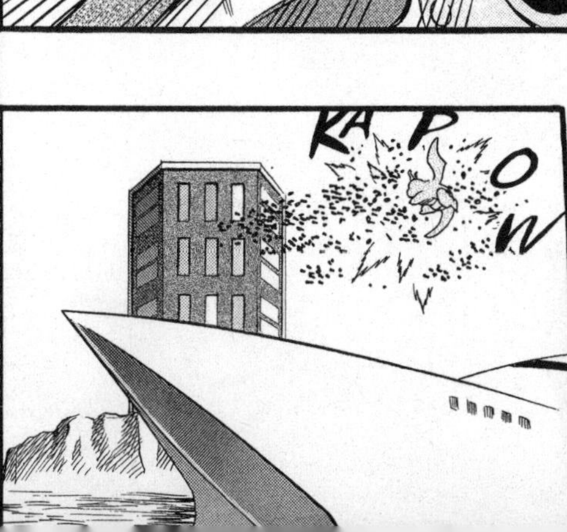
KAPOW

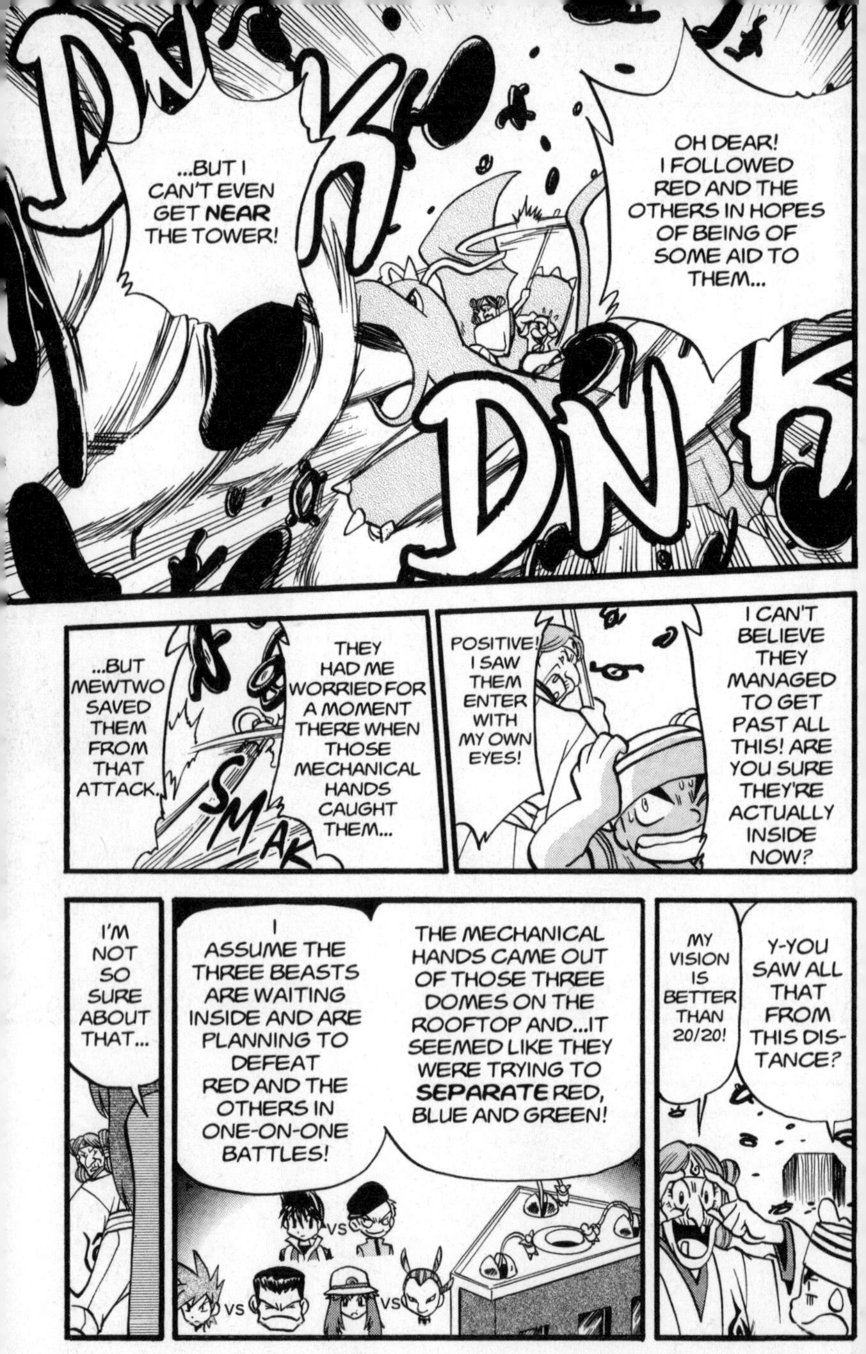
OH DEAR! I FOLLOWED RED AND THE OTHERS IN HOPES OF BEING OF SOME AID TO THEM...
...BUT I CAN'T EVEN GET NEAR THE TOWER!
DN
DN
I CAN'T BELIEVE THEY MANAGED TO GET PAST ALL THIS! ARE YOU SURE THEY'RE ACTUALLY INSIDE NOW?
POSITIVE! I SAW THEM ENTER WITH MY OWN EYES!
THEY HAD ME WORRIED FOR A MOMENT THERE WHEN THOSE MECHANICAL HANDS CAUGHT THEM...
...BUT MEWTWO SAVED THEM FROM THAT ATTACK.
SMAK
Y-YOU SAW ALL THAT FROM THIS DISTANCE?
MY VISION IS BETTER THAN 20/20!
THE MECHANICAL HANDS CAME OUT OF THOSE THREE DOMES ON THE ROOFTOP AND...IT SEEMED LIKE THEY WERE TRYING TO SEPARATE RED, BLUE AND GREEN!
I ASSUME THE THREE BEASTS ARE WAITING INSIDE AND ARE PLANNING TO DEFEAT RED AND THE OTHERS IN ONE-ON-ONE BATTLES!
VS
VS
VS
I'M NOT SO SURE ABOUT THAT...

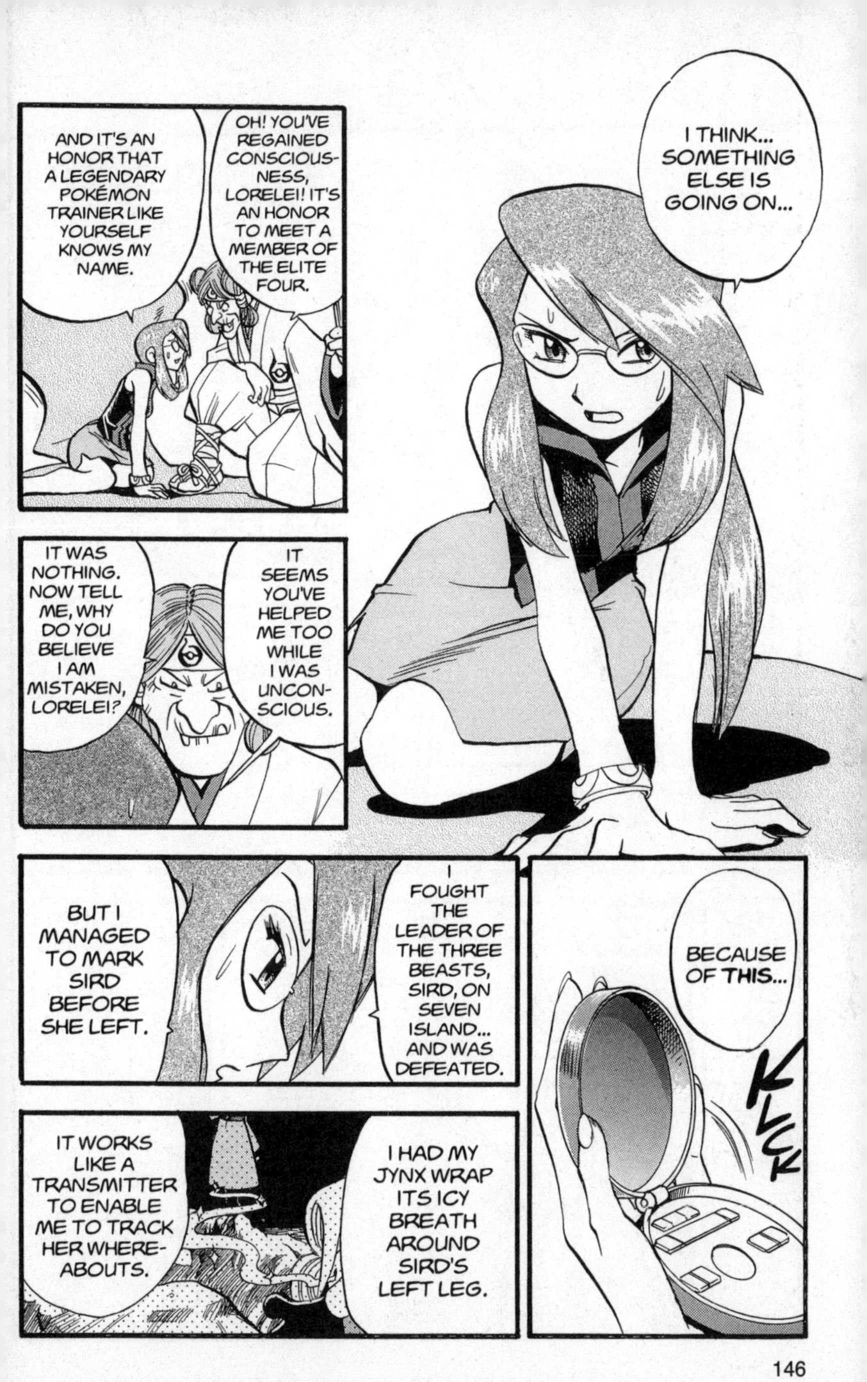
I THINK... SOMETHING ELSE IS GOING ON...
OH! YOU'VE REGAINED CONSCIOUS-NESS, LORELEI!! IT'S AN HONOR TO MEET A MEMBER OF THE ELITE FOUR.
AND IT'S AN HONOR THAT A LEGENDARY POKÉMON TRAINER LIKE YOURSELF KNOWS MY NAME.
IT SEEMS YOU'VE HELPED ME TOO WHILE I WAS UNCON-SCIOUS.
IT WAS NOTHING. NOW TELL ME, WHY DO YOU BELIEVE I AM MISTAKEN, LORELEI?
BECAUSE OF THIS...
KLICK
I FOUGHT THE LEADER OF THE THREE BEASTS, SIRD, ON SEVEN ISLAND... AND WAS DEFEATED.
BUT I MANAGED TO MARK SIRD BEFORE SHE LEFT.
I HAD MY JYNX WRAP ITS ICY BREATH AROUND SIRD'S LEFT LEG.
IT WORKS LIKE A TRANSMITTER TO ENABLE ME TO TRACK HER WHERE-ABOUTS.

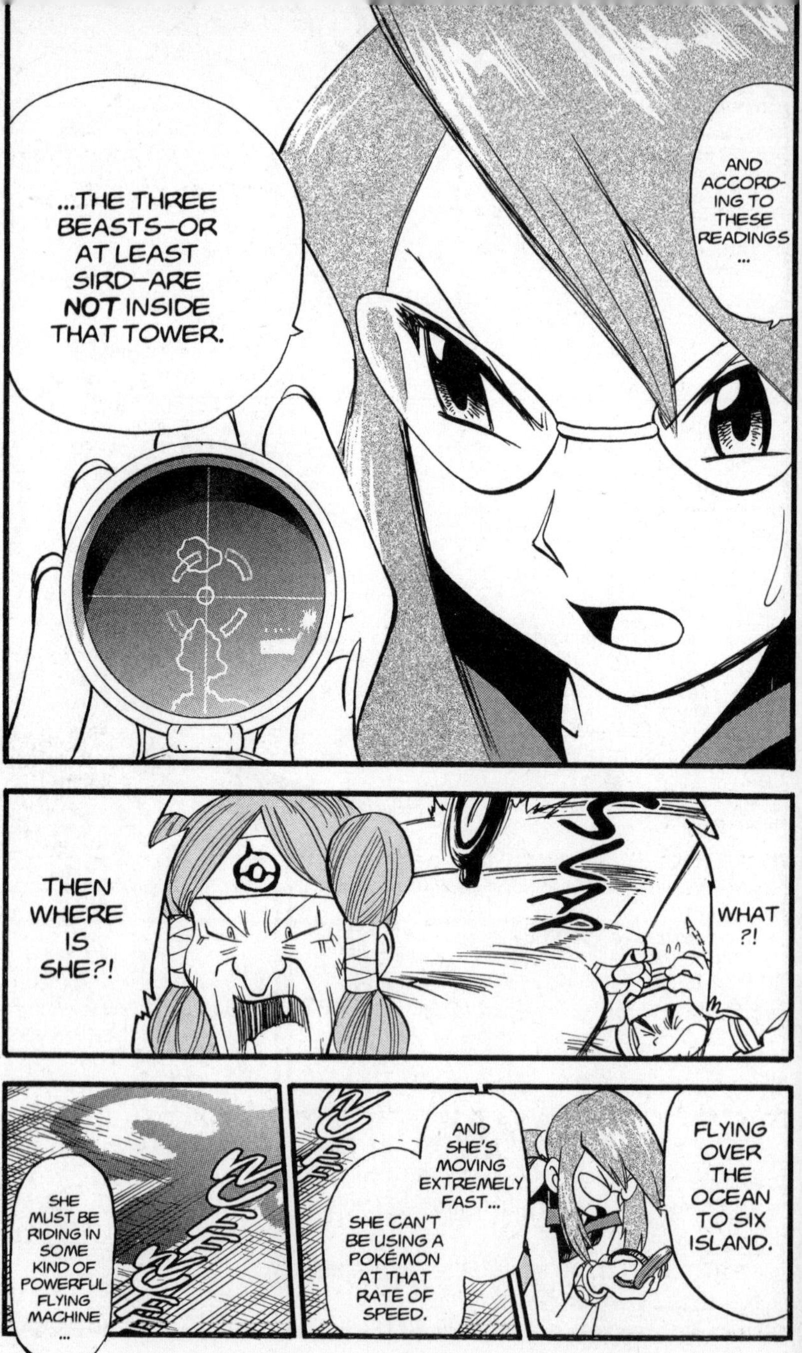
AND ACCORDING TO THESE READINGS...
...THE THREE BEASTS—OR AT LEAST SIRD—ARE **NOT** INSIDE THAT TOWER.
WHAT?!
THEN WHERE IS SHE?!
FLYING OVER THE OCEAN TO SIX ISLAND.
AND SHE'S MOVING EXTREMELY FAST...
SHE CAN'T BE USING A POKÉMON AT THAT RATE OF SPEED.
SHE MUST BE RIDING IN SOME KIND OF POWERFUL FLYING MACHINE...

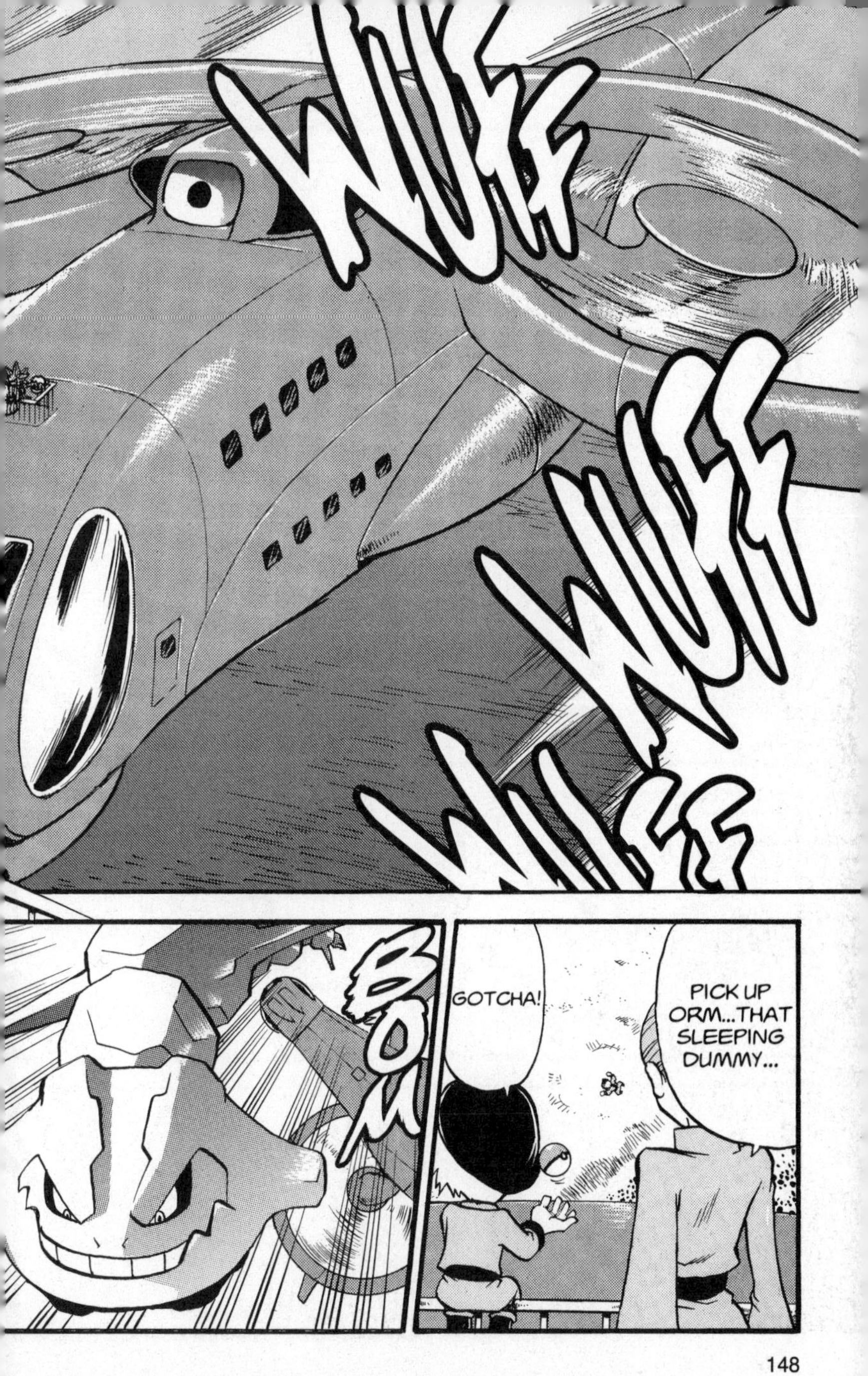
WUFF
WUFF
WUFF
PICK UP ORM...THAT SLEEPING DUMMY...
GOTCHA!

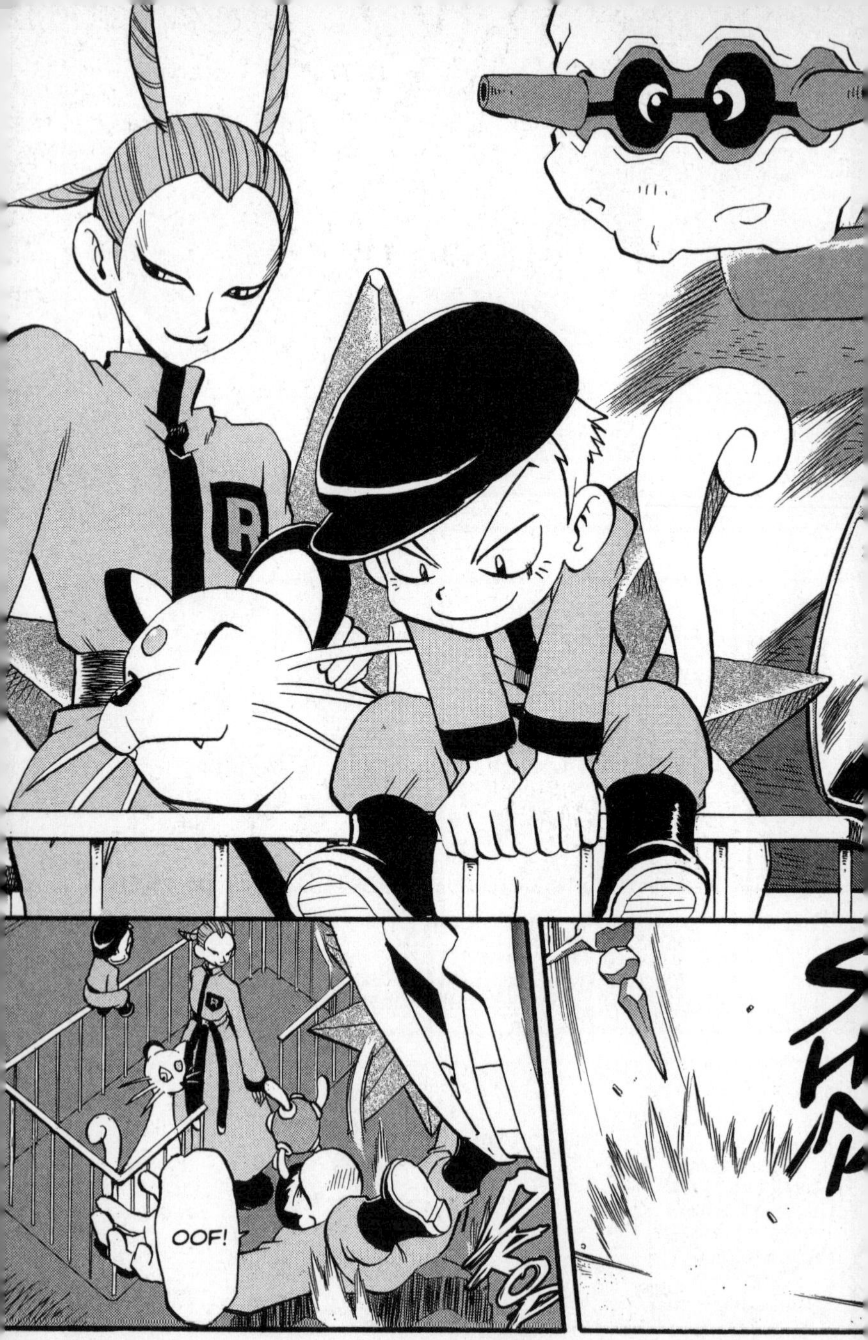
SHAK
OOF!

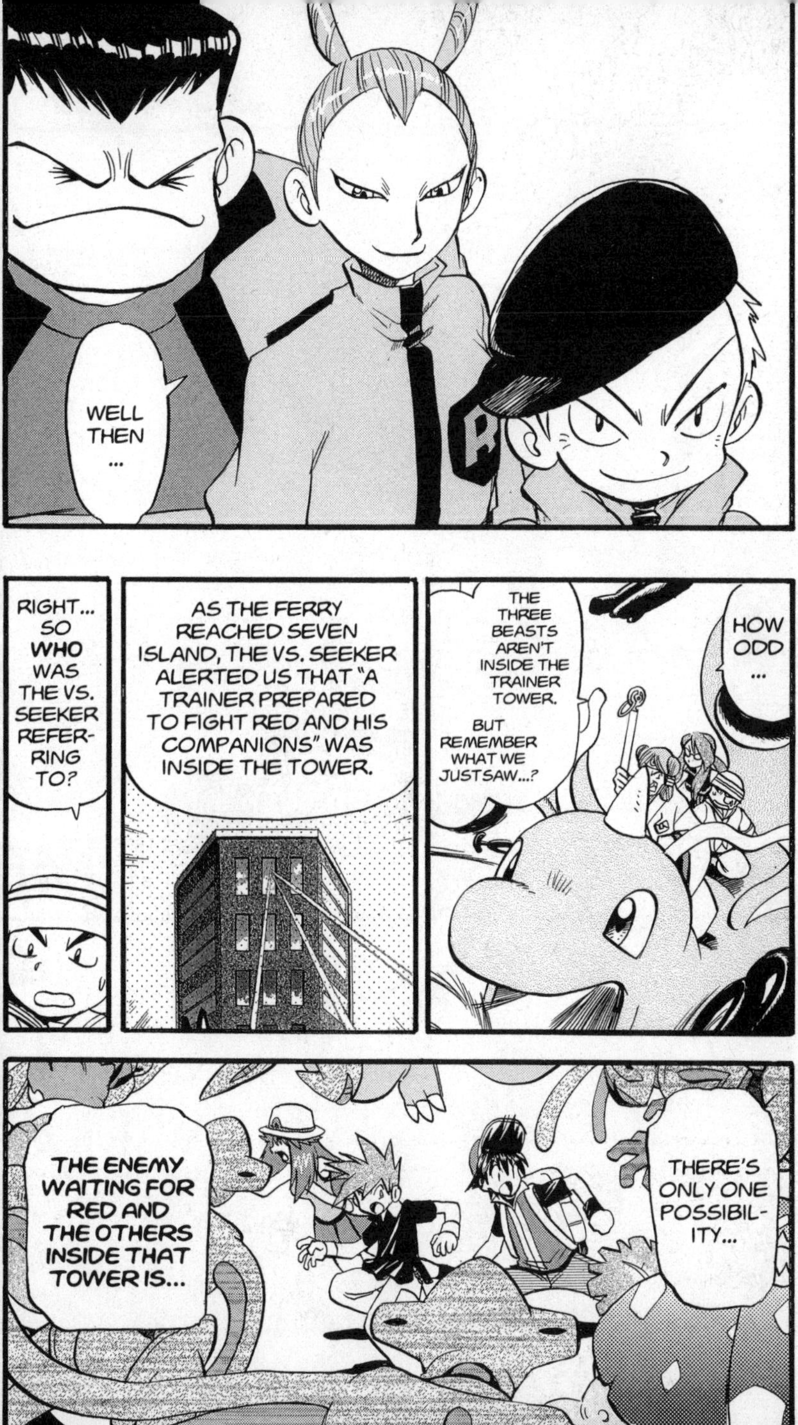
WELL THEN ...
HOW ODD ...
THE THREE BEASTS AREN'T INSIDE THE TRAINER TOWER.
BUT REMEMBER WHAT WE JUSTSAW...?
AS THE FERRY REACHED SEVEN ISLAND, THE VS. SEEKER ALERTED US THAT "A TRAINER PREPARED TO FIGHT RED AND HIS COMPANIONS" WAS INSIDE THE TOWER.
RIGHT... SO **WHO** WAS THE VS. SEEKER REFER-RING TO?
THERE'S ONLY ONE POSSIBIL-ITY...
THE ENEMY WAITING FOR RED AND THE OTHERS INSIDE THAT TOWER IS...

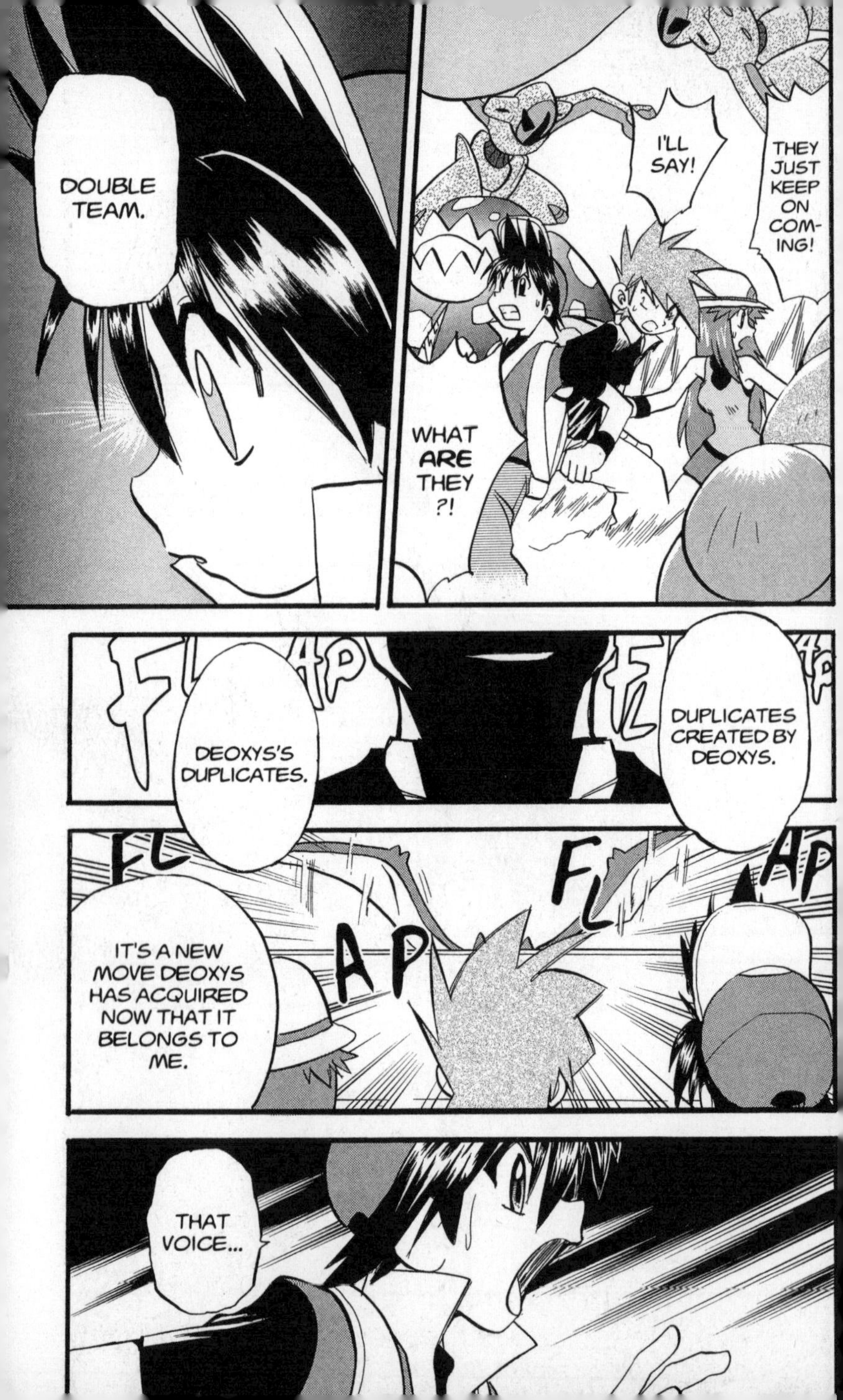
THEY JUST KEEP ON COMING!
I'LL SAY!
WHAT ARE THEY ?!
DOUBLE TEAM.
FLAP
FLAP
DUPLICATES CREATED BY DEOXYS.
DEOXYS'S DUPLICATES.
FLAP
FLAP
IT'S A NEW MOVE DEOXYS HAS ACQUIRED NOW THAT IT BELONGS TO ME.
THAT VOICE...

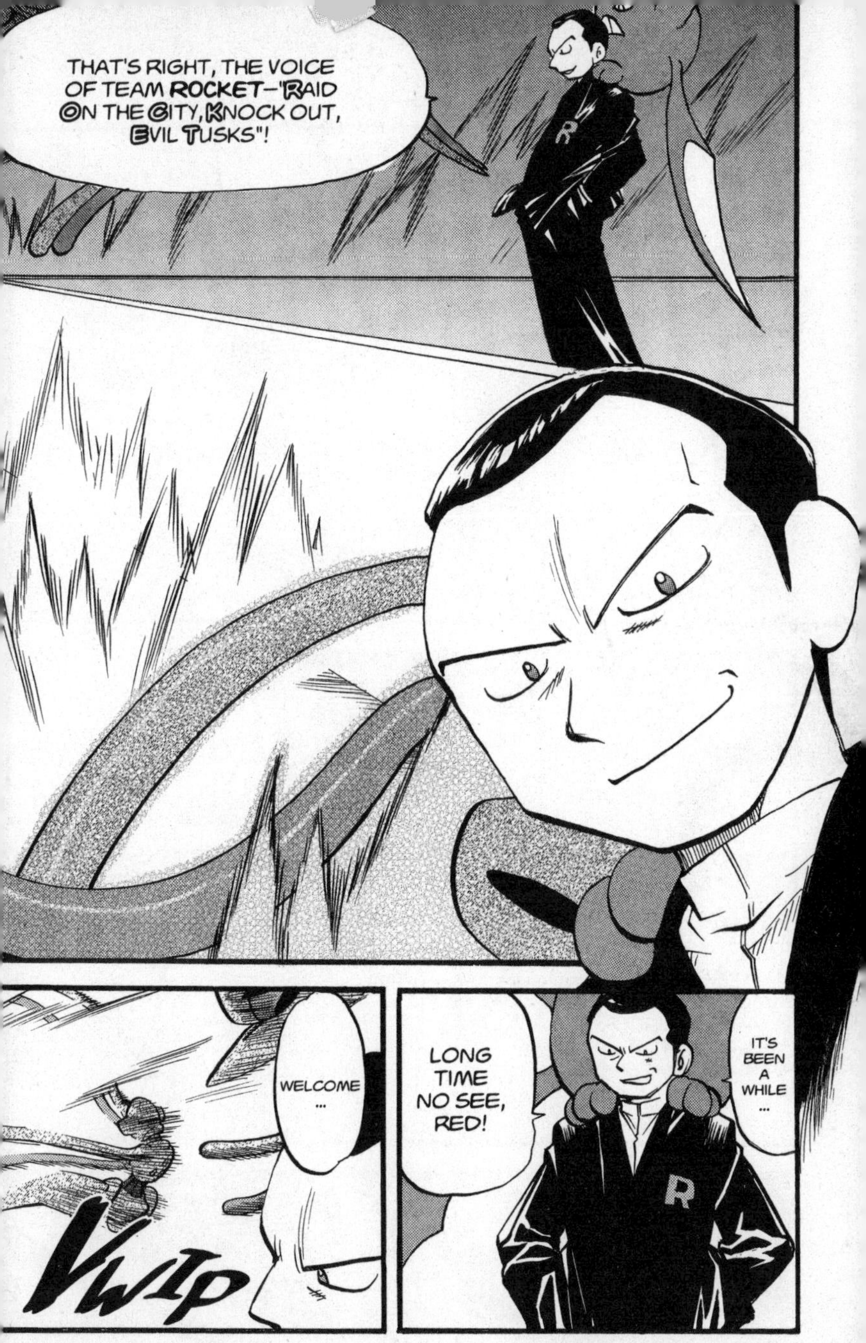

THAT'S RIGHT, THE VOICE OF TEAM ROCKET—"RAID ON THE CITY, KNOCK OUT, EVIL TUSKS"!
IT'S BEEN A WHILE ...
LONG TIME NO SEE, RED!
WELCOME ...
VWIP

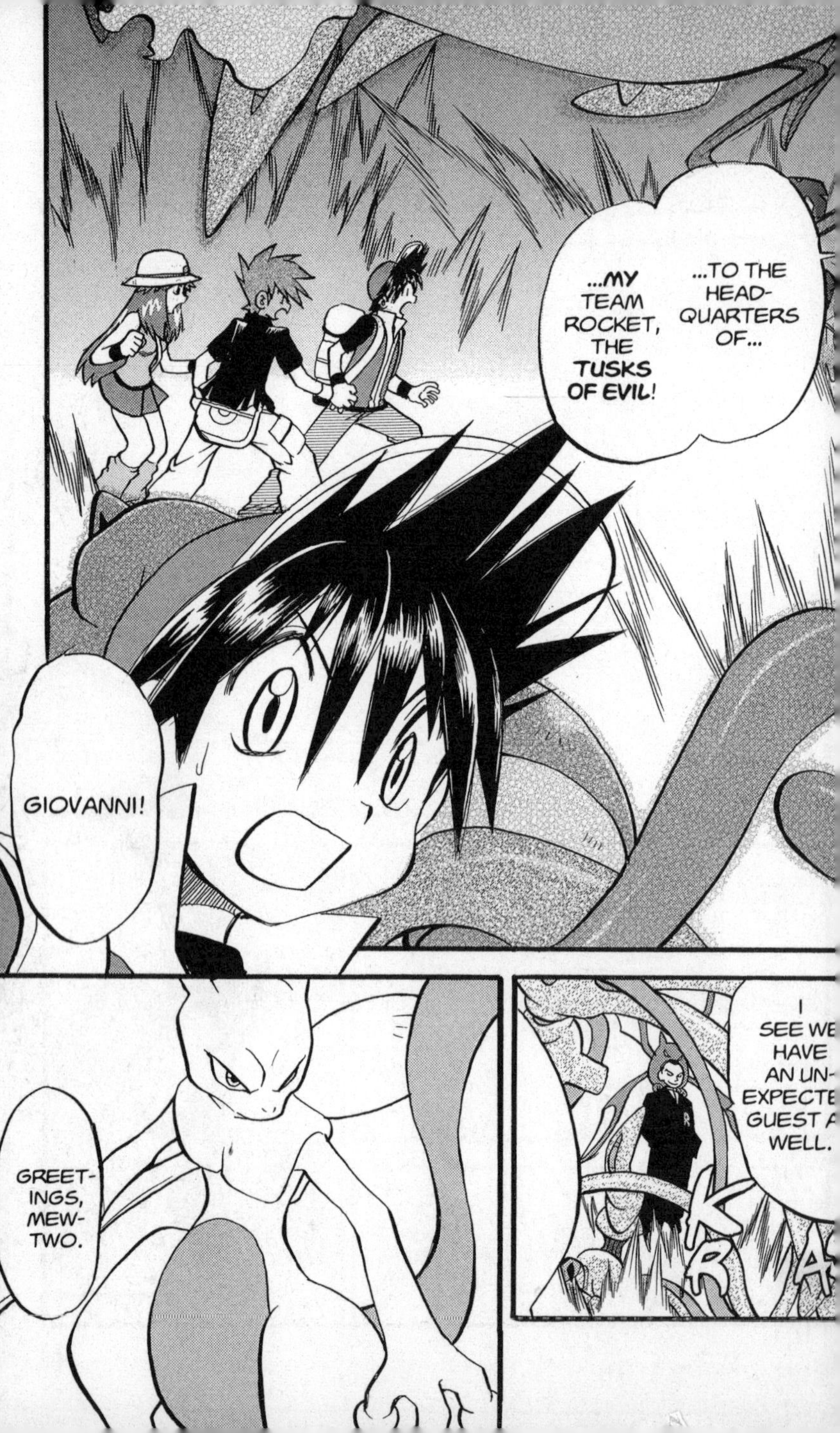
...TO THE HEAD-QUARTERS OF...
...MY TEAM ROCKET, THE TUSKS OF EVIL!
GIOVANNI!
I SEE WE HAVE AN UN-EXPECTE GUEST A WELL.
KRA
GREET-INGS, MEW-TWO.

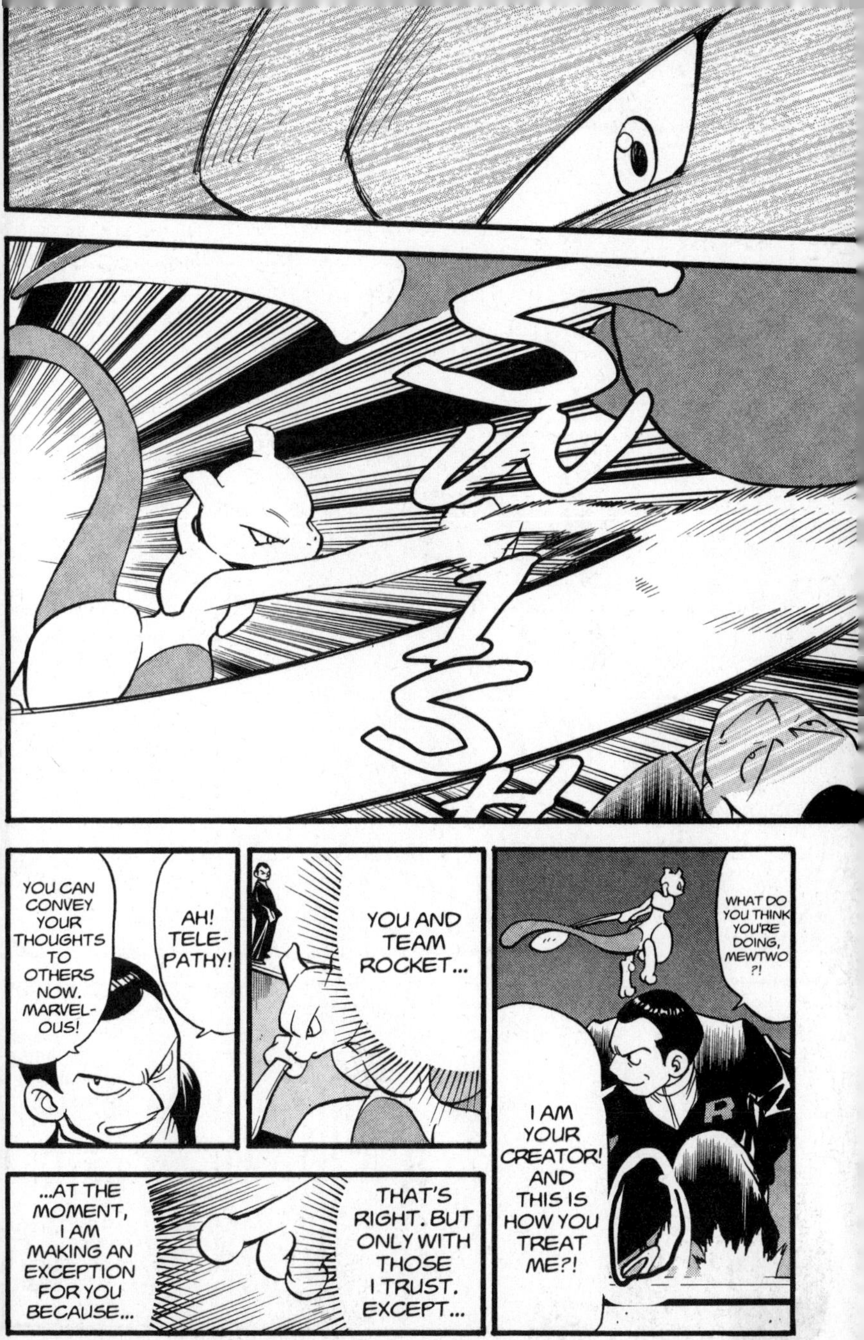
SWISH
WHAT DO YOU THINK YOU'RE DOING, MEWTWO?!
I AM YOUR CREATOR! AND THIS IS HOW YOU TREAT ME?!
YOU AND TEAM ROCKET...
AH! TELE-PATHY!
YOU CAN CONVEY YOUR THOUGHTS TO OTHERS NOW. MARVEL-OUS!
THAT'S RIGHT. BUT ONLY WITH THOSE I TRUST. EXCEPT...
...AT THE MOMENT, I AM MAKING AN EXCEPTION FOR YOU BECAUSE...

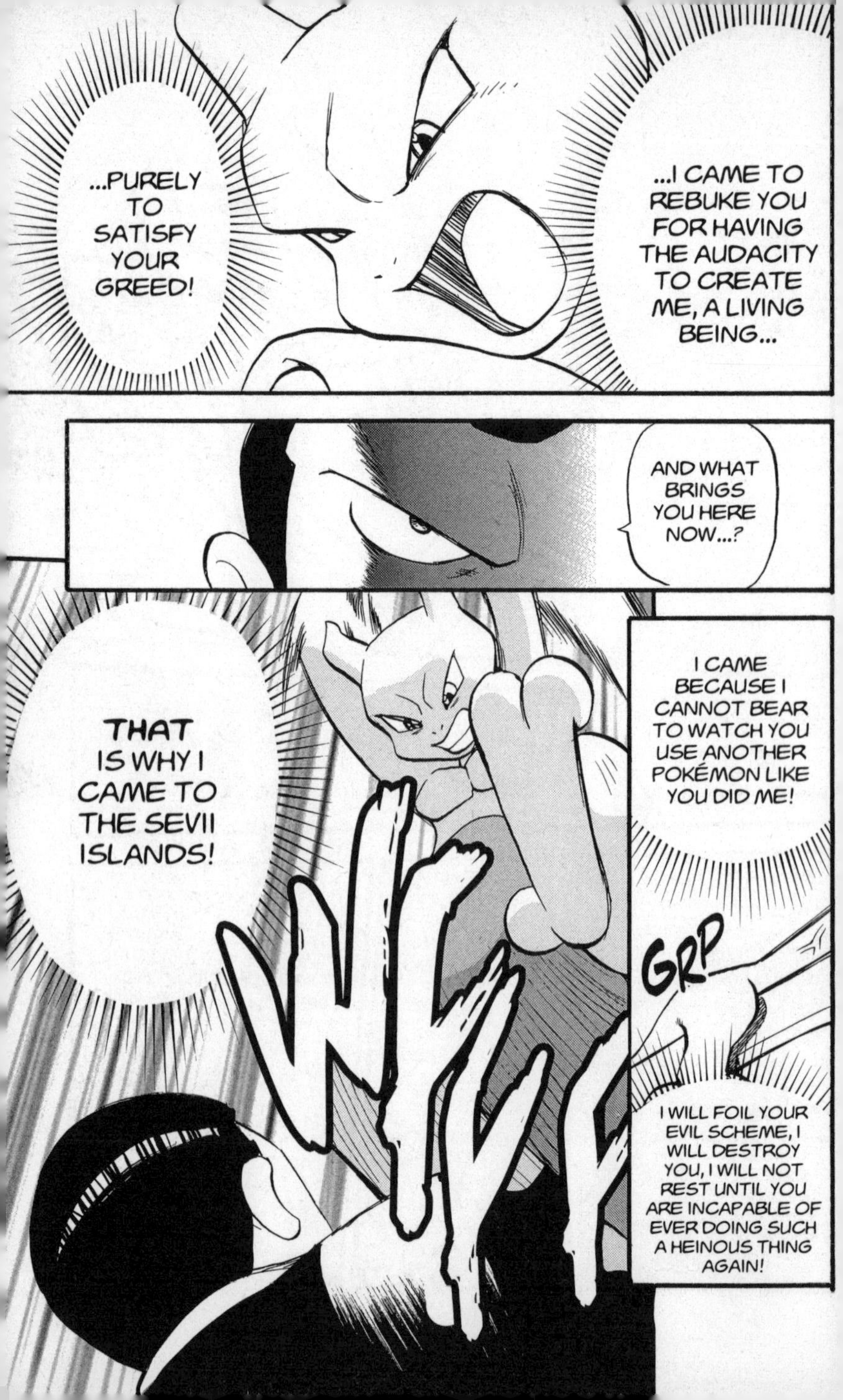
...I CAME TO REBUKE YOU FOR HAVING THE AUDACITY TO CREATE ME, A LIVING BEING...
...PURELY TO SATISFY YOUR GREED!
AND WHAT BRINGS YOU HERE NOW...?
I CAME BECAUSE I CANNOT BEAR TO WATCH YOU USE ANOTHER POKÉMON LIKE YOU DID ME!
THAT IS WHY I CAME TO THE SEVII ISLANDS!
GRP
I WILL FOIL YOUR EVIL SCHEME, I WILL DESTROY YOU, I WILL NOT REST UNTIL YOU ARE INCAPABLE OF EVER DOING SUCH A HEINOUS THING AGAIN!

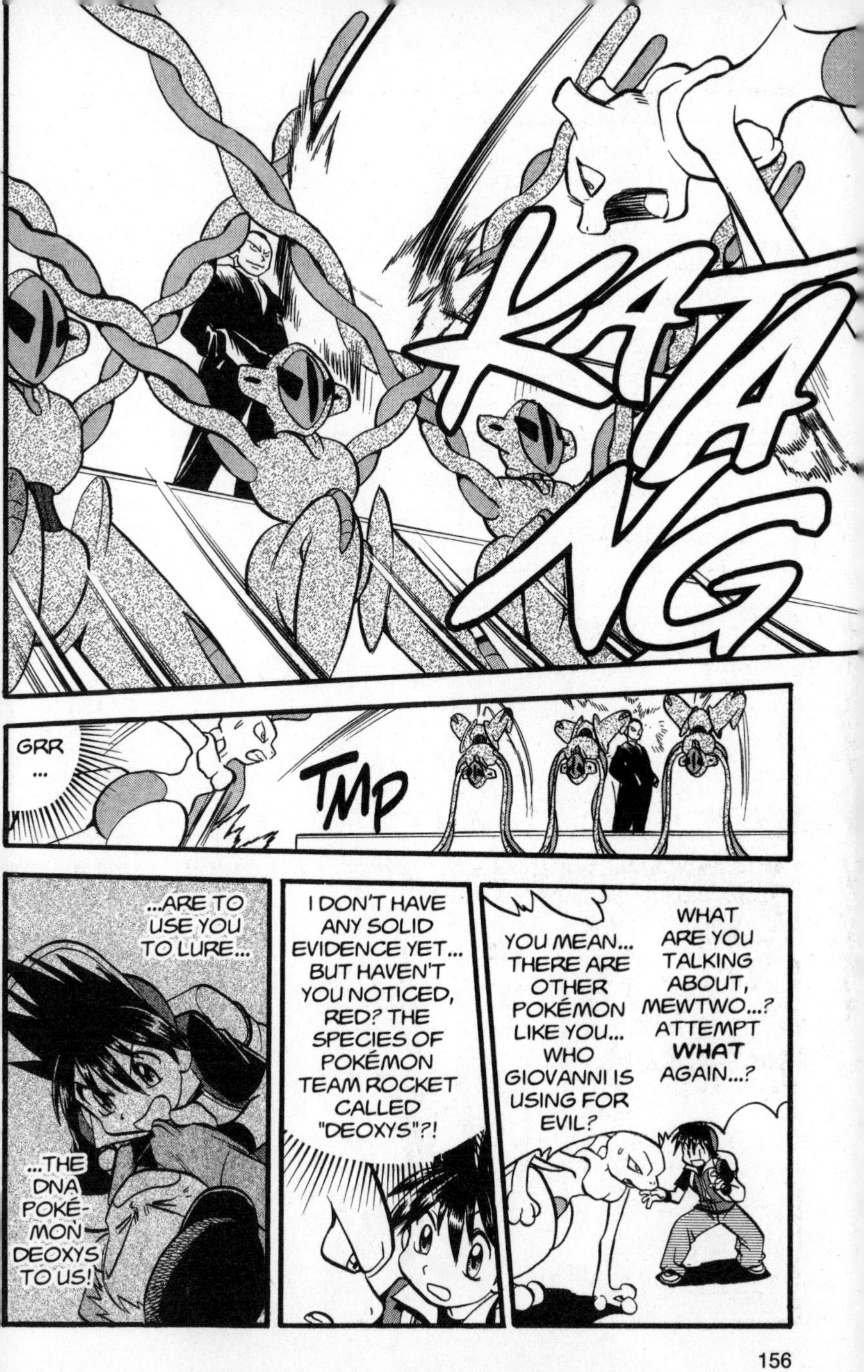
KAZANG
TMP
GRR ...
WHAT ARE YOU TALKING ABOUT, MEWTWO...? ATTEMPT **WHAT** AGAIN...?
YOU MEAN... THERE ARE OTHER POKÉMON LIKE YOU... WHO GIOVANNI IS USING FOR EVIL?
I DON'T HAVE ANY SOLID EVIDENCE YET... BUT HAVEN'T YOU NOTICED, RED? THE SPECIES OF POKÉMON TEAM ROCKET CALLED "DEOXYS"?!
...ARE TO USE YOU TO LURE...
...THE DNA POKÉ-MON DEOXYS TO US!

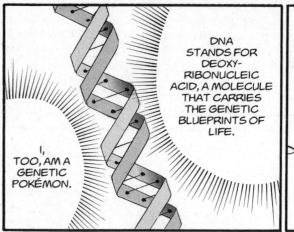

A DNA POKÉMON ...
DNA STANDS FOR DEOXY-RIBONUCLEIC ACID, A MOLECULE THAT CARRIES THE GENETIC BLUEPRINTS OF LIFE.
I, TOO, AM A GENETIC POKÉMON.
DNA POKÉMON AND GENETIC POKÉMON ARE SIMILAR SPECIES' NAMES.
THAT IS WHAT HAS BEEN WEIGHING HEAVILY ON MY MIND.
SO YOU SEE **YOURSELF** IN DEOXYS, DO YOU?
BUT YOU AND DEOXYS ARE VERY DIFFER-ENT...
LET ME EXPLAIN ...
A CERTAIN SPACE VIRUS WAS EXPOSED TO A LASER BEAM...
...AND THAT VIRUS MUTATED INTO THIS POKÉMON—ONE THAT NO ONE HAD EVER SEEN BEFORE.

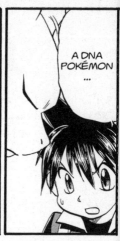

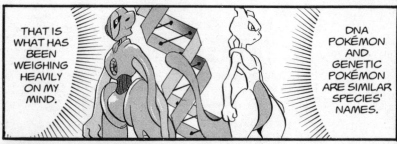

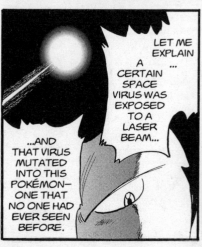

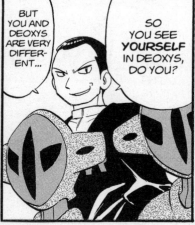

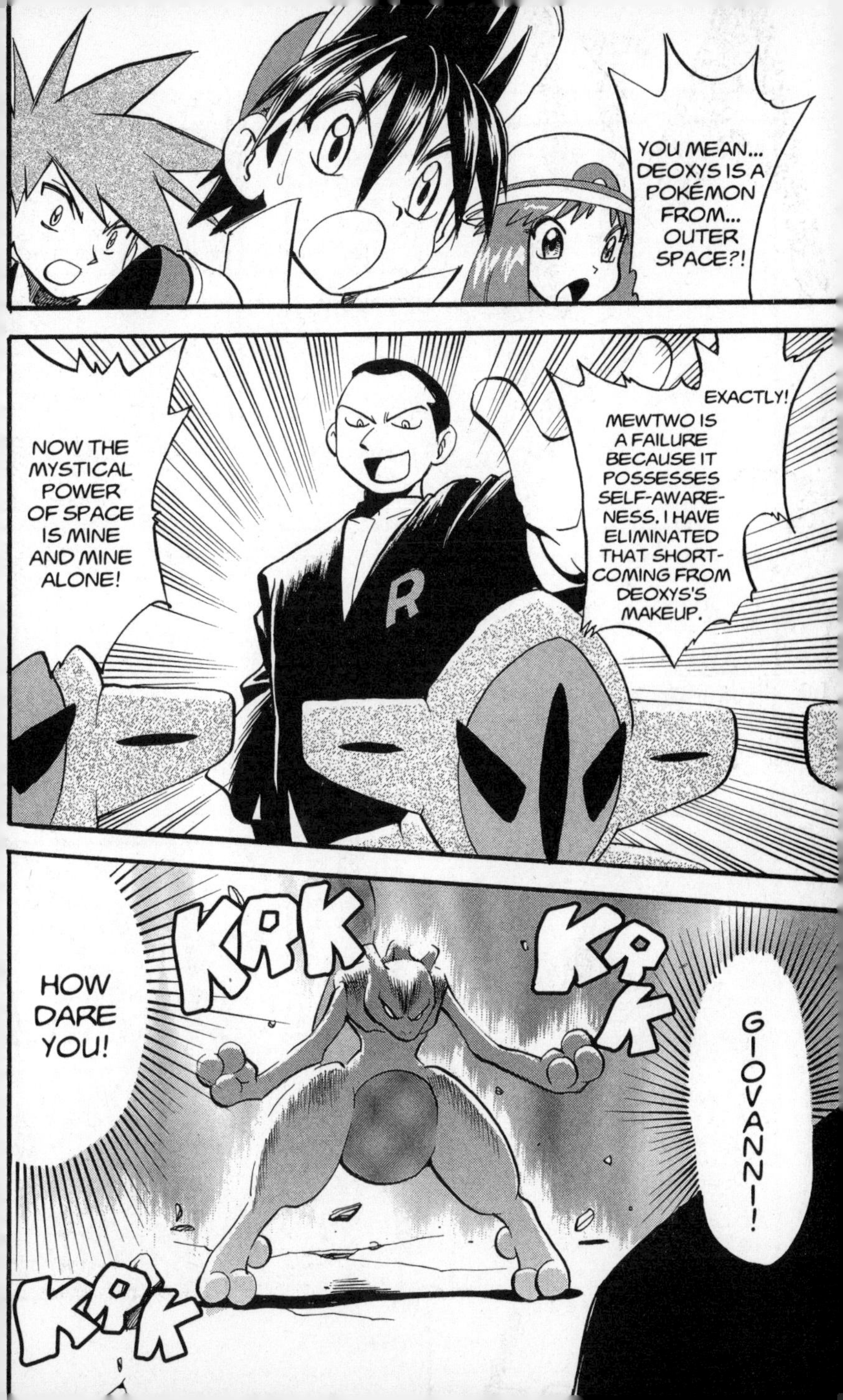

YOU MEAN... DEOXYS IS A POKÉMON FROM... OUTER SPACE?!
EXACTLY!
MEWTWO IS A FAILURE BECAUSE IT POSSESSES SELF-AWARE-NESS. I HAVE ELIMINATED THAT SHORT-COMING FROM DEOXYS'S MAKEUP.
NOW THE MYSTICAL POWER OF SPACE IS MINE AND MINE ALONE!
R
KRK
GIOVANNI!
KRK
HOW DARE YOU!
KRK

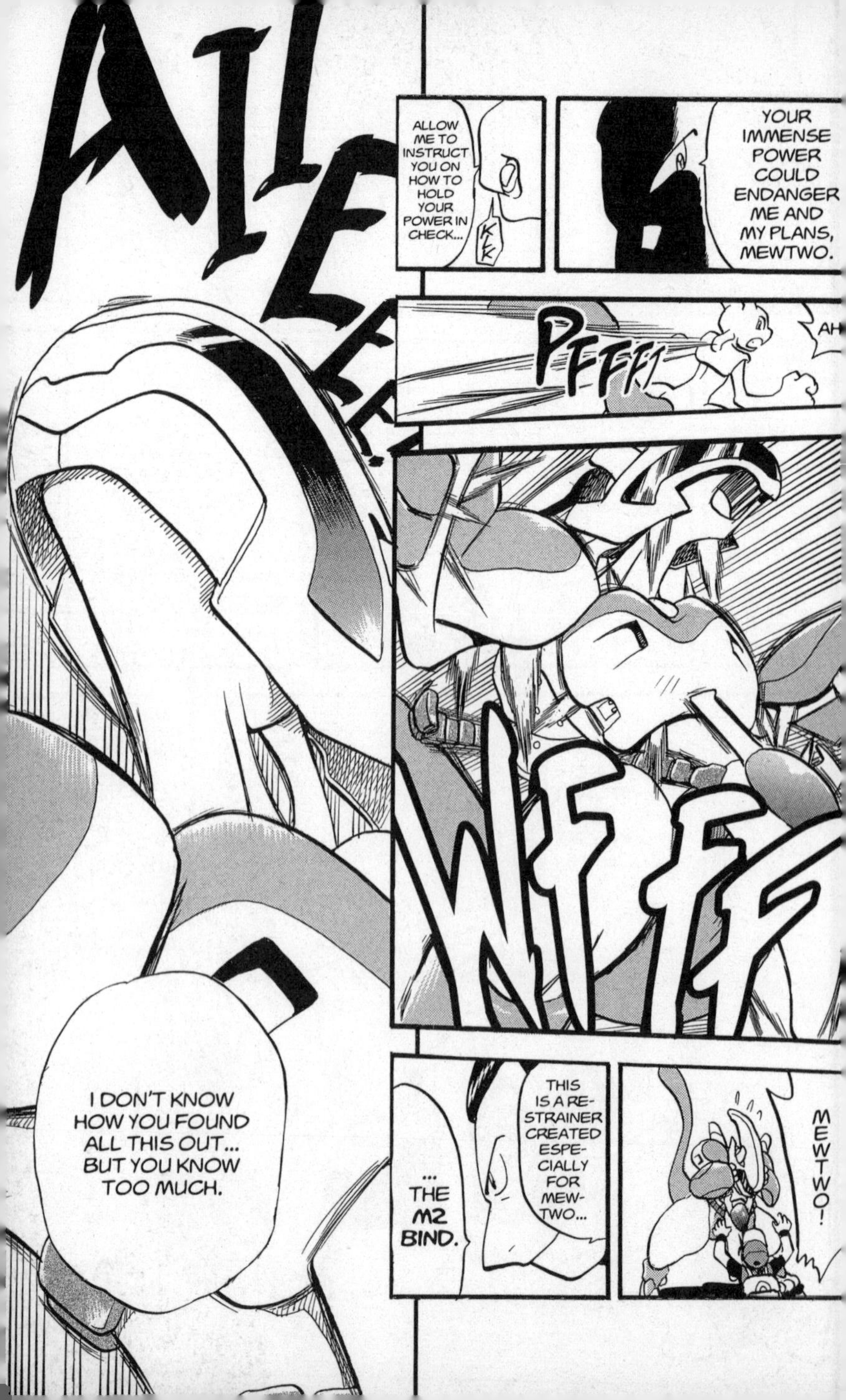
YOUR IMMENSE POWER COULD ENDANGER ME AND MY PLANS, MEWTWO.
ALLOW ME TO INSTRUCT YOU ON HOW TO HOLD YOUR POWER IN CHECK...
KKK
AH
PFFFT
WIFF
MEWTWO!
THIS IS A RE-STRAINER CREATED ESPE-CIALLY FOR MEW-TWO...
...THE M2 BIND.
AIIEE
I DON'T KNOW HOW YOU FOUND ALL THIS OUT... BUT YOU KNOW TOO MUCH.

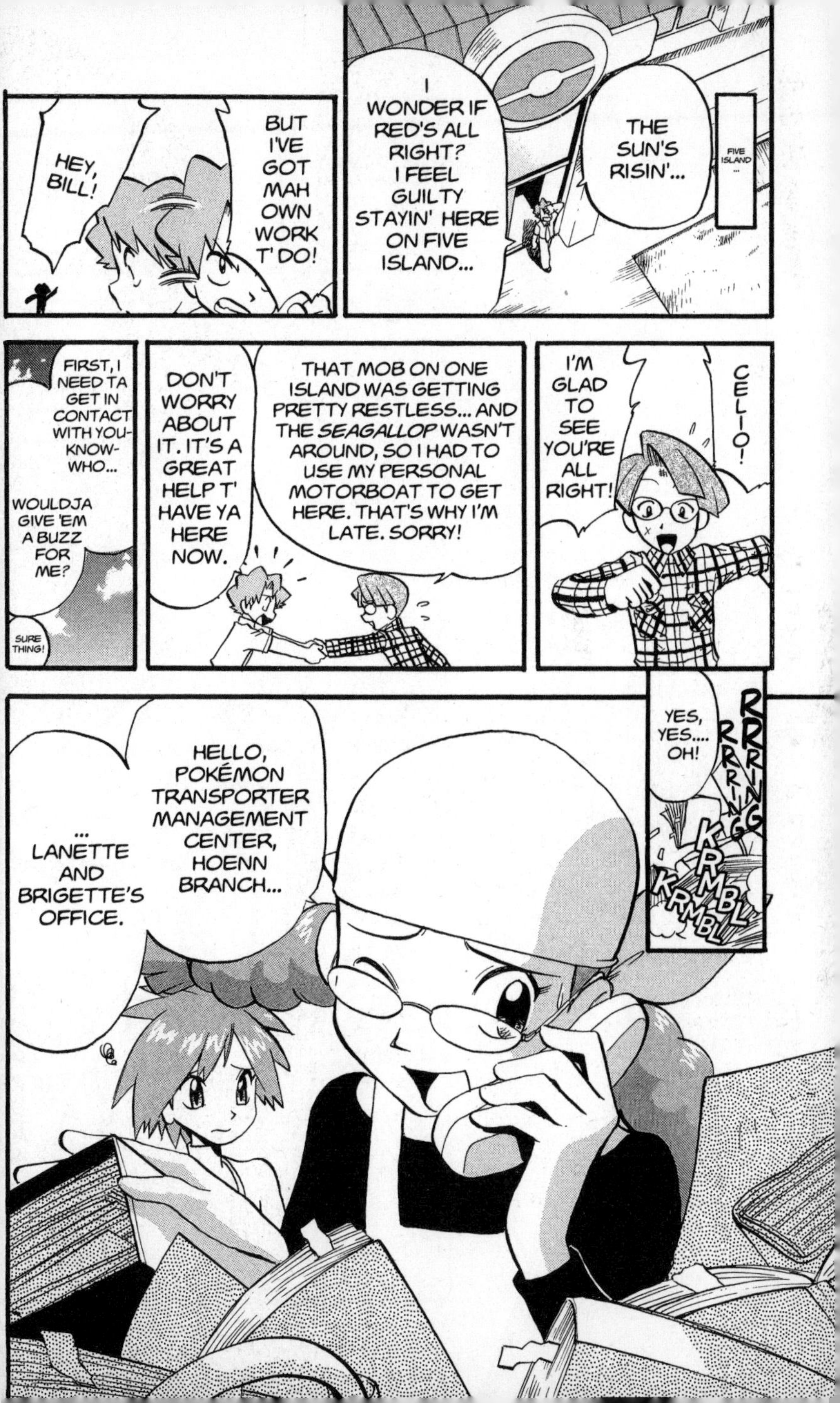
FIVE ISLAND ...
THE SUN'S RISIN'...
I WONDER IF RED'S ALL RIGHT? I FEEL GUILTY STAYIN' HERE ON FIVE ISLAND...
BUT I'VE GOT MAH OWN WORK T' DO!
HEY, BILL!
CELIO!
I'M GLAD TO SEE YOU'RE ALL RIGHT!
THAT MOB ON ONE ISLAND WAS GETTING PRETTY RESTLESS... AND THE *SEAGALLOP* WASN'T AROUND, SO I HAD TO USE MY PERSONAL MOTORBOAT TO GET HERE. THAT'S WHY I'M LATE. SORRY!
DON'T WORRY ABOUT IT. IT'S A GREAT HELP T' HAVE YA HERE NOW.
FIRST, I NEED TA GET IN CONTACT WITH YOU-KNOW-WHO...
WOULDJA GIVE 'EM A BUZZ FOR ME?
SURE THING!
RRRING
RRRING
YES, YES.... OH!
KRMBL
KRMBL
HELLO, POKéMON TRANSPORTER MANAGEMENT CENTER, HOENN BRANCH...
... LANETTE AND BRIGETTE'S OFFICE.

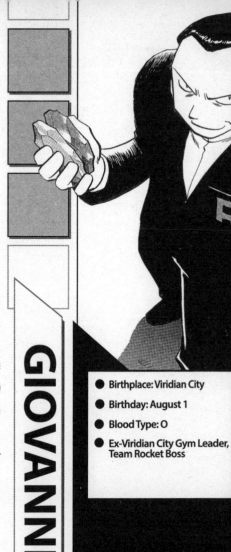

GIOVANNI

- Birthplace: Viridian City
- Birthday: August 1
- Blood Type: O
- Ex-Viridian City Gym Leader, Team Rocket Boss

GIOVANNI FOUNDED THE SECRET SYNDICATE TEAM ROCKET, WHICH IS OFTEN AT WORK BEHIND THE SCENES IN THE KANTO REGION—AND NOT FOR THE BENEFIT OF ITS CITIZENS! HE WAS ONCE THE GYM LEADER OF VIRIDIAN CITY GYM, IS A SPECIALIST IN GROUND-TYPE POKÉMON, AND IS KNOWN AS "GIOVANNI OF THE LAND." GIOVANNI SET OUT ON A JOURNEY TO IMPROVE HIS SKILLS AFTER HIS BATTLE AGAINST RED FIVE YEARS AGO WHEN TEAM ROCKET WAS TEMPORARILY DISBANDED. NOW TEAM ROCKET HAS RISEN AGAIN WITH NEW MEMBERS—INCLUDING THE THREE BEASTS: SIRD, CARR AND ORM—AND HAS CAPTURED DEOXYS ON THE SEVII ISLANDS. GIOVANNI SUCCESFULLY USED RED WITHOUT HIS KNOWLEDGE TO GATHER DATA ON DEOXYS AND CAPTURE IT. WHAT IS GIOVANNI'S ULTIMATE MOTIVE?!

•Adventure 287•
Secrets from Sneasel

POKéMON ADVENTURES
FIRERED & LEAFGREEN
The Fifth Chapter

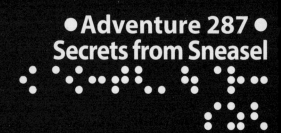

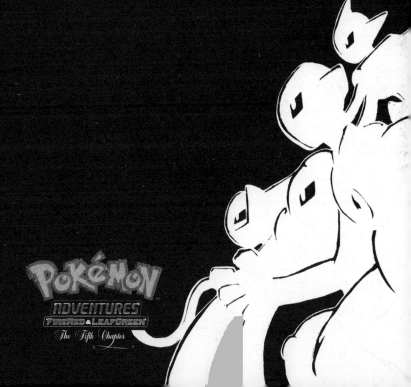

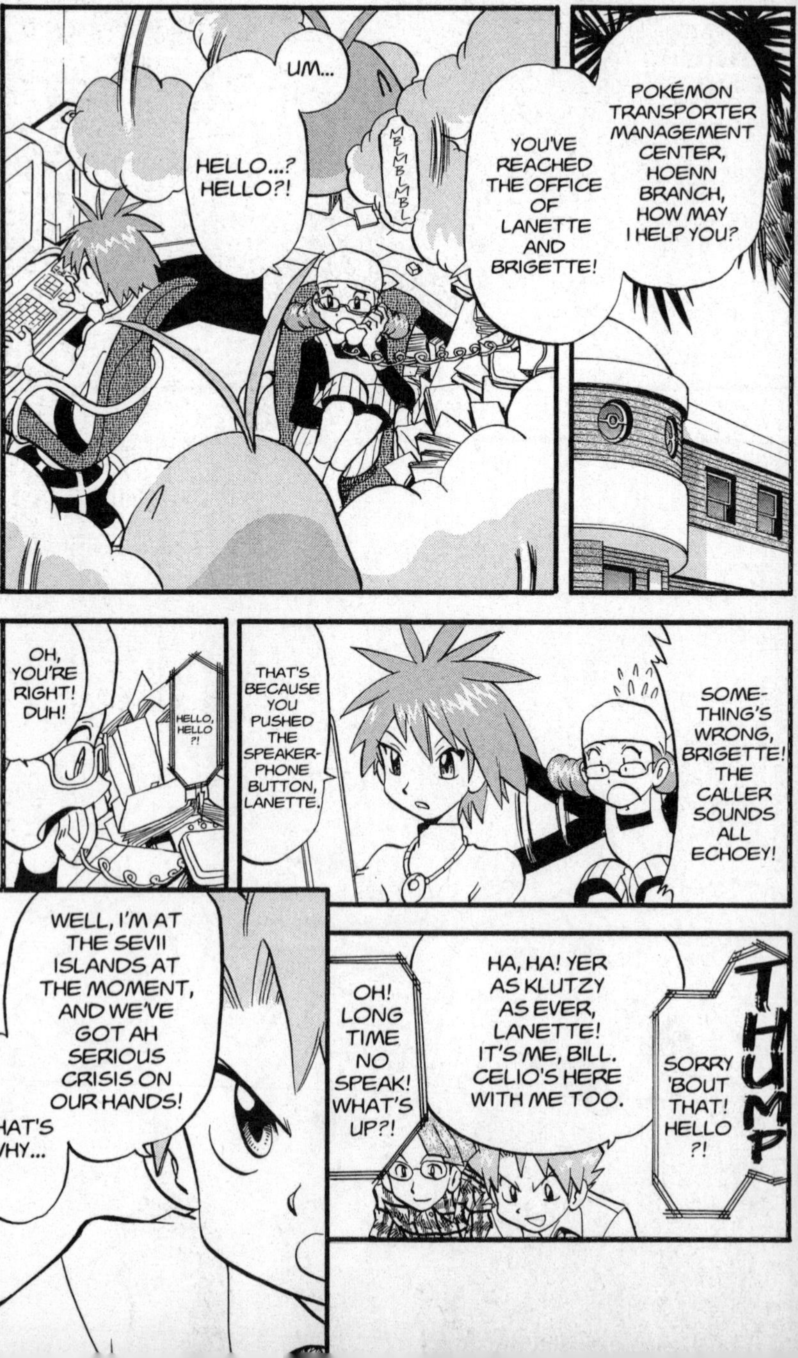

POKÉMON TRANSPORTER MANAGEMENT CENTER, HOENN BRANCH, HOW MAY I HELP YOU?
YOU'VE REACHED THE OFFICE OF LANETTE AND BRIGETTE!
MBLMBLMBL
UM...
HELLO...? HELLO?!
SOME-THING'S WRONG, BRIGETTE! THE CALLER SOUNDS ALL ECHOEY!
THAT'S BECAUSE YOU PUSHED THE SPEAKER-PHONE BUTTON, LANETTE.
HELLO, HELLO ?!
OH, YOU'RE RIGHT! DUH!
THUMP
SORRY 'BOUT THAT! HELLO ?!
HA, HA! YER AS KLUTZY AS EVER, LANETTE! IT'S ME, BILL. CELIO'S HERE WITH ME TOO.
OH! LONG TIME NO SPEAK! WHAT'S UP?!
WELL, I'M AT THE SEVII ISLANDS AT THE MOMENT, AND WE'VE GOT AH SERIOUS CRISIS ON OUR HANDS!
THAT'S WHY...

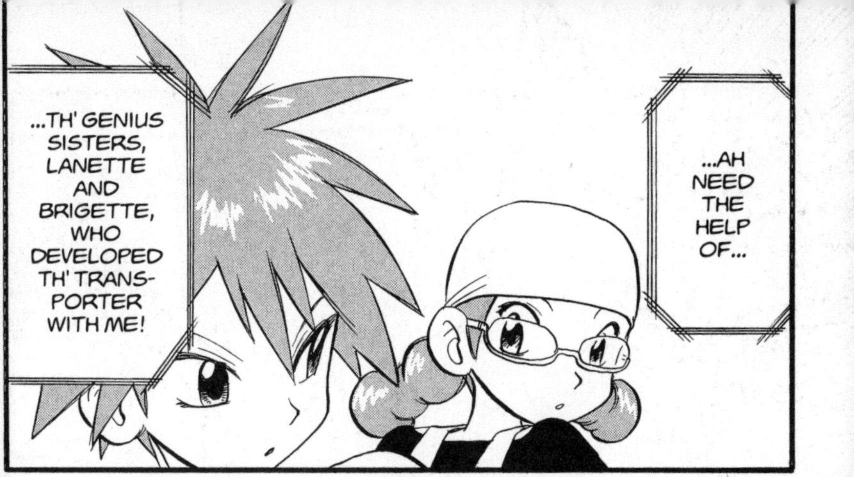
...AH NEED THE HELP OF...
...TH' GENIUS SISTERS, LANETTE AND BRIGETTE, WHO DEVELOPED TH' TRANS-PORTER WITH ME!
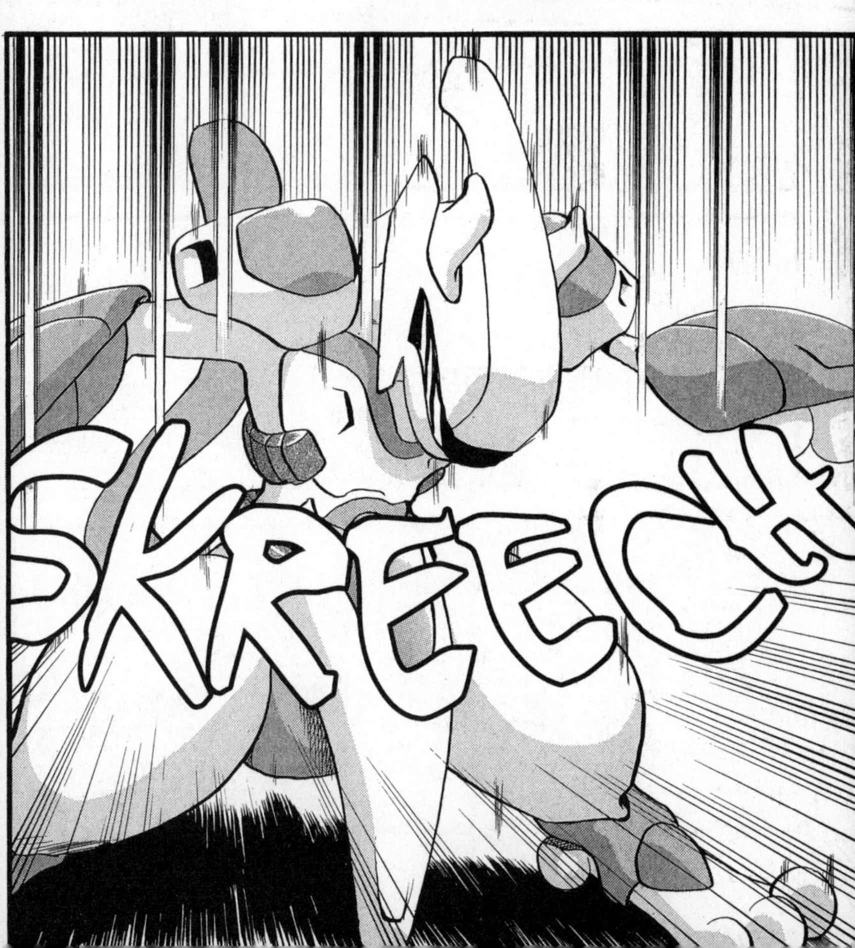
SKREECH

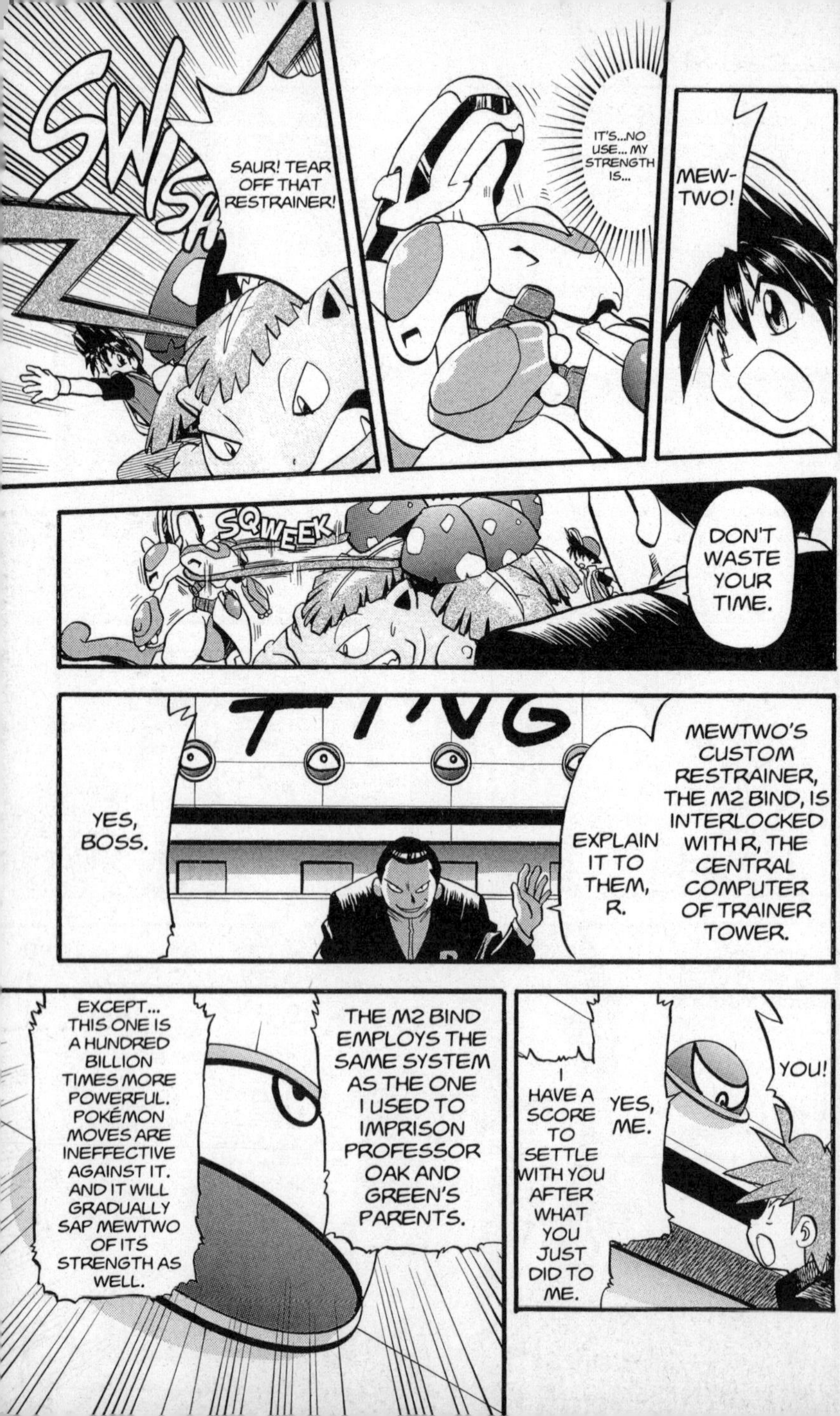
MEW-TWO!
IT'S...NO USE... MY STRENGTH IS...
SAUR! TEAR OFF THAT RESTRAINER!
SWISH
DON'T WASTE YOUR TIME.
SQWEEK
MEWTWO'S CUSTOM RESTRAINER, THE M2 BIND, IS INTERLOCKED WITH R, THE CENTRAL COMPUTER OF TRAINER TOWER.
EXPLAIN IT TO THEM, R.
TING
YES, BOSS.
YOU!
YES, ME.
I HAVE A SCORE TO SETTLE WITH YOU AFTER WHAT YOU JUST DID TO ME.
THE M2 BIND EMPLOYS THE SAME SYSTEM AS THE ONE I USED TO IMPRISON PROFESSOR OAK AND GREEN'S PARENTS.
EXCEPT... THIS ONE IS A HUNDRED BILLION TIMES MORE POWERFUL. POKÉMON MOVES ARE INEFFECTIVE AGAINST IT. AND IT WILL GRADUALLY SAP MEWTWO OF ITS STRENGTH AS WELL.

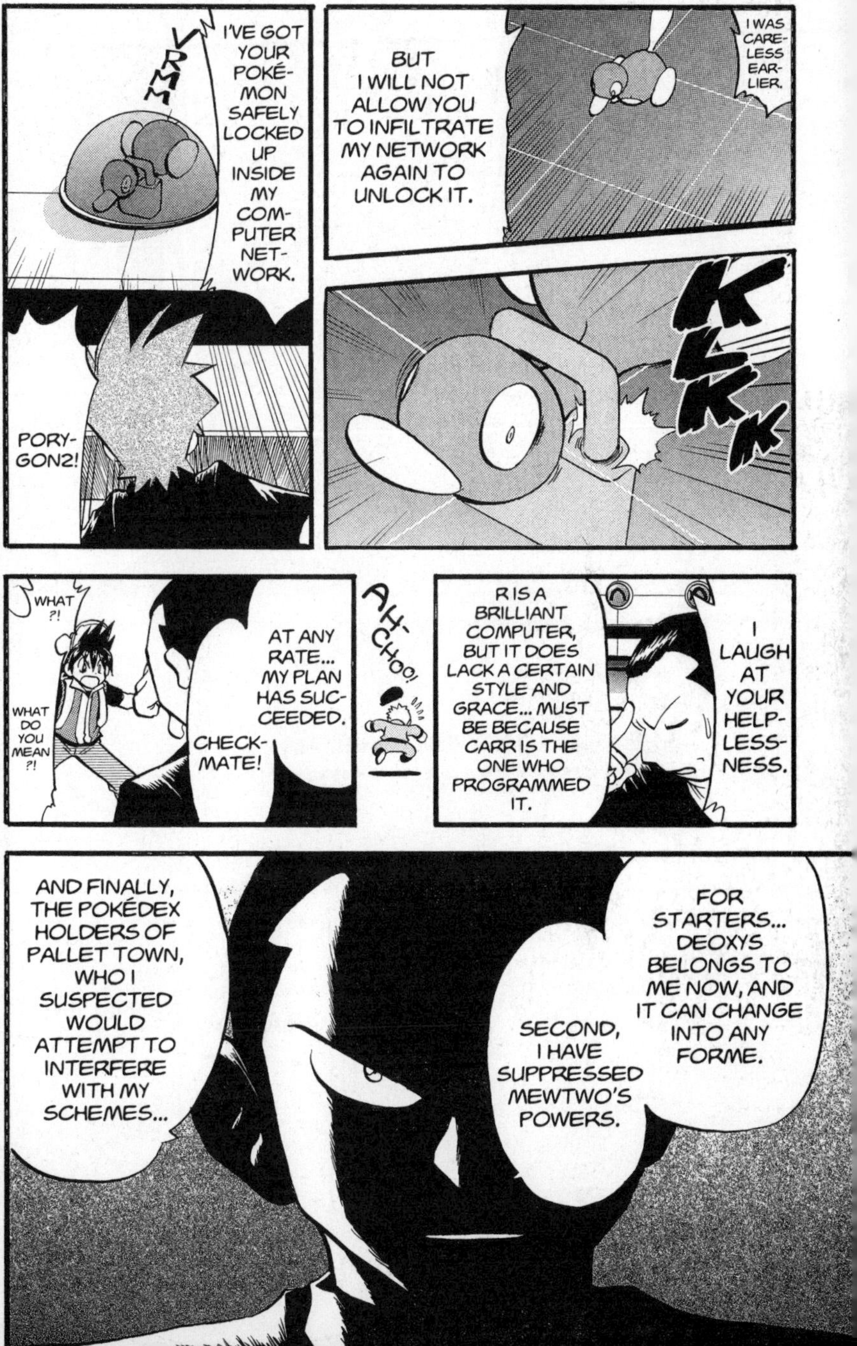
I WAS CARELESS EARLIER.
BUT I WILL NOT ALLOW YOU TO INFILTRATE MY NETWORK AGAIN TO UNLOCK IT.
VRMM
I'VE GOT YOUR POKÉMON SAFELY LOCKED UP INSIDE MY COMPUTER NETWORK.
KKKK
PORYGON2!
I LAUGH AT YOUR HELPLESSNESS.
R IS A BRILLIANT COMPUTER, BUT IT DOES LACK A CERTAIN STYLE AND GRACE... MUST BE BECAUSE CARR IS THE ONE WHO PROGRAMMED IT.
AH-CHOO!
AT ANY RATE... MY PLAN HAS SUCCEEDED.
CHECKMATE!
WHAT?!
WHAT DO YOU MEAN?!
FOR STARTERS... DEOXYS BELONGS TO ME NOW, AND IT CAN CHANGE INTO ANY FORME.
SECOND, I HAVE SUPPRESSED MEWTWO'S POWERS.
AND FINALLY, THE POKÉDEX HOLDERS OF PALLET TOWN, WHO I SUSPECTED WOULD ATTEMPT TO INTERFERE WITH MY SCHEMES...

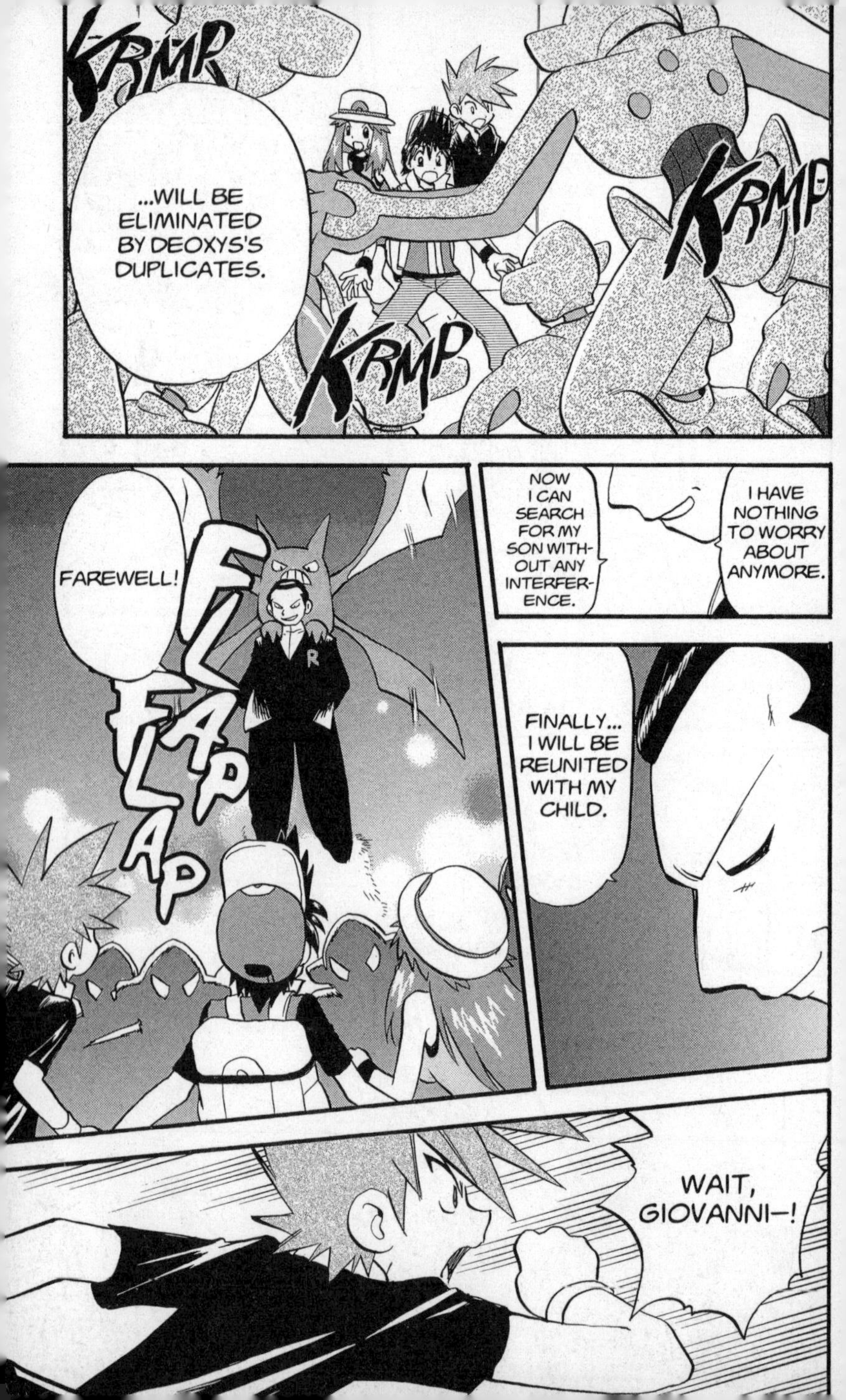
KRMP
KRMP
...WILL BE ELIMINATED BY DEOXYS'S DUPLICATES.
KRMP
I HAVE NOTHING TO WORRY ABOUT ANYMORE.
NOW I CAN SEARCH FOR MY SON WITH-OUT ANY INTERFER-ENCE.
FINALLY... I WILL BE REUNITED WITH MY CHILD.
FAREWELL!
FLAP
FLAP
WAIT, GIOVANNI—!

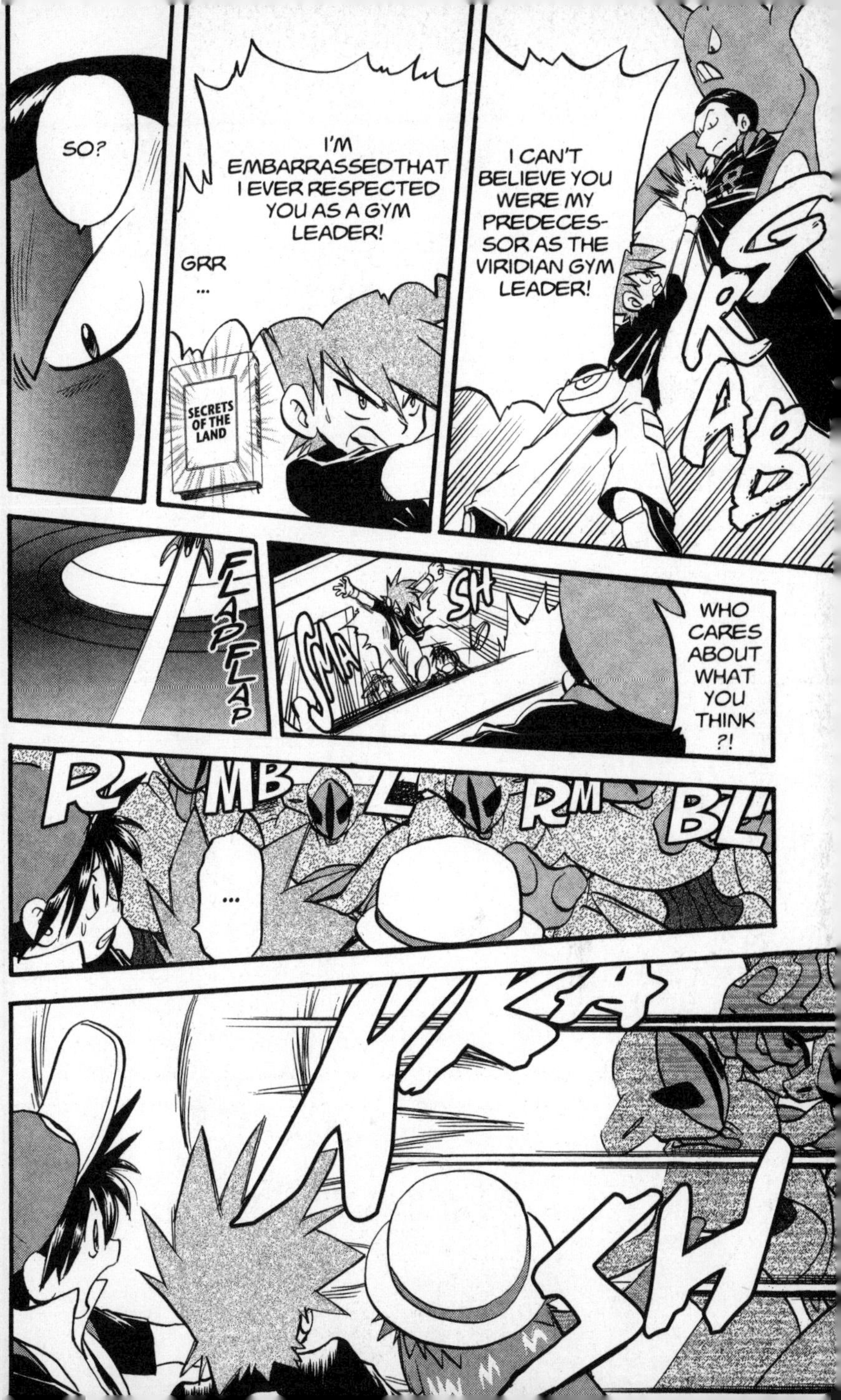
GRAB
I CAN'T BELIEVE YOU WERE MY PREDECES-SOR AS THE VIRIDIAN GYM LEADER!
I'M EMBARRASSED THAT I EVER RESPECTED YOU AS A GYM LEADER!
GRR ...
SECRETS OF THE LAND
SO?
WHO CARES ABOUT WHAT YOU THINK ?!
SH
SMA
FLAP FLAP
R MB L RM BL
...
SH

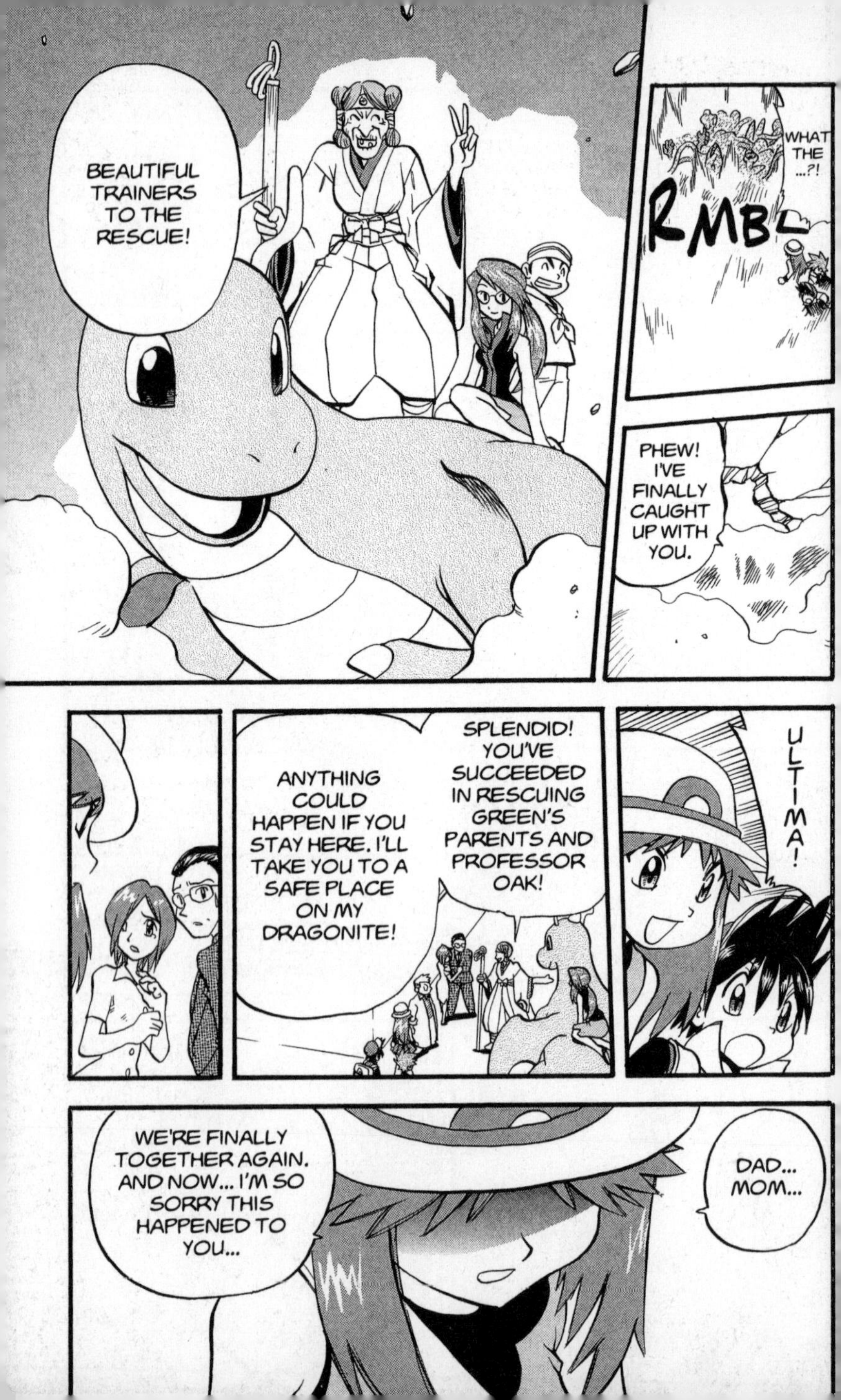
WHAT THE ...?!
RMBL
PHEW! I'VE FINALLY CAUGHT UP WITH YOU.
BEAUTIFUL TRAINERS TO THE RESCUE!
ULTIMA!
SPLENDID! YOU'VE SUCCEEDED IN RESCUING GREEN'S PARENTS AND PROFESSOR OAK!
ANYTHING COULD HAPPEN IF YOU STAY HERE. I'LL TAKE YOU TO A SAFE PLACE ON MY DRAGONITE!
DAD... MOM...
WE'RE FINALLY TOGETHER AGAIN. AND NOW... I'M SO SORRY THIS HAPPENED TO YOU...

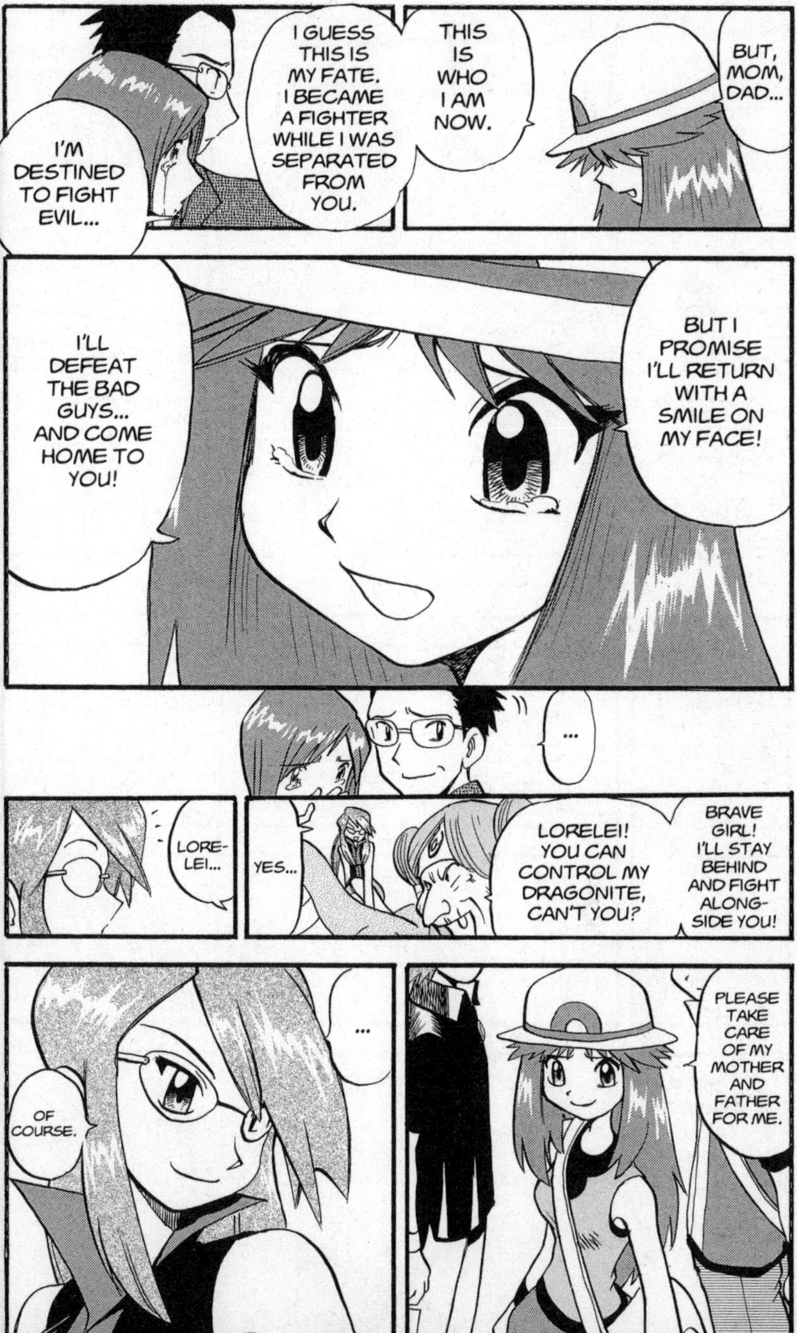
BUT, MOM, DAD...
THIS IS WHO I AM NOW.
I GUESS THIS IS MY FATE. I BECAME A FIGHTER WHILE I WAS SEPARATED FROM YOU.
I'M DESTINED TO FIGHT EVIL...
BUT I PROMISE I'LL RETURN WITH A SMILE ON MY FACE!
I'LL DEFEAT THE BAD GUYS... AND COME HOME TO YOU!
...
BRAVE GIRL! I'LL STAY BEHIND AND FIGHT ALONG-SIDE YOU!
LORELEI! YOU CAN CONTROL MY DRAGONITE, CAN'T YOU?
YES...
LORE-LEI...
PLEASE TAKE CARE OF MY MOTHER AND FATHER FOR ME.
...
OF COURSE.

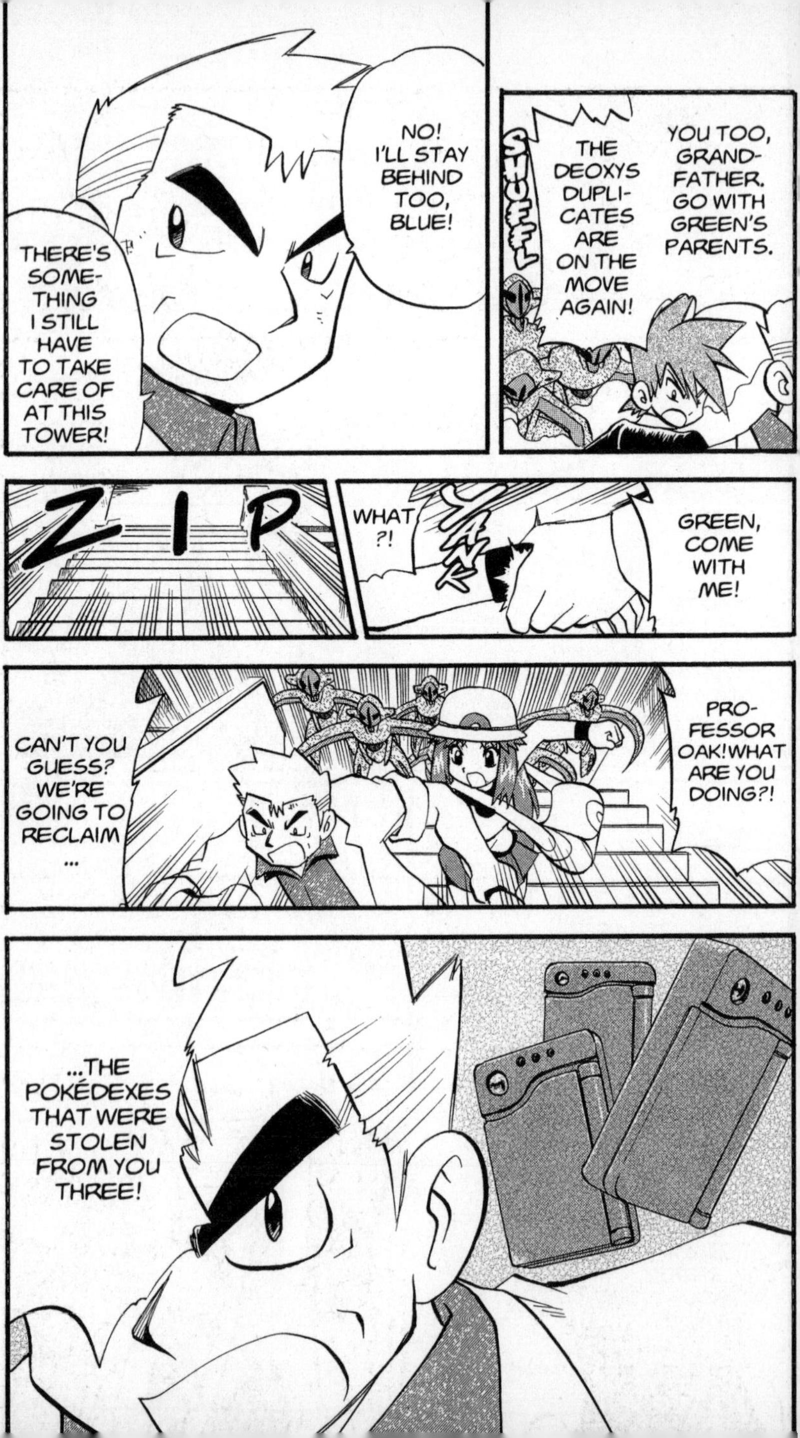
YOU TOO, GRANDFATHER. GO WITH GREEN'S PARENTS.
THE DEOXYS DUPLICATES ARE ON THE MOVE AGAIN!
SHUFFL
NO! I'LL STAY BEHIND TOO, BLUE!
THERE'S SOMETHING I STILL HAVE TO TAKE CARE OF AT THIS TOWER!
GREEN, COME WITH ME!
YANK
WHAT?!
ZIP
PROFESSOR OAK! WHAT ARE YOU DOING?!
CAN'T YOU GUESS? WE'RE GOING TO RECLAIM...
...THE POKÉDEXES THAT WERE STOLEN FROM YOU THREE!

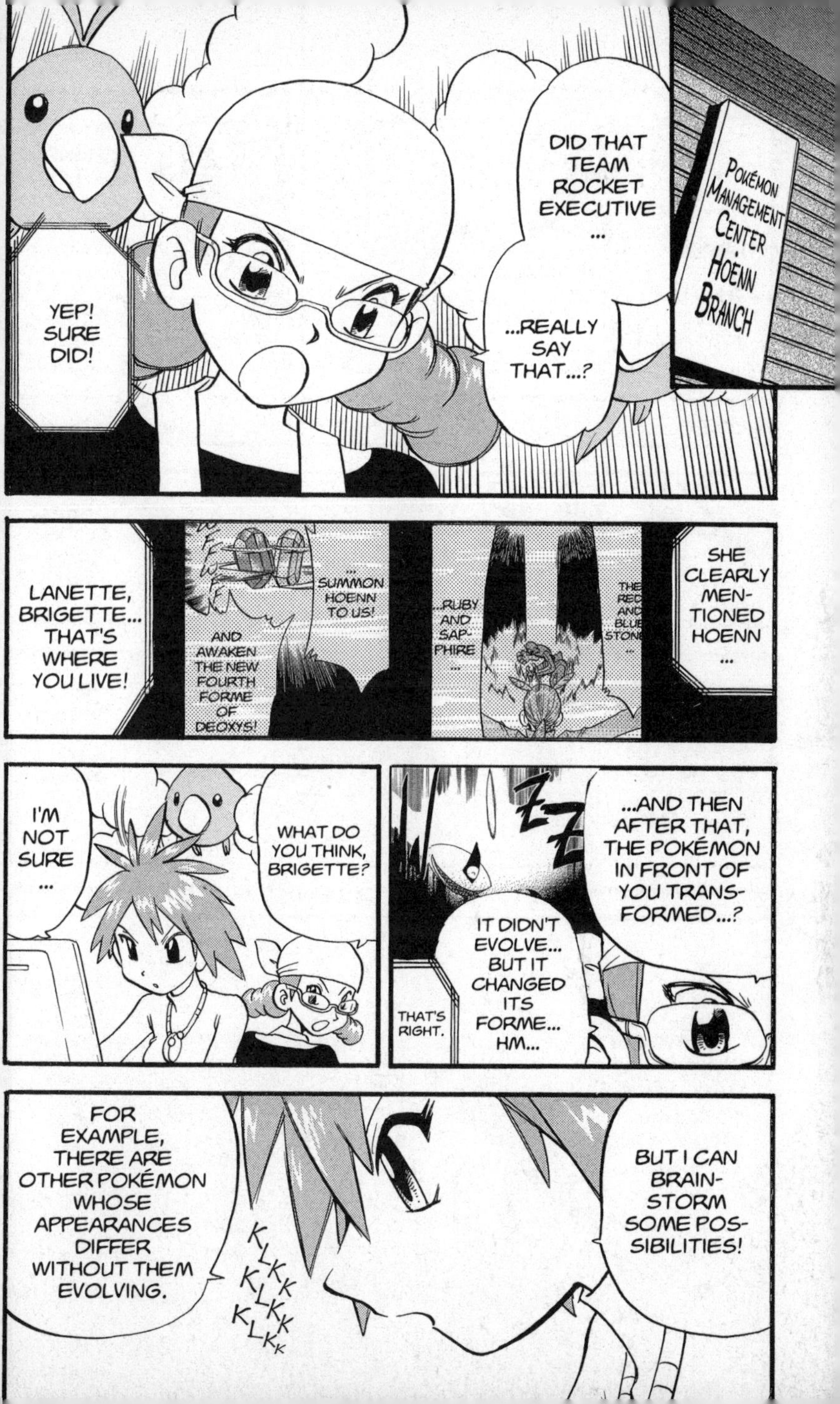
DID THAT TEAM ROCKET EXECUTIVE ...
...REALLY SAY THAT...?
POKÉMON MANAGEMENT CENTER HOENN BRANCH
YEP! SURE DID!
SHE CLEARLY MEN-TIONED HOENN ...
THE RED AND BLUE STONE ...
...RUBY AND SAP-PHIRE ...
... SUMMON HOENN TO US!
AND AWAKEN THE NEW FOURTH FORME OF DEOXYS!
LANETTE, BRIGETTE... THAT'S WHERE YOU LIVE!
...AND THEN AFTER THAT, THE POKÉMON IN FRONT OF YOU TRANS-FORMED...?
IT DIDN'T EVOLVE... BUT IT CHANGED ITS FORME... HM...
THAT'S RIGHT.
WHAT DO YOU THINK, BRIGETTE?
I'M NOT SURE ...
BUT I CAN BRAIN-STORM SOME POS-SIBILITIES!
KLKK KLKK KLKK
FOR EXAMPLE, THERE ARE OTHER POKÉMON WHOSE APPEARANCES DIFFER WITHOUT THEM EVOLVING.

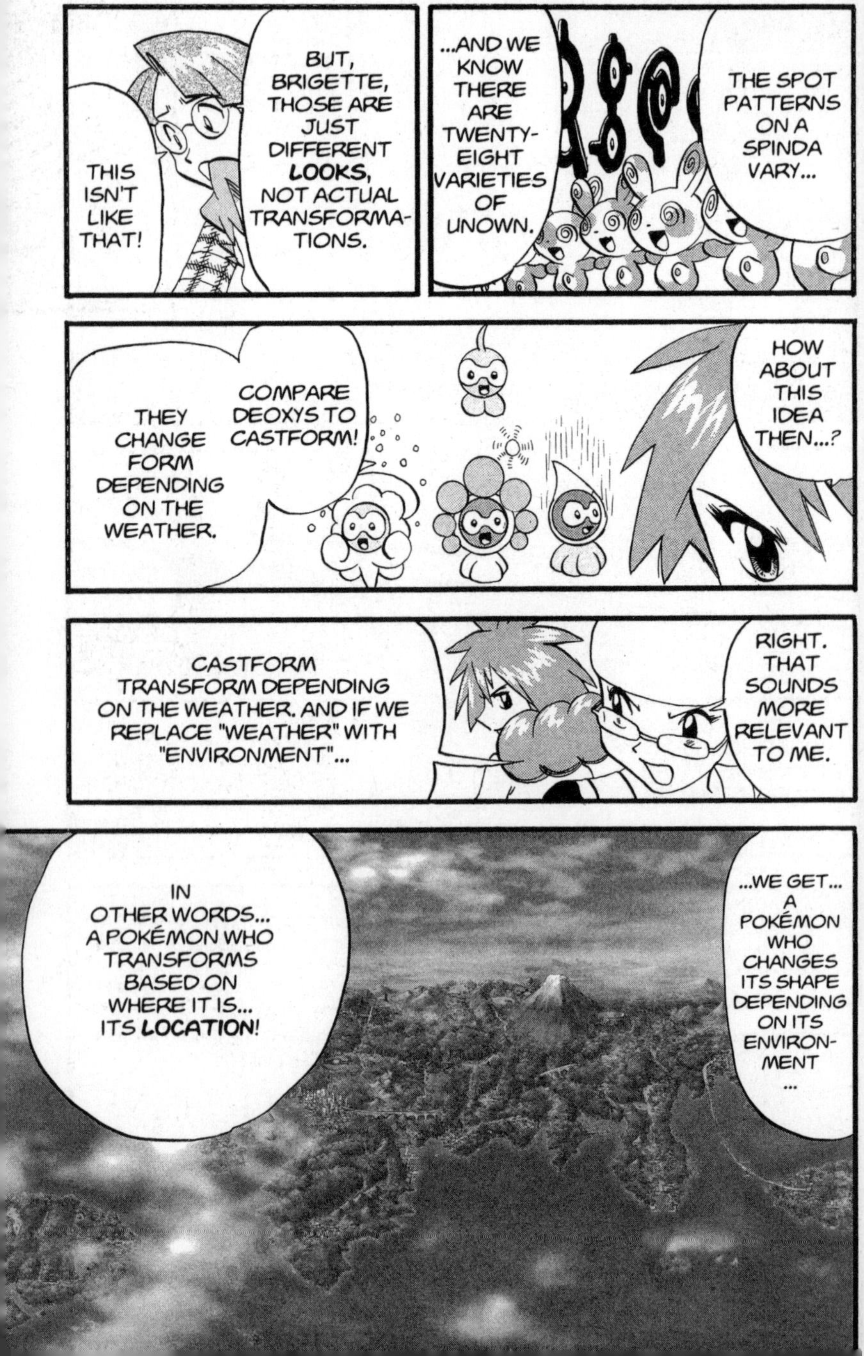
THE SPOT PATTERNS ON A SPINDA VARY...
...AND WE KNOW THERE ARE TWENTY-EIGHT VARIETIES OF UNOWN.
BUT, BRIGETTE, THOSE ARE JUST DIFFERENT **LOOKS**, NOT ACTUAL TRANSFORMATIONS.
THIS ISN'T LIKE THAT!
HOW ABOUT THIS IDEA THEN...?
COMPARE DEOXYS TO CASTFORM!
THEY CHANGE FORM DEPENDING ON THE WEATHER.
RIGHT. THAT SOUNDS MORE RELEVANT TO ME.
CASTFORM TRANSFORM DEPENDING ON THE WEATHER. AND IF WE REPLACE "WEATHER" WITH "ENVIRONMENT"...
...WE GET... A POKÉMON WHO CHANGES ITS SHAPE DEPENDING ON ITS ENVIRONMENT...
IN OTHER WORDS... A POKÉMON WHO TRANSFORMS BASED ON WHERE IT IS... ITS **LOCATION**!

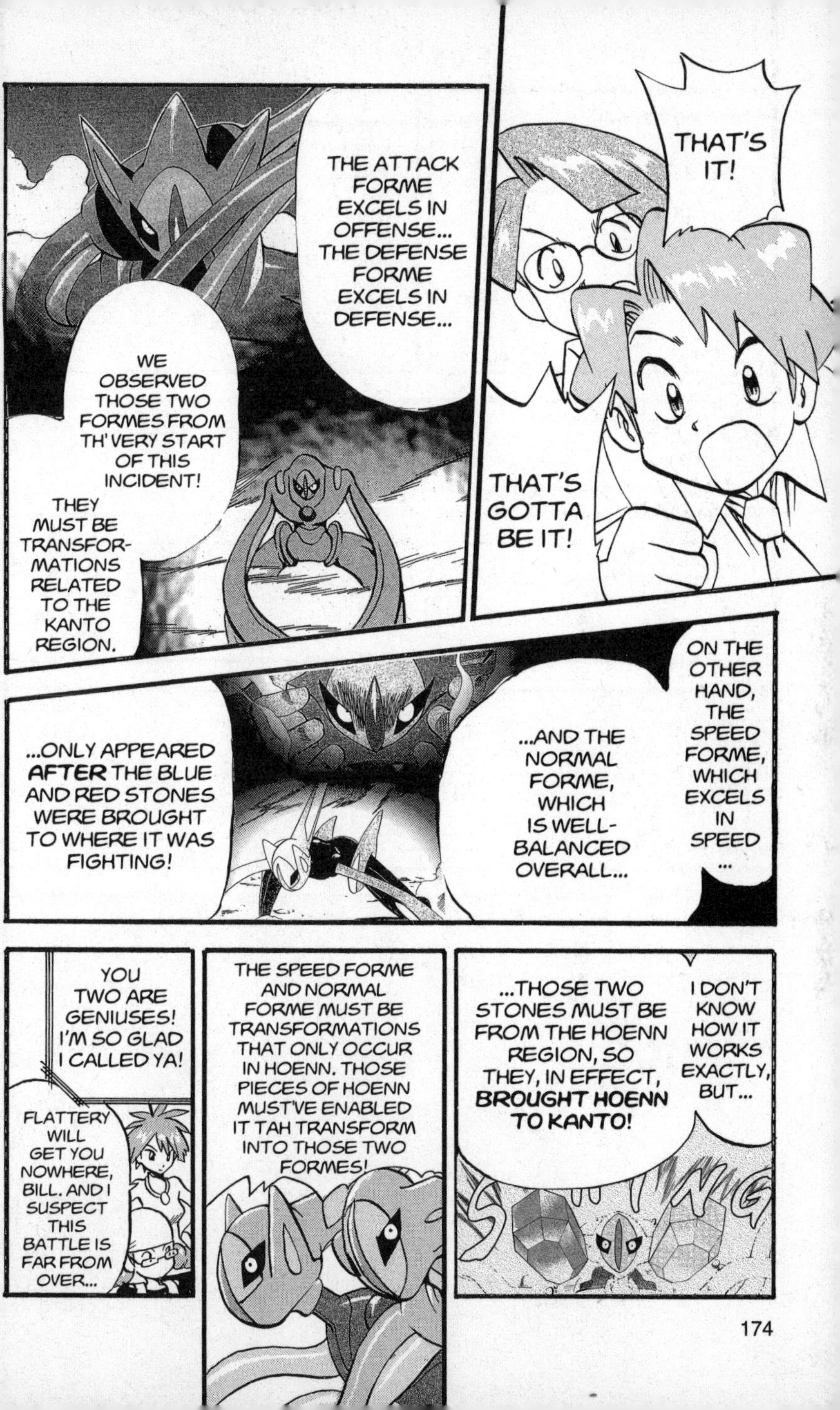
THAT'S IT!
THAT'S GOTTA BE IT!
THE ATTACK FORME EXCELS IN OFFENSE... THE DEFENSE FORME EXCELS IN DEFENSE...
WE OBSERVED THOSE TWO FORMES FROM TH' VERY START OF THIS INCIDENT!
THEY MUST BE TRANSFORMATIONS RELATED TO THE KANTO REGION.
ON THE OTHER HAND, THE SPEED FORME, WHICH EXCELS IN SPEED...
...AND THE NORMAL FORME, WHICH IS WELL-BALANCED OVERALL...
...ONLY APPEARED AFTER THE BLUE AND RED STONES WERE BROUGHT TO WHERE IT WAS FIGHTING!
I DON'T KNOW HOW IT WORKS EXACTLY, BUT...
...THOSE TWO STONES MUST BE FROM THE HOENN REGION, SO THEY, IN EFFECT, BROUGHT HOENN TO KANTO!
THE SPEED FORME AND NORMAL FORME MUST BE TRANSFORMATIONS THAT ONLY OCCUR IN HOENN. THOSE PIECES OF HOENN MUST'VE ENABLED IT TAH TRANSFORM INTO THOSE TWO FORMES!
YOU TWO ARE GENIUSES! I'M SO GLAD I CALLED YA!
FLATTERY WILL GET YOU NOWHERE, BILL. AND I SUSPECT THIS BATTLE IS FAR FROM OVER...

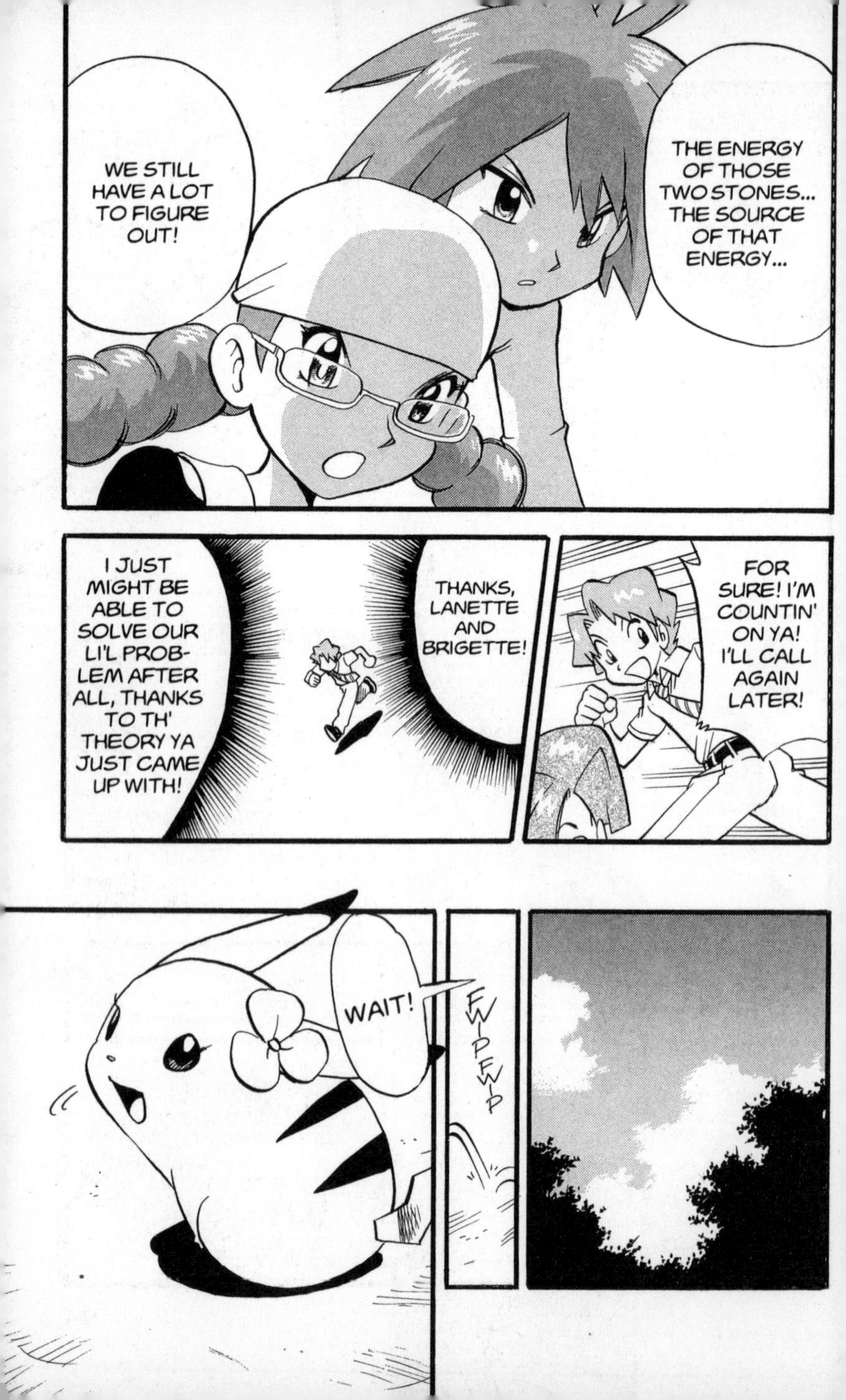
THE ENERGY OF THOSE TWO STONES... THE SOURCE OF THAT ENERGY...
WE STILL HAVE A LOT TO FIGURE OUT!
FOR SURE! I'M COUNTIN' ON YA! I'LL CALL AGAIN LATER!
THANKS, LANETTE AND BRIGETTE!
I JUST MIGHT BE ABLE TO SOLVE OUR LI'L PROB-LEM AFTER ALL, THANKS TO TH' THEORY YA JUST CAME UP WITH!
FWIPFWIP
WAIT!

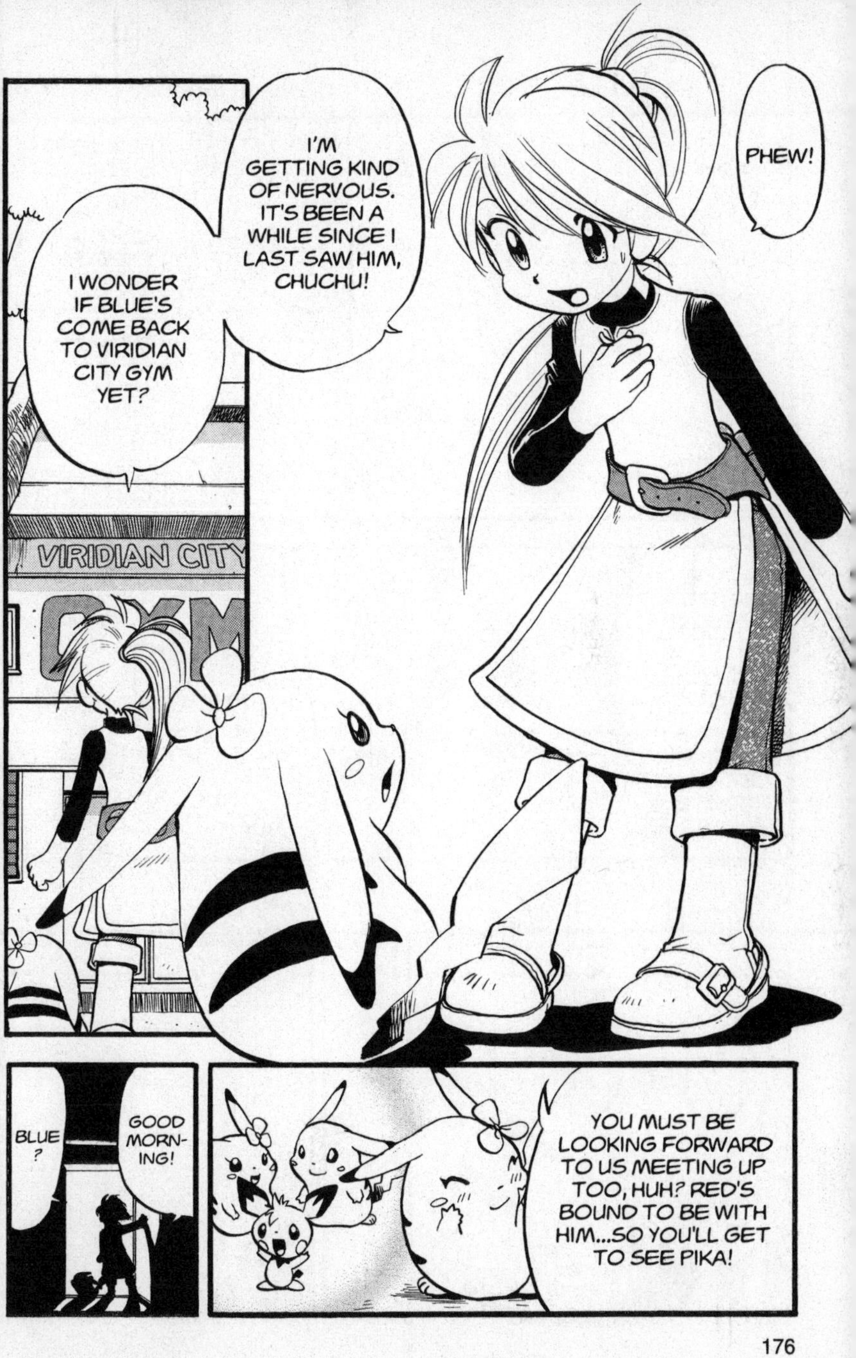
PHEW!
I'M GETTING KIND OF NERVOUS. IT'S BEEN A WHILE SINCE I LAST SAW HIM, CHUCHU!
I WONDER IF BLUE'S COME BACK TO VIRIDIAN CITY GYM YET?
VIRIDIAN CITY
YOU MUST BE LOOKING FORWARD TO US MEETING UP TOO, HUH? RED'S BOUND TO BE WITH HIM...SO YOU'LL GET TO SEE PIKA!
GOOD MORN-ING!
BLUE?

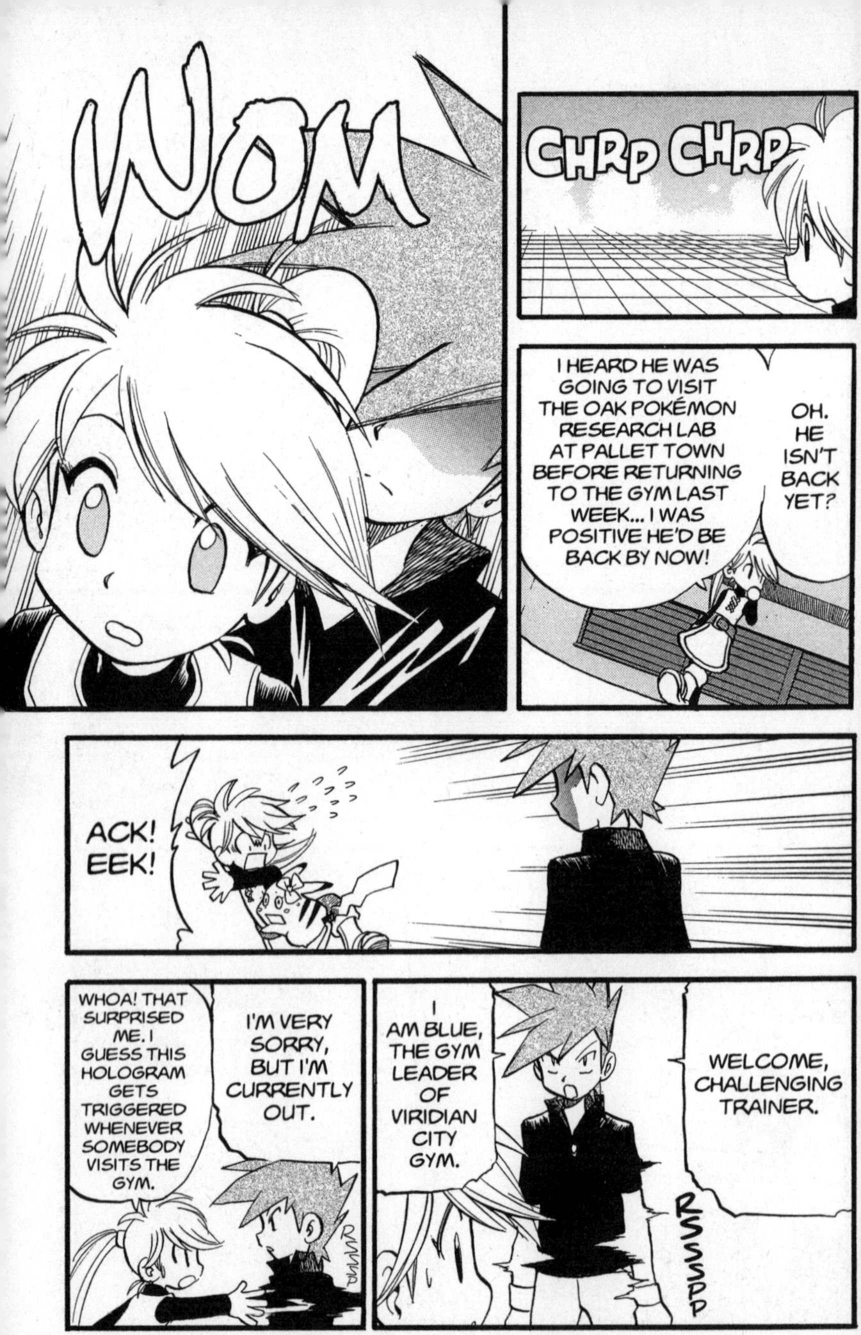
CHRP CHRP
OH. HE ISN'T BACK YET?
I HEARD HE WAS GOING TO VISIT THE OAK POKÉMON RESEARCH LAB AT PALLET TOWN BEFORE RETURNING TO THE GYM LAST WEEK... I WAS POSITIVE HE'D BE BACK BY NOW!
WOM
ACK! EEK!
WELCOME, CHALLENGING TRAINER.
I AM BLUE, THE GYM LEADER OF VIRIDIAN CITY GYM.
RSSSPP
I'M VERY SORRY, BUT I'M CURRENTLY OUT.
WHOA! THAT SURPRISED ME. I GUESS THIS HOLOGRAM GETS TRIGGERED WHENEVER SOMEBODY VISITS THE GYM.

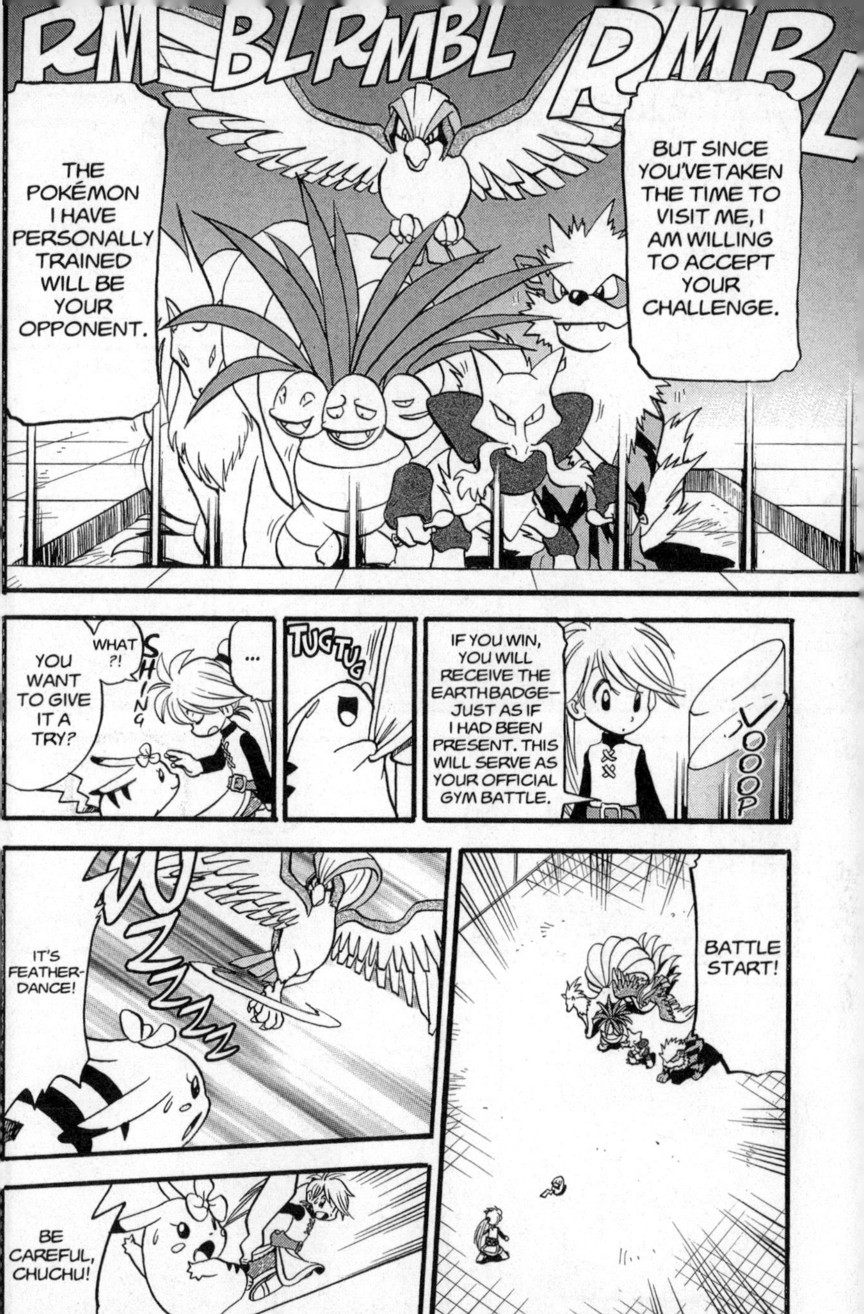
RM BLRMBL RMBL
BUT SINCE YOU'VE TAKEN THE TIME TO VISIT ME, I AM WILLING TO ACCEPT YOUR CHALLENGE.
THE POKÉMON I HAVE PERSONALLY TRAINED WILL BE YOUR OPPONENT.
IF YOU WIN, YOU WILL RECEIVE THE EARTHBADGE— JUST AS IF I HAD BEEN PRESENT. THIS WILL SERVE AS YOUR OFFICIAL GYM BATTLE.
VOOOOP
TUGTUG
...
SHING
WHAT ?!
YOU WANT TO GIVE IT A TRY?
BATTLE START!
IT'S FEATHER-DANCE!
BE CAREFUL, CHUCHU!

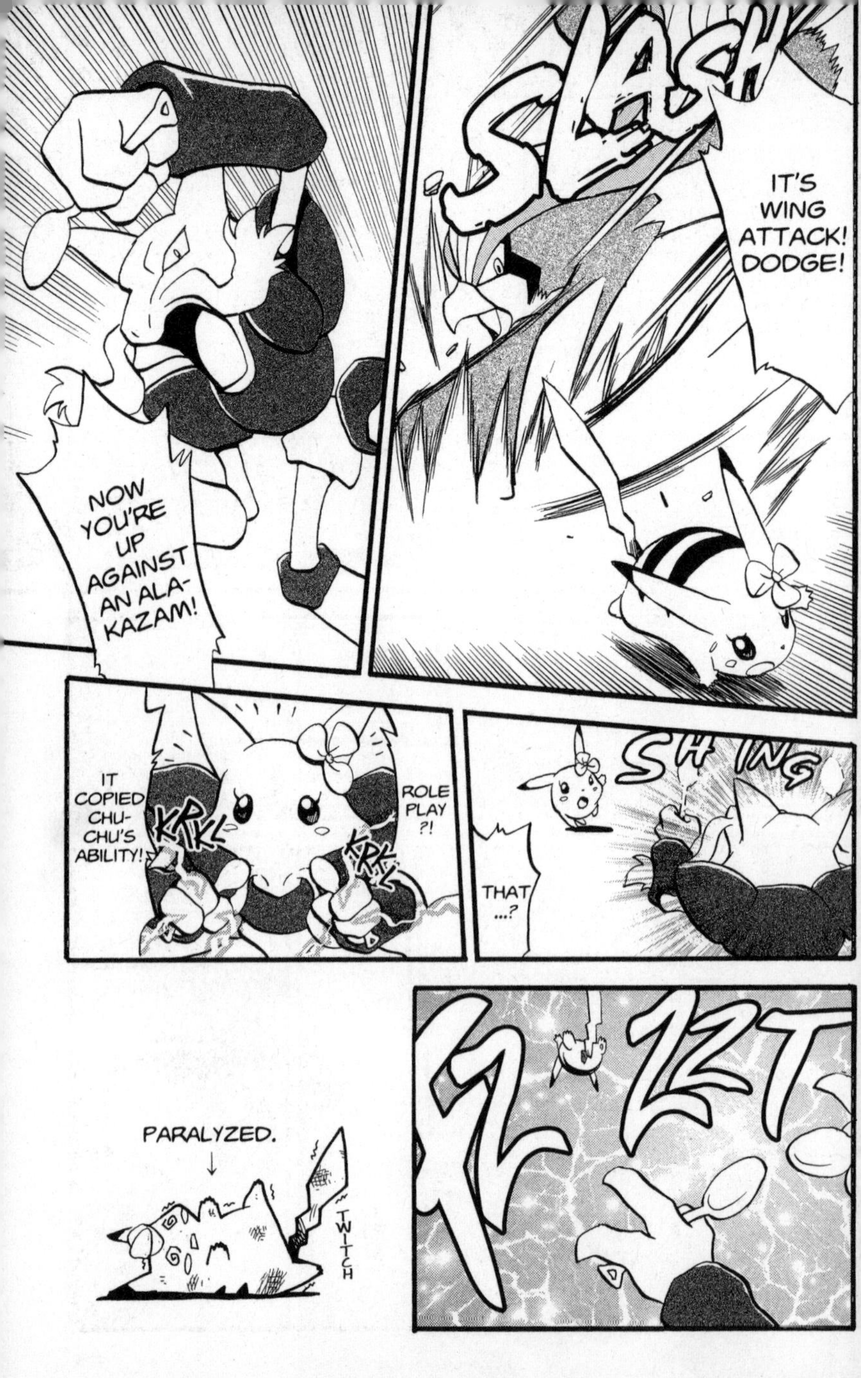
SLASH
IT'S WING ATTACK! DODGE!
NOW YOU'RE UP AGAINST AN ALA-KAZAM!
SHING
THAT ...?
ROLE PLAY ?!
KRKL
KRKL
IT COPIED CHU-CHU'S ABILITY!
ZZZT
PARALYZED.
TWITCH

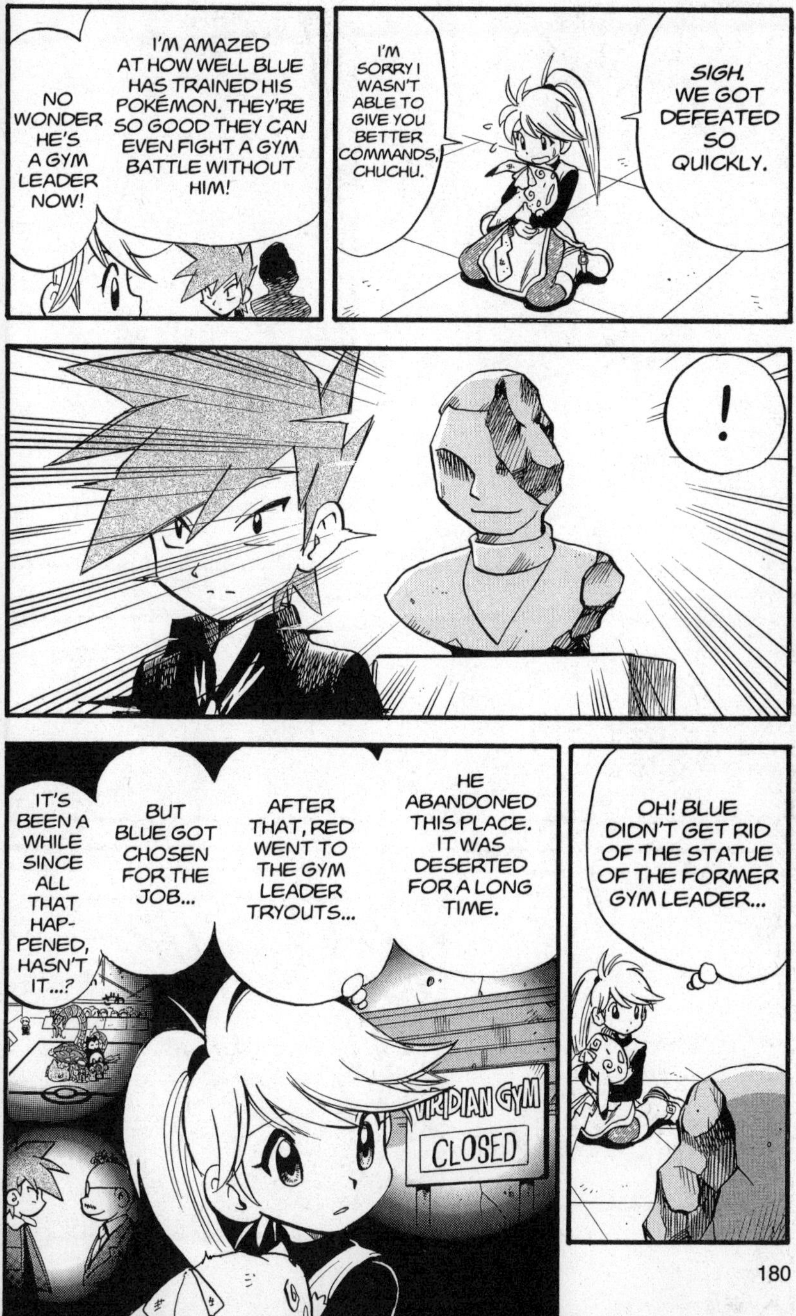
SIGH. WE GOT DEFEATED SO QUICKLY.
I'M SORRY I WASN'T ABLE TO GIVE YOU BETTER COMMANDS, CHUCHU.
I'M AMAZED AT HOW WELL BLUE HAS TRAINED HIS POKÉMON. THEY'RE SO GOOD THEY CAN EVEN FIGHT A GYM BATTLE WITHOUT HIM!
NO WONDER HE'S A GYM LEADER NOW!
!
OH! BLUE DIDN'T GET RID OF THE STATUE OF THE FORMER GYM LEADER...
HE ABANDONED THIS PLACE. IT WAS DESERTED FOR A LONG TIME.
AFTER THAT, RED WENT TO THE GYM LEADER TRYOUTS...
BUT BLUE GOT CHOSEN FOR THE JOB...
IT'S BEEN A WHILE SINCE ALL THAT HAP-PENED, HASN'T IT...?
VIRIDIAN GYM
CLOSED

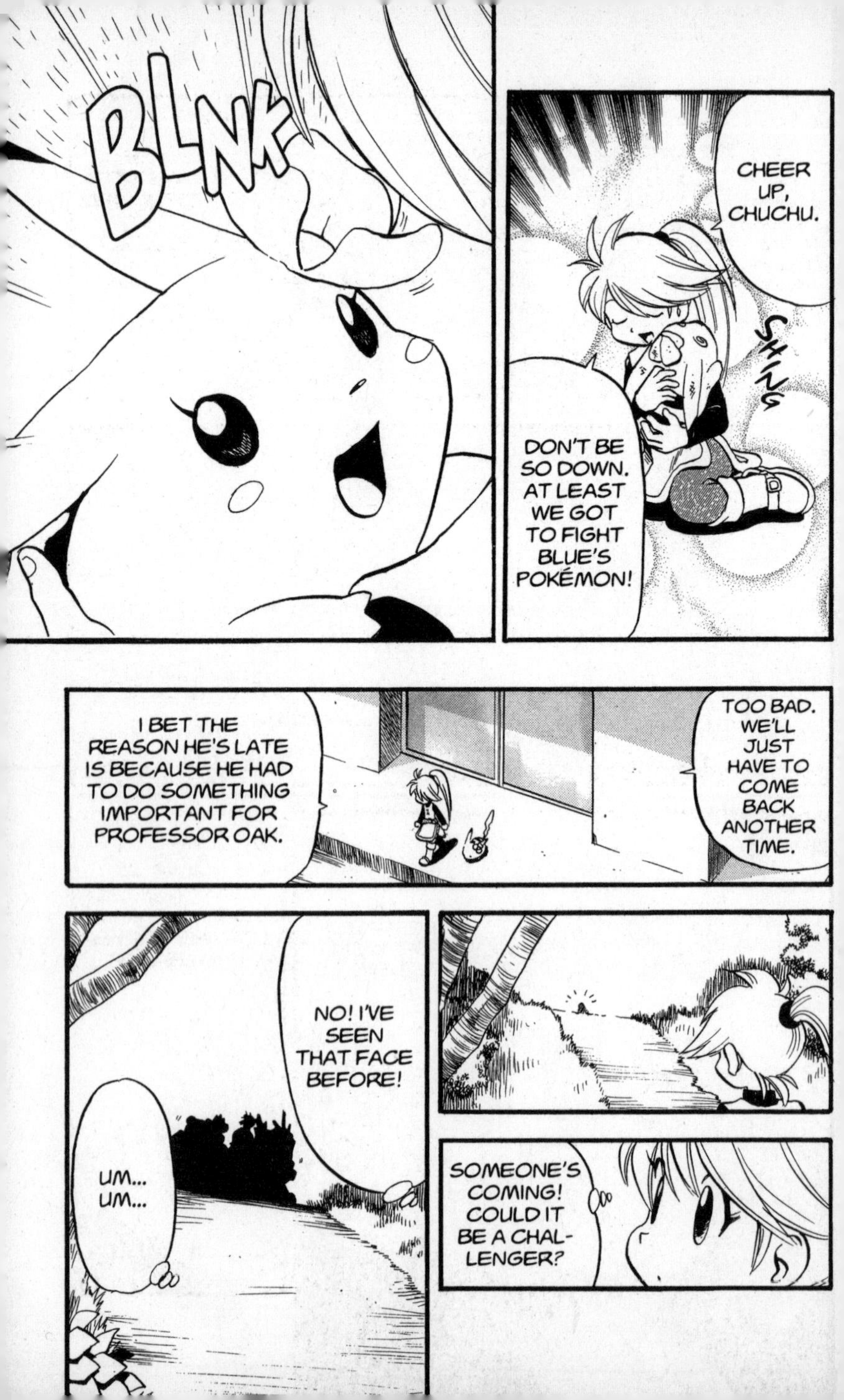
CHEER UP, CHUCHU.
SHING
DON'T BE SO DOWN. AT LEAST WE GOT TO FIGHT BLUE'S POKÉMON!
BLNK
TOO BAD. WE'LL JUST HAVE TO COME BACK ANOTHER TIME.
I BET THE REASON HE'S LATE IS BECAUSE HE HAD TO DO SOMETHING IMPORTANT FOR PROFESSOR OAK.
SOMEONE'S COMING! COULD IT BE A CHAL-LENGER?
NO! I'VE SEEN THAT FACE BEFORE!
UM... UM...

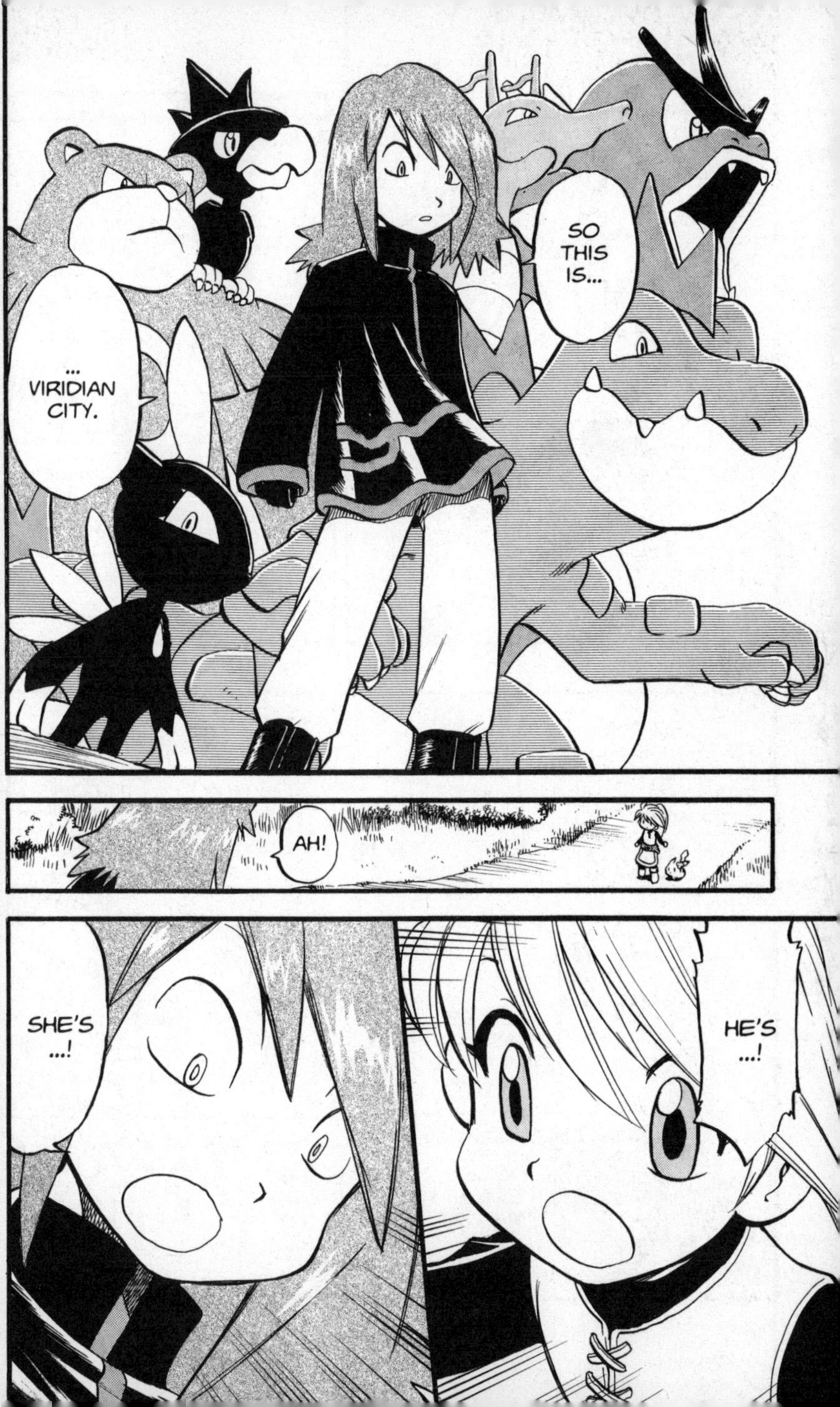
SO THIS IS...
...VIRIDIAN CITY.
AH!
HE'S ...!
SHE'S ...!

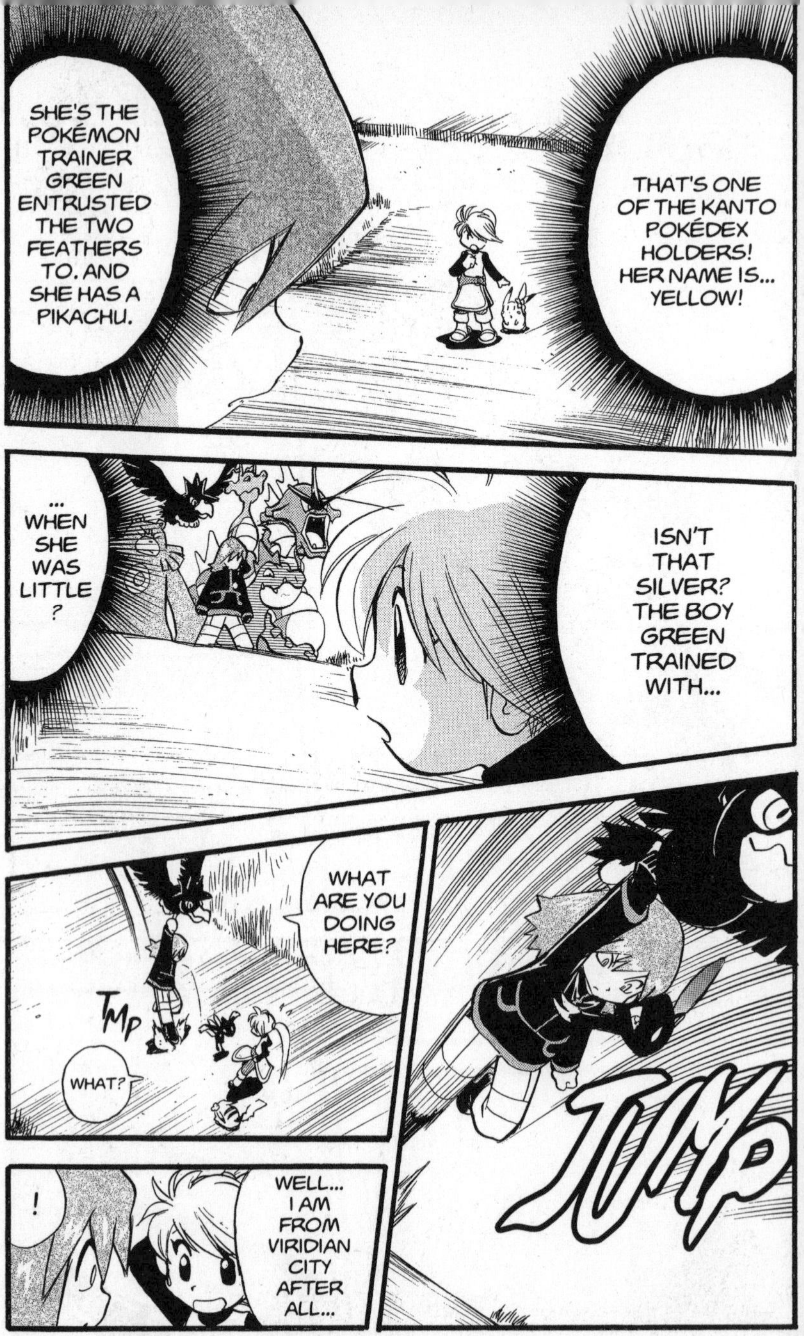
THAT'S ONE OF THE KANTO POKÉDEX HOLDERS! HER NAME IS... YELLOW!
SHE'S THE POKÉMON TRAINER GREEN ENTRUSTED THE TWO FEATHERS TO. AND SHE HAS A PIKACHU.
ISN'T THAT SILVER? THE BOY GREEN TRAINED WITH...
... WHEN SHE WAS LITTLE ?
JUMP
WHAT ARE YOU DOING HERE?
TMP
WHAT?
WELL... I AM FROM VIRIDIAN CITY AFTER ALL...
!

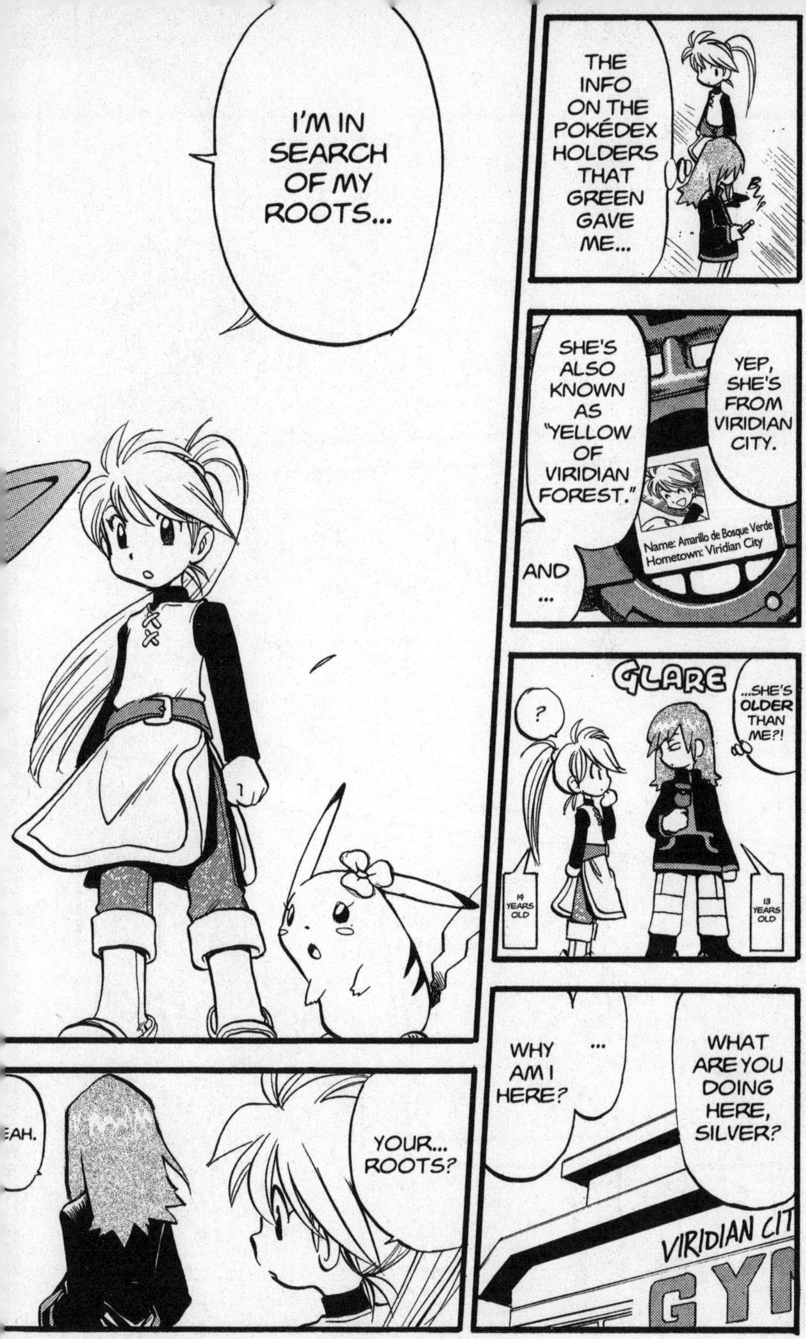
THE INFO ON THE POKÉDEX HOLDERS THAT GREEN GAVE ME...
YEP, SHE'S FROM VIRIDIAN CITY.
SHE'S ALSO KNOWN AS "YELLOW OF VIRIDIAN FOREST."
Name: Amarillo de Bosque Verde
Hometown: Viridian City
AND ...
GLARE
...SHE'S OLDER THAN ME?!
?
13 YEARS OLD
14 YEARS OLD
WHAT ARE YOU DOING HERE, SILVER?
...
WHY AM I HERE?
VIRIDIAN CIT
GY
I'M IN SEARCH OF MY ROOTS...
YOUR... ROOTS?
EAH.

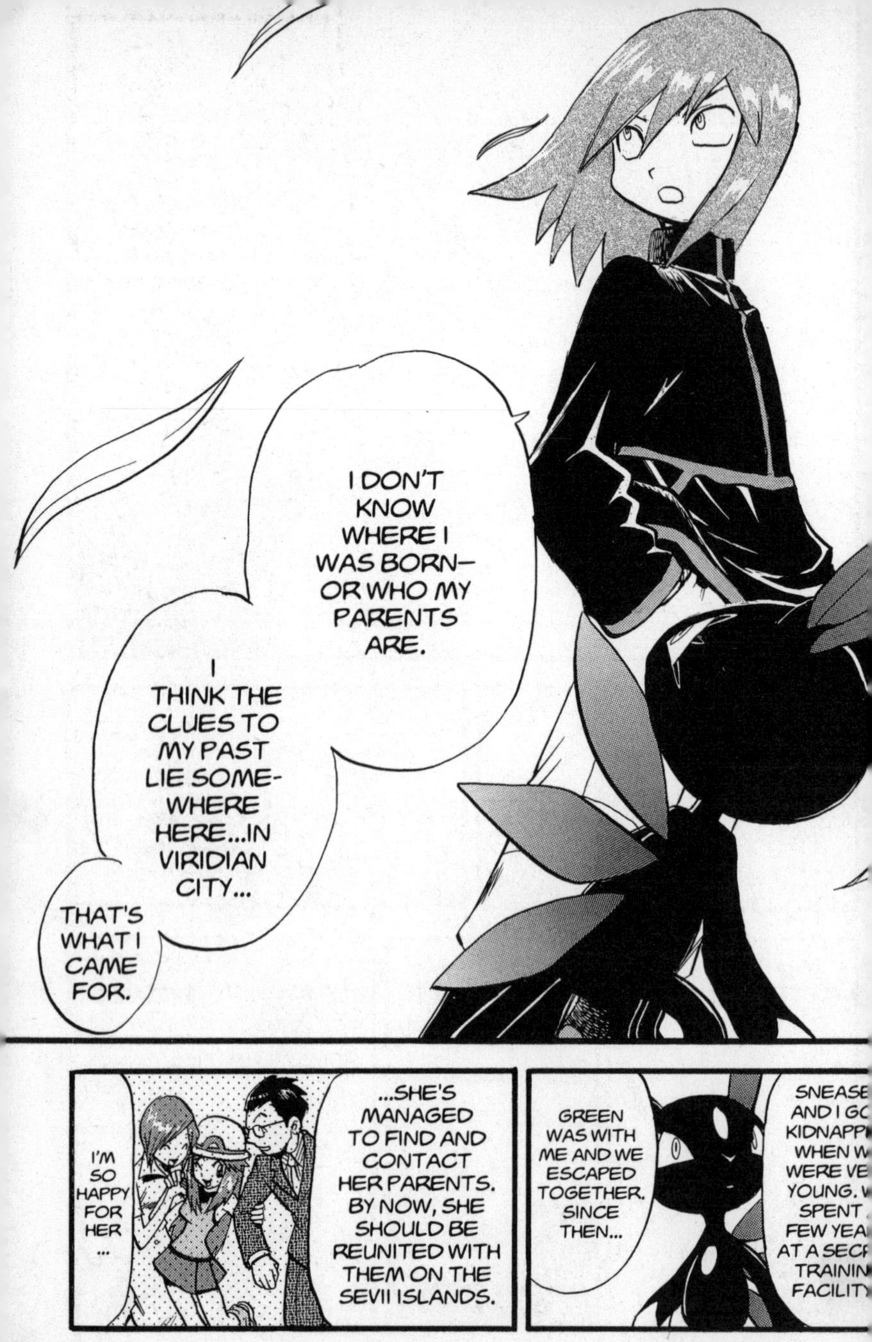
I DON'T KNOW WHERE I WAS BORN–OR WHO MY PARENTS ARE.
I THINK THE CLUES TO MY PAST LIE SOME-WHERE HERE...IN VIRIDIAN CITY...
THAT'S WHAT I CAME FOR.
SNEASE AND I GO KIDNAPP WHEN W WERE VE YOUNG. W SPENT FEW YEA AT A SECR TRAININ FACILITY
GREEN WAS WITH ME AND WE ESCAPED TOGETHER. SINCE THEN...
...SHE'S MANAGED TO FIND AND CONTACT HER PARENTS. BY NOW, SHE SHOULD BE REUNITED WITH THEM ON THE SEVII ISLANDS.
I'M SO HAPPY FOR HER ...

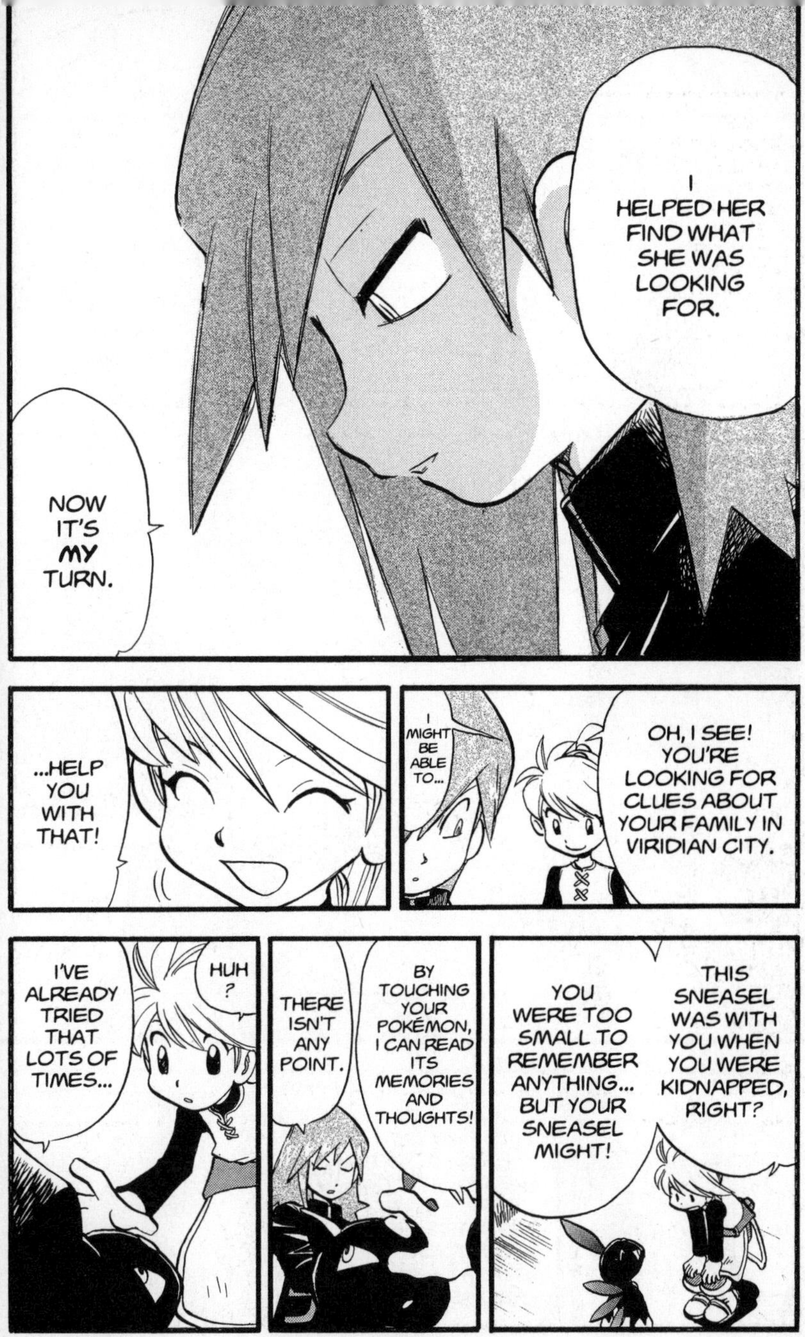
I HELPED HER FIND WHAT SHE WAS LOOKING FOR.
NOW IT'S **MY** TURN.
OH, I SEE! YOU'RE LOOKING FOR CLUES ABOUT YOUR FAMILY IN VIRIDIAN CITY.
I MIGHT BE ABLE TO...
...HELP YOU WITH THAT!
THIS SNEASEL WAS WITH YOU WHEN YOU WERE KIDNAPPED, RIGHT?
YOU WERE TOO SMALL TO REMEMBER ANYTHING... BUT YOUR SNEASEL MIGHT!
BY TOUCHING YOUR POKÉMON, I CAN READ ITS MEMORIES AND THOUGHTS!
THERE ISN'T ANY POINT.
HUH?
I'VE ALREADY TRIED THAT LOTS OF TIMES...

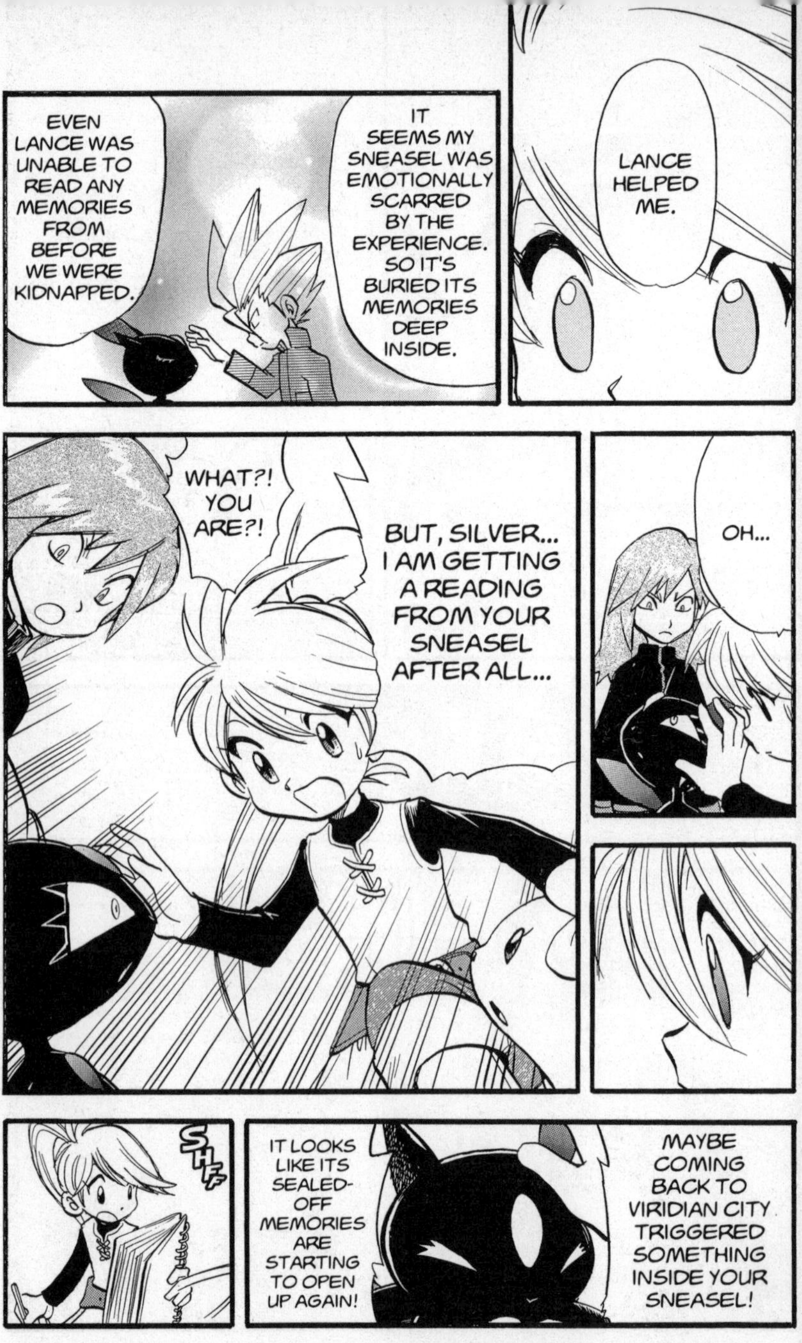
LANCE HELPED ME.
IT SEEMS MY SNEASEL WAS EMOTIONALLY SCARRED BY THE EXPERIENCE. SO IT'S BURIED ITS MEMORIES DEEP INSIDE.
EVEN LANCE WAS UNABLE TO READ ANY MEMORIES FROM BEFORE WE WERE KIDNAPPED.
OH...
BUT, SILVER... I AM GETTING A READING FROM YOUR SNEASEL AFTER ALL...
WHAT?! YOU ARE?!
MAYBE COMING BACK TO VIRIDIAN CITY TRIGGERED SOMETHING INSIDE YOUR SNEASEL!
IT LOOKS LIKE ITS SEALED-OFF MEMORIES ARE STARTING TO OPEN UP AGAIN!
SHFF

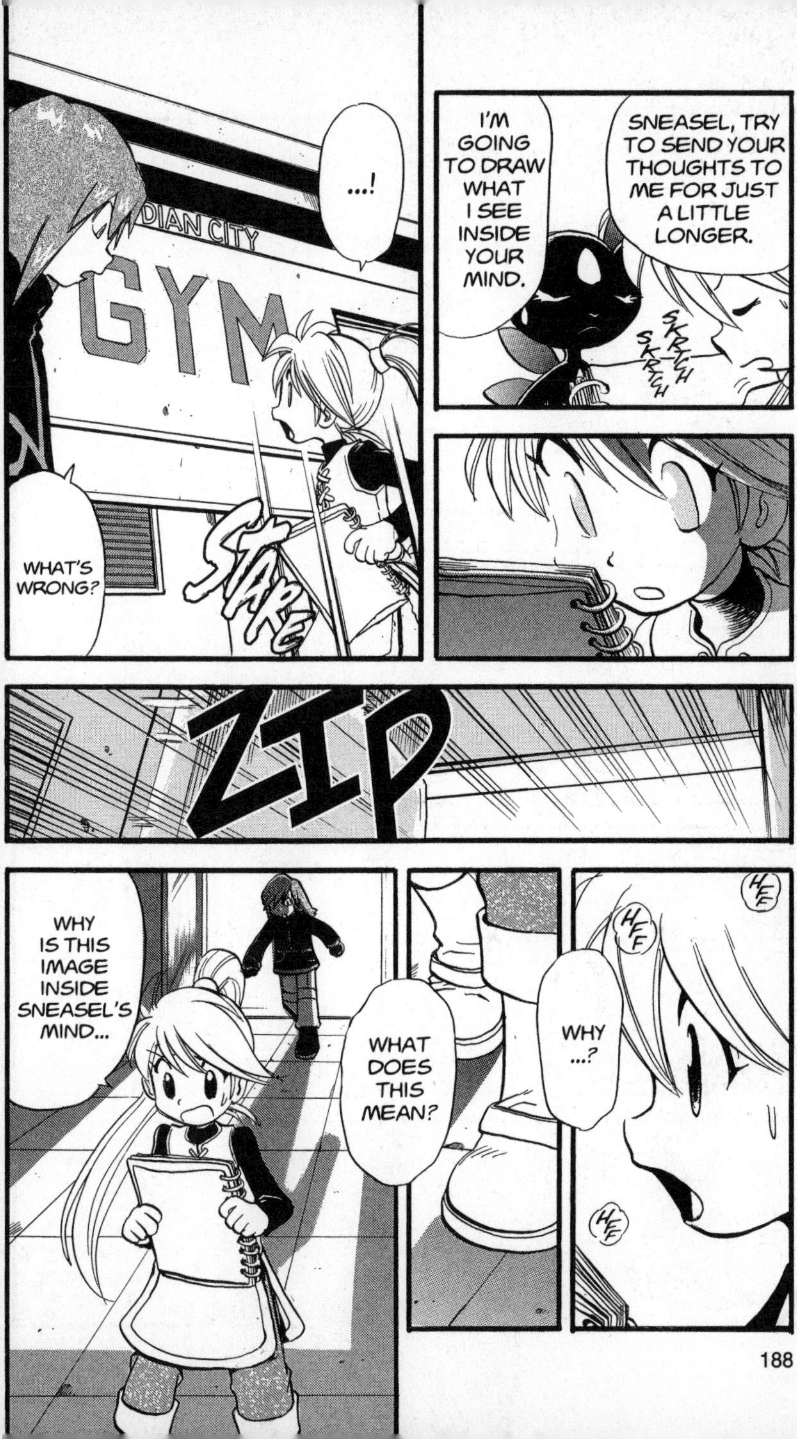
SNEASEL, TRY TO SEND YOUR THOUGHTS TO ME FOR JUST A LITTLE LONGER.
I'M GOING TO DRAW WHAT I SEE INSIDE YOUR MIND.
SKRITCH SKRITCH
...!
STARE
WHAT'S WRONG?
ZIP
HFF
HFF
WHY ...?
HFF
WHAT DOES THIS MEAN?
WHY IS THIS IMAGE INSIDE SNEASEL'S MIND...

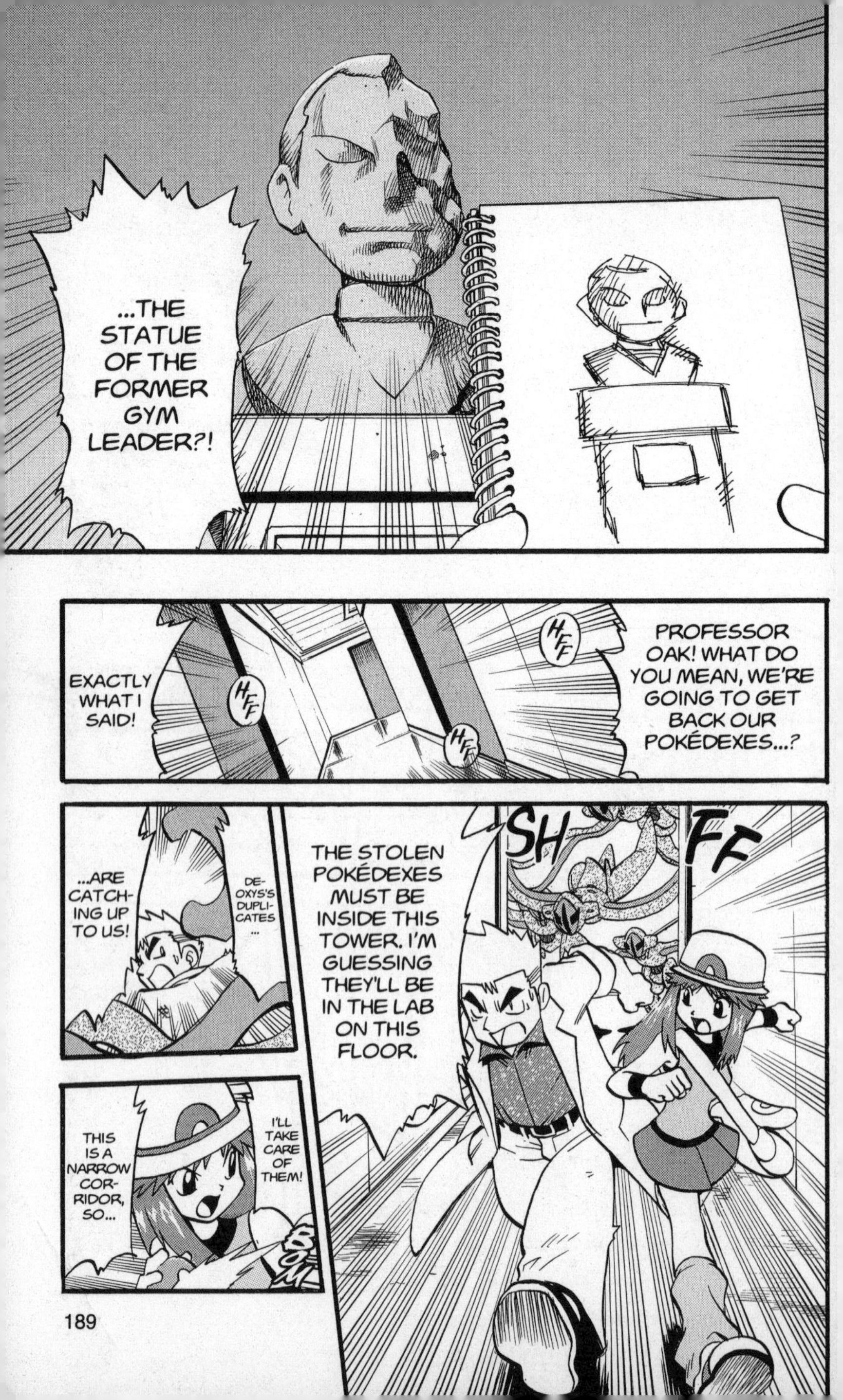
...THE STATUE OF THE FORMER GYM LEADER?!
PROFESSOR OAK! WHAT DO YOU MEAN, WE'RE GOING TO GET BACK OUR POKÉDEXES...?
HEF
HEF
HEF
EXACTLY WHAT I SAID!
SHFF
THE STOLEN POKÉDEXES MUST BE INSIDE THIS TOWER. I'M GUESSING THEY'LL BE IN THE LAB ON THIS FLOOR.
DE-OXYS'S DUPLI-CATES...
...ARE CATCH-ING UP TO US!
THIS IS A NARROW COR-RIDOR, SO...
I'LL TAKE CARE OF THEM!
BOOM

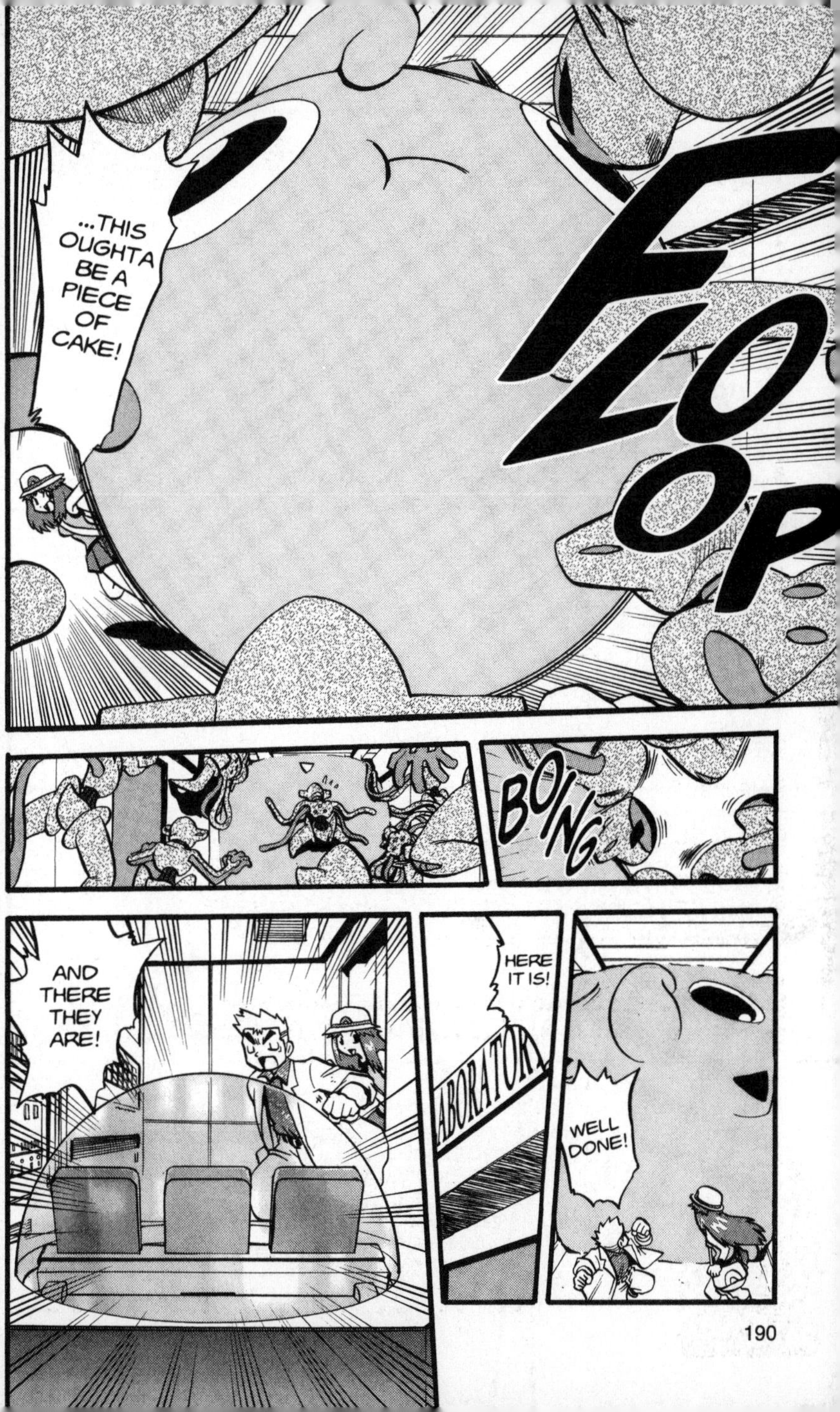
FLOOP
...THIS OUGHTA BE A PIECE OF CAKE!
BOING
WELL DONE!
HERE IT IS!
ABORATOR
AND THERE THEY ARE!

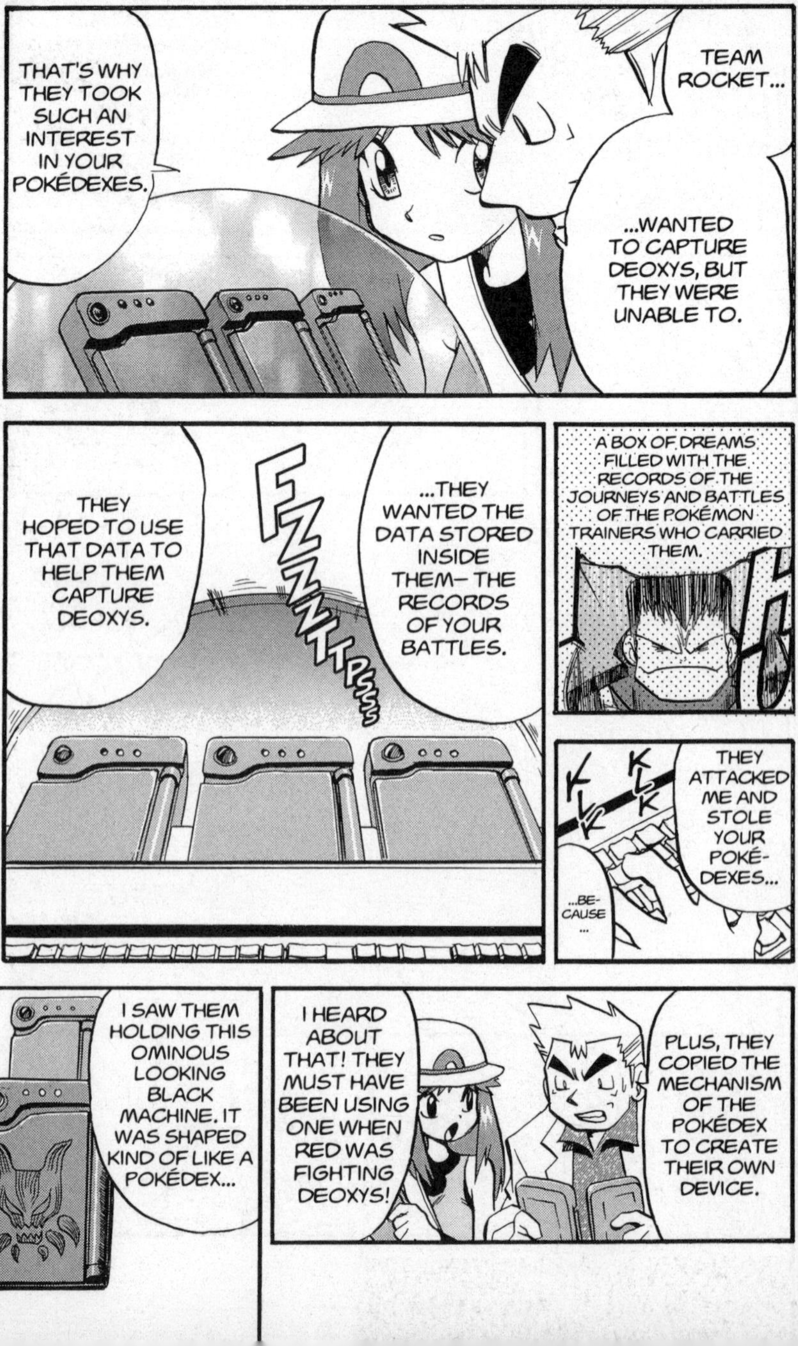
TEAM ROCKET...
...WANTED TO CAPTURE DEOXYS, BUT THEY WERE UNABLE TO.
THAT'S WHY THEY TOOK SUCH AN INTEREST IN YOUR POKÉDEXES.
A BOX OF DREAMS FILLED WITH THE RECORDS OF THE JOURNEYS AND BATTLES OF THE POKÉMON TRAINERS WHO CARRIED THEM.
THEY ATTACKED ME AND STOLE YOUR POKÉ-DEXES...
KLK KLK
...BE-CAUSE ...
...THEY WANTED THE DATA STORED INSIDE THEM— THE RECORDS OF YOUR BATTLES.
FZZZT PSSS
THEY HOPED TO USE THAT DATA TO HELP THEM CAPTURE DEOXYS.
PLUS, THEY COPIED THE MECHANISM OF THE POKÉDEX TO CREATE THEIR OWN DEVICE.
I HEARD ABOUT THAT! THEY MUST HAVE BEEN USING ONE WHEN RED WAS FIGHTING DEOXYS!
I SAW THEM HOLDING THIS OMINOUS LOOKING BLACK MACHINE. IT WAS SHAPED KIND OF LIKE A POKÉDEX...

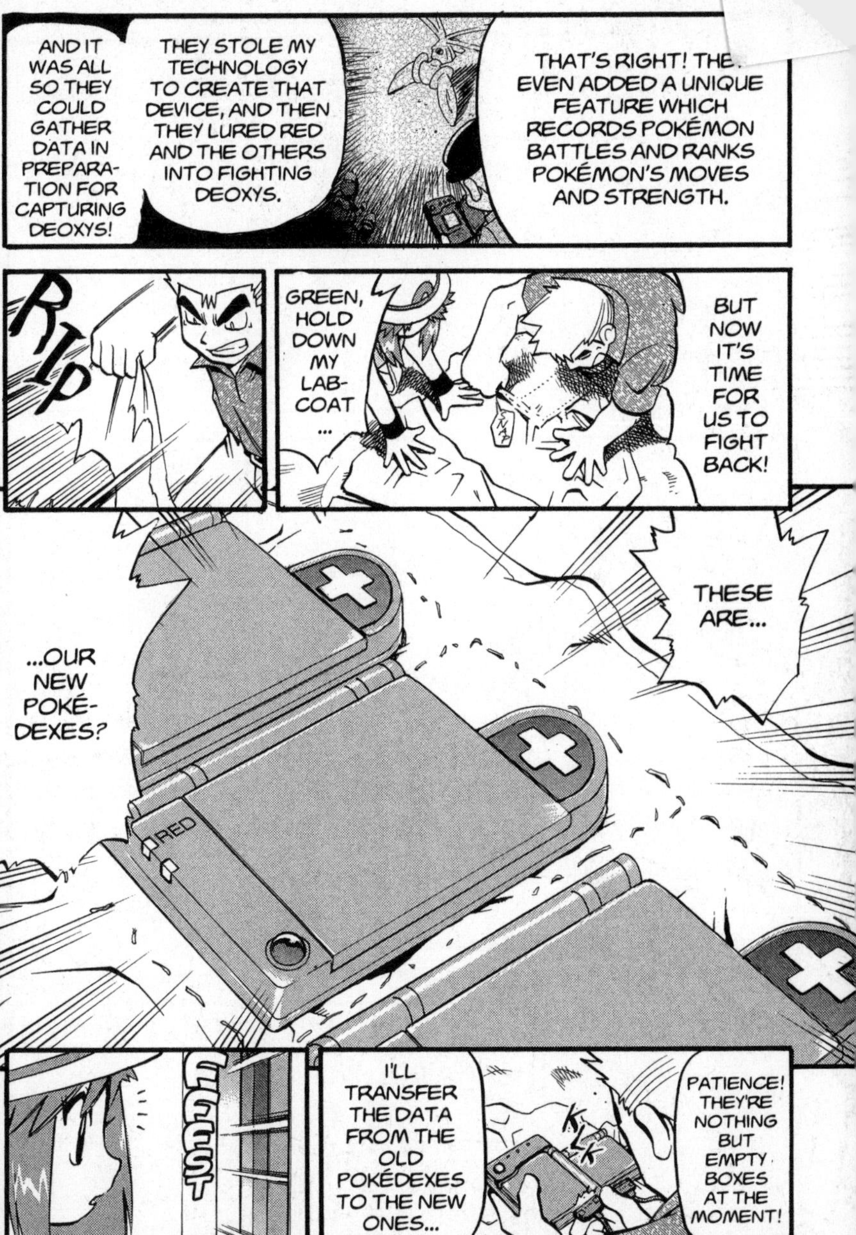
THAT'S RIGHT! THE EVEN ADDED A UNIQUE FEATURE WHICH RECORDS POKÉMON BATTLES AND RANKS POKÉMON'S MOVES AND STRENGTH.
THEY STOLE MY TECHNOLOGY TO CREATE THAT DEVICE, AND THEN THEY LURED RED AND THE OTHERS INTO FIGHTING DEOXYS.
AND IT WAS ALL SO THEY COULD GATHER DATA IN PREPARATION FOR CAPTURING DEOXYS!
BUT NOW IT'S TIME FOR US TO FIGHT BACK!
GREEN, HOLD DOWN MY LAB-COAT...
RIP
THESE ARE...
...OUR NEW POKÉ-DEXES?
RED
PATIENCE! THEY'RE NOTHING BUT EMPTY BOXES AT THE MOMENT!
KLK
I'LL TRANSFER THE DATA FROM THE OLD POKÉDEXES TO THE NEW ONES...
FEEST

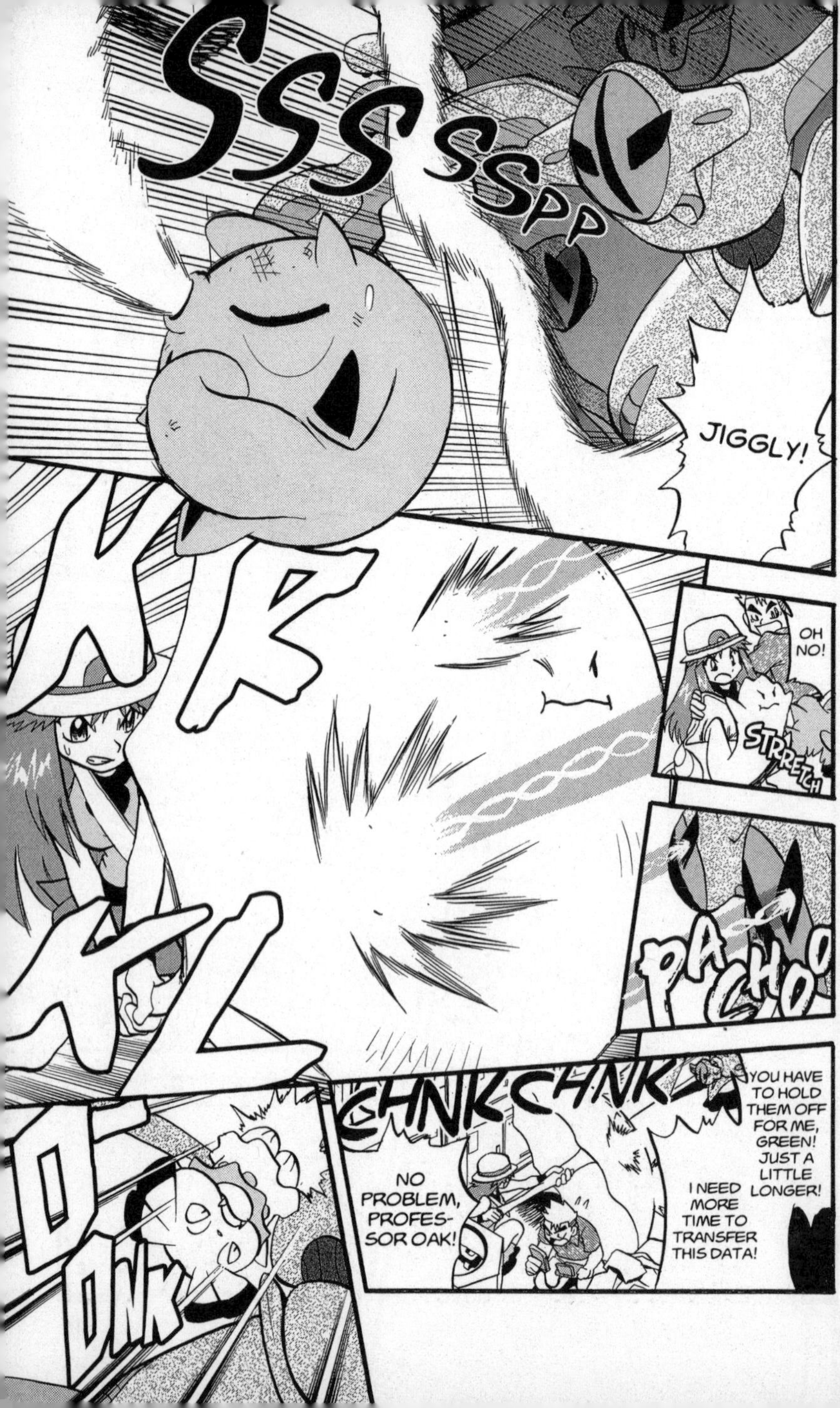
SSSSSPP
JIGGLY!
OH NO!
STRRETCH
PACHOO
CHNKCHNK
YOU HAVE TO HOLD THEM OFF FOR ME, GREEN! JUST A LITTLE LONGER!
I NEED MORE TIME TO TRANSFER THIS DATA!
NO PROBLEM, PROFES-SOR OAK!
DONK

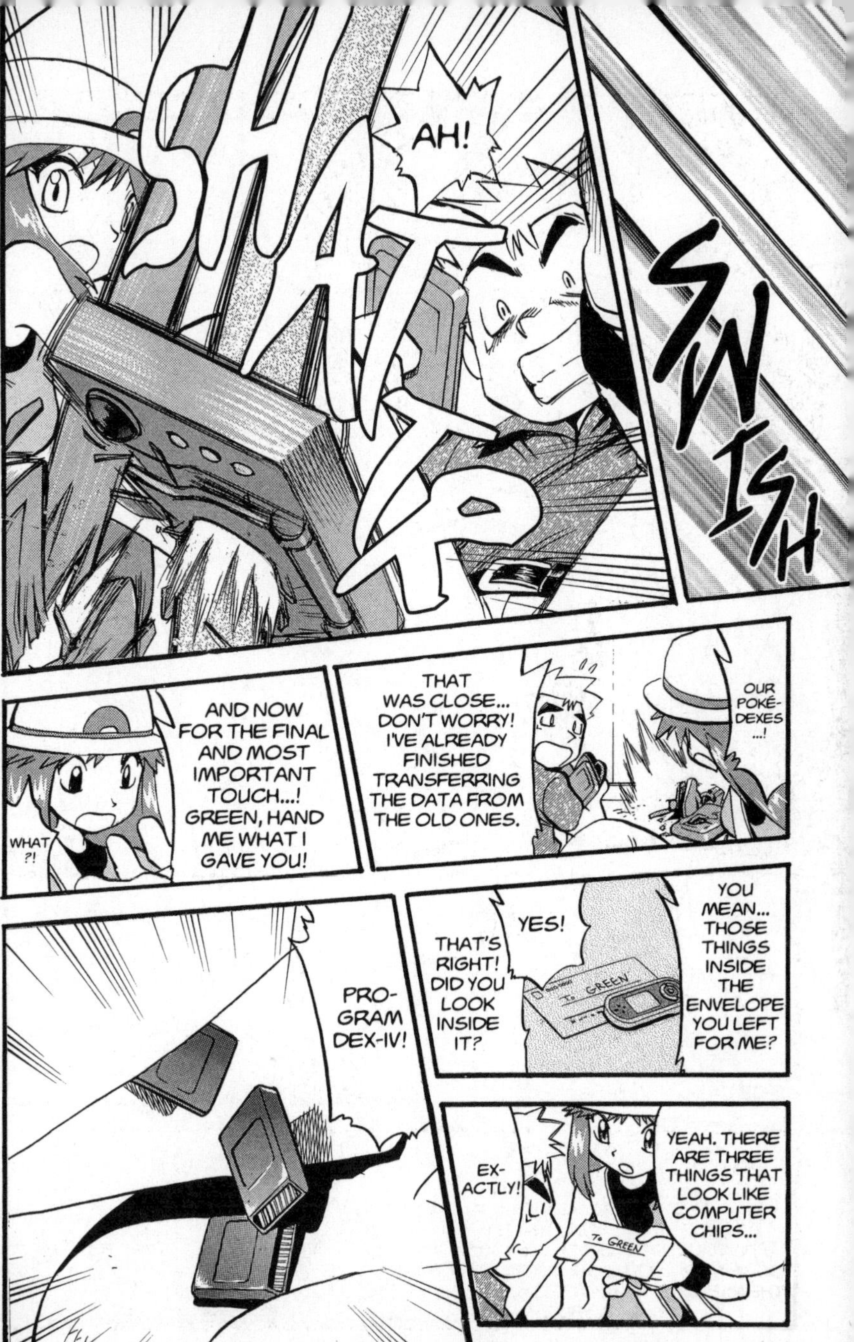
AH!
SWISH
SHATP
OUR POKÉ-DEXES...!
THAT WAS CLOSE... DON'T WORRY! I'VE ALREADY FINISHED TRANSFERRING THE DATA FROM THE OLD ONES.
AND NOW FOR THE FINAL AND MOST IMPORTANT TOUCH...! GREEN, HAND ME WHAT I GAVE YOU!
WHAT?!
YOU MEAN... THOSE THINGS INSIDE THE ENVELOPE YOU LEFT FOR ME?
YES!
THAT'S RIGHT! DID YOU LOOK INSIDE IT?
To GREEN
YEAH. THERE ARE THREE THINGS THAT LOOK LIKE COMPUTER CHIPS...
EX-ACTLY!
To GREEN
PRO-GRAM DEX-IV!

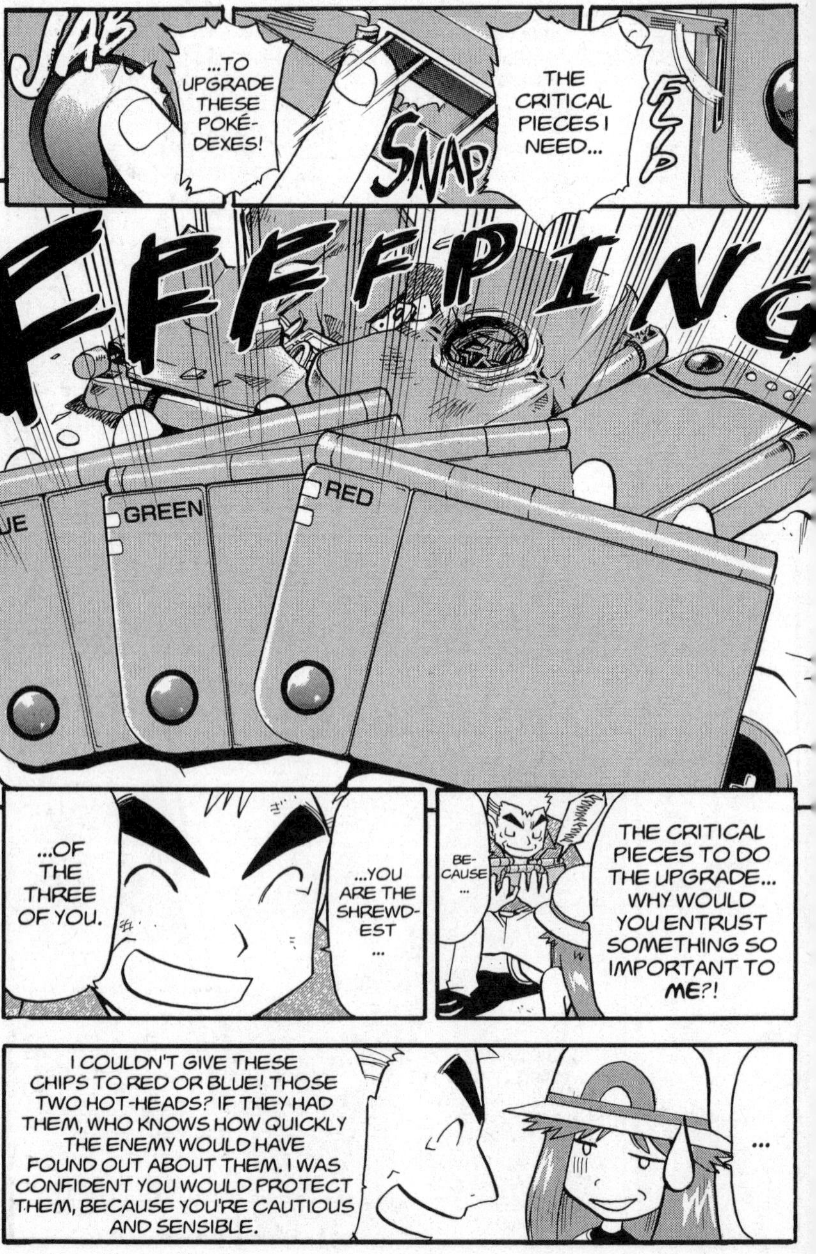
FLIP
THE CRITICAL PIECES I NEED...
SNAP
...TO UPGRADE THESE POKÉ-DEXES!
JAB
FFFFPING
BLUE
GREEN
RED
THE CRITICAL PIECES TO DO THE UPGRADE... WHY WOULD YOU ENTRUST SOMETHING SO IMPORTANT TO ME?!
BE-CAUSE ...
...YOU ARE THE SHREWD-EST ...
...OF THE THREE OF YOU.
...
I COULDN'T GIVE THESE CHIPS TO RED OR BLUE! THOSE TWO HOT-HEADS? IF THEY HAD THEM, WHO KNOWS HOW QUICKLY THE ENEMY WOULD HAVE FOUND OUT ABOUT THEM. I WAS CONFIDENT YOU WOULD PROTECT THEM, BECAUSE YOU'RE CAUTIOUS AND SENSIBLE.

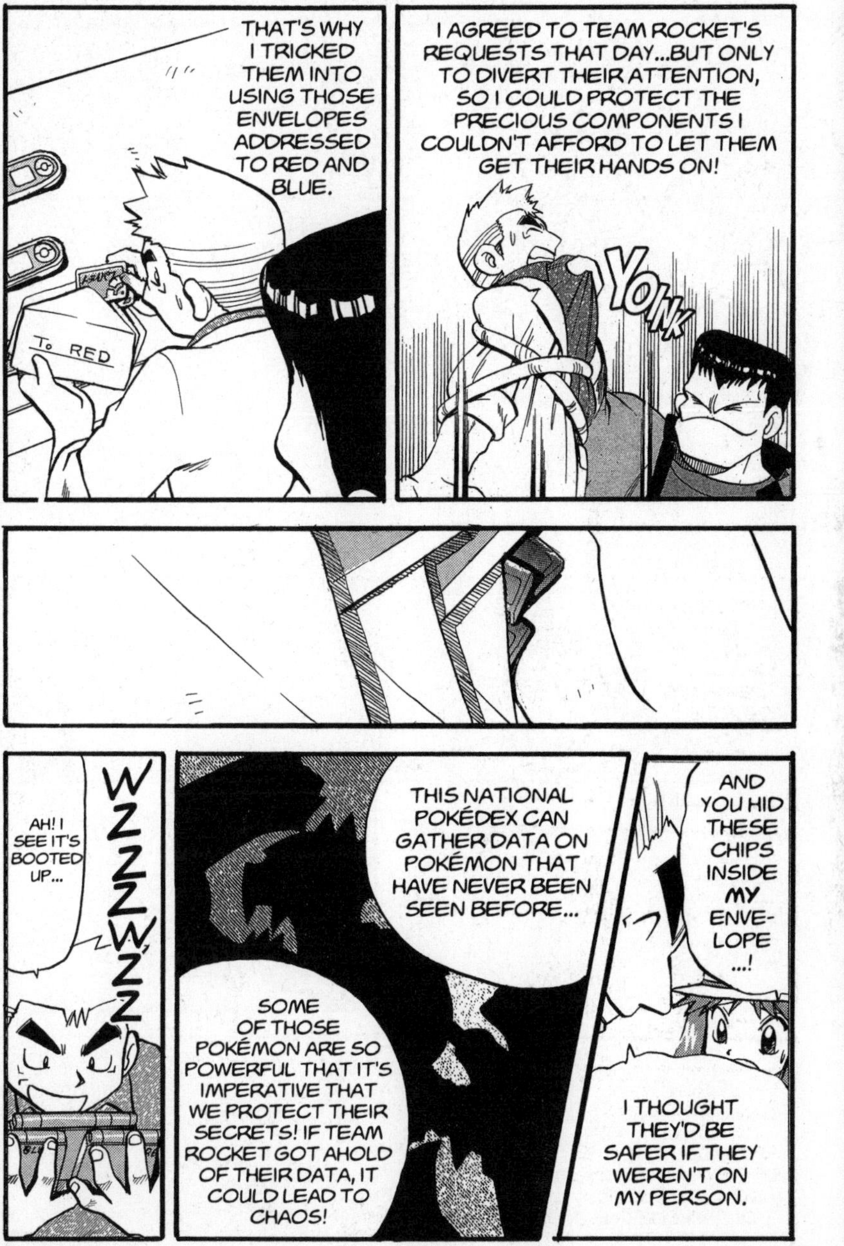
I AGREED TO TEAM ROCKET'S REQUESTS THAT DAY...BUT ONLY TO DIVERT THEIR ATTENTION, SO I COULD PROTECT THE PRECIOUS COMPONENTS I COULDN'T AFFORD TO LET THEM GET THEIR HANDS ON!
YOINK
THAT'S WHY I TRICKED THEM INTO USING THOSE ENVELOPES ADDRESSED TO RED AND BLUE.
To RED
AND YOU HID THESE CHIPS INSIDE MY ENVELOPE...!
I THOUGHT THEY'D BE SAFER IF THEY WEREN'T ON MY PERSON.
THIS NATIONAL POKÉDEX CAN GATHER DATA ON POKÉMON THAT HAVE NEVER BEEN SEEN BEFORE...
SOME OF THOSE POKÉMON ARE SO POWERFUL THAT IT'S IMPERATIVE THAT WE PROTECT THEIR SECRETS! IF TEAM ROCKET GOT AHOLD OF THEIR DATA, IT COULD LEAD TO CHAOS!
WZZZWZZ
AH! I SEE IT'S BOOTED UP...

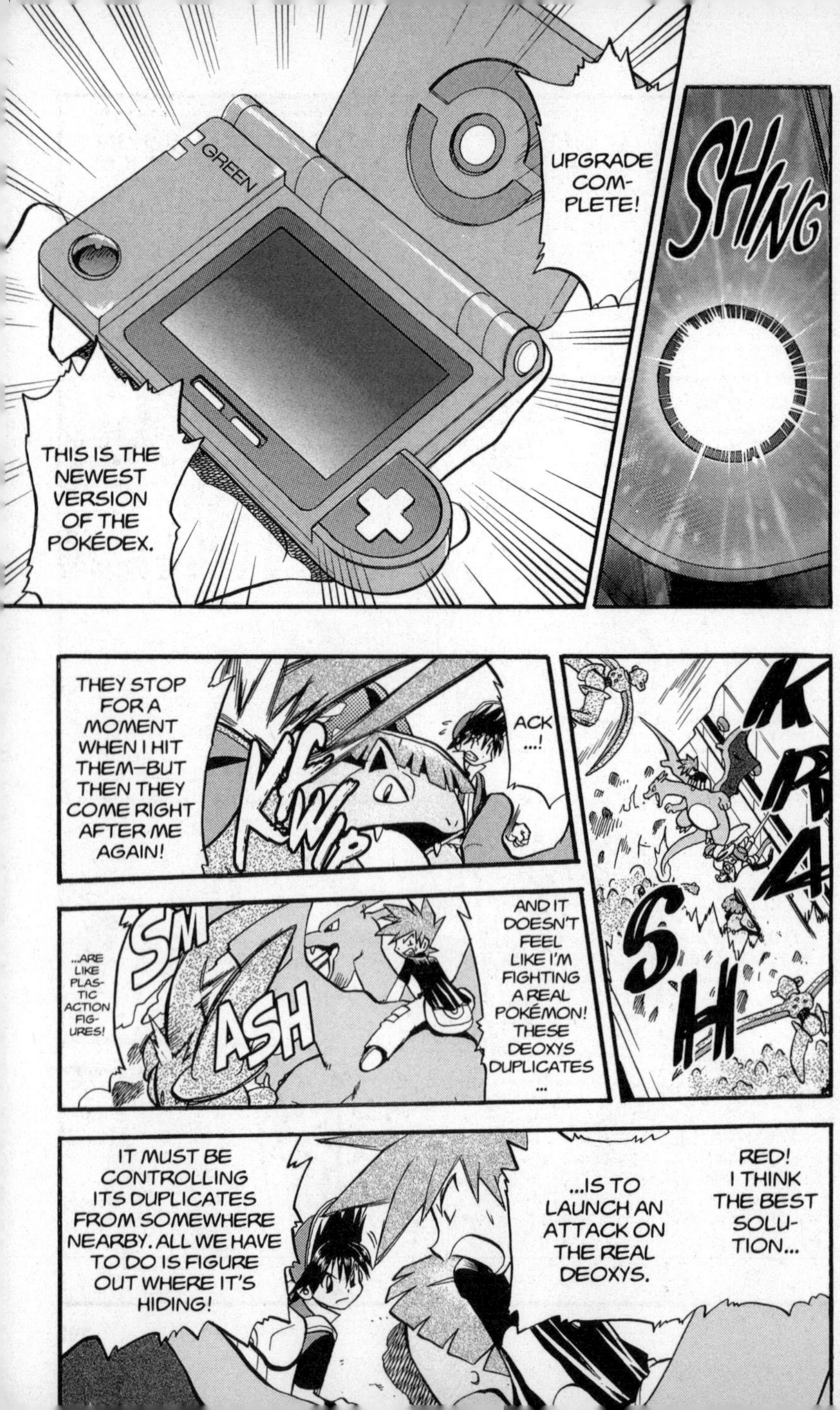
SHING
GREEN
UPGRADE COMPLETE!
THIS IS THE NEWEST VERSION OF THE POKÉDEX.
KRASH
ACK ...!
THEY STOP FOR A MOMENT WHEN I HIT THEM—BUT THEN THEY COME RIGHT AFTER ME AGAIN!
KWIP
AND IT DOESN'T FEEL LIKE I'M FIGHTING A REAL POKÉMON! THESE DEOXYS DUPLICATES ...
SMASH
...ARE LIKE PLASTIC ACTION FIGURES!
RED! I THINK THE BEST SOLUTION...
...IS TO LAUNCH AN ATTACK ON THE REAL DEOXYS.
IT MUST BE CONTROLLING ITS DUPLICATES FROM SOMEWHERE NEARBY. ALL WE HAVE TO DO IS FIGURE OUT WHERE IT'S HIDING!

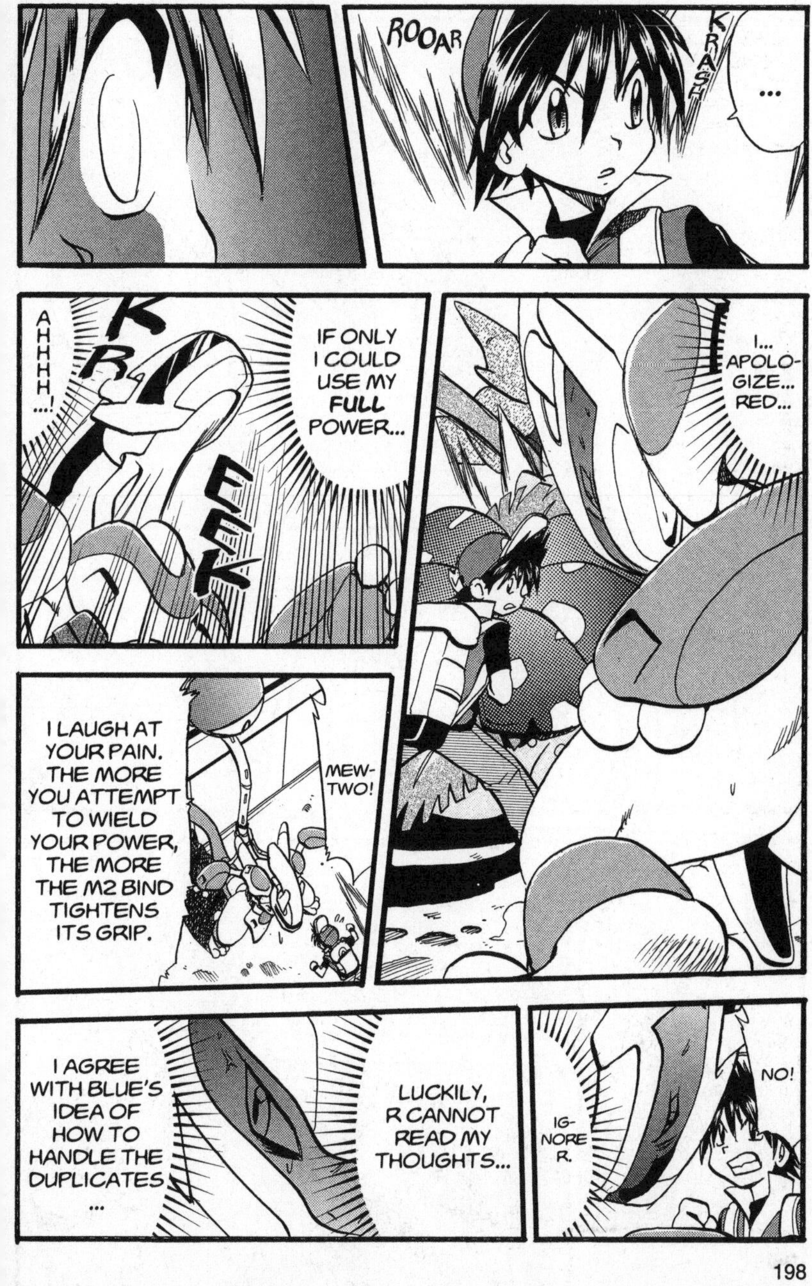

ROOAR
KRASH
...
I... APOLOGIZE... RED...
IF ONLY I COULD USE MY **FULL** POWER...
KREEK
AHHHH....!
MEW-TWO!
I LAUGH AT YOUR PAIN. THE MORE YOU ATTEMPT TO WIELD YOUR POWER, THE MORE THE M2 BIND TIGHTENS ITS GRIP.
NO!
IG-NORE R.
LUCKILY, R CANNOT READ MY THOUGHTS...
I AGREE WITH BLUE'S IDEA OF HOW TO HANDLE THE DUPLICATES ...

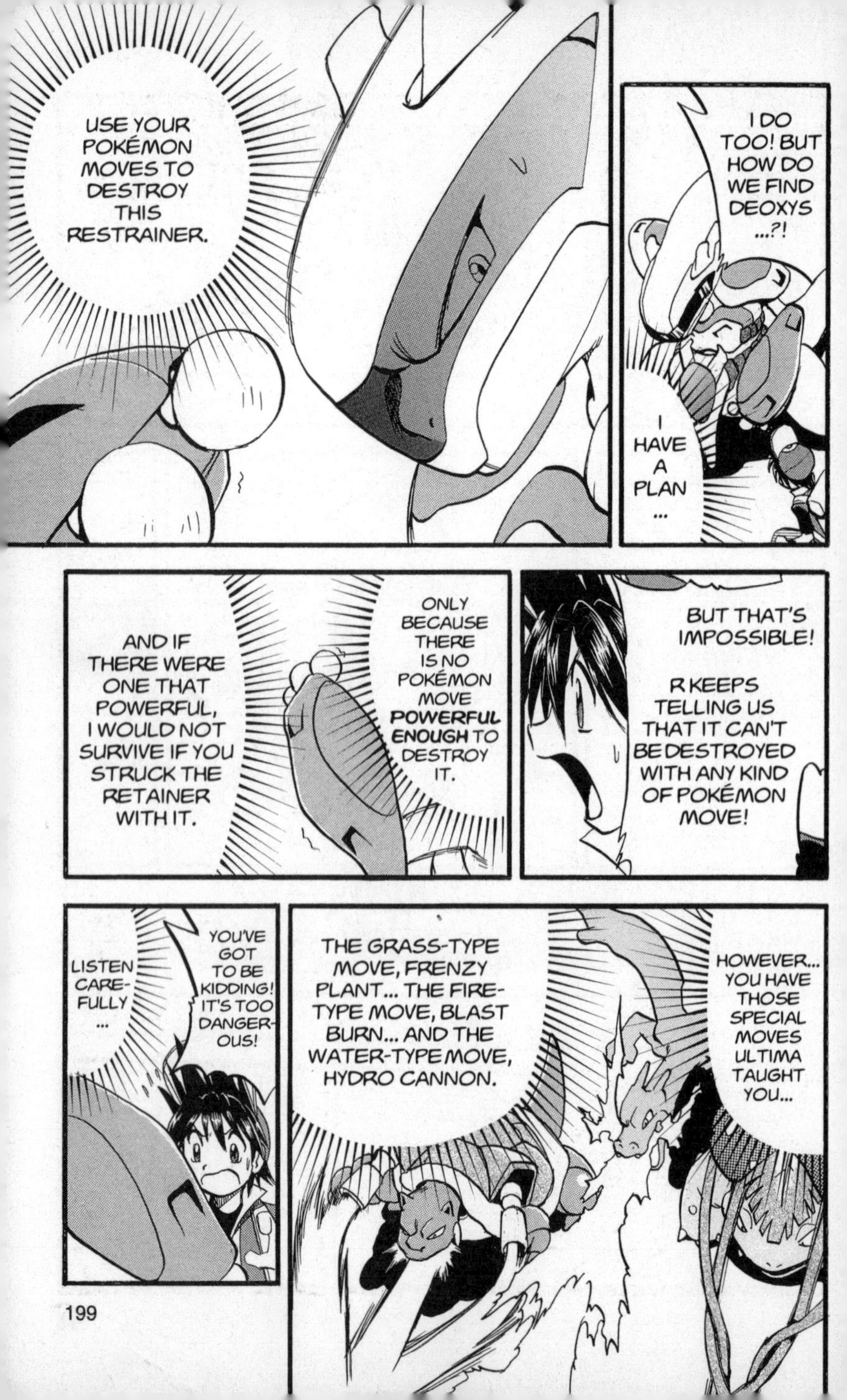
I DO TOO! BUT HOW DO WE FIND DEOXYS ...?!
I HAVE A PLAN ...
USE YOUR POKÉMON MOVES TO DESTROY THIS RESTRAINER.
BUT THAT'S IMPOSSIBLE!
R KEEPS TELLING US THAT IT CAN'T BE DESTROYED WITH ANY KIND OF POKÉMON MOVE!
ONLY BECAUSE THERE IS NO POKÉMON MOVE **POWERFUL ENOUGH** TO DESTROY IT.
AND IF THERE WERE ONE THAT POWERFUL, I WOULD NOT SURVIVE IF YOU STRUCK THE RETAINER WITH IT.
HOWEVER... YOU HAVE THOSE SPECIAL MOVES ULTIMA TAUGHT YOU...
THE GRASS-TYPE MOVE, FRENZY PLANT... THE FIRE-TYPE MOVE, BLAST BURN... AND THE WATER-TYPE MOVE, HYDRO CANNON.
YOU'VE GOT TO BE KIDDING! IT'S TOO DANGEROUS!
LISTEN CAREFULLY ...

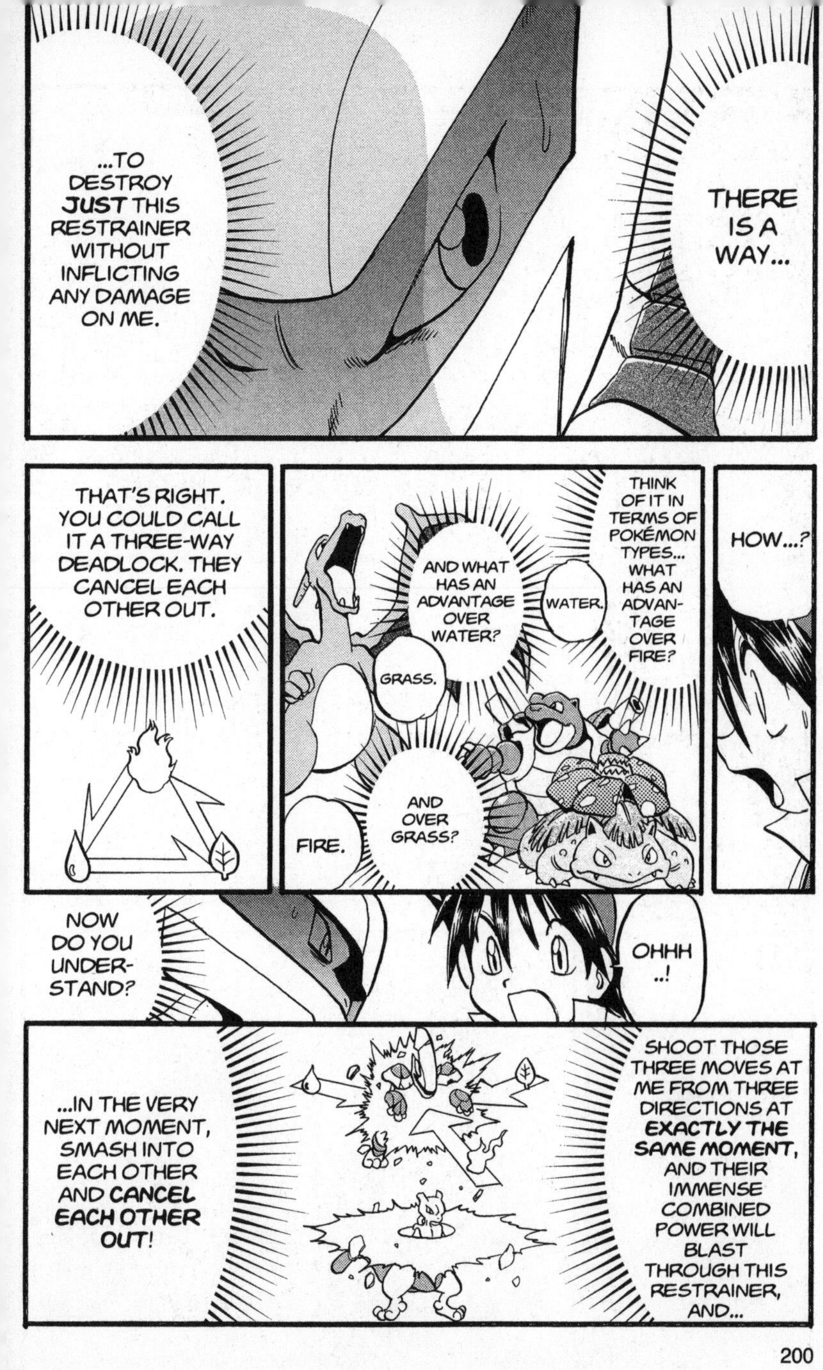
THERE IS A WAY...
...TO DESTROY JUST THIS RESTRAINER WITHOUT INFLICTING ANY DAMAGE ON ME.
HOW...?
THINK OF IT IN TERMS OF POKÉMON TYPES... WHAT HAS AN ADVANTAGE OVER FIRE?
WATER.
AND WHAT HAS AN ADVANTAGE OVER WATER?
GRASS.
AND OVER GRASS?
FIRE.
THAT'S RIGHT. YOU COULD CALL IT A THREE-WAY DEADLOCK. THEY CANCEL EACH OTHER OUT.
OHHH ..!
NOW DO YOU UNDERSTAND?
SHOOT THOSE THREE MOVES AT ME FROM THREE DIRECTIONS AT EXACTLY THE SAME MOMENT, AND THEIR IMMENSE COMBINED POWER WILL BLAST THROUGH THIS RESTRAINER, AND...
...IN THE VERY NEXT MOMENT, SMASH INTO EACH OTHER AND CANCEL EACH OTHER OUT!

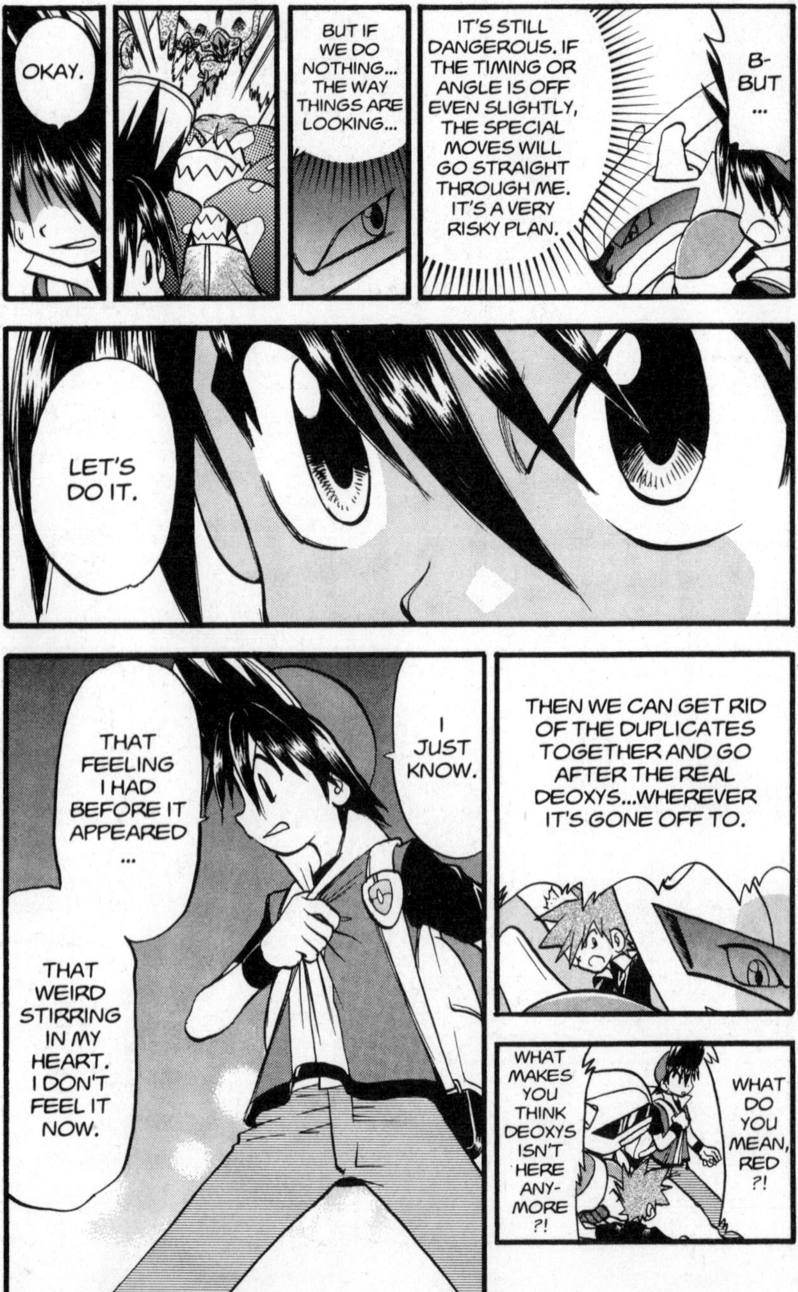
B-BUT...
IT'S STILL DANGEROUS. IF THE TIMING OR ANGLE IS OFF EVEN SLIGHTLY, THE SPECIAL MOVES WILL GO STRAIGHT THROUGH ME. IT'S A VERY RISKY PLAN.
BUT IF WE DO NOTHING... THE WAY THINGS ARE LOOKING...
OKAY.
LET'S DO IT.
THEN WE CAN GET RID OF THE DUPLICATES TOGETHER AND GO AFTER THE REAL DEOXYS...WHEREVER IT'S GONE OFF TO.
WHAT DO YOU MEAN, RED?!
WHAT MAKES YOU THINK DEOXYS ISN'T HERE ANY-MORE?!
I JUST KNOW.
THAT FEELING I HAD BEFORE IT APPEARED...
THAT WEIRD STIRRING IN MY HEART. I DON'T FEEL IT NOW.

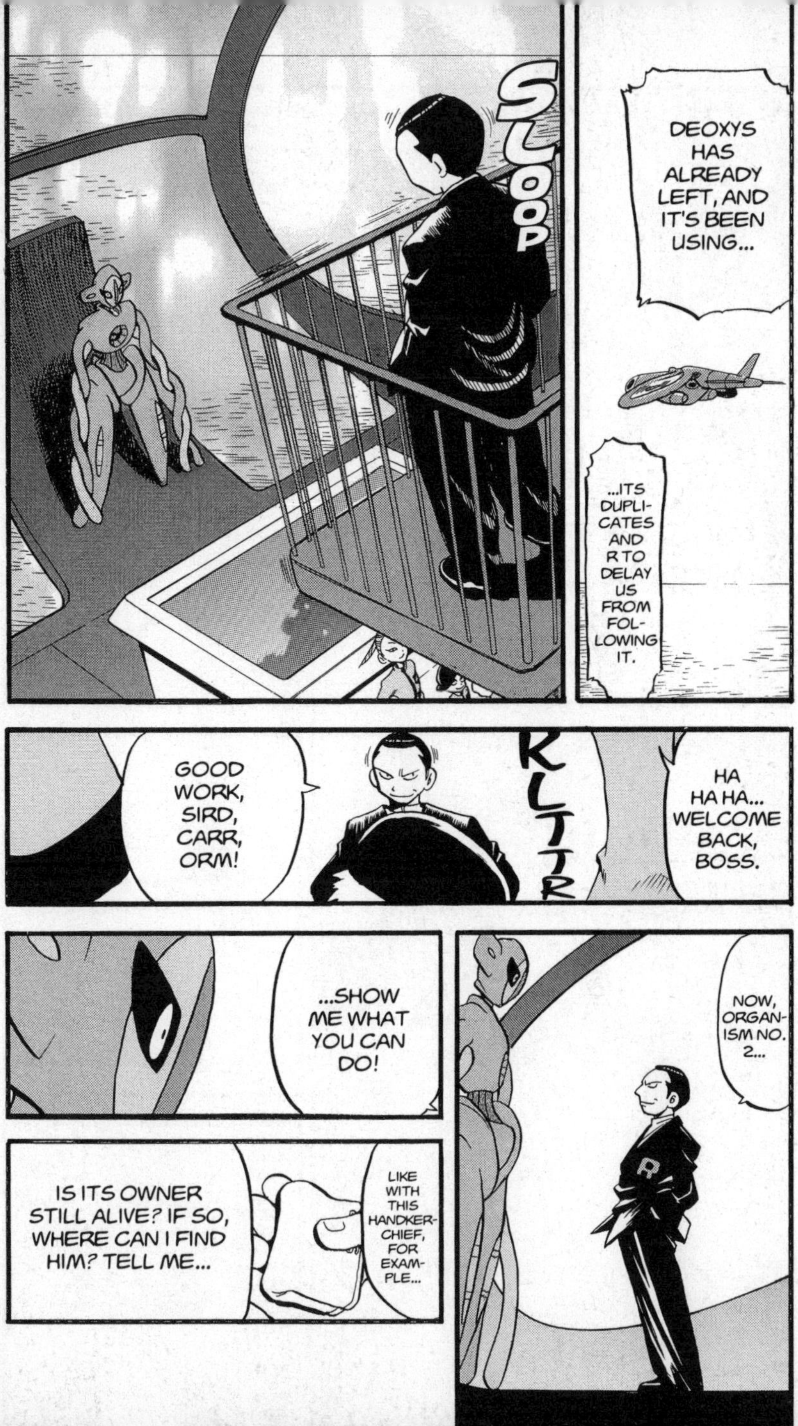
DEOXYS HAS ALREADY LEFT, AND IT'S BEEN USING...
...ITS DUPLICATES AND R TO DELAY US FROM FOLLOWING IT.
SLOOP
HA HA HA... WELCOME BACK, BOSS.
KLTTTR
GOOD WORK, SIRD, CARR, ORM!
NOW, ORGANISM NO. 2...
...SHOW ME WHAT YOU CAN DO!
LIKE WITH THIS HANDKERCHIEF, FOR EXAMPLE...
IS ITS OWNER STILL ALIVE? IF SO, WHERE CAN I FIND HIM? TELL ME...

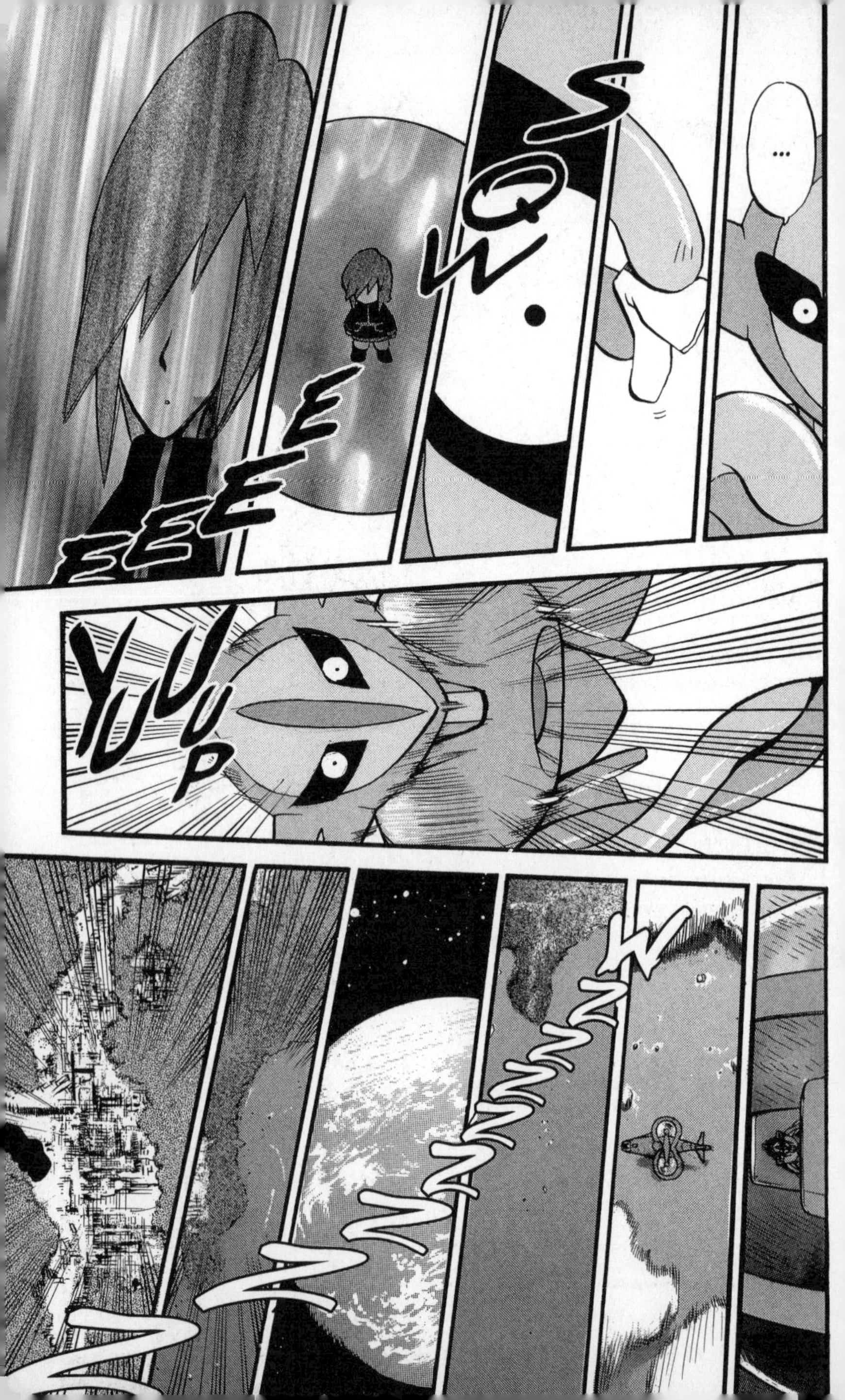
...
SQWEEEEE
YUUUUP
ZZZZZZZZW

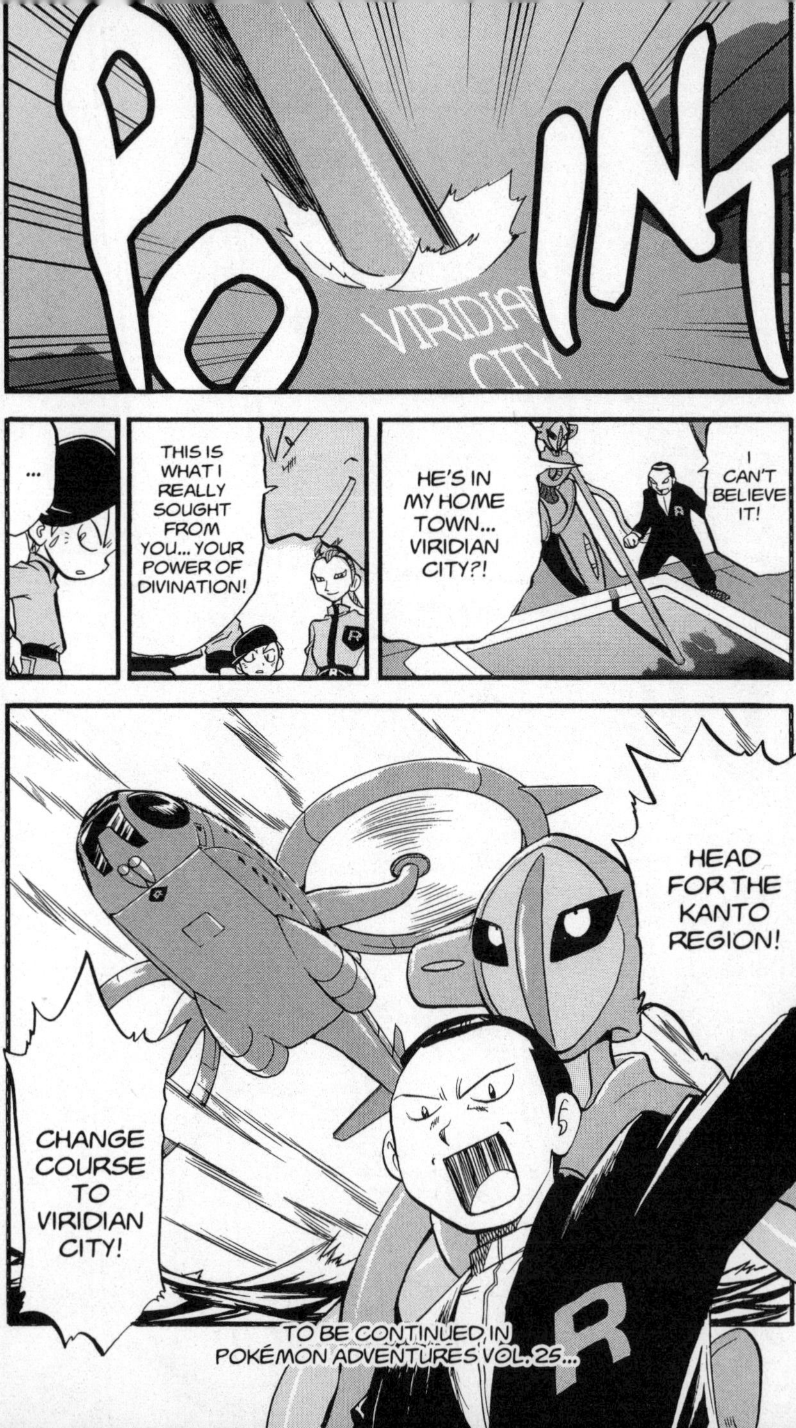
POINT
VIRIDIAN CITY
I CAN'T BELIEVE IT!
HE'S IN MY HOME TOWN... VIRIDIAN CITY?!
THIS IS WHAT I REALLY SOUGHT FROM YOU... YOUR POWER OF DIVINATION!
...
HEAD FOR THE KANTO REGION!
CHANGE COURSE TO VIRIDIAN CITY!
TO BE CONTINUED IN POKÉMON ADVENTURES VOL. 25...

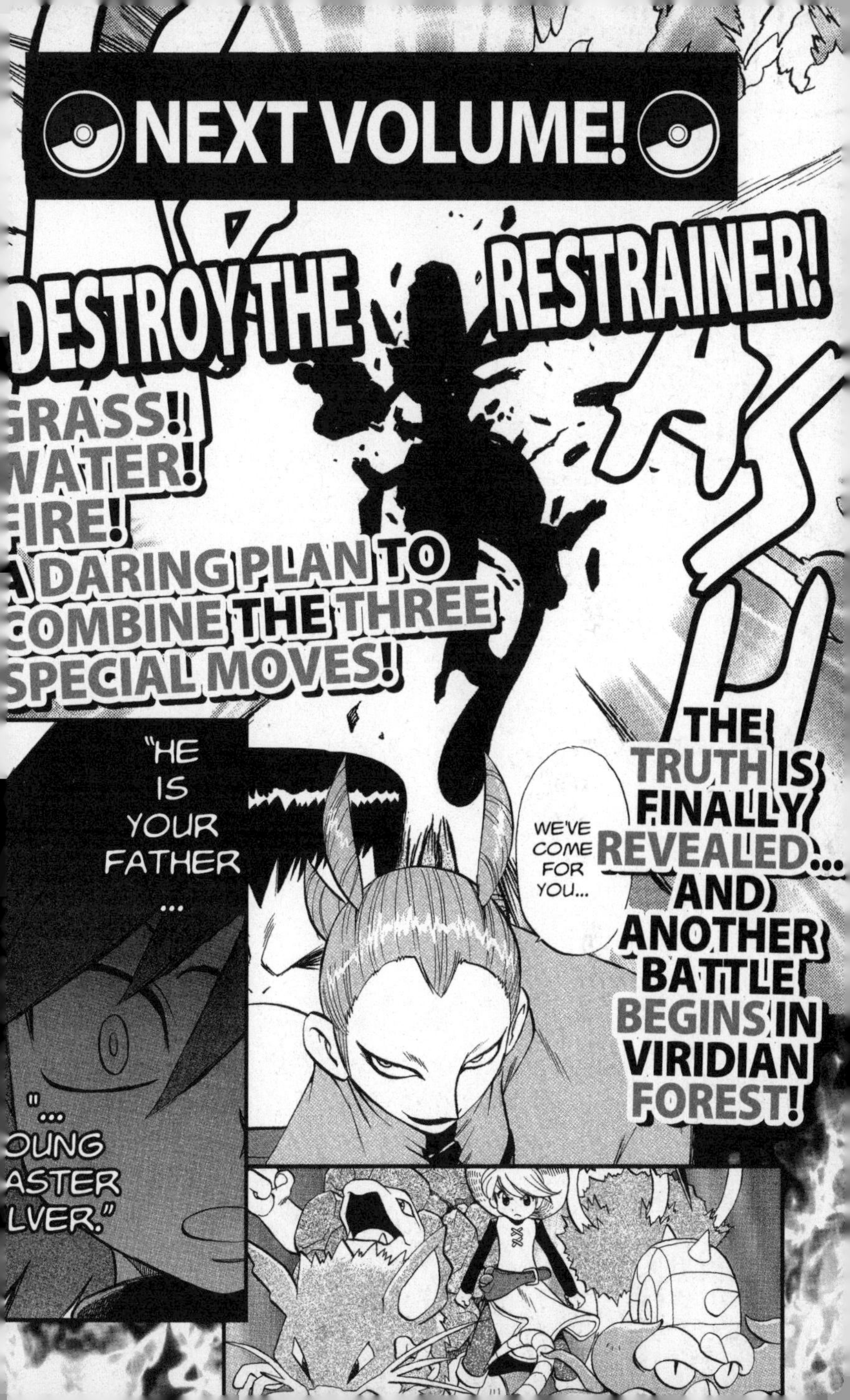
NEXT VOLUME!
DESTROY THE RESTRAINER!
GRASS! WATER! FIRE! A DARING PLAN TO COMBINE THE THREE SPECIAL MOVES!
THE TRUTH IS FINALLY REVEALED... AND ANOTHER BATTLE BEGINS IN VIRIDIAN FOREST!
WE'VE COME FOR YOU...
"HE IS YOUR FATHER ...
"... OUNG ASTER LVER."

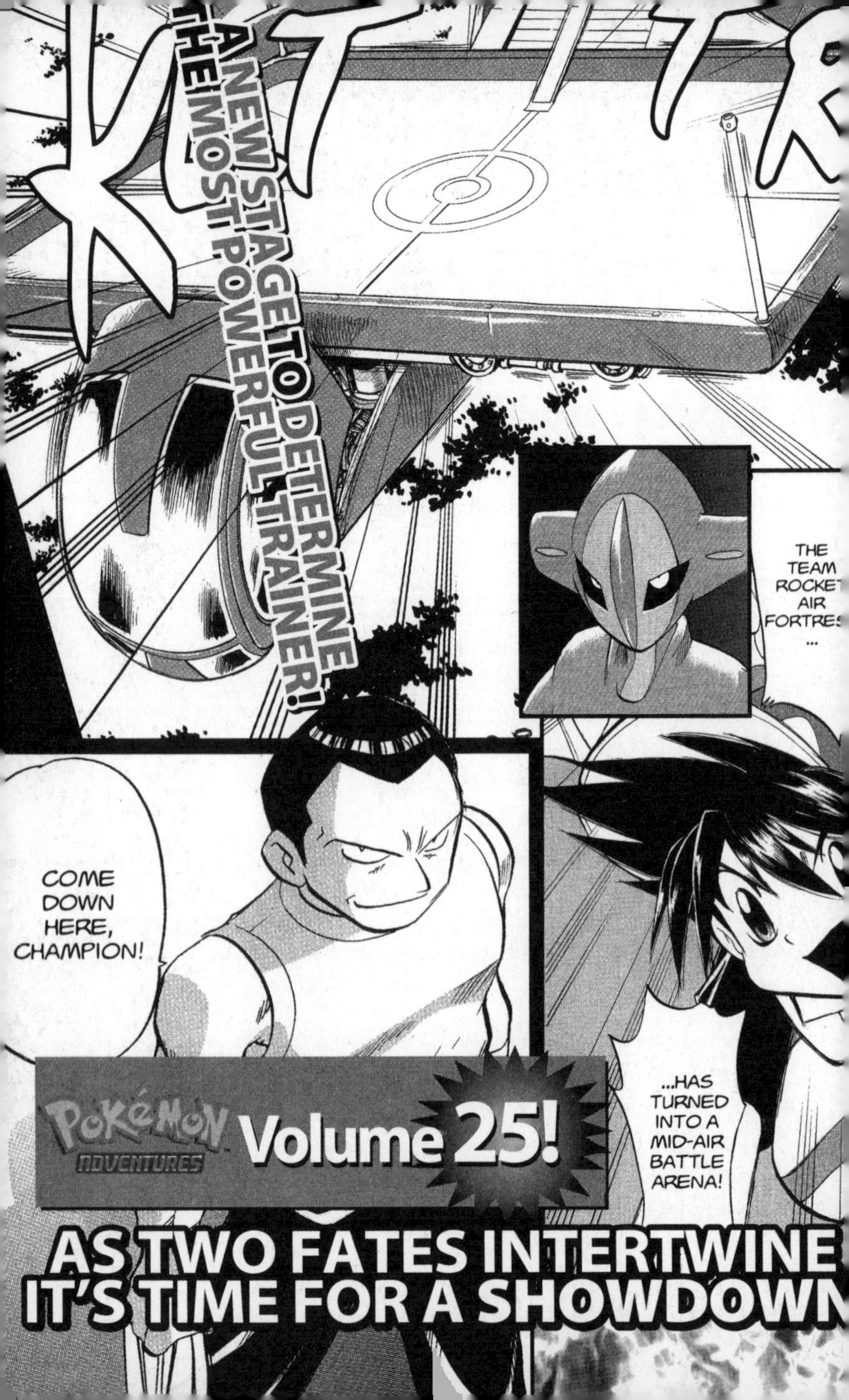
A NEW STAGE TO DETERMINE THE MOST POWERFUL TRAINER!
THE TEAM ROCKET AIR FORTRES ...
...HAS TURNED INTO A MID-AIR BATTLE ARENA!
COME DOWN HERE, CHAMPION!
POKéMON ADVENTURES Volume 25!
AS TWO FATES INTERTWINE IT'S TIME FOR A SHOWDOWN

Message from
Hidenori Kusaka

The year 2006 was filled with all kinds of new games for Pokémon fans: *Pokémon Ranger*, *Pokémon Diamond & Pearl* and *Pokémon Battle Revolution*. These games came out for the Nintendo DS and Wii. I still remember the Gameboy days, and I'm amazed at the progress. On the other hand, the *Pokémon Adventures* series has hardly changed since it began. Hm... In the manga, we can't increase the file size of the images or change the controls like they can in the games...so the most important things are the story and the characters!

*This note was written in 2006 when this manga was first published in Japan!

Message from
Satoshi Yamamoto

I like to draw people with flaws. In the beginning of this story arc, Red was an optimistic, carefree, cheerful guy, who seemed a bit unapproachable. But as I drew his crushing defeat and showed his distress in the beginning of vol. 24, I felt that I was finally able to get close to Red. I hope readers feel the same.

More Adventures Coming Soon...

One of Team Rocket's Three Beasts turns against their leader Giovanni and seeks to usurp his power. Silver learns a shocking secret about his family. Red and Mewtwo hazard a daring escape. And—whoa! The Team Rocket airship is about to crash-land!

Then, in a battle between powerful Mewtwo and Mythical Pokémon Deoxys, who will triumph...?!

AVAILABLE NOVEMBER 2014!

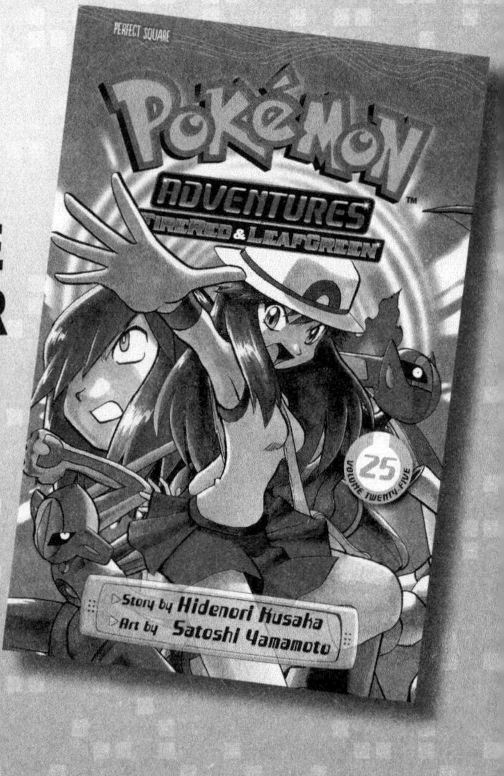
PERFECT SQUARE
POKéMON
ADVENTURES
FIRERED & LEAFGREEN
25
VOLUME TWENTY-FIVE
Story by Hidenori Kusaka
Art by Satoshi Yamamoto

The Struggle for Time and Space Begins Again!

Pokémon Trainer Ash and his Pikachu must find the Jewel of Life and stop Arceus from devastating all existence! The journey will be both dangerous and uncertain: even if Ash and his friends can set an old wrong right again, will there be time to return the Jewel of Life before Arceus destroys everything and everyone they've ever known?

POKéMON
ARCEUS
JEWEL OF LIFE
A TALE UNTOLD. A LEGEND UNLEASHED.

POKéMON
ARCEUS
AND THE
JEWEL OF LIFE

POKÉMON
BLACK AND WHITE

MEET POKÉMON TRAINERS
BLACK AND WHITE

THE WAIT IS FINALLY OVER!
Meet Pokémon Trainer Black! His entire life, Black has dreamed of winning the Pokémon League... Now Black embarks on a journey to explore the Unova region and fill a Pokédex for Professor Juniper. Time for Black's first Pokémon Trainer Battle ever!

Who will Black choose as his next Pokémon? Who would *you* choose?

Plus, meet Pokémon Snivy, Tepig, Oshawott and many more new Pokémon of the unexplored Unova region!

Story by
HIDENORI KUSAKA

Art by
SATOSHI YAMAMOTO

$4.99 USA | $6.99 CAN

Inspired by the hit video games
Pokémon Black Version and *Pokémon White Version!*

Available Now
at your local bookstore or comic store

www.vizkids.com   www.viz.com/25years

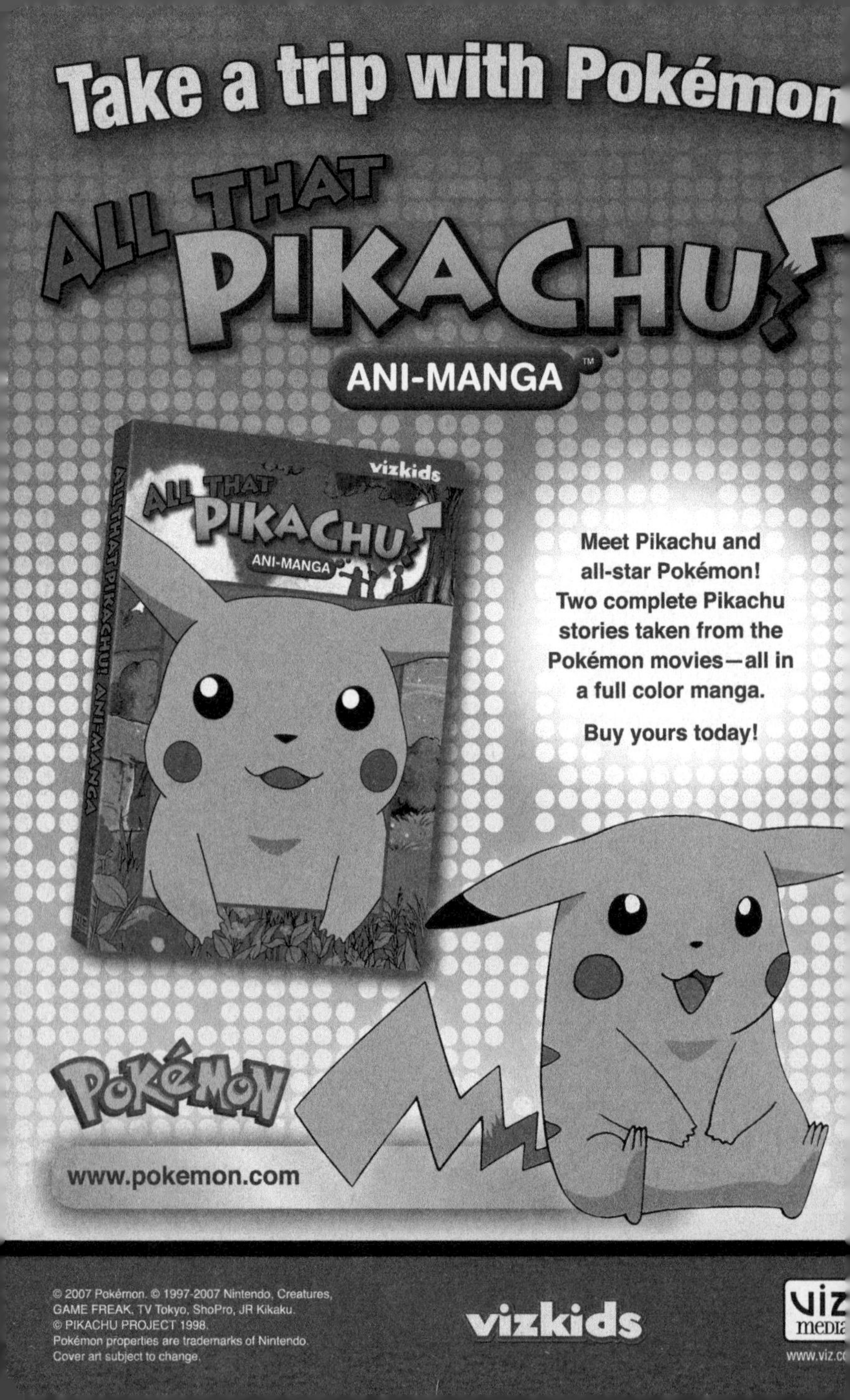
Take a trip with Pokémon
ALL THAT PIKACHU!
ANI-MANGA™
vizkids
ALL THAT PIKACHU!
ANI-MANGA
ALL THAT PIKACHU! ANI-MANGA
Meet Pikachu and all-star Pokémon! Two complete Pikachu stories taken from the Pokémon movies—all in a full color manga.
Buy yours today!
POKéMON
www.pokemon.com
© 2007 Pokémon. © 1997-2007 Nintendo, Creatures, GAME FREAK, TV Tokyo, ShoPro, JR Kikaku. © PIKACHU PROJECT 1998. Pokémon properties are trademarks of Nintendo. Cover art subject to change.
vizkids
VIZ media

NOW THE WORLD IS IN DANGER!

Long ago, the mighty Pokémon Arceus was betrayed by a human it trusted. Now Arceus is back for revenge! Dialga, Palkia and Giratina must join forces to help Ash, Dawn and their new friends Kevin and Sheena stop Arceus from destroying humankind. But it may already be too late!

een the ovie? ead the anga!

Story and Art by
Makoto Mizobuchi

Original Concept by Satoshi Tajiri
Supervised by Tsunekazu Ishihara
Script by Hideki Sonoda

POKÉMON ARCEUS AND THE JEWEL OF LIFE

MANGA PRICE: $7.99 usa $9.99 can
ISBN-13: 9781421538020 • IN STORES FEBUARY 2011

Check out the complete library of Pokémon books at VIZ.com

www.vizkids.com   www.viz.com   ratings.viz.com

© 2011 Pokémon.
© 1997-2011 Nintendo, Creatures, GAME FREAK, TV Tokyo, ShoPro, JR
Kikaku, © Pikachu Project 2009.
Pokémon properties are trademarks of Nintendo.
ARCEUS CHOUKOKU NO JIKUU E © 2009 Makoto MIZOBUCHI/Shogakukan

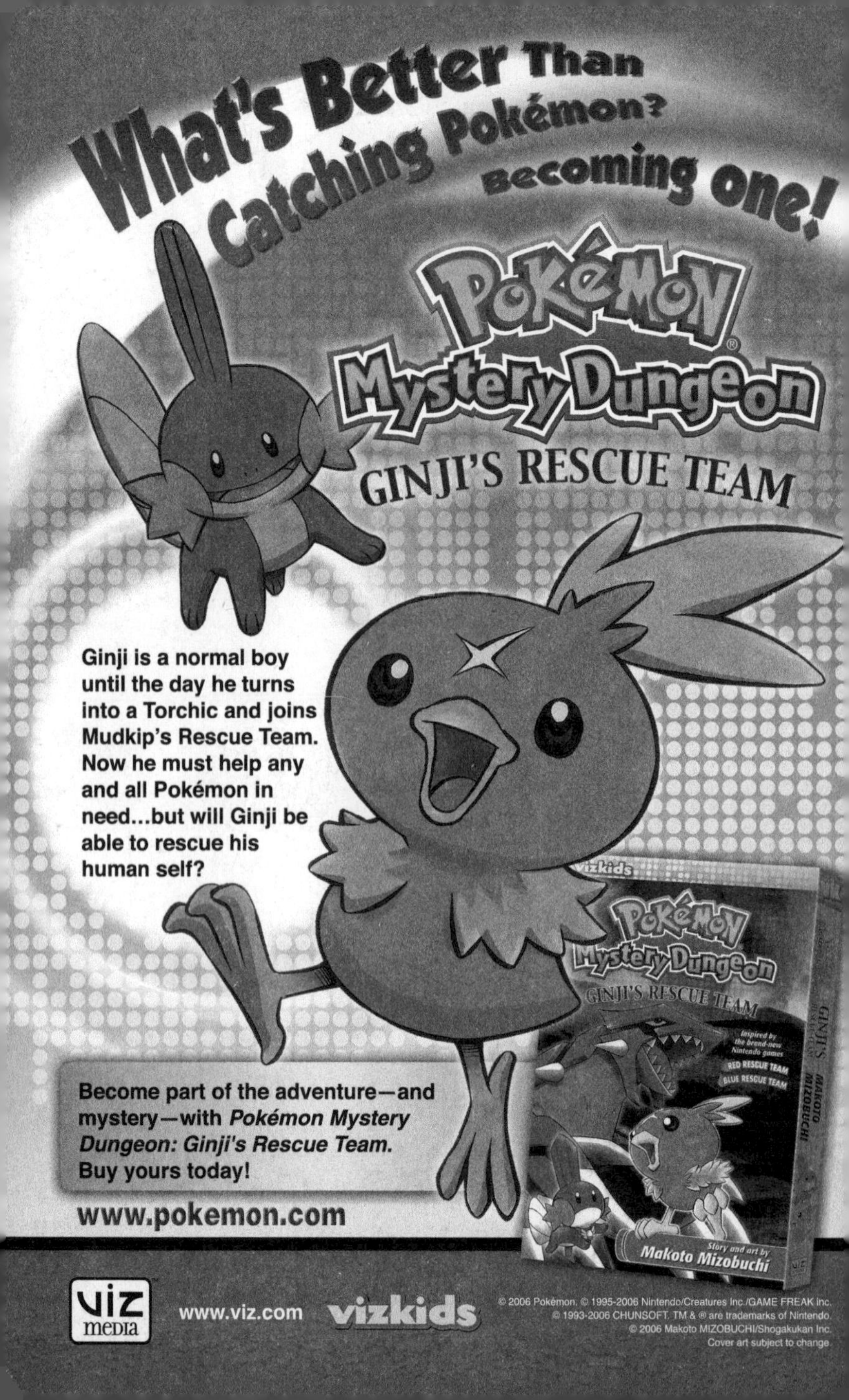
What's Better Than Catching Pokémon?
Becoming one!
Pokémon Mystery Dungeon
GINJI'S RESCUE TEAM
Ginji is a normal boy until the day he turns into a Torchic and joins Mudkip's Rescue Team. Now he must help any and all Pokémon in need...but will Ginji be able to rescue his human self?
Become part of the adventure—and mystery—with Pokémon Mystery Dungeon: Ginji's Rescue Team. Buy yours today!
www.pokemon.com
vizkids
Pokémon Mystery Dungeon
GINJI'S RESCUE TEAM
Inspired by the brand-new Nintendo games
RED RESCUE TEAM
BLUE RESCUE TEAM
Story and art by
Makoto Mizobuchi
VIZ media
www.viz.com
vizkids
© 2006 Pokémon. © 1995-2006 Nintendo/Creatures Inc./GAME FREAK inc.
© 1993-2006 CHUNSOFT. TM & ® are trademarks of Nintendo.
© 2006 Makoto MIZOBUCHI/Shogakukan Inc.
Cover art subject to change.

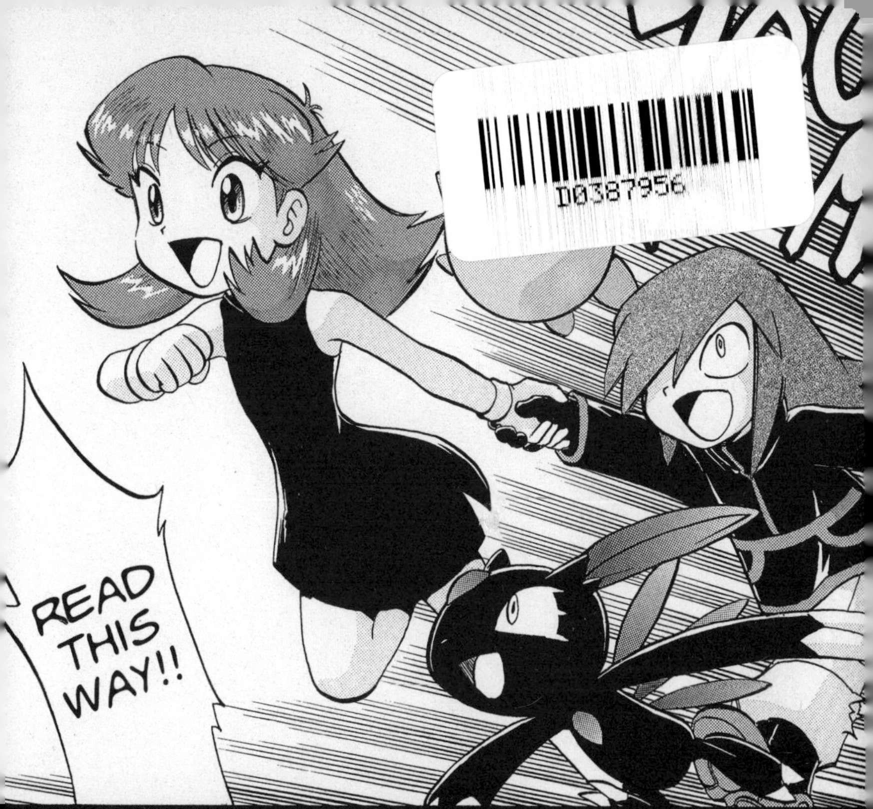
READ THIS WAY!!

THIS IS THE END OF THIS GRAPHIC NOVEL!

To properly enjoy this VIZ Media graphic novel, please turn it around and begin reading from right to left.

This book has been printed in the original Japanese format in order to preserve the orientation of the original artwork.

Have fun with it!

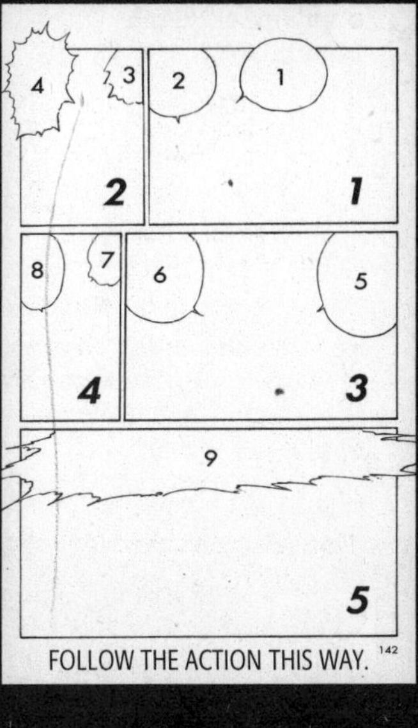
FOLLOW THE ACTION THIS WAY.